BY THE SWORD

BY THE SWORD

EMPRESS BOOK TWO

J. V. Simms

Podium

BY THE SWORD

Everly's World

Years from now . . .

I was seven years old and didn't know anything else but the Katharos. Or the *inheritors*, as they preferred to be called. Ever since I'd been born, they'd always been there. To me, they were a universal constant, as inevitable as sunset and the receding of the tides. I accepted their existence. What other choice was there? I couldn't deny the reality of sickness or death. I couldn't deny violence and the shame I felt when I had to endure it. I couldn't deny the world as it was, and so I couldn't deny the Katharos either. They simply were.

My dad did, though. It was hard for him. He'd been some sort of fighter when he was younger. Part of something called the military, which was like a snatching crew but bigger. Bigger than anything I could imagine. Bigger than a town. Maybe bigger than a city? And they didn't answer to anyone except someone who was 'lected. Is that the word? I think so. Someone got 'lected every four years on the old calendar, and everyone paid tribute to him. He was called the Unprecedented, and the military was his fist. I think.

My dad's crew was called the rapid militia. And he said they were the bravest of the brave. He said if anyone acted unlawfully, that was when he and his guys got the call. "Something gets fucked up, we went in and unfucked it," he said proudly. I didn't know what that meant, but I knew my dad was strong. No one in the resettlement messed with him. He was a respected man, feared even, and I loved him. But he did not love his life. He was there when the Katharos first came through the portal they opened from Oldstead. They tore a hole in the air itself and came marching in like they owned the place. Which they did, I guess. My dad and his crew were strong, but the Katharos say there are limits to what mortal men can do.

They tell us that all the time.

And occasionally, they show us. Just like they showed him.

He never told me how he lost his hand. Only that it happened fast. The ugly scars he received when his rifle burst in his face. That happens when a sword slashes through a chambered bullet so quickly that it detonates the gunpowder. The Katharos didn't like guns. For them, killing was something you did face-to-face. They understood the tactical necessity of ranged weaponry in war, but they only let their conscripts handle such things. It was a mortal insult to them to imply they couldn't do their own work up close and personal.

The Katharos poured through the portal and quickly took the city, led by Grail himself. The militia did their best, but they were swept aside like they were nothing. It was those Aegis guards the Katharos wore. They looked like silver medallions, pinned to their shoulders. A quick tap on them put up something called a *variable dispersal field*. It blocked stuff. Stopped bullets cold, deflected light, protected them from heat and flame. Effortless.

The only way to get through the field was with slower, cruder methods. They could still be suffocated or slowly crushed. They could be stabbed and slashed. You just had to be willing to fight them on their level. Which was still no guarantee you'd survive, because these things—I'm sorry, I'm sorry, the Katharos—were not only a culture dedicated to melee perfection.

They could read our minds.

Try fighting someone who could anticipate your every movement, who could whisper to you everything you were afraid of, who, within moments of crossing blades with you, understood you better than you understood yourself. It was impossible. Our best fighters were toys to them. First, their most experienced warriors came in the first wave and took our own veterans apart. And then, during the cleanup phase, they sent out their apprentices to practice on the remnants of our defenders.

They culled us like sheep. Maybe that's why they called us *lambs*.

My dad was no lamb. Even with twenty years spent under their boots, he didn't stop finding ways to fight them. To resist. He and others like him did their absolute best to be as uncooperative and unproductive as they could be. Kelthay was our home. No one had the right to come in and tell us where we could live and what we could think. To let us reproduce on a scheduled basis like pedigreed dogs, and to keep human children collared like pets. He said this was savagery, something we evolved past centuries ago. They didn't care. They let him fight. They *loved* that he kept fighting. They liked hurting him.

I don't know if it was a cultural thing or a genetic flaw, but the Katharos didn't process emotions the same way we did. Maybe it was due to them being telepaths? They couldn't feel emotions themselves; they felt it *through* others, and the sensation of it stimulated them. Love, anger, hate—these were intoxicants to those creatures. Especially the more negative feelings. The more intense the emotions produced by their victims, the greater their high was. Not only had we become a cheap source of labor and entertainment to the freaks; we were their *drugs*. They drank our very souls. The worst of them indulged in depravity that couldn't be described and, in a just world, would never be experienced.

Once every few weeks, they'd take my dad away. They'd haul him and the other noncompliant humans to the countess's estate and bring them before Claudia herself. The Empress's beloved sister. The smiling princess.

Then they'd do things to their *minds* . . .

When they dropped him off, Dad wouldn't speak for days, and if anyone so much as touched him, they were risking their lives. They kept taking him over and over again, and he kept fighting back. Over time, he started to change. Forget things, forget my name, forget where he was. He was always scared, always angry. And it got worse and worse. All because he wouldn't back down. Between him and the Katharos, something had to give. And in the end, it was him.

One night, he had a nightmare. His screams racked our entire dwelling and practically made the windows shake. Mom tried to snap him out of it. Tried to wake him up. She shouldn't have done it. She shouldn't have touched him.

I won't say what he did. But he did it fast, and my mom was gone. Just like that. I don't know if they loved each other. I don't know if they even really *knew* each other. They were paired together because the Katharos wanted them to be. They produced three children, who were inspected, approved, then taken away. Then they had me. Whatever it was my siblings had, I didn't. I was considered ancillary, so they let me stay home. My mom never talked to me, never even smiled at me. She was younger than my dad, born during the rising, raised and educated by them. Claimed she'd known the countess herself. That Claudia kept her as a pet before she was replaced and tossed into the resettlement.

Mom never got over how far she'd fallen in life. Never got over her resentment toward my dad. Now she was dead, and I'd never truly know her.

Dad held her and screamed her name. He screamed even louder than when he'd been dreaming. That was when I realized he'd been well and truly broken. He'd snapped and was just a shell of a man, lashing out on instinct. He was now useless to them. An overseer came in to investigate, irritated at being called from his bed. He saw Dad cradling my mother, took his bronze-colored helmet off, and laughed. Seeing an inheritor in person without their face covered was always surreal. They were all so beautiful. Those strange hazel eyes and golden-white hair. It was only when they were in their armor that you feared them. When you saw their faces, it was hard to believe these angelic creatures could harm anyone at all.

They say demons once served the gods.

"Matthew, what have you done?" he asked my dad with a knowing smile. "She belonged to the Empress. As do you. Will you please come with me? Claudia will want to speak with you about your unruly behavior."

"Nooooo," said my dad. "No, no, no."

"Asking was a courtesy, Matthew. You *will* come with me."

My dad was on him in an instant. He let my mother go, raced to the overseer, and slammed him into the wall. He headbutted the creature, grabbed a knife off the tabletop, and then slashed it across his enemy's face. He then reversed his grip and plunged it toward the overseer's throat. But before it could penetrate his skin, the overseer grabbed Dad by the wrist, quick as a snake. My dad pushed with all the strength and leverage he could muster, but the overseer's grip wouldn't budge.

The overseer closed his eyes and breathed in deeply, then licked the blood trickling down from his cut face, sighing intensely with pleasure. Then with his other hand, he grabbed my dad by his throat, lifted him into the air, and brutally choke-slammed him to the kitchen floor. The air was knocked from my dad's lungs, leaving him sputtering for breath.

The overseer knelt and gently held my father's head in his lap, while stroking his hair like an old dog, murmuring gently as he did so.

"Matthew . . ." he said, once more wearing that smile of endearment on his beautiful face. "Matthew. Thank you for sharing this with me." Then he slit Dad's throat with his own knife.

I've heard people talk about cutting throats like it was a means of killing someone instantly. That might be true for animals, but not for humans. It's messy, sure, but it's not actually a fast death at all. It's more of a slow suffocation. The blood doesn't just spout outside, it also goes down your esophagus and slowly fills your chest. You'll choke and drown in your own blood, and it takes a long time to happen. That's how my dad went out, and all the while the Katharos that butchered him drank in his fear and desperation to live. Then it was done, and that was how I lost both of my parents.

The overseer shivered in pleasure and rose to his feet. "Everly's blessings upon you. It was a good night, after all," he said happily, rubbing a finger gently against his wounded face. "Very good, indeed."

That was when he saw me.

"Oh," he said. "I hadn't noticed you there, lamb. You must be Matthew's get. What's your name, girl?"

I couldn't say anything to him. I backed against the wall, shaking uncontrollably. He smiled and continued talking. "No name, then? Oh, that's right. I'd forgotten. You were the runout. The unremarkable remnant. There's nothing special about you at all, is there? Not like your wonderful siblings, yes?"

He gripped my chin and turned my head left and right, scrutinizing me. "No point in taking you to Claudia. I can already tell your mind is below her standards. I could dispose of you, if you'd prefer. It's very difficult out in the world for a lamb that's lost its flock. Would you like that? Would you like to join your parents? I could do that for you, if you'll only say please. Go ahead. Say, *please kill me.* Say it! Say it just like your father did . . ."

"He did not! He did not!" I sobbed.

"Yes, he did. He said it with his thoughts. He was happy when I finished him. Do you know why? Because he knew he'd never have to see *you* again . . ."

Fear left me in an instant. Hate replaced it, hate so potent and hot I could feel it burning me from the inside. Rage like I'd never felt before, like I'd never known I could produce. It poured from my soul and hit his mind like a closed fist. *This*, he did not enjoy.

"Argh!" he screamed, covering his face as though I'd thrown acid on it. I pushed past him and raced to the door, leaving him rolling on the ground, shrieking in pain. Out into the dark I ran, just a kid with no one left in the world to look after me. Another lost lamb. I was going to have to get by on my own from now on. It wouldn't be easy. Terra was more of a nightmare than I ever knew. But through the degradation and the pain, through the desperation and fear, one thing kept me going. It was my hate. My hate was the greatest gift my parents had ever given me. It was my sword and my shield, and with that anger, I could *hurt them.*

And one day, I'd do so much more than merely hurt them.

Whatever I had to do to survive, from that point on, I'd do it. Anything that made me stronger. More capable. Anything that let me match them. I'd never be a slave. I'd never again be one of their lambs. I would be so much more. After all, *someone* had to teach them how to feel on their own. Feel *fear,* that is. And I would be that teacher.

I would be a lamb no longer. I'd become a butcher. And I'd make them all pay! All the monsters that were ruining this world!

General Grail. Tybalt the Rat. Conservator Laurel. Discordia. Countess Claudia.

And her.

Especially, her . . .

Empress Everly. The devil herself.

You'll all pay for what you've done.

One day, I'll have you all . . .

The Village

The village at night had become as still and unsettling as a graveyard. Thea fought hard to resist the urge to turn back to her hiding spot and huddle beneath her blankets. Although the urge to wait until sunrise was powerful in her, she knew she had to set aside such a childish urge. There was no time that was safe, day or night. In fact, the night offered her the best chance for escape. She just had to be brave enough to seize this moment.

She never thought she'd be in a situation like this. Did anyone?

Everyone is counting on me, she thought miserably to herself. *I must escape here. I must find an adventurer! If not, that beast will eat us all up. First the grown-ups, then the other children! Gods save us all; I need to move!*

Thus resolved, Thea made her way forward as quietly as could be, fearing the idea of making the slightest bit of noise. The monster's ears were beyond sharp and would surely notice her if she gave cause. Silence would guard her far better than any weapon could.

Sticking to the shadows as fearfully as any mouse that lived, Thea slowly made her escape. After what seemed like hours, the village was finally behind her. Just as it seemed she'd finally be able to release the breath she'd been keeping inside her lungs all night, a horrendous scream tore through the air. A *child's* scream.

She knew that voice. It was Adriette. They'd both committed to the decision to run tonight; Adriette would escape to the north, and Thea would take the southern route, and whoever managed to avoid the beast's detection would be the one to bring help.

From the intensity of the screams, it appeared that Adriette had not only been caught but was also receiving a severe punishment. *Chastisement*, the fiend liked to call it. Those who disappointed the creature received an agonizing death, pain beyond description.

Thea shuddered to think of the methods involved.

Still, even though she wanted to weep for her poor friend, even though she wanted to lie in the dirt and sob until her heart gave out, the fact that the monster was such a merciless sadist could play to her advantage. Now that it was occupied by playing with its food, Thea could run as fast as she liked. It would be too distracted in its killing frenzy to even notice her.

Gods above, forgive my cowardice; I pray that you welcome Adriette into paradise for her bravery, Thea thought as she desperately raced through the night. *Please, let me find help, please-please-please! Please, don't let this be for nothing! Please, let me save the children; please, let me save all that yet live!*

Another bloodcurdling scream sounded throughout the night air. But this one wasn't a scream of fear and pain as Adriette's had been. It was a howl of rage and hunger. The cry of the beast. It sounded once, distantly, behind her. And then it did so again but was much closer. And that was when Thea knew *that it was chasing her.*

Of course. *Of course!* The fiend could read the thoughts of living men. It had probably torn the very memory of their plan right out of Adriette's skull even as it feasted on her flesh and blood. It knew about Thea! And now it was hunting her down!

Oh gods, oh gods, oh gods, oh gods! She whimpered inwardly, now too terrified to properly pray. Instead, she raced for her life as quickly as she could, knowing that if her feet dared fail her, she would soon join her friend in the beast's maw.

Another sound soon reached her ears. The sound of the raging river that divided the two great territories that bordered it. A recent deluge of rain and melting snow had made the river perilous for those who fell in it. But in her desperation to defeat the speed of the monster that was swiftly closing the ground between them, that river now represented the best hope Thea had for survival.

"I can smell you, girl!" a cheerful voice called to her. "I can *smell* you! You're going to join your friend as my toy, you cowardly, simpering little thing! And when I get bored, *I'M GOING TO EAAAAAAAAAAT YOOOOOOOOOU ALIVE!"*

"NOOO!" Thea screamed in panic, now no longer able to contain her fear. Without looking backward, fully aware of what she would see coming toward her if she did, Thea leaped into the dark, freezing river and was immediately swept away, desperately trying to keep afloat even as she was rammed mercilessly into rocks, felled trees, and other dangerous objects trapped in the water with her.

In a moment of perfect clarity given only to those who've realized that they are about to perish, Thea now knew that the choice between the river and the monster had merely been a decision between how she wanted to die: being eaten alive or drowned in terrible darkness.

As the current began to pull her under, Thea sorrowfully asked her friends and the spirits of her family to forgive her. She'd failed them. She'd failed all of them. No one would avenge them. No one would save them. No one would even know that she ever existed.

" . . . I'm sorry," she said to the lonely night. "I'm so sorry . . . "

Then down she went.

Gone into eternity.

From the darkness, a cruel figure with bloodied talons emerged. His glittering eyes observed the girl's descent. He waited patiently to see if she would emerge again. When she didn't, he smiled, pleased with the results of his hunt.

He would have liked to have taken her alive. He'd barely been able to enjoy the other one before her terrified thoughts of her friend had alerted him to this one's attempted escape. Oh, well.

He'd just have to pick a fresh one from the larder, wouldn't he?

Silly little things.

He enjoyed them so.

Everly was a girl who loved living in the moment. Like, *the* moment. That very particular point in time when the past was firmly behind her and the future was nothing but an undecided possibility, leaving only the very real, the very urgent *now*. For in that moment, there was nothing left to do but to do *it*.

Whatever *it* just happened to be.

"STUPID GIRL! I SMASH YOU GOOD!"

Everly's *it* of this moment was killing a troll.

It wasn't like she'd sought out this troll in particular. She'd been minding her own business and had been enjoying her walk down the king's road on her journey to Oldstead, not realizing that the troll had been lurking under the old stone bridge she was crossing, waiting to snatch someone up at random to make a meal of them, as trolls are known to do.

His error had been selecting Everly for that meal.

On paper, it made sense. Everly was tall for her age, at five feet eleven, and very well physically conditioned. Endless hours spent alone in the woods of her hometown of Anders while gleefully engaged in relentless calisthenics, weight lifting, and swordplay had put a surprising amount of muscle on her lithe frame. From the troll's perspective, the young blond teenager must have seemed like an utter snack.

An *excellent* source of protein.

What the poor troll couldn't have known was that Everly was no ordinary exercise enthusiast with an unhealthy obsession with bladed weaponry. In addition to being an extremely capable combatant with a sword or her bare hands, having long surpassed the vaunted title of sword king, Everly was also an extremely powerful magic user. Possibly the strongest one on the entire planet. The skills she excelled at were earth magic and spiritual manipulation.

Which is to say, she was a psionic behemoth who could destroy a person's mind as easily as she could bring down a mountain range. (Which would have been *very* easy for her.) Everly considered herself quite the complete package, which was why she'd decided a while ago to declare herself the Empress of the world at a future point in time and rule with tyrannical impunity since no one was strong enough to oppose her.

The troll didn't know *any* of this. He just wanted lunch. What he got instead was the most difficult fight of his miserable life.

He wasn't enjoying any of it.

Everly was, though. She *really* loved a good fight; it could be said that her nature was combative, with a real emphasis on *combat*. There was something about seeing something strong and self-assured and then grinding it to dust beneath the heel of her boot that really *spoke* to her.

The words it spoke were usually some permutations of *do it.*

"STOP MOVING!" the troll roared in frustration when she avoided another one of its sluggish strikes. The creature was a massive thing, standing nearly twenty feet in height and coated in matted hair atop the rippling fat that covered its large but spindly limbs. "WHY WON'T YOU STOP MOVING?!"

"Because the rhythm is *nigh!*" Everly called back. "The rhythm is nigh, and I'm letting it carry me away!"

To emphasize her words, she gracefully danced away from another of the troll's clumsy blows with an expertly timed dodge that bordered between being breathtakingly precise and suicidally overconfident. The troll began to scream and stomp with homicidal rage.

Everly, stop playing with this monstrosity and take it down, NOW! said the stern voice of Grail, her mentor since childhood and unwilling conscript in her mad-but-undeniably-fun scheme for world domination. *Drawing the fight out like this makes a mockery of your training. A sword king finishes the battle with one swift and decisive blow.*

"Aww, I thought I was making a mockery of the other guy," Everly smirked as she effortlessly cartwheeled away from another wild swipe. "Why you gotta be so down on me, teach? I'm just having some fun."

Combat is not about fun, *Everly. It's about respecting the line between life and death and responding to your enemy with earnestness. You might think you're belittling him, but you're making yourself look arrogant.*

"I *am* arrogant," Everly said with a wicked grin. "And powerful! Stylish! Talented! And undeniably cool!" Everly emphasized each of these sentences with a brilliant slash of her sword, which she drew and swung so swiftly that the blade seemed to vanish from sight with each impossibly quick movement.

Five scarlet lines appeared on the poor troll's body, beneath its throat and on its four limbs, that soon began gushing blood. Everly kept the edge of her sword supernaturally sharp; the slightest tap of it would be enough to chip stone. To say the troll's limbs had been severed would have been as obvious as denoting the wetness of water.

"Wuuuut," gasped the dying monster as it lay dying on the bridge, seeing nothing else but the unbearably bright sun it had avoided its entire life.

"What?" Everly asked it as she sheathed her blade. "You're dying, big guy. *That's* what. Got any final words?"

The troll pondered his killer's question. Then he said:

"I regret that until this very moment, I had never truly beheld the majesty of the sun at its noontime apex. How many precious moments did I squander hiding in the lonely darkness of this aging bridge when I could have sat beneath the sky's gentle warmth and reveled in the beauty of the day? Could even a loathsome beast such as myself have found peace under the gaze of such all-seeing magnificence? Truly, I was beyond foolish. What a sad thing it is to realize your own absurdities . . . only when it's too . . . late . . . to *change* . . ."

That having been said, the troll closed his eyes and breathed no longer.

"Well, okay, then," Everly said after a suitable number of moments had passed. "Yeah, I really didn't see that coming. Jesus, he kind of put a damper on the whole thing, didn't he?"

A malicious attempt to ruin your fun, that's what I say, said Eris, the spirit elemental who had served Everly since childhood. *He couldn't defeat you in fair combat, so he decided to haunt you with his words. What a conniving tactic!*

Aww, now I feel bad for trolls, said Titania, the other elemental who served Everly and the younger sister of Eris. *Can't we, like, liberate them or something? Show them they don't have to live under bridges and in sewers and all those other awful places?*

How is the embodiment of the very earth such a ridiculous softy? Eris said. *The way of the world is to kill or be killed. Why do you concern yourself so often with the feelings of those who serve the cycle of life and death?*

I don't know, maybe because you're a mean bitch? Did that ever occur to you? Titania answered sullenly.

Why, you little worm! How dare you disrespect me in front of the others! I have half a mind to twist your arm behind your back until you squeal like a dog in a bathtub!

Bring it on, nerd! I'll take you down to taco town! Destination: my foot up your ass!

Everly mentally muted the sisters so that they could carry on with their argument as they had done a thousand times before, without it bothering her. They were loyal to her and loyal to each other, but they were also extremely disagreeable at times. As all tight-knit siblings knew, it didn't take much to get them at each other's throats. Sometimes Everly discouraged it, sometimes she egged it on.

Today, she was distracted.

"Grail?" she asked as she stood at the edge of the bridge and looked down. "Do my eyes deceive me or is that a dead body floating in the river?"

Your assessment is correct, he replied. *Perhaps it was one of the troll's victims?*

"I'm curious," Everly said. "Let's find out, why don't we?"

Fishing the dead girl out of the water hadn't taken much effort. Using a giant hand of stone that emerged from the very earth itself, Everly carefully placed the corpse on the grass growing just past the embankment.

"Let's *seeeee,*" Everly said to herself. "Okay, so if I'm remembering my *Law & Order: SVU* correctly, she couldn't have died that long ago because she's not bloated or rotting. Still has her eyes . . . very identifiable, I'm sure. Yeah, no fish have been nibbling on her. I bet she was alive as recently as yesterday."

Pretty good guess, boss, Titania said cheerfully. *Her decaying cells just told me she died last night at eleven thirty. Got dragged down by the current. Yep.*

"You can just talk to her body, and it'll tell you when she died?" asked Everly.

Well, yeah. I can talk to anything that comes from the earth. All the various cells, acids, and assorted squigglies involved in animal reproduction and maintenance are built up from consumed food, and all food comes from the earth, so I can pretty much get answers to any question I desire.

"Could you ask a stone that was used to bash in a man's skull who it was who swung it?"

Yup, Titania said immodestly.

"Damn, T. You'd be a scary witness for the prosecution," Everly said with genuine admiration.

Well, thank goodness I'm an outlaw, Titania said smugly.

"Damn straight," Everly said with a smile. "So, what was she doing in the water? Why did she drown? She looks only a little younger than me. Old enough to know better than to play near a raging river."

She was running from something, Everly, Titania said. This time all the humor had fled the elemental's voice. *Something nasty was on her heels. She was trying to get help and had to choose between death in the water or a worse death facing whatever was after her.*

"Is that right?" Everly said with a frown.

Yeah.

"And her body can't tell you what it was that hounded her?"

No. Only that it was cruel. And that it likes to eat children.

"Hmm," Everly said to herself.

This was obviously a complicated issue. The sort of entanglement that Everly didn't personally wish to involve herself in. Killing monsters was a job for heroes. Everly knew herself too well to ever fantasize about being such a noble soul. The fact of the matter was, she was a bad person. An *awful* person. And joyfully so. Solving issues for others was white-knight territory, and the future Empress of the world was most certainly not one of those.

If anything, she probably had more in common with the monster. When it came down to it, Everly was a villain at her core. Her goal in life was to thwart justice and rule through tyranny, after all.

At the same time, however, she had personal standards. Sure, Everly was a bad person, but that didn't necessarily mean she marched lockstep with all manner of vileness. She believed in gradations of villainy and felt that while it was possible to be evil *and* happy, that didn't mean she had to countenance *all* evil. Just the parts she herself enjoyed. Being a villain didn't mean you had to be accepting of others, and it didn't mean you had to pass a litmus test of darkness.

In other words, just because she liked crushing heroes and wanted to turn the world into a theocracy that worshipped her didn't mean she had to be okay with something eating small children.

When it came to her principles, you either got on board with them or you drowned. That's all there was to it.

Though, now that she thought about it, using a drowning analogy next to a girl who had recently died that way could be viewed as being in bad taste. Low-hanging fruit, as it were.

"Oh, whatever," she muttered to herself. "Titania, do the thing."

Huh?

"You know, *the thing*. She looks fresh enough to be brought back relatively intact. So wake her up from her sleep so she can lead us back to where she came from. I want to have a talk with her about this child-gobbling fiend that's been plaguing her home."

So we're not calling it necromancy anymore? We're just calling it 'the thing'?

"Titaniaaaaa, just *do* it," Everly groaned.

Heh, heh, right on it, boss.

Reviving her didn't take long at all. Although Everly didn't understand the particulars of how Titania's talent for earth manipulation translated into being able to raise the dead, she was glad to have it in her arsenal.

The girl, Thea, soon awakened back to life without any traumatizing memories of how her first stint at it had failed. The cold of the river had done her a service. It had preserved her body so well that Titania hadn't had to go to any extra effort to restore her. Everly only had to tell one mild fib about finding her floating unconscious on her back to make her believe she'd survived fleeing the creature that had been after her.

"Are you really an adventurer?" Thea asked hopefully after everything had been carefully explained to her.

"Sure. I have adventures all the time. That's a prerequisite, right?" Everly said.

"I'm sure it is, but I just . . . I mean, what I'm asking you to do is very dangerous! If you're not prepared for it, you really could be killed!"

Everly smiled at the other girl's worry and patted her hand gently. "*Me?* Killed? Dear friend, you may not be aware of the nature of the reality we inhabit, but I genuinely don't believe that there's anything in existence that could possibly *end my life.* I've lately begun to suspect that I'm the only thing that truly exists, you see, and therefore, death is a meaningless concept reserved solely for background characters such as yourself. Whatever the perils that assail the little people, *I'll* surely be fine."

Everly, are you certain you want to do this? Eris's voice buzzed through her mind. *Your charmingly arrogant self-confidence notwithstanding, there's no need to put yourself in danger unnecessarily.*

It's not arrogance if it can be demonstrably proven, Everly shot back. *Eris, stop being such a nanny! This is* adventuring! *What could possibly go wrong?*

Everly, according to the information I've absorbed about popular entertainment in your world, the prelude to every horrific death in every horror movie that ever existed begins with someone saying, what could possibly go wrong if I do this?

So you agree that I'm correct!

I . . . What? No. No, I most certainly do not! I was suggesting we ignore this child's request. If your goal is to participate in the summer campaign before your academic year begins, then you really need to stop being sidelined by all these . . . these . . .

Side quests? Everly offered.

Yes! Exactly the term I was looking for. You need to stop being distracted by all these meaningless side quests! Are you a warrior or a cat distracted by shiny objects?

Can't I be both?

Well . . . yes? But it's annoying.

Is it really?

Yes!

Well, then I'm absolutely going to do it. Thanks for your advice, dear servant! But Grail the Golden Wanderer could no more turn from a maiden in need than she could ignore a puppy locked in a hot car.

Everly . . . what do puppies have to do with anything? And why do you insist on using MY name whenever you want to play at being heroic? Grail's complaining voice interjected.

Never question me, old man! Everly commanded.

"Uh, Everly?" Thea hesitatingly cut in.

"Yes?" Everly answered. "Wait, let me guess. You saw me standing perfectly still and found it slightly unnerving, and you also noticed that I seemed to be talking to myself quietly as though I were having a conversation with several invisible entities. Well, have no fear, it was just a mental exercise that I do to refresh myself daily. A strengthened mind is a *powerful* mind!"

"Oh. Oh, good, I'm glad!" Thea said enthusiastically.

"Yes, gratitude is entirely what's called for," Everly said with a nod. "For I have decided to lend my sword to your service. Lead the way, Thea. Let's go fumigate your village."

"Thank you!" the girl said excitedly. "Oh, thank you so much! This is what I hoped would happen. Save us, Mistress Grail! Save our home!"

"Kid, you only had to ask," Everly said with a smile and a wink. "Trust me, I'm great at everything I do. This will work out just fine."

As they made their way to her home, Thea told the sorry tale of what happened. Of how Mister Whisper came to take up residence in the village.

"He looked so old when he first arrived," Thea said. "Just a little old man. He claimed he was a retired merchant from the capital who wanted to retire to the countryside and enjoy his remaining years in tranquility. The mayor and the village council gave him permission to stay."

"Your village was big enough to have a mayor, huh?" Everly asked. "And he just let a random stranger take up residence?"

"Mister Whisper had . . . He had a lot of gold," Thea said. "More wealth in his one pocket than I've ever seen in my life. The mayor said you can trust a man with money. They have no reason to lie. The village council agreed with him. And we needed that money on account of the poor yield we got from this year's harvest."

"So, your idiot leaders let a monster buy his way in. That's a shame. I take it they didn't make it?"

"No. I mean, yes. No, what I mean is, my father is dead. He realized the mistake that had been made and tried to stop it. But the council is fine. They're now sleeping. The mayor and all the other important villagers. One night they went to bed and they haven't woken since."

"So, *none* of the other adults have died?" Everly asked with a raised eyebrow.

"Oh, lots of them," Thea said sadly. "Mostly the ones who tried to protect their kids, like my dad. Mister Whisper would leave them hanging in the village center. The ones who tried to fight, the ones who tried to take their children and run, he made examples of them all."

"But not any of the councilors," Everly said.

"No, ma'am."

It would seem a pact was made, Eris said darkly. *I suspect if you ask for further details, the people who began disappearing first would be from the poorer sections of the village. Invalids, orphans, disruptive elements, and any other undesirables.*

Is that how it works? Everly wondered.

It's in accordance with nature, Titania said sadly. *Genuine predators prefer targets that are either too young to defend themselves or too old. In mortal society, it's even better if they're the dregs. No one cares what happens to the poor.*

"When did you start to notice people were missing?" Everly asked Thea.

"All throughout the winter. Folks stopped coming to church. Stopped coming to meetings. They just started dropping out of sight. At first, it was the poorest of us—"

See? Told you, Eris said.

Shush, Everly told her.

"Then it started moving closer to the center of the village, where the most prosperous of us abide, while slowly getting worse. And all throughout, Mister Whisper began to change. He grew hale, stronger, uh . . . *younger,* if you can believe it. The longer the season of death continued, the more refreshed he became. We knew what was happening. We knew it was *him* somehow, but the council . . . our *leaders* wouldn't believe us. They didn't care."

"A lot of gold buys a lot of complicity," Everly said neutrally.

"He was *eating* us!" Thea said with a sickened, strained voice. "We told the mayor we had to stop him, and he said it didn't matter if a little trash got sacrificed for the greater good of the community! He slapped me across the face when I told him we needed help! Said I'd be ruining a good thing for everyone."

"Sounds like something that needed ruining," Everly said sympathetically.

"It did!" Thea said tearfully. "On the day the council went to sleep and didn't awaken, Mister Whisper called us all to the center and said he was in charge now. And if we were good and obedient, then it wouldn't hurt when he came for us. Harl Ebens started crying when he said that. He was only eight years old! He started crying and it annoyed Mister Whisper so much that he grabbed him and right in front of us he opened his mouth and—"

Thea began to shake at the memory. Her body trembled as tears glistened in her eyes. Everly began to feel uncomfortable in her presence. How does one go about comforting a troubled young person? It would be the height of insincerity to merely pat her on the back and say *there, there.* Embarrassing too.

No, the truth was that trauma is very particular to the people who suffer it. She couldn't say or do anything to provide genuine comfort. She could only keep her word and deal with the creature.

So that was what she would do.

When the two of them arrived, they found the village covered in a dismal mist that obscured their vision and made their forward progress uncertain. Everly found it extremely annoying yet thematically appropriate. It certainly set the *mood* for this confrontation. What better setting than this for the tale of a haunted village?

The center was empty. The houses were quiet. Even the animals that remained had fallen into silence. Their footsteps across the cobbled streets echoed loudly throughout the air, violating the stillness of the place. Everly saw that Thea was growing increasingly terrified. She'd been surviving for months by attempting to make less noise than anyone else to keep from drawing this Mister Whisper's attention. Everly's blatantly careless stride went against every instinct Thea possessed.

"Don't be afraid, Thea. *I'm* here now. Whoever he is, whatever he is, he doesn't matter anymore. I'll show you."

She gestured to the mist that surrounded them and said with a magnified voice, *"MISTER WHIIIIIIIIIISPER! HELLO!"*

Her greeting reverberated throughout the village center, loud as could be, as though Everly had projected it with a speaker and a microphone. It washed over the entire area, bathing it with the sound of her voice. The tone was flippant, irreverent, and *contemptuous.* An open challenge for those who heard it.

A challenge that was swiftly accepted.

"Hello," said the elegantly dressed man who appeared before them, seemingly out of nowhere. He was handsome, young, and pale. *Severely* pale. Distractingly so. *Extremely distractingly so.*

Everly didn't want to focus on that one aspect of this loathsome bastard—she really didn't—but she couldn't help herself.

He was *so* pale.

"Holy shit, man. Is pigmentation your kryptonite?" Everly asked him.

"I . . . What?" he asked.

"You look like a vegan covered in chalk."

"What do you . . . huh?" he said with increasing irritation.

"I can see more blue veins on your face than in an expensive cut of foreign cheese," Everly continued.

"Have you any idea who you're talking to, girl?" he snarled at her. "This glib mockery only whets my appetite for your suffering."

"Do you sweat milk?" Everly asked him with utter sincerity.

Mister Whisper closed his eyes and breathed deeply to settle his temper. Then he looked past Everly to face Thea. "Ah, our lost little doe has returned to the herd. I could have sworn I saw you drown, though. Well, no matter. What a wonderful reunion this will be, Thea. I'm so excited to see you once more—"

Everly ripped his head off and then mashed it beneath her boot. Then she had Titania drag the body into the very center of the world, where flowing magma hotter than the surface temperature of a star incinerated it completely.

No more Mister Whisper.

"Ignoring people is rude," said Everly with a frown.

"Uh," said Thea in surprise.

The fog quickly dissipated.

I mean, I'm just saying it was a bit anticlimactic is all, Eris said later as they entered the mayor's home. *He was a very mysterious creature, wasn't he?*

"I suppose," Everly said uncaringly.

You have to admit there was a lot of foreshadowing involved, Eris continued. *I mean, narratively speaking, wouldn't it have made more sense to draw things out? We didn't even know what sort of creature he was. Weren't you the least bit curious about his background?*

"Nah, he was gross. Fuck him," Everly replied as she walked into the mayor's bedroom. "There are some people who just aren't worth knowing."

Seeing the mayor snoring peacefully in his bed, Everly drew her sword and dispatched him with a thrust through the neck, then left him to choke to death on his own blood, just as she had with his fellow conspirators.

Everything on her list had been neatly checked off.

"I mean, when the mood takes me, I'm all for some fun banter and all, but these guys . . . This whole thing . . . Yeah, I just don't know. I thought it would be more fun than this. But when I wasn't looking, someone flipped the setting from light to heavy. I think after this one, we'll need to go on a, you know, more *lighthearted* romp. More trolls, less Pennywise the dancing clown."

Don't let the trolls have last words, though; they'll seriously harsh us out, Titania reminded her.

"So noted," Everly said with a nod.

Regardless of your motivations, you've done a good thing today, Grail said to her quietly. *Confronting the darkness of this world and putting it in its place was a noble deed.*

"Ugh. Gag me with a spoon while you're at it, old man," Everly said with disgust.

So, what now? Titania asked. *You saved the girl and killed the monster. You even punished the greedy fools who let things get so out of hand. But the village population has decreased significantly; entire families have been wiped out. Plus, there'll be loads of orphans as well. It's a real mess.*

"Yeah? Kind of sounds like a local problem to me," Everly said indifferently. "Not all the adults were killed. We'll leave it to them to deal with. They still have all the gold Whisper was throwing around, so I'm sure they can figure something out. I'm going to go ahead and call this a successful conclusion to an otherwise regrettable affair."

Aww, we're not even going to say goodbye, Titana whined. *I hate all that mysterious-wanderer stuff. Getting credit and receiving thanks makes me feel pretty good! Can't we at least see some of the smiles on the faces of the children?*

"The faces of the children who now get to grow up with the immense mental trauma of having seen their friends and family slowly eaten alive by some hideous thing?" Everly asked pointedly.

Oh. Well. Yeeeah, when you put it that way, maybe it's best to just quietly disappear, Titania decided.

"I thought you'd see it my way," Everly smirked.

Too bad, though. Whatever qualities existed that drew Mister Whisper here have *surely been magnified by his long presence,* said Grail as they made their discreet exit. *This place could be even more vulnerable to attack with no one left to protect it.*

"Who said we were leaving it without a protector?" asked Everly.

Weeks later.

"How disappointing," said Lady Murmur as she surveyed the village, noting its gradual restoration. "I came here seeking the company of my brother, who told me this place had been thoroughly pacified. Instead, he is gone, and the prey roams free of the larder. How unsightly."

Behind her stood ten more of her kind. The entire clan.

All here to finish what Whisper had begun.

"Get out of here!" Thea said hysterically as the elegant-looking woman slowly approached her. "Leave us alone! You have no place here!"

Somehow Thea had known this would happen. Now, in the dead of night, she stood alone, facing them.

"No place here, child? *Noooo.* Quite incorrect. My place is wheresoever I wish. Just as your place shall soon be inside . . . *me*," the ethereal-looking creature said, before her face quickly transformed into a razor-fanged horror. "Now come to me, dear girl . . . Come to me and—"

Thea put her fist through the monster's head. When she removed her hand, Lady Murmur's face had been replaced with a cavernous hole from which various fluids now dripped messily.

Her body dropped to the ground, twitched once, then ceased its motion.

Thea stared at her hand in surprise, then made another fist with it. She had felt strange ever since she'd met Lady Grail. She felt somehow greater than what she had been before, but it was difficult for her to articulate the difference that she now felt between who she had once been and what she had now become.

Had she been reborn? Was she the same person?

Was she still Thea? Or was she the *inheritor* of her place?

Did it matter?

"Who's next?" she growled at the remaining creatures, who had all begun gradually backing away.

It didn't save them.

That night, in the name of vengeance and justice, Thea played her own games with those that had dared torment her and the community she loved.

Like Everly on the bridge, she danced with the monsters, let herself be swept away with the rhythm of violence, and asserted herself over them.

She played a melody of discordant rhythms whose patterns only *she* knew.

Discordia was what she had become.

CHAPTER TWO

Down

The kingdom of Winstead continued to reign as the mightiest power on the continent. A land where power was held in the hands of a small but dangerous aristocracy whose command of magic through their elemental familiars made them all a force to be feared. These merciless overlords clung tenaciously to their power and ruthlessly purged anyone who resisted them. In that sense, Winstead could be called a paradise for the strong and a hell for the weak.

Everly had been reborn into this world sixteen years ago after concluding that life on planet Earth was no longer suitable to her needs as a future tyrant. She wanted a place where she could flourish and truly spread her wings. And in this new world, she found it.

She still remembered the first time she touched magic. The excitement of experiencing *harada*. The pleasure of claiming her first kill. It had all been so glorious. She'd never felt so complete before . . .

Everly? Are you going to stay in bed again? Titania asked her uncertainly.

Everly ignored the voice of her most trusted servant and pulled the blankets back over her head. She was tired and didn't want to do anything today. That was all.

It was a strange malaise that had come over Everly recently. Like nothing she'd ever before experienced. Everly was someone who had never experienced a moment of doubt in her life. She shunned weakness in all its forms and scorned those who succumbed to it. And why shouldn't she? Suffering was a core aspect of the human experience. Having the will to overcome your troubles and return stronger than before was what separated those who were meant to rule from those who were meant to be *ruled.* Everly was strong. She was better than this.

Yet, despite her resolve, for the last two months, Everly had been unable to leave the room she'd been renting at the Wayward Leaves Inn, at the very edge of Belsar County, where her birth father, a high-ranking member of the nobility, ruled. She'd come into the inn, despondent for reasons she found difficult to articulate, and mentally dominated the staff into giving her a room free of charge. Then she went to bed and refused to leave.

Everly strongly believed in the principles of survival. The strong lived and the weak perished. That was an immutable law of nature that existed long before she'd come along. Why should she spend even a moment second-guessing the decision she had made?

Why did the expression Fenneth wore as she died haunt her so much?

I didn't even know her. She was nothing to me. I didn't do anything wrong.

Despite how often she told herself that, it never seemed to ring true.

As time continued to pass, the collection of friends and servants she'd acquired during her new journeys began to grow concerned. Everly had never been like this before. To be fair, she was an awful person. Someone who refused to learn from her past mistakes based on the nebulous logic of being perfect and therefore incapable of *making* them. More than once, she'd blasphemously declared herself to be a divinity who deserved the right to rule over all others because they were too weak to stop her.

But more than anything else, Everly was a relentless gadfly who couldn't resist the urge to rile up other people and watch them explode into anger for her personal amusement. She was a remorseless, terrible human being.

Her servants loved her very much.

"What can we do for her?" Titania asked fretfully one night in the memory palace.

"We have to shake her out of it," Eris said. "Our Empress must not be allowed to continue this miserable decline. She hasn't done anything wrong! Why should she suffer like this?"

Carter and Grail said nothing. The two of them were more experienced in the ways of the world than the elemental sisters and already knew that some wounds only healed with time.

"She'll bounce back eventually, right?" Titania asked. "I mean, nothing keeps her down. She just needs to be left alone, that's all."

One morning, Everly surprised everyone by crawling out of bed and coming to the inn's main floor for breakfast. She was still in her nightclothes and her hair was a tangled mess, but this was the first time she'd left her room in weeks. She stumbled her way to a table and sat down ungracefully. Then she raised her arm to gain a servant's attention.

Throughout the bustling room, people turned to give her snide looks and to make unfriendly jokes at her expense. Everly paid them no mind. She just wanted a heaping portion of whatever it was she smelled wafting through the air to her nostrils.

"What are you making for breakfast?" she asked the young maid who came to take her order.

"Fresh biscuits with mushroom and sausage gravy," she answered politely.

"Gimme four plates and a pitcher of pressed apple juice," Everly mumbled.

"That's a lot of food, miss. Are you sure?" the waitress asked.

Everly made an impatient gesture with her hand and the maid quickly set off to fulfill her request. When her food arrived, she tore into it with animal gusto, shoving it into her mouth and swallowing it as quickly as she could, searing her tongue with the heat of it and licking her plate when she was finished. Everyone who saw her eat was both amazed and repulsed.

"Damn, little girl," snickered a middle-aged man sitting at a table adjacent to hers. "You must have some swine in your ancestry to pack away a meal like that."

The three other men seated with him chortled nastily at his stupid joke.

"Maybe I do," Everly said absentmindedly as she raised a hand to signal for more food. "It must be how you recognized me."

"Hmm?" the man asked in reply. "I'm afraid I don't follow you."

"Shouldn't swine recognize their own kind? I'm grateful for your acknowledgment, Elder Pig."

An ugly frown creased the brows of the men sitting at that table. Elder Pig in particular began to redden with anger.

Once the maid returned to Everly's table, she was quick to sense the mood and tried to calm the situation down before it could escalate.

Everly paid her words no mind and told her to bring her more food. Her high-handed manner seemed to incense Elder Pig and his friends even more. She didn't care.

When she received her food and resumed eating, the other men began commenting on how disgusting she was and how repulsive her manners were. Her genuine indifference to their presence began to offend them even more than her imperious mannerisms had.

Finally, Elder Pig himself slammed his hand on her table and angrily told her to leave. "Get out of here!" he ordered her. "The way you eat is making our drinks taste bad."

Everly turned to regard the owner of the hand that had placed itself at the center of her table. "It's a little early in the day for that, isn't it?" she asked him.

"What are you implying?" he demanded to know.

"That you're an unemployed drunkard," Everly said indifferently. "No one with any pride in themselves would indulge in day drinking if they had any place to go. You're too young to be retired, so you're either too lazy to find work, or you're too stupid to keep it when you have it. You're also a grown man picking a fight with a teenage girl, so you clearly lack dignity as well."

Everly sopped up the remainder of the gravy with her last biscuit and swallowed it with one bite. Then she wiped her mouth on her sleeve and continued. "Is this really where life has brought you? Was this all your dreams amounted to? It's so pathetic, I could cry. Elder Pig, would you please become my mentor? Would you teach me everything I need to know so that I'll never end up like you?"

It was a sincere offer. Everly never made them *solely* for the purpose of crushing another person's spirit. That was merely a pleasant bonus. While it was true that Everly believed herself incapable of making mistakes due to her status as a superior being, she still enjoyed learning from the missteps and misfortunes of others. If Elder Pig had possessed genuine wisdom, she would have rewarded him lavishly for his services with gold. She would have built him a peerless mansion that even royalty would have envied. If it was lust that motivated him, her necromantic abilities could create peerless beauties of whichever gender he preferred that would have mindlessly existed for no purpose other than to bring him pleasure.

All these things and more could have been his if Elder Pig had only possessed the grace to humble himself before her, say yes, and offer himself to her in eternal servitude. Instead, he allowed his pride to be rankled by her cruel words. Instead of recognizing her patronizing tone and dismissive attitude as the supreme right bestowed upon her by destiny itself, he chose to be offended and slapped her across the face.

Everly blinked in surprise. Had that been the reaction that she'd intended to provoke? It was difficult to say. These last two months had been hazy and bleak. Even on her best days, she barely understood herself and her desires. Lately, she understood herself even less.

She rubbed her cheek gently where the fool had struck her and smiled warmly. She'd been so absentminded lately that she hadn't even bothered maintaining a shield of *harada* to protect herself. His clumsy blow had *hurt* her, which was . . . nice. Pleasant, even. For far too long, she'd been wallowing in emotional turmoil over what she'd been forced to do to resolve a dangerous situation brought on by a certain someone whose face and name she refused to recall.

How nice was it to realize that she didn't have to live solely in her head to experience a little suffering? She could just get it the old-fashioned way. "Do that again," she ordered Elder Pig once the stinging in her cheek had subsided. He stared blankly at her in dumb confusion, uncertain of why she was reacting like this instead of breaking down into tears as he'd expected.

Everly was annoyed by his reluctance to commit to his role.

"I want you to hit me *again*," she explained to him with exaggerated patience. When he gave her another bewildered look, she seized control of his body and forced him to do it herself. First, he slapped her. Then he punched her. Then he threw her from her seat to the floor and began madly pummelling her while she squealed and laughed through her bloodied teeth at the relief his fists brought her.

His friends eventually pulled him off her but not before he grabbed her head and slammed it brutally against the floor, smashing her unconscious.

For the first time in two months, Everly slept restfully, wearing a contented smile on her battered face.

When she awoke the next morning, Everly was surprised to discover herself locked away in a cell, lying on a filthy floor surrounded by other wretched people. This certainly wasn't her comfortable bed, which she had assumed she'd be carried to. Instead, she was apparently being jailed. She wondered what crime she'd committed. Sleeping too soundly or waking up refreshed in an offensive manner? The laws that governed others could be mystifying at times. Which was why the only laws she ever respected were the ones she created herself.

"Ah, there she is," said an unfamiliar voice. Everly looked up to see a handsome, lightly armored man sitting behind a desk in front of the cell where he could closely observe his prisoners while remaining comfortably seated. "Welcome back to the living, Princess."

"And what exactly am I doing here?" Everly asked her jailer as she slowly climbed to her feet.

"Funny you should ask." He smiled at her. "The local constabulary received word yesterday that a young girl had provoked a tavern goer into beating the light out of her. *He left her halfway dead* was what the poor maid who reported this indecency said. *You* are supposed to have a broken face and jaw. By all rights, you should be wheezing or dead."

Everly raised her eyebrow. "You said *the local constabulary.* Are you saying you're not one of them?" she asked the stranger.

"I'm afraid not," he replied with a smile. "I'm just a knight on my way to Count Van Belsar's estate to pay my respects to his mourning wife. The tale of your little misadventure reached my ear when I stopped by the inn for my lunch."

"And what tale is that, precisely?" Everly asked him.

"The story of a mysterious girl who's apparently been living at the inn free of charge for months, although no one can remember signing her in. Apparently, she had the staff under her spell up until the moment she was beaten into unconsciousness by an unemployed lumberman. They're calling you a witch, girl. And your pretty face with nary a bruise or cut is all the proof they need. Which honestly squares with my own theory. You're a runaway, aren't you?"

"Your meaning, sir?" Everly asked with a frown.

"Don't be coy. Belsar County is very close to the first border with Oldstead. Your sort is commonly hunted down here desperately trying to seek refuge in that nation of traitors. Too bad I happened to be here, or your little game could have gone on indefinitely."

Now Everly understood. The Republic of Oldstead was a breakaway nation formed primarily of citizens of Winstead who'd been enslaved by the kingdom's nobles for possessing magic without being a member of their social class. Mages who weren't nobles must either serve them or perish. That was the law in Winstead.

That meant this fool believed that Everly was some runaway commoner seeking her fortune in Oldstead before she could be chained by servitude to her betters.

Everly smiled wickedly to herself. Now, *that* was the sort of interesting background story that a devoted lover of role-playing such as herself could really sink her teeth into! Why pretend to be a wandering adventurer when she could instead be a persecuted weakling in search of freedom? That would lend her all kinds of sympathy from the audience, who now wouldn't be so quick to judge her. It would be like how Magneto from the *X-Men* comics would sink naval ships and drown hundreds of innocent sailors when he was having a snit, but would instantly get a free pass from the readers by mentioning that he was a Holocaust survivor.

Everly was in. *She loved it.* She decided at that moment that she wanted to be a downtrodden victim too. Co-opting the suffering of others for her own amusement and profit sounded quite villainous, and she was now in the mood to once more be *bad*.

"Wh-what are you going to do with me?" she sniffled in fear.

CHAPTER THREE

Clean Boots

The young knight who'd taken Everly into his custody called himself Sir Kelton Tome, which she thought was a passable if not stuffy-sounding sort of name. It made him seem like the kind of person who preferred study time in the library over playing outside with his friends, which he probably didn't have very many of while growing up due to being saddled with an awful name like *Kelton Tome.*

The other children wouldn't have been kind to him, she thought sadly. *She* certainly wouldn't have been. She'd have called him *Kelpie* or *Kelly* and would have tormented him for hours. Not because she was a bully, but because there were certain protocols that all children were expected to follow, and one of them was making fun of weird names.

"Why are you looking at me like that?" Sir Kelton suddenly asked her.

"Hmm?" Everly said as she snapped out of her thoughts. "Oh, I'm sorry. I didn't realize I was staring."

"Right," Kelton said doubtfully. "So, why were you doing it?"

"Well, I was just thinking that you were someone who's probably had a lot going on in his life," Everly told him with some empathy in her voice. "I'm available to listen in case you ever want to get anything off your shoulders."

"Shut up," Sir Kelton glowered.

"Or I could do that," Everly conceded.

Everly decided that she pitied this man and would only kill him if circumstances demanded it or if he was terribly annoying.

Sir Kelton informed her that he'd be taking her with him to the count's estate, where he would leave her fate in his hands. He didn't seem to approve very much of people fleeing the country in search of liberty and told her in no uncertain terms that he'd strike her down if she tried to escape.

For her part, Everly thought he was cute when he tried to sound threatening. Like a little puppy that growled whenever someone approached his owner. She found it very difficult to take him seriously but kept a straight face so that she wouldn't break character.

Sir Kelton then told her that the dungeons were surrounded by his men and that any attempt to flee would be foolish. They were leaving first thing in the morning, so she should try to get some rest for her audience with the count.

On that note, he departed for the inn without wishing her a good night. Which was rude, but she decided to forgive him for this impertinent display thanks to the inspiration he'd provided for her. Inspiration wasn't something anyone should take for granted. It wasn't an infinite resource that you could count on forever, like oil or fresh water. Everly had been feeling a little down on herself for a while now and was grateful to suddenly have something that she wanted to focus on.

Everly had mixed feelings about returning to her father's home. She'd recently had to take some unfortunate actions there for the purposes of preemptive self-defense that resulted in the passing of a certain someone who had interested her. Someone that she would . . . miss? Not that it mattered, of course. Everly knew for a fact that souls were real and continued to exist after death, so it wasn't as though she'd done lasting damage to the person who she'd murdered. It was just that . . . she hadn't really wanted to murder her?

It was confusing. Everly didn't quite know how to feel about it. On the one hand, she was incapable of making human errors because she existed beyond the realm of humanity. But on the other hand, she felt as though her hand had been forced and she *hated* that. The main reason she'd sought this world out was because she never wanted to feel compelled against her will to do something she didn't want to. She'd come here seeking *freedom*.

There was also the matter of her accidentally/intentionally killing her stupid older brother, Aiden. Well, not killing him so much as figuratively tearing him apart like a human-shaped pastry and smearing red jam all over the furniture. She hadn't approached him with the *intention* of doing such an awful, tragic, *oh, my goodness, think of the children* sort of thing to him, but given his personality, she doubted many would mourn him.

Honestly, Everly sincerely doubted anyone else in her position would hesitate to do the same. Aiden was just . . . Well, maybe you had to be psychic to truly understand what an absolute little stain he'd been.

It's been said before that some people were just better off being dead. But in Aiden's case, most people were better off *with* him being dead.

That was just a fact.

Still, while Everly didn't believe there was any way that she could be person-ally connected to the deed, that didn't necessarily mean that she wanted to return to the scene of the crime. That was something serial killers liked to do. They always had to revel in the memories of their trespasses and got off on the atten-tion it brought them.

Which was a very good reason why they so often got caught.

"Eris, how many guards are watching the cells right now?" she asked her servant.

Ten inside the building, seven positioned around it was the answer she received.

"Put them all to sleep for an hour or so. I assume you put a marker on Elder Pig?"

You know me well, Everly.

"I suppose I do, don't I?" Everly smirked.

With no one to impede her, Everly had no difficulty finding her way outside the jail and on her way to Elder Pig's home, which Eris had helpfully highlighted with a towering pillar of light extending skyward from it that only she could see.

It really was a shame that she had to pay a visit to his home like this. That knockout blow he'd delt her had provided the best sleep she'd enjoyed in a while. Deep rest unencumbered by any nightmares or hints of regret to peck away at her. It had been nice. Very nice.

But unfortunately, he hadn't attacked her with the intention of helping her rest, had he? Nope, that was an act of violence and intimidation. And as a proud and confident young person of today, Everly couldn't let such behavior slide. What sort of example would that be setting for others? The responsible thing to do in a situation like this was to calmly confront your assailant and then gently correct their behavior.

When she arrived at the doorstep of his poorly maintained property, she gave Elder Pig's front door a jaunty little knock and waited for him to respond. He came stumbling to the door a few minutes later, cursing blearily and wondering who the hell was knocking at this time of night.

"What the hell are *you* doing here?" he asked with wide-eyed surprise when he realized who it was that stood at his doorstep.

"Cleaning up," she said cheerfully. Which was an ironic thing to say, consid-ering the mess she proceeded to make of him.

A few pleasantly spent minutes later, she had Titania bring her a pail of well water, which she used to clean the mess off herself. After that was finished, she next had Titania make her some fresh clothing. Then she walked back to the jail, being careful to step around the body so that she didn't get any blood on her boots.

Once back in her cell, Everly tried to process her feelings about finally meeting her father face-to-face. It hadn't been something she was looking forward to. From what she'd been able to piece together from infrequent conversations she'd had with her mother, Lyona, over the years, her father was a cold, distant man. Someone obsessed with maintaining the reputation of his household and slow to forgive any slight against his honor. In short, the sort of stereotypically distant father that loads of female protagonists in fantasy stories were stuck with. A foreboding, dignified figure who would be quick to speak disdainfully to her and say things like, "Be silent in my presence, you ungrateful whelp!"

Everly really hoped she wouldn't have to kill him as well. But could it really be helped if he was as much of a prick as her imagination insisted?

One of the character archetypes that Everly most enjoyed was the frowning, foreboding fantasy father who'd relentlessly tell his children how disappointed he was in them, and how much he wished they'd never been born. Everly *loved* characters like that! They existed for no other purpose than to be awful for no reason and to get the audience to despise them. It was a form of villainy that she deeply respected. What motivated someone to improve more than a horrible parent or a similar figure of authority?

Everly often wondered what sort of mother she'd be if she ever decided to have kids. It was difficult to decide. On the one hand, being an Uncle Vernon type was tremendously appealing. But on the other hand, spoiling her children with all the pleasures the world could offer while slowly corrupting them into becoming miniature versions of herself had a lot going for it as well. How could she possibly decide?

What if she had twins? Oh, twins would be excellent! Then she could just openly favor one over the other while slowly setting them against each other. It'd be like the Winstead civil war all over again, but so much worse because her progeny would undoubtedly be little demigods! Oh, she could already imagine all the explosions and screaming.

Yeah, kids were great. Everly had been one herself a couple of times. Childhood was always a fun time in life.

But then again, just because Everly would have enjoyed role-playing as a domineering mother, that didn't mean she would be willing to tolerate being looked down upon by her own parents. That wouldn't do at all. Everly had no reason to believe that anything she did was less than brilliant, and even if she couldn't properly articulate her argument to back up her beliefs, she was still fully capable of reinforcing her point of view with overwhelming violence. Which she would have no problem inflicting on the count if he started going in on her about being an embarrassment to his precious bloodline or whatever.

She really didn't like being talked down to.

Oh, well. How things turned out would be a problem for tomorrow. Everly considered herself more of a creature of the moment. She preferred to keep her future goals nebulous and ill-defined so that she could be free to live her daily life with uncaring impulsivity.

Whether or not she'd kill her daddy would be determined by her mood and his tone. Until their encounter occurred, why waste even a moment of thought on it? She may as well get some shut-eye for the big trip tomorrow. It was going to be an interesting day!

"I don't want to die," sobbed the quavering voice of Elder Pig in her dream as he tried to crawl away from her on his ruined legs.

"Most people don't," Everly grinned as she slowly reached for his eyes.

It hadn't been personal. She'd genuinely enjoyed the slap he'd given her. But she didn't want anyone to think she was going soft. Even if those people didn't yet realize who she would become, she still couldn't let things slide.

Reputation matters.

The next morning, true to his word, Sir Kelton returned to escort her to the count's mansion. Her hands were bound in rope, the end of which was tied to the saddle of his horse. Then he and his men began their journey with her in tow. It was a pleasant walk, so she didn't raise any objections.

No one thought to ask how Everly had cleaned herself up and gotten fresh clothing.

No one cared.

CHAPTER FOUR

Reunion

As Everly approached her father's receiving room, she wondered if this was what trepidation felt like.

Ordinary people placed in situations such as this would undoubtedly feel all sorts of intense, conflicting emotions. Anger, anticipation, nervousness, perhaps even regret. But Everly didn't consider herself ordinary in the slightest, which was why her own reaction surprised her.

Her father had never bothered trying to form any sort of emotional attachment with her. She'd never even seen him before. At the time, she couldn't have cared less, but now that the moment had arrived for their first face-to-face meeting, she didn't quite know what to expect, or even how she'd react. It was . . . unsettling?

The idea that she could be unsettled by *anyone* was infuriating. It was *Everly* who unsettled other people and not the other way around. She was no victim of circumstances; she was the circumstance that created victims! Loads of them! She wasn't nervous at all!

"Feeling nervous, runaway?" snickered Sir Kelton as he guided her down the hall of the manor.

"I just *said* I wasn't!" snapped Everly irritably.

"Huh? You didn't say anything!" said the knight in confusion.

"If you're too ignorant to read the signs, then stick to being a background character," Everly said archly.

Sir Kelton had no idea what that meant. Perhaps fear of her looming punishment was making the girl a bit unhinged. It made sense. To a certain extent, he even felt bad for her.

After all, no one grew up *wanting* to be forced into lifelong servitude to their betters, but the laws that governed Winstead had made the kingdom strong and prosperous for centuries. Her bondage would contribute to a far greater good. She'd realize that in time and perhaps even feel grateful for having a part to play.

But first, they were going to have to break that haughty pride she exuded. Sir Kelton looked forward to that.

He couldn't stand arrogant women.

The count's receiving room was a splendid-looking place filled with tastefully selected, lavish furniture and art. Carefully arranged platters of fruit and cheese with some mulled wine had been placed there as well. Sir Kelton found this slightly confusing.

The receiving room was a place normally reserved for visiting nobility or other notable guests. Sir Kelton found himself wondering why he'd been directed to bring the girl here. Normally, handing over a runaway would have consisted of releasing the girl into the custody of the count's personal jailor so that she could languish in his cells for a bit.

If he didn't know any better, he'd think the count was trying to make this brat feel welcome.

Suddenly, a door opened, and an extremely handsome man wearing nothing but silken undergarments, an open robe that showed off his chiseled physique, and a pair of dark spectacles whose tinted lenses covered his eyes stepped into the room.

His mussy hair was the same shade of burned gold as the girl's.

The man paused to stare at her. She stared back.

They stood that way for a bit.

"Ah," he finally said. "How unexpected. Didn't think I'd have company until later."

"How much later?" she asked innocently.

"*Much* later," he replied. Two women walked into the room, each wearing garments so scant that they left very little to the imagination. One of them wrapped her arms around the man's waist, while the other reached for a bit of cheese and nibbled it in a . . . suggestive manner.

"Well, *damn*." The girl smiled as she gave each of the women an appreciative look.

"Hey! *Mine*," the man said defensively as he spread his arms wide to cover his . . . friends.

"It was a compliment," the girl pouted. "No harm in looking, right?"

"Just so long as we keep things that way," the older man said. He then turned to his companions and whispered to them. One giggled and turned to leave, but not before nibbling on one of his ears. She then took the other woman by the hand and they both left. A few moments later, the door reopened, and a shirt and pair of slacks were thrown in.

With no apparent embarrassment, the other man dressed himself while he and the girl continued to stare curiously at each other.

Sir Kelton continued to stand there in embarrassed bewilderment.

That whole exchange had felt a bit awkward. Okay, more than a bit. Far more. However, he was quick to regain his senses and quickly dropped to one knee. "Your Excellency! I've brought the girl to you as requested. The runaway mentioned in my message?"

Kelton turned to the girl, angered by her audacity in continuing to stand in the presence of Count Marcis Van Belsar, the ruler of Belsar County and one of the most powerful men in the kingdom. "Girl! On your knees! Do you even realize who it is you dare stand before?"

"I kind of have an idea, yes?" the girl replied dryly.

Marcis waved his hand dismissively toward Sir Kelton and said, "Okay. All right. I'll take it from here. Good job, Colton. You may leave."

"It's . . . ahem! It's *Kelton*, Excellency."

"Huh?" Marcis asked.

"My name is *Kelton*, Excellency. Not Colton," Sir Kelton said. "Uh, people get it wrong all the time, I just thought I'd . . . You know, in case you have need of me later, I just thought I'd let you know the correct pronunciation of my name . . . "

"Oh," Marcis said with a nod. "Well, how about that? That would be genuinely embarrassing if I were someone who gave a damn what your name was, wouldn't it, Connie?"

"Uh, *Kelton*, sir . . . ?"

"Why, so it is! Please get out," Marcis said as he pulled back a chair at the table and sat down. As he began greedily devouring mouthfuls of fruit, he suddenly said, "Oh, thank you for your service, by the way. Will you be staying long?"

"Uh, yes, yes, Excellency, if you'll permit it," Sir Kelton quickly stammered. "My men are here from the Godwell dukedom to offer our sincerest condolences to you and your lady wife for the loss of your son and heir—"

"Sir, please don't mention Aiden while I'm eating," Marcis interrupted him. "That was a standing rule in this household even when he was alive. Something about that boy puts me off my appetite, always has. Just another reason not to like the little shit."

"Sir!" said Sir Kelton, his expression aghast at the words the count chose. "Lord Aiden was your son!"

"From my perspective, that feels less like an obvious fact and more like an accusation," Marcis said grimly. "My wife, Countess Anne, is away now, conducting some undoubtedly *grave* and *important* Godwell business, despite now bearing my last name. If you insist on dispensing sympathy to her, you and your men may stay however long you like. See my steward, Kelser, about lodging."

"We are grateful, Count Van Belsar," Sir Kelton said with a stiff bow. "And what would you have us do with this girl in the meanwhile? Shall I escort her to your cells?"

"Hmm. *Tempting . . .*" Marcis said contemplatively.

"Hey!" Everly said.

Marcis sighed. "No, no dungeons for this one. Pull her a seat at my table, please."

"Sir?" Kelton asked, confused once more.

"She's my *daughter*, you fool," Marcis grumbled as he reached for another grape. "Can't you see the resemblance?"

Everly happily preened at the confused knight. "Don't forget the shackles," she added.

"So. Everly. What brings you by, sweetness?" Marcis asked his child after his servants entered the room, bringing with them two heaping plates of eggs, bacon, and seared steak, which they placed before father and daughter before discreetly making their exit.

Everly said nothing. Instead, she continued to stare at her father. She'd had many ideas about what he would look like, how he would act, and how she'd react accordingly. Today he'd defied those expectations effortlessly, leaving her feeling somewhat confused. He was also an enormous eater, and she hadn't been prepared for that at all. She was used to being the biggest eater in the room, but his appetite clearly dwarfed hers.

"Hey," he said, interrupting her thoughts. "It's too late to pretend you're mute. I asked you what brought you by today. You weren't really trying to escape into Oldstead, were you? That would have been a mistake if you had. That place sucks."

"Oldstead . . . sucks?" Everly asked him, surprised at his turn of phrase.

"That's a bit of terminology I once heard a drifter use as he passed through on a pilgrimage throughout the kingdom," Marcis said. "He was upset by how the town guards treated him for being a stranger in those parts. He said their behavior *sucked.* I at once grasped his meaning and adopted its usage into my own vocabulary."

"Why?" Everly asked.

"Because so many things *do* in fact . . . suck. Taxes suck. Work sucks. Marriage sucks. Kids *especially* suck. Now, before I decide whether or not to add you to the massive collection of nouns that I regard as being suckful, I insist you answer my question. Were you really seeking shelter in Oldstead?"

"Nooo," Everly admitted. "I was just passing by. I was going to participate in the summer campaign."

"Participate in what way?" Marcis wondered.

"I'm going to fight, duh!" Everly replied. "I'm *freakishly* strong."

"You consider yourself a warrior?" Marcis said.

"Tch, I'm a veritable goddess of death, Daddy," Everly answered without humility.

"Oh. Cool."

"Cool?"

"Yes. Another pilgrim phrase I acquired in my youth. It denotes my approval. If I think something is *cool*, I'll label it as such. You being a fighter? I think that's *very* cool. Though, I'm surprised your mother permits it."

"I don't need anyone's permission to do anything," Everly said with a slight crease on her brow.

"Is that a fact?" her father asked her in a slightly chilly tone.

"It *is*," Everly said, matching his stare without flinching.

"Well, good," Marcis said as he resumed cutting into his steak. "They say it's better to beg for forgiveness than ask for permission. I hate doing either, and I despise those that do. Life is so . . . pointless. And *boring.* Do whatever you want. Fuck the consequences. Find what you enjoy and stick with it. This kingdom sucks."

Everly was stunned. "Uhhh?"

"What?" Marcis said as he leaned back in his chair. "What? Were you expecting some useful tidbit of practical advice that would make life seem more navigable? It isn't navigable, Everly. It's *stupid.* Man is a cursed beast who desperately seeks order and meaning in this wild patch of chaotic randomness we call existence. It isn't there. We want it to be, but it isn't. There are no rules except the rules we create for others to follow in order to make our own lives easier. That's it. That's all there is."

"Sir, this is a Wendy's," Everly said quietly.

"If that's so, then where's the beef?" her father sneered.

"Oh, fuck," Everly said.

"Fuck *yeah*, you mean," her father smirked.

"You've never met a traveling drifter dropping American slang before, have you?" Everly asked him.

"I actually have," the count said as he tapped a finger against his own temple. "I pulled the information directly out of his mind and absorbed it. I've done so dozens of times. It's *addictive.* I know for a fact that there are worlds other than this one and that for some mysterious reason, people who come from those worlds are occasionally reborn here. I know all kinds of interesting things happen because of that."

"Then you know what I am," Everly said.

"Yep. You're a murdering psychopath," the count said nonchalantly. "Eh, comes with being a Van Belsar."

"I'm *not* a psychopath," Everly said defensively. "I have strict rules that govern my behavior!"

"Yeah, okay, Dexter," her father said mockingly.

"Don't compare me to fictional people!" Everly shouted.

"Isn't that what you like to do yourself?" Marcis asked her. "*What would Kang the Conqueror do in such and such situations? Maybe I should be like Maleficent and poison a spindle needle? Time to be like Krang and cruuuush some turrrrrrtles!* Fiction is your guiding path in life, my black-winged little angel. I'm not judging you for it. I'm *amused* by it."

"Are you trying to pick a fight with me?" Everly asked him darkly.

"Hardly! You're a *lot* stronger than I am," the count chortled. "Besides, fathers and daughters shouldn't fight. It'd tear my *heart* out if you hated me. Just like poor little what's-her-name? You know who I mean. Anne's little grand-get. Farrah? Funnel cake? Something like that."

"Stop," Everly said. "Stop doing that. Stop *mocking* her."

"It makes you angry, doesn't it?" Marcis asked her. "I can tell. Your father is like a fat boy after a long day of school, Everly. I'm an *emotional eater.*"

Everly leaped over the table, her hands extended toward Marcis's throat. She was going to throttle this smug bastard to death, punish him with oblivion for daring to bring up her recent troubles just so he could *laugh* at her over them.

But before she could reach him, his hand swept outward and sent her sailing backward until she smashed painfully into a wall.

"Okay," Marcis said as he blew on his hand and shook it gingerly. "I was kind of being a dick. That's on me. God, that hurt! Listen, I've been wanting you to visit for years, but now that you're finally doing it, it's only because you're in the middle of some weird scheme. You didn't even give me a hug! And don't think I didn't notice you checking out my ladies earlier. Kid, that's a no-fly zone if ever there was one. Don't poach from your old man! It's uncalled for!"

"How do you *know* all this?" Everly asked as she dusted herself off. "How do you know I . . . killed her?"

"The same way I know you killed your brother," Marcis said. He then pushed away his plate of food. "I don't want that anymore. You stepped on it."

"DAD!" Everly yelled.

Marcis sighed. "It's my elemental gift, silly. Like you and your sister, I use spirit magic. It manifested differently from yours, though. Gave me two uncommon abilities. I can empower myself with the emotions of others, which I've just demonstrated for you. I literally eat negative feelings. It's . . . *quite* enjoyable. It makes me strong and fast to degrees that are impossible for ordinary people to comprehend."

Marcis held up a butter knife. He placed it upside down in the center of the table. Then he lightly tapped it with his pinky. It shot through the table with a sound like a bullet being fired and embedded itself into the floor below.

"Anger, fear, jealousy, you know, all those *girly* emotions. They pump me up like you wouldn't believe," he said to her smugly.

"What's your other gift?" Everly demanded.

"It's a *seeecret*," he said playfully.

"I really will kill you this time," she warned him.

"Okay! Fine! Jeez," he said. "It's called psychometry. To put it simply, I can take information from anything I touch. Anything or *anyone*. That includes bodies. Like poor little Fenneth. Everly, you might attack me again upon hearing this, but I really can't stop myself from saying it. Fenneth liked you. That's why she reacted so negatively to your behavior. You really disappointed her."

Marcis tensed, expecting another violent reaction from his daughter. Instead, she stood there unblinking for a long moment. Then she sat on a couch and slumped dejectedly.

"*Fuck,*" she said miserably.

She was surprised a few moments later when her father sat beside her and threw an arm carelessly around her shoulders.

"Yeah. It sucks, right?" he asked her. "You have power. And power separates us from conventional morality in a way that others can't understand. I understand your feelings very well. I didn't want to be a count, you know."

"Really?" Everly asked him.

"Really. I liked traveling. Seeing the land. It's my passion in life. But my older brother didn't believe me when I assured him that I was no threat to his inheritance. I had to kill him because *he* intended to kill me. Then I had to kill my father because he intended to avenge his favorite son. Then I had to kill my uncles when they disputed my claim. My gifts made me too powerful for them to defeat, but they also left me incapable of being merciful. Because I always know when someone's lying. And in the circles of power in which I dally, *everyone always lies.* You can't spare nobles, Everly. They're jackals waiting for an opportunity to pounce. Trust me."

"Why don't you care that I killed Aiden?" asked Everly.

"Because I held him the moment he was born. And it was a happy, joyous moment," Marcis said quietly. "And then my gift activated and told me who he really was. What he was capable of. Aiden had a mind that *crawled*, Everly. He was diseased in ways I cannot describe. I would have thrown him from a window if not for Anne. I warned her what he was, but she believed she could change his nature. Nothing can change our natures, daughter. You did the world a favor, even if that wasn't your intent."

"Does anyone else know what I've done?"

"I told Anne it was the work of an old enemy. She's out there now, on the eastern continent, preparing to *avenge* our boy."

"Why would you do such a thing?"

"You're the only kid I've got who takes after me. As if I'd give you to the fucking Godwells. You're my *reflection*, Everly. Besides . . . I'm not just comforting you. Now that I've touched you, I see exactly how enormous your potential is."

"What does that mean?"

"I wasn't joking when I said I hated this world, my brilliant little angel. And I think a girl like you is *exactly* what this sad little kingdom needs to once more become an interesting place to live. This world will be a million times better with you in it. Bet me!"

Everly turned to stare at her father. He was so handsome. Beautiful, really. The kind of beauty they once sculpted statues of during the Middle Ages. And his smile was welcoming and endearing. But it also seemed so hollow. She reached forth slowly and removed his glasses from his face and was unsurprised to see that his irises were colored an icy blue that seemed to shine vividly even in the brightness of day.

"Dad, are you a bad person?" Everly asked him.

"Not as much as I'd like to be. But I'm working on it. And I'm only going to get worse as I age," he promised her. Then he kissed her on the forehead. "I'm really glad you came home, Everly."

"I'm not staying for long," she said.

"Of course not," he chided her. "You're starting school next month."

"*Seriously?*" Everly asked in surprise.

CHAPTER FIVE

Claudia

O h, don't be so surprised, angel," Marcis snickered once Everly had regained her composure. "It's the law of the land for all the dear children of the nobility to receive their formal education in the capital. Well, those of you blessed with elemental gifts, anyway. I don't know what we do with the more useless variety of children. What did we do with Aiden? I really can't recall."

Marcis leaned back in his seat and furrowed his brow as he tried to recover the necessary memories. Then he shrugged his shoulders and gave up.

"Bleh, I suppose it doesn't matter. Oh, good job killing Casten Meers, by the way. I've been wanting to do that for *years*. I even made the attempt a short while back, but then Anne started giving me such a scolding before I was halfway through strangling the wretch. The man was an absolute *poodle*."

He sighed dramatically and poured himself another glass of wine. "I deeply approve of how you handled him, my girl. You slapped his face backward! That had me tittering for days! Staring at his own ass is a suitable fate for a fellow like that. Would you like to do the same to Sir Kelton?"

"I thought his name was Colton?" Everly asked.

"Do the names ever really matter?" Marcis mused.

"Dad, I don't want to go to *schooool*," Everly moaned piteously.

"Sorry, kitten. Daddy can't do anything about that," Marcis said apologetically. "The state likes to monitor the children of all we rich, powerful maniacs and make certain that we're good, loyal little drones prepared to give our all for the kingdom. May the gods bless Winstead, blah, blah, blah. It'll be a good experience for you! You'll meet lots of fun and interesting people. You might even get to kill a few, if you're sneaky enough."

"But I don't feel like I accomplished anything during my journey," Everly whined.

"Everly, you obliterated the entire town of Bremburg in one fell swoop and defeated a cardinal sin! That's achievement enough to have your name placed in a song. I mean, considering the collateral damage you caused, I'm certain the lyrics wouldn't be very *flattering*, but the fact remains you can't claim you didn't do anything notable. Then there was that lovely defender of the temple whom you crushed with your merciless hand . . ."

"Dad, I won't tell you again. Stop making jokes about her," Everly said furiously.

"Kitten! I was talking about Sarah! *Poor little Sarah!* The Godwells were *infuriated* when they found her in that state. They'll be recalibrating and reprogramming that poor creature for ages to get her back into a semblance of semi-functionality. In the meanwhile, the temple has been forced to appoint a new paladin of the north. What did you *do* to her, anyway?"

"Couldn't you have touched her and found out?" Everly asked.

"Ewww. Didn't want to. I'm not certain if you're aware, my girl, but that kid was dirt-eating mad *before* you laid your fists upon her. Whatever you've done to her since, I don't want an *inch* of it slithering around my memories."

"All I did was take her somewhere quiet to have a long chat, that's all," Everly said.

"Oh? Where was that, I wonder?" asked her father.

"It's called the rat room."

"Ha!" he laughed. "Of *course* it is. Heh, Septis would love that. Maybe I'll give him the idea at our next encounter."

"Who?"

"Everly, brush up on the basics, sweetie," her father said. "Septis is the king of Winstead. I understand not bothering to learn the names of the various . . . How do you refer to them? Background characters? Yes, I understand not wanting to bother with learning the names of the various background characters you encounter, but if your final goal is to rule these lands, then at least remember *his* name. He's rather a big deal around these parts."

"Why bother?" Everly snorted. "I'm just going to kill him and take his stuff anyway."

"Septis is scrappier than you think, angel. Even with your power, you'll need a proper strategy to defeat his forces and supplant him."

"Tch, *Dad*," Everly said with a roll of her eyes. "I can just raise an endless army of the dead and overwhelm the capital. I could make it right now, go to bed, and wake up in the morning as the new monarch if I felt like it."

"Ohhhh," her father said after he finished processing her words. "Well, I suppose that's completely true. So, in that case, why *don't* you?"

"Well," Everly said thoughtfully. "It's not that I don't want to rule over everything and everyone, but I want to do it in accordance with the principles I believe in. I want to gradually crush everyone's hopes and dreams, but not all at once, you see. Plus, I want my enemies to think they have a fighting chance so they'll keep trying their hardest to defeat me. I don't even mind pretending to lose on occasion if it keeps the game going. It's not about the conquest, see? I just want to be the villain of the story. THE villain."

Marcis smiled at his child's earnest words and found himself throwing his arms around her to hug her tightly. "By the gods, you're mad," he said admiringly.

"No, I'm not," she mumbled with her face squeezed against his chest. "My motivations are completely logical to my nature."

"They really are, aren't they?" he asked with a smile. "Oh, Everly, we *really* need to get you to the capital. Let me introduce you to one of Septis's children. You'd be a good match for either of them. Selphie is a timid little thing—I think you'd trample all over her nicely—but Seraphine fancies herself a warrior in the image of the holy maiden. You could have a lot of fun breaking her."

"I don't think I'm ready for a relationship, Dad," Everly said reluctantly.

"Hmm. Really? Well, I suppose I understand. Women are wonderful, but there's something to be said for having a man in your life, isn't there? Did you know that Septis has recently adopted his nephew? The son of the very brother whose blood he shed to secure his throne! Prince Ian has returned to the kingdom."

"Ian?" Everly asked curiously.

"Oh, but I don't know if you'd really like that one," Marcis said with a cunning smile on his face. "Prince Ian is a very kind young man. The hardships he suffered growing up in the frozen north have made him caring and compassionate! He believes fervently in his father's dreams of peace and equality and is quick to draw his sword in defense of the weak and downtrodden. The people of the land call him a hero! The first true one to appear in generations."

"He's . . . heroic?" Everly asked quietly.

"He has the purest heart I've ever seen," Marcis whispered into her ear. "Oh, Everly. He shines so brightly. In his reassuring presence, one can't help but believe that everything will work out in the end. What *sort* of monster would someone have to be to oppose him? Only the *cruelest* tyrant possible would look upon him and see an enemy."

"Daaaad . . ." Everly said excitedly.

"He'll be attending the academy with his sisters," Marcis said. "The three great hopes of the kingdom, all gathered in one place. Oh, I *pray* no one appears before them with any sort of villainous agenda. Can you imagine the tragedy?"

Everly said nothing but blushed furiously as her mind began to wander. Marcis smiled, knowing that he had won.

"Well, I'm glad we got that sorted. I think you'll take to academy life like a fish to water! The fish in this case being some manner of massive man-eating predator. Whatever, I'll make sure Claudia takes good care of you."

"Who?" Everly asked suspiciously.

"*Claudia*, sweetie," Marcis said patiently. "Your sister. I can't remember if she's your older or younger one. Completely slips my mind, I'm afraid."

"You can't tell which of us is older?" Everly said in exasperation.

"I was a very busy man in the months preceding your birth, angel. Your mothers were both ovulating, and I was trapped inside all winter still recovering from my duel with the Mountain Splitter, when—"

"No. Stop. You lost me at *your mothers were both ovulating*," Everly said quickly. Marcis scoffed at this provincial display.

"Don't be prudish Everly," he said. "There's nothing wrong with having an awareness of the wonders of biology. It's very practical! Your mother and I greatly enjoyed each other's company. I'll have you know that the sex that produced you was absolutely *spectacular*! Both Lyona and I had wobbling knees for days afterward. Would you like to know what position we were in when we conceived you?"

"Never in this life, no," Everly answered immediately.

She'd have to speak to Eris later about preparing some mind bleach.

"Oh, very well. Anyway, let's go ahead and introduce you to your sister. You'll love her! She's *great*."

"Is she really?" Everly asked.

"Oh, dear god, no," he said at once. "But she'll be the academy's problem starting next month, so there's that to look forward to."

Everly began to frown.

Marcis led Everly through the corridors of the mansion to a wing of the great house she'd never been to before. Through the seemingly endless hallways and twisting corridors, he eventually brought her to the massive personal quarters reserved exclusively for his daughter.

"Ah, here we are," he said cheerily as he began to rap his knuckles against the closed wooden door.

"Claudia? Lambkin? Sweetie pie? It's your father! I have someone I'd like you to meet! Won't you please open your door?"

Marcis stood there and waited patiently for over a minute before trying again. "Claudia? Lambkin? Sweetie pie? It's still your father! I really do have someone I'd like you to meet! Won't you please open the door?"

This time there was a response.

Several women appeared as if from nowhere, each dressed in the uniform of a maid, but for some reason they were brandishing the razor-sharp cutlery they carried threateningly at Marcis and Everly as they spoke.

"I don't want to talk to you! You're a vile pervert!" one of them hissed.

"You slept with one of my maids again, you nasty bastard! You *know* I can see their memories! Those stains don't wash out, you rutting old goat!"

"Well, if we're being honest, I slept with *two* of your maids this morning, but in my defense, they were *really* into it," Marcis replied shamelessly.

"Nauseating!" shrieked one maid.

"Respect my boundaries, you prick!" wretched another.

"Oh, don't talk to *me* about boundaries, you little brat," Marcis sneered. "What three consenting adults, with a fourth to sit there and watch, do for fun is their own business. Besides, you're hive-minding the help again! *What* have I said about that?!"

"Stop telling me what to do!" one maid yelled.

"I'll be an adult soon!" said another.

"I can't wait to get out of here! All you do is stifle me!" added a third.

"Dearest, smothering the spark of independence is what parents who *care* do. Now, seriously, come out at once. I want you to meet Everly."

"Who's that?" yelled one. "Another one of your harlots?"

"Gross. No, thank you!" another said forcefully.

"You're *really* crossing a line now, libertine scum," concluded another. The original three maids had now grown into a veritable mob of enraged femineity, who all directed their angry faces toward the count and spoke with one voice.

He, in turn, began to sigh wearily.

"Oh, to hell with this. Now I'm starting to feel tired," Marcis said. "Everly, can you handle the rest?"

"What?" Everly asked in confusion. "Why are you dragging me into this? You're the one she's pissed with!"

"Yeeeeah, but you seem *so* capable, Everly. You're just *so* mature," her father told her. "I have this feeling that this whole thing could be resolved peacefully if you were to take up the wheel. Besides, I'm still feeling peckish. You *did* step on my breakfast platter earlier. So in a sense, you owe me? Have fun. I love you both!"

In response, the maids all began throwing their knives after Marcis, which he nimbly evaded before making good on his escape.

"I'll find you, Daddy! I'll make you pay!" they all shouted at his retreating figure.

"Wow, what a piece of work," Everly said with an odd feeling of admiration mixed evenly with revulsion.

"God, you're telling me," glowered the maids. Then they turned to face her. "So, who the hell are you supposed to be? His latest toy? And he really thought I wanted to *meet* you? Please don't feel flattered."

"Gross, no," Everly said. "It's not like that at all. I'm actually your—"

"New maid? No. Uh-uh. Absolutely not," the maids said forcefully. "I seriously can't handle another memory of him seducing one of my servants. Does that bastard not realize the psychic trauma caused by seeing one of your parents naked? *Through a first-person view?* Killing him can't even be called patricide. It's clearly self-defense!"

"Holy shit," Everly said. "You sound like you've had it rough."

"You have no idea!" the maids said at once. "Listen, you seem sweet, you really do. Tell me where you're from and I'll see you're sent home with some gold in your pocket. Oh, I'll have to erase your memories too, but you won't really care about that part. Can't have any embarrassing stories getting out about the family, can we?"

"Hey! *Listen*, please," Everly said, now truly feeling annoyed. "I'm not our dad's sidepiece, and I'm not your new maid, okay? I'm your sis—"

"What did you mean by *our* dad?" the maids said angrily. "Do you mean to say . . . Oh, no, he makes you call him *daddy!* GROSS! Son of a bitch, I'm really going to KILL him this time! Father! Get back here at once," they screamed as they began running in the direction the count had fled.

Soon, the corridor was empty.

"I somehow feel outdone," Everly said to the empty hallway.

Wasn't *she* supposed to be the crazy one? It seemed that her title was now in contention.

Everly kicked the door to the bedroom down and stepped inside to finish giving her greetings.

"Hey! What do you think you're doing?" snapped the bedroom's inhabitant, a young blond woman around her own age, who shared the facial features that Marcis and Everly possessed with a slightly rounder frame. She was also notably shorter.

"Making my introductions, duh?" Everly replied as she stepped farther into the room. "Oh, wow, you're adorable! You look like a little doll."

"What kind of a knuckle-dragging thug are you?" the other girl, Claudia, snapped back. "Do you often find yourself smashing your way into the bedrooms of other people? Reconsider your lifestyle!"

In response, Everly placed her hands firmly on her hips and said, "If my life didn't involve constantly kicking doors open and marching in like I owned the place, I wouldn't want to live it." She then looked around and said, "Man, I thought I had a nice room back home, but this is practically palatial. What do you do with this much open space?"

"Whatever the hell I feel like," Claudia said. "Why did you break my door?"

"To talk to you?" Everly said. "You didn't really expect me to go chasing your maids around, did you? I mean, *you're right here.* That would just be silly."

"What would we *possibly* have to discuss?" Claudia demanded of her.

"I dunno," Everly said. "Do you like boys? Girls? Sword fights? *Ponies?*"

"None of the above and especially not ponies!" Claudia said dismissively. "You feeble commoner! *I* am a kingdom unto myself! I reign, godlike, over the meager lives of my subjects! My every whim is an unbroachable commandment to them, which they are unable to refuse! Tell me why a sacred existence such as myself should waste even a moment of her time conversing with a nobody like you?"

"God *damn*, you are adorable," Everly said. "Seriously, I just want to grab you up right now and snuggle until you die."

"Don't get impetuous with me!" Claudia warned her. "I wield dominion over the soul itself! Why, if I wanted to, I could break your mind like an eggshell! Crush your very will and reduce you to a—what are you DOING?!"

"Ahhh, it's too much!" Everly said happily. Before the other girl realized what had happened, she'd been snatched from her bed and given a devastating hug that nearly squeezed the very life from her body. "Special attack! GLOMP STORM! *Gloooooomp!*"

Everly began joyfully rubbing her cheek against Claudia's face, refusing to let go, and spinning her around in her arms until the other girl was too dizzy to resist. When she'd temporarily passed out, Everly spotted a nearby chair and sat down on it with her sister on her lap. Then she began blissfully playing with the other girl's hair.

Claudia regained consciousness a few moments later and was alarmed to discover her hair being brushed.

"What are you doing?" she asked.

"I cannot resist messing with such gorgeous hair," Everly confessed. "God, it's so soft! Like running my fingers through silk. You are just a perfect little thing! I could do this *forever*."

"I'm definitely going to kill you for this intrusion into my personal space," Claudia vowed. "I'm serious. You're *so* dead."

"Really?"

"Yep. Hey! I didn't say stop brushing."

"You got it."

"Why are you being so forceful, anyway?" Claudia wondered. "You're a lot weirder than any of my old man's other plunge-buddies."

"Do you really think I'm weird?" Everly asked her.

"Who wouldn't? And how are you this damn strong, anyway? You look as much like a doll as I do, but you have the brawn of a gorilla."

"That's insulting, Claudia. I possess the brawn of a *thousand* gorillas," said the displeased Everly. "A nation of them, in fact."

"Don't use my first name so casually, girl. *I'm* the daughter of a count!"

"Yeah? Well, so am I!"

"What? Which one?"

"Van Belsar."

Claudia's head snapped back in surprise. She then suddenly stood up and pushed Everly back against the chair while she stared at her. With their faces inches apart, she looked at the other girl with large eyes.

"Boo!" Everly suddenly said, then giggled when her sister sprang back in alarm.

"Why can't I hear your thoughts?" Claudia asked. "Are you a spirit user too?"

"You guessed it!" Everly said. She then jumped from her seat and embraced the other girl again. "This is so amazing! The perfect gift I never even knew I wanted! An adorable little sister who's also a complete monster. The dichotomy is *beyond* delightful. I *never* wanna let you go!"

"Shut UP!" Claudia shouted as she helplessly tried to pry herself free. "And unhand me! You can't expect me to go along with this! I refuse to acknowledge you!"

"Why not? I'm right here," Everly asked her.

"Your *location* has nothing to do with it, fool! The Van Belsars need only *one* daughter in their household!"

"Okay. I'll have my name changed, then," Everly said as she put the other girl down. "I don't mind going by my mother's last name. Skolder's good enough for her, so it's good enough for me."

"What?" Claudia asked in confusion. "Why would you do that?"

"To make you happy," Everly replied. "If my cute sister wants to be the only Van Belsar daughter, then that's what she'll be."

Claudia stared at her suspiciously. "Okay, what's the catch?"

"No catch."

"There's *always* a catch!"

"Usually, yes, but not today!" Everly declared. She grabbed the other girl by her hands and stared merrily into her eyes. "I *like* you, Claudia. I really, really like you. I can tell just by that look in your eyes that we have so much in common beyond dear old Daddy. I look at you and I see . . ."

"What?" Claudia asked, now curious despite herself. "What do you see?"

"*A collaborator*," Everly said gleefully. "A willing participant in *so* many fun things to come! And I'm so glad of it too! Until this moment, I'd never even realized I wanted a sister as badly as I now do."

"Is your skull cracked or something?" Claudia asked after a few moments had passed.

"Nope!"

"I don't even know your name, stupid," Claudia said.

"I'm Everly! Everly Skolder," Everly said enthusiastically. "I'm your *sister*."

"Yeah, yeah, yeah," Claudia said, flicking her hand dismissively. "I got that already. Listen, Everly, you seem . . . interesting for a provincial girl. I get that you'd want to be around me. I am a *sterling* example of what it means to be a noble. But there are things about me you just don't know, kid. I'm *dangerous*."

"I figured. The way you can control a whole mob of people at once is impressive!"

"I'm not just talking about my powers, sis. I'm talking about the company I keep," Claudia said airily. "My name is known and feared even among demonkind. I've associated with some extremely dangerous beings in my time . . . even one of the cardinal sins themselves."

"No!" Everly said, with widened eyes.

"Oh, yeah. Only Lady Anne knows the full extent of the dark circles in which I've dallied," Claudia said smugly. "It might be pretty dangerous for you to associate with me."

"Which one of them was it?" Everly asked.

"Which one?"

"Which one of the cardinals was it?"

"Oh! Well, it was none other than Acedia. The incarnation of sloth itself!"

"No way," Everly said breathily.

"*Yes*, way," Claudia said proudly. "So, as you can see, I'm not certain you're quite at the level necessary to—"

"Yeah, I totally killed that guy," Everly said, cutting her off.

"WHAT?!"

CHAPTER SIX

On Bad Terms

After leaving his children to get to know each other, Marcis returned to his study to enjoy a light snack. Parenting was often a challenging role. Tiring as well. As a man who preferred never to challenge himself and to rest whenever he made the slightest exertion, Marcis felt that he had earned a proper respite for being able to introduce his daughters to one another while narrowly avoiding being stabbed. A fitting reward was clearly called for.

Upon entering his study, to his surprise, he saw another man sitting in his chair, apparently awaiting his arrival. Marcis did *not* approve of people sitting at his desk. He angrily opened his mouth to order this impertinent intruder to depart when he suddenly realized who it was that had come to pay him a visit.

An anticipatory smile soon spread across his face. Oh, this was going to be *fun*.

"My word, it's *you*," Marcis said as he stepped over to his shelf and poured himself a glass of wine. "How delightful to see you again, Louis! How long has it been since good King Septis saw fit to send you off to that hellish banishment to the north? I see you've been keeping trim. If you don't mind my saying so, you seem a bit younger! Perhaps the cold is keeping you spry?"

Grail said nothing in reply but glared angrily at the other man, who smiled at his reaction before suddenly striking his palm against his forehead as though he'd made an embarrassing faux pas.

"Oh, dear! Please accept my sincerest apologies," Marcis said. "You're not actually *him*, are you? Just a mere simulation of my old friend's memories. A *simulacrum*, if you prefer. Goodness, what did they call creatures like you in the world Everly's soul hails from? Artificial? Yes, that sounds about right. You're an artificial man, aren't you? Um, *Grail*, was it?"

"I don't care what you call me, Van Belsar," Grail said to him. "But you and I need to speak."

"Is that right?" Marcis asked. "Well, in that case, I think I'll call you *Louie*. Oh, I like that! A nice term of endearment to be shared between old friends."

"You know damn well that we were never friends, Marcis," Grail said bitterly. "Don't think I don't remember who you are. The real you slithering beneath that pleasant facade. The hedonistic bully. The unwanted student whom I was obliged to accept due to the request of the former king."

"Well, it never hurts to be good friends with a prince." Marcis smiled with a nonchalant shrug. "Still, I'm a little hurt by your assessment of our relationship, Louie! Wasn't I the most talented of that crop? Even Septis couldn't equal me. He still can't, either, although I'd *never* say that aloud."

"You just did," Grail said without humor.

"Well, so I did. How about that?" Marcis replied carelessly. "Would you care to explain the purpose of this visitation, though? Pleasant though your company is, I'm about to enjoy my evening meal, and I'd prefer to eat alone. Does Everly even know that you're here?"

"Don't think I've forgotten what a poisonous influence you had on Prince Septis, Van Belsar," Grail said while ignoring the other man's question. "How his character changed once he met you. You darkened his soul with your foul presence and turned him against his own brother."

Marcis smiled with delight at the accusation.

"Oh, Louie. Do you *still* blame that exciting little war on me? How can you be so unreasonable? I was so young back then. We all were! I merely introduced Septis to a little bit of my personal philosophy; how can it possibly be *my* fault that he took to it so readily?"

"There didn't have to be a war," Grail said heatedly. "There was a plan in place—"

"What? Shared rulership of the kingdom? Oh, *please*," Marcis said, his voice now dripping with contempt. "Louie, that was a fantasy from the start. A kingdom needs a king. *A* king. Not *two*. That would have been a ridiculous constraint upon them both. It disappoints me that you feared the spilling of blood so much that you attempted to wrangle their father into that desperate compromise. Thank goodness Septis saw reason and decided to assert his rights, otherwise this boring little land would have been even *more* insufferably dull."

"You were the war's architect!" Grail shouted, now no longer able to contain his anger. "Everything that happened stemmed from your friendship with the prince! If you had never been there—"

"But I *was*, Louie. I *was* there. So, there's no point in dwelling on the how and why of our dear king's decision-making," Marcis said with a malignant grin.

"It happened because you *corrupted* him!" Grail yelled.

"You give me entirely too much credit, old man. The darkness in His Majesty's soul is greater than you know. I merely helped him realize his own potential like a good friend should. Where his instincts took him from there was his own business."

"And now you'd do the same with Everly," Grail said.

"Ahhh, now we've come to it!" Marcis said with an insolent grin. "Louie, as dear as you are to me, I must warn you, it's a foul thing to come between a father and his beloved child. Propriety insists that you take a step back, old man."

"Shut up!" Grail said. He was across the room in a moment and slapped the glass of wine from Marcis's hand before grabbing him by the shirt to glare into his eyes. "Everly doesn't need you in her life, you vile serpent! After she leaves for the capital, you're not to contact her ever again!"

"Oh, *Louie*," Marcis moaned. "It's been so long since you last manhandled me with your strong, *strong* hands! I've forgotten how enjoyably *rough* you can be! Chastise me more!"

"It was fate that spared you that night in Redmane's fields," Grail said with a murderous whisper. "I nearly had your head then, you little wretch. I'm sorely tempted to take it now."

"Oh, that fight was the making of me, Louie. It really was. Sure, I lost. Some would say badly, but the entire experience was of *such* intensity. Too bad I've grown so powerful since then. I really don't think I'll ever be able to experience another night quite like it," Marcis said dreamily.

"What are you babbling about—" Grail began to say before he was sent flying back with a shove.

He recovered his balance immediately, but before he could retaliate, Marcis was upon him, now with a sword in hand. Despite his resolve to wield only an axe in battle, a lifetime of practice caused Grail to snatch a mounted sword off a wall and parry the thrust that had been aimed at his neck. "How *dare you*," he growled, enraged at being forced to break his vow.

"I *am* a little scamp, aren't I?" Marcis grinned. He then began his attack, one hand behind his back as he began making rapid thrusts with the single-edge saber he carried, his movements so quick that even Grail found it difficult to defend against them.

This was another reason that Grail despised this man. Even though Marcis couldn't even use *harada*, he was somehow able to match those who could in single combat. His strength and speed had always been astonishing, and even at the peak of Grail's power as the Mountain Splitter, defeating him had been a close call.

It seemed that the years since their duel hadn't slowed the bastard one iota. Indeed, he seemed even stronger than before.

It was *infuriating*.

"Hmm. You seem a bit off your game, Louie. I'm disappointed! If you're going to come into a man's home and threaten his life, at the very least you should be able to back your words up!" Marcis taunted him.

"Enough!" Grail roared. From his body sprang plates of heavy armor that sheathed around him, making him impenetrable to harm. In moments, a giant horned figure towered over the count, staring balefully at him with eyes that emitted fire.

"Oh, my. Didn't expect you'd do that," Marcis said just before Grail seized him by the neck and hurled him through a window to land on the lawn outside.

"Hmm. I think I *may* have touched a nerve," Marcis said to himself as he lay in the dirt. He rose unsteadily to his feet as Grail's footsteps pounded toward him. "Ah, Louie, old friend? What say we call this off for now? Wouldn't the evening be better spent enjoying a good meal and reminiscing about the good old days?"

"I'm going to pull your head off and place it on an ant hive," Grail responded grimly as he lifted the man up once more.

"Well, that's always an option too, but how are you going to explain my demise to Everly?" Marcis wondered. "I mean, it's not as though you can keep any secrets from her. She'd be awfully sore if you did such a thing to me, wouldn't she?"

"She'd get over it. She's resilient."

"Of course she is! She takes after her father," Marcis replied cheekily. "But she *still* doesn't like it when people ignore her wishes, does she? How do you think she'll react to this bit of unilateral homicide?"

"Swear you'll stay away from her!" Grail demanded.

"I can't do it, old man. She's far too interesting," Marcis said apologetically. "I'd rather be dead than bored, so go ahead and do what you must. My only regret in life is not being more selfish!"

"Have it your way, bastard," Grail said as he reached for the other man's head.

"Though . . . now that I think about it, even if you *do* kill me, my dearest daughter will simply resurrect me from the grave. Build me a new, immortal body just like yours and that Nalec chap's, wouldn't she? Then I'd have *eternity* to do as I like? Oh, I like that! I like that a lot! Go on, Louie! Finish me off!"

He then bared his neck to make it easier for Grail to strike.

"What a ridiculous bluff," Grail frowned. "She hasn't copied your mind."

"Can you be *certain* of that?" Marcis asked him quietly.

Grail paused. Then he stared hatefully at this ridiculously evil man, torn between the desire to destroy him and the fear that he was being deadly serious. Indecision gripped him in that moment, leaving him unable to decide the best course of action.

Finally, although it frustrated him greatly, he hurled Marcis back onto the lawn, battered but alive. Then he retracted his armor.

"If you do *anything* to impede Everly, if you dare use her to enact even one of your miserable schemes, then I'll come for you no matter what. Do you understand me, Marcis?" Grail asked him.

"Of course, of course," Marcis replied. "Wouldn't even *dream* of doing such a thing, Louis. A father's job is to encourage his child's dreams. I just want to see my little angel *soar*, that's all. Any *real* father would."

"I love her as dearly as if she were my own blood," Grail said.

"But she *isn't*, is she? And that's a boundary you should respect," Marcis said with an unbearably knowing smirk.

"You little *bastard*," Grail said vehemently as he took a step toward the other man.

"Ah, ah, ah, I was merely offering an opinion, my friend. No more tussling for me tonight," Marcis said. "Thank you for the exercise, though! It was quite invigorating. That'll aid my appetite well, I think."

Marcis began heading to the house while whistling a jaunty tune when Grail cut him off once more. "Everly deserves better than you, monster," he said to him in a low voice.

"Yes, I expect she does," Marcis replied. "Funny how life goes, isn't it? I'll let the guards know not to attack you if they should sight you. If I were you, though, I'd retreat to that wonderful memory palace my daughter created. Wouldn't want her wondering what you've been up to, would we?"

"One day, Van Belsar . . ." Grail said to him.

"Of course, of course, whatever you say," Marcis said dismissively as he walked past him.

There in the dark, Grail stood for some time.

Angry and alone.

CHAPTER SEVEN

Killjoy

The sound of a rooster crowing directly into her ear caused Riley Kilo to awaken with a start and also caused her to stumble out of her bed to the cold wooden floor.

"Graaah! What the hell!" she said as she stared around the room with wild eyes after assuming a defensive position with her ring out. "Bruticus? Was that you?"

"Yes," said an extremely deep and unpleasantly aggressive-sounding voice.

"Why did you do that?" she demanded as she stood up and gingerly rubbed her forehead where she'd accidentally smacked it against the floor. "That freakin' hurt!"

"Good. Let your momentary pain be a reminder to immediately awaken when your preset alarm activates."

"And you *had* to scream in my ear over that?" Riley asked with a frown growing on her brow.

"I didn't have to. I *wanted* to. Punctuality can be a matter of life or death on the battlefield."

"In exactly *what* way?"

"I may be forced to terminate you in the future if you refuse to awaken when I tell you to."

"Bruticus, have any of your previous partners ever called you a mean asshole before?"

"Every single one of them," he said in a thoroughly pleased tone of voice.

"Yeah, I bet," Riley muttered. She stood on her tiptoes and stretched her arms toward the ceiling. Then she fell forward and began doing a set of push-ups to warm up her body and force the sleepiness out of her head. Bruticus was being a pain like always, but her partner made a good point. She wasn't in the academy anymore; she had to start exercising better awareness of her surroundings. In a serious situation, Bruticus would have her back, but it wasn't fair to put everything on him.

She wasn't a cadet anymore. Big girls carried their own weight.

"Ser Riley. The human male you rutted with last night has awakened and is currently observing you. Would you like me to terminate him?"

"What?!" Riley said in alarm before jumping to her feet with an embarrassed blush on her face. She was a pretty girl with a head of blazing red hair, cut short, which perfectly complimented her pale skin and freckles. She was currently dressed in underwear and a T-shirt and had assumed she'd gone to bed alone last night.

That was apparently not the case.

"Did we really?" she asked in a high-strung voice.

"Yes, you did."

"Why didn't you stop me?"

"You were highly inebriated and told me to piss off and let you *have some fun.*"

"And you *listened* to me?!"

"You *are* my commanding officer, after all."

"Are you certain we—"

"Would you like me to activate a [Black Light]?"

"Daaaaaamn you!" Riley cried out ferociously while shaking an angry fist toward the sky.

"Who're you talking to?" asked the man in her bed.

Riley turned to him and saw to her absolute horror that he was handsome and fit looking but also *very* youthful. Too youthful! She pounced on him in a state of near panic, and with her face inches from his, asked him desperately, "Hey, buddy! Uh, how old are you?"

Oh god, please be eighteen, oh god, please be eighteen, oh god, please be eighteen . . .

"I'm nineteen," he said with a smirk.

"Hallelujah!" Riley cried out rapturously to the heavens while hopping on the bed in ecstatic relief. Then she paused, suddenly suspicious, and pointed her hand at the man. "Say that one more time, please."

"Uh, I'm nineteen," he repeated.

"Bruticus, [**Lie Detector**]."

"He's telling the truth, Ser Riley," Bruticus promptly informed her. He sounded disappointed that she wasn't going to continue freaking out.

Riley collapsed on the bed, now suddenly exhausted. "Bruticus, add honey mead to the list of things I hereby refuse to ever again drink in excess."

"Why bother? You'll break your vow the moment it inconveniences you."

"Lies!" Riley said with great personal determination. "From now on, I am a good girl and vow to live as such from here on out!"

"Okay," said her bedmate as he quickly stood up and dressed. "Well, uh, I'll see myself out, okay? You have a good day."

"Huh?" Riley said as she sat up and swept her bangs out of her eyes. "Hey, uh, have you had breakfast yet?"

"Well, y'know, I kind of ditched my crew to hang out with you, so I should go meet up with them. I mean, I had fun, but uh, I can see you've . . . got a lot going on," he said.

"What? No, I've got nothing going on! I mean, if you change your mind . . ." Riley said.

"Yeah, no, I'm probably not going to do that. But hey, have a good one," said the man as he quickly walked out of the inn room, leaving Riley by herself.

"Well, *that* could have gone better," she sighed to herself.

"That could have gone MUCH better," Bruticus agreed. **"I feel embarrassed for you, Ser Riley. If I were an inferior organic life-form, I would give serious consideration to self-deletion after a rejection like that."**

"You're a real pal, do you know that?" Riley asked him with a cocked eyebrow.

"I am a rose that blooms in all seasons," Bruticus said loftily.

"You know plants grow out of shit too, right?" Riley said in annoyance. Then she flopped onto her stomach and wearily declared that she was going back to sleep.

"Do as you wish. But the battle royale begins in forty minutes. Your bedmate will be participating."

"What battle royale?" Riley asked irritably.

"You signed up to participate last night while inebriated. It's a national contest to find a temporary replacement for the so-called *paladin of the north* while the current one recuperates from wounds received in battle."

"Why would I do something as dumb as that?" Riley wondered to herself.

"Because you were trying to impress Eric with your prowess. You said *I could do that, I'm SUCH a badass!*"

"Did I really say that?" she asked him meekly.

"You did. I don't have a body, so I could not cringe on your behalf. I would have, though. I would have."

"Who the hell is *Eric*?"

"The boy who just patronizingly dumped you moments ago after your one-night stand."

"Oh," Riley said. "Well, I suppose I should kick his ass, then, at the very least."

"I currently have him targeted. At your command, I will erase him from existence with a devastating air-to-surface strike."

"What's the projected collateral damage?"

"Extensive."

"Denied."

"You're the only one who gets to have fun," Bruticus complained.

"Yeah, well, I'm the one wearing the forge ring, pal," smirked Riley Kilo, Knight-Binary-Minor of the order of forge knights. "Set me up a [**Shower**], will you? I guess we have a contest to win."

Half an hour later, Riley made her way to the staging grounds of the tournament, sipping a mug of hot cocoa and watching everyone getting ready for battle. She was now dressed in belted trousers, a pair of worn but comfortable boots, and a jerkin, over which she wore the traditional red cloak of her order.

She didn't think she stood out too much, but from the glares that she was receiving from her mostly male competitors, it was easy to guess that women didn't commonly participate as combatants in this sort of thing.

"Well, look at me, breaking the ceiling for the ladies." She smirked to herself while continuing to enjoy her sweet drink. "I guess that makes me a pioneering girl boss! How about that, Bruticus?"

"Unlikely," her ring's artificial intelligence said scornfully. **"The prior paladin was also a woman of considerable ability, as are two of the remaining three."**

"Huh?" Riley asked in confusion. "Then why is everyone flashing me such shitty expressions?"

"You're dressed in male clothing and sipping cocoa. Your opponents may consider your attitude and demeanor irreverent and disrespectful of their warrior traditions."

"Wow. These stage-two civilizations really like falling back on those boring old tropes, huh?" she asked. When she finished with her drink, she promptly created a [**Waste Basket**] to dispose of her cup, then [**Recycled**] both back into the soil.

After that, she wandered around the area, saying hello to the various participants who responded with either creatively descriptive threats or cold silence. Eventually, she found Eric and gave him a wry grin when he was startled at the sight of her.

"Hey, bud. Relax. From what I remember of it, last night was fun," she said to him casually. "You don't have to run. We're copacetic, trust me."

"Oh. Okay, good," Eric said, breathing out a sigh of relief. "I'm sorry if I was . . . uh, abrupt. You were just talking to yourself a bunch, and I was a little unsure of what was happening."

"Yeah, I'm a little out there," Riley said with a shrug.

"So, you're participating in the temple's battle royale, huh?" Eric said. "Listen, don't feel you have to go through with this just to impress me. I'm a seasoned adventurer, you know. And even I'll be in danger with this collection of animals running wild."

"Oh, an *adventurer*," Riley said admiringly. "That sounds like a cool job. Gathering herbs for healers and collecting wool for farmers. Hey, do you do any escort quests? I hear those are a blast!"

"Uh, I'm a little past the rookie stage," Eric said with a slightly strained smile. "I'm Eric of the Brave Quartet! Surely you've heard of me. One of the brave survivors of the massacre of Bremburg?"

"Sorry, I'm not familiar with that," Riley said. "I'm a late arrival to this dimension, you could say."

"Well, I'm sort of a big deal, and I've rightfully earned a fair bit of fame," Eric said crossly. "Listen, this brawl is going to get nasty. Being a paladin, even a temporary one, would be a feather in the cap of many a proud warrior. I hope you don't expect me to take it easy on you just because we had a little fun together. That was a pleasure, but *this* is business."

"Hey, I wouldn't dream of it," Riley said obligingly. "I've got no dog in this race. Maybe I'll just keep the prize money when I win and let the runner-up have the title."

She said this loudly enough to let her voice carry. If the expressions that greeted her earlier were angry before, now they were positively *murderous*.

"You're not going to make too many friends with an attitude like that," Eric muttered to her before walking away.

"Pfft, their loss. I'm great once you get to know me," Riley said to his departing back.

Ten minutes later, a man in ostentatious white robes approached the stage to the cheers and adulation of the rowdy crowd, which was excited to see what would surely become the event of the year.

The robed man spoke of past tragedies and the loss of someone named Dame Fenneth, which had some of the crowd in tears. Next, he spoke of the loss of Bremburg and some kind of invasion that had recently taken place. Honestly, it was all a little difficult for Riley to keep track of.

Finally, the robed man spoke of Bremburg being avenged.

"With the loss of her dear cousin weighing heavily on her heart, and the demons arrogantly massing from the gates of the town to spread their foul miasma throughout our beloved kingdom, Lady Sarah made the decision then and there to turn the tide! With the power of the light to illuminate her path and the will of the gods to guide her righteous hand, she smote the hellish invaders with relentless divine fury and crushed their fiendish leader in personal combat!"

The crowd cheered uproariously at this part and deliriously chanted the woman's name for nearly a full five minutes. "Sarah! Sarah! *Sarah!*"

"Man, this old guy is no slouch at spinning a yarn," Riley said. "The order ought to snatch him up for our public relations department. He's got a gift for propaganda."

"He's lying about everything," Bruticus said with absolute certainty. **"His heart rate and breathing patterns have given him away. Something is being covered up."**

"Could it possibly affect our mission?"

"Unlikely."

"Then who cares? We're just having some fun while we work," Riley said.

"I hate it when some aether-corrupted demihuman mutant attempts to deceive me," Bruticus seethed. **"A mere four thousand years ago we would have slated the entire population of this mud pit for extermination and sanitized the surface from orbit."**

"Jeez, you old-timers really hate magic, don't you, partner?" Riley asked him chirpily.

"It corrupts everything. It distorts reality. It is an abomination. As are all these creatures assembled here."

"That's a snap judgment, Bruticus. That's why the order sent us here for this surveying gig. However long it takes, we need to ascertain if the people of this world are a potential pandimensional threat."

"They are. I recommend immediately initiating extermination protocols."

"*Denied,*" Riley said. "We've only been here for two days, B. Let's try shepherding a little before we jump straight to the butchery."

"Rrrr. Organics always lack resolve."

"When it comes to depopulating a planet? Goddamn right, we do," Riley said with a frown.

They'd warned her before accepting her commission that Bruticus was a hard case. *Intractable* was practically his middle name. He was a third-generation forge ring and thus older than some solar systems. Normally, such a long-lived and experienced mind would have long since retired from frontline operations to live in harmony with his siblings as a revered icon of the order.

The reason he didn't was because his siblings *despised* him. And rightfully so. Bruticus was an *ass*. He was stubborn, difficult to work with, frequently critical of his partners, and believed resolutely in overwhelming violence as the best possible solution for every possible situation. He was a complete nightmare to be around, and his partnerships rarely lasted longer than a handful of months.

Somehow, Riley had been with the old goat for nearly four years. She'd received him when she was fifteen. Now, at the age of nineteen, their partnership had somehow become the longest-lasting relationship either of them had ever been in.

Before being recruited into the order, Riley had grown up in a Massachusetts town called Sandwich, which she frequently had to insist to disbelievers was an actual place that existed. She was the only daughter in a tight-knit family with seven older brothers. They never took it easy on her for being a girl, and she learned early on how to use her wits and her fists to survive growing up with a bunch of hockey-loving lunatics who didn't mind sending slap shots in her direction if she couldn't get out of the street in time.

A key part of her boisterous upbringing had been her grandfather, a first-generation American straight from the Emerald Isle itself. A kindly, neighborly man for the most part, but also the meanest bastard in town if you caught him on a bad day. Sensing she'd need the help, he'd taken his granddaughter under his wing and instilled in her the values every young person needed to know to get by in this crazy thing called life.

Such as when to elbow an idiot in the throat when he wouldn't back off, and how to offer a credible argument of self-defense if you decided to attack someone from behind with a baseball bat because you caught them wearing a Lakers jersey in public and they wouldn't apologize.

Riley loved her grandfather dearly and missed him when he passed. And so, despite his anti-organic, extremely paranoid, sadism-prone, ill sense of humor, alongside his relentless suggestions for species-wide extermination of whatever the local flora and fauna happened to be, Riley got along with Bruticus just fine.

He reminded her of her grandpa. So he became family.

For his part, Bruticus was extremely suspicious of Riley's willingness to put up with him. But after a while, he merely accepted that she was probably deficient in some manner particular to organics, and so he resolved himself to look out for her. And to mock her at every available opportunity for being inferior to him.

So, in that sense, she became *his* family as well.

Partnerships can be complex things. Or they can be as simple as two souls connecting in the spirit of true friendship and finding something in the other that they lacked in themselves. Bruticus was a mean old bastard. But he was also seasoned, capable, and a ferocious combatant.

Riley could be deadly if the situation called for it, but she was also kind and patient and willing to accept other people for who they were. She was the first cadet to ever reach the vaunted rank of Knight-Binary before graduating.

Any opponent who underestimated her because of her age did so at dire peril. That no-nonsense aspect of her personality was perhaps why she and Bruticus were able to work so well together.

Sometimes, people just *click*.

"Bruticus, prep a [**Stealth Screen**], a pair of [**Air Walkers**], a [**Matter Phaser**], a [**Stun Glove**], and a [**Sound Dampener**]," Riley said as the announcer continued. "Activate them as soon as I snap my fingers."

"I recommend aerial support as well. Stealth drones."

"Good idea. Make sure their weaponry is non-lethal."

"FINE," he said grouchily.

"And so, let this battle for glory and honor begin!" the man in white said to rapturous applause.

With that said, a loud bell began to toll thunderously in the background.

Throughout the announcer's speech, Riley had begun slowly backing away from the center of the arena, where the fighting would surely be at its fiercest. Many of her opponents, Eric included, realized what she was doing and began sneering at her in derision. As soon as the bell rang, they turned toward her to attack, sensing easy prey.

The poor, poor things.

Riley smiled at them cheekily and gave them a jaunty wave in farewell. Then she snapped her fingers and vanished from view.

"What the hell?" said the fighter closest to her position, an imposing brute who stood nearly seven feet tall, wielding a massive club. "Where the hell did she go?"

"She's cloaked! It's a rogue's trick," said another. "Just check the sand for her footprints."

"I *know*," bellowed the first brute. "There ain't no footmarks! The little cow just vanished!"

Calling a young lady who cares about her personal fitness and engages in regular heavy calisthenics a *little cow* is a cruel thing to do. For his careless words, and in the name of justice for people everywhere who didn't want to be referred to as bovines, Riley poked him on the chest with the finger of her stun glove.

"Bloop!" she said to him.

ZAP!

The overly muscled oaf went sailing through the air and landed, unconscious.

He'd been very close to finding her. It just wouldn't have done him any good. First, her stealth screen masked her perfectly from view. Next, the matter-phasing unit she was using allowed her to walk through solid matter as though it were thin air. The big man had passed through Riley several times and never even noticed.

The air walkers she now wore were a personal antigravity unit worn like a pair of boots, which levitated her several inches above the ground and allowed her to walk without so much as disturbing a leaf. The sound dampener negated any noise she made, and the stun glove on her left hand was an automatic one-hit knockout. Well, a *one-tap* knockout, anyway.

If Riley wasn't enjoying herself so much, she could have ended the melee at any time by having her stealth drones open fire with their tranquilizing shots; she could have brought the curtain down on everyone in an instant.

In other words, this was neither a fight nor a competition.

This was just her having a little fun.

For the next twenty minutes, Riley sauntered through the midst of the other combatants casually poking anyone who caught her eye, pausing to watch one-on-one fights that looked exciting, intervening whenever anyone was ganged up on only to dispatch the victim herself after his attackers had been defeated, and just generally enjoying the vibe of the moment. She had her earbuds in, she was listening to her tunes, and she was giving considerable thought to whipping up another cup of cocoa.

Yeah, this was a good day.

Soon, the other participants had been whittled down to three other fighters. To Riley's surprise, Eric was one of them.

"Wow, I guess he was as good as he said he was," she said with mild surprise.

"That just means the rest of them were worse than they realized," said the unimpressed Bruticus.

"Perhaps, but this setup has hilarious possibilities. Deactivate the cloak and the matter phaser and set me up with a [**Personal Force Field**]."

"Done," Bruticus said at once.

"Awesome sauce," she said.

The two warriors behind her continued to advance on Eric, who looked tired but determined. The odds weren't looking too good for him when Riley suddenly appeared behind his opponents and crept forward with comically exaggerated motions to tap each one on the shoulder.

"Bloop and bloop," she said smugly as they passed out at her touch. "Heeeey, bud. Looks like it's you and me, huh?" she asked him as the crowd went wild at her sudden appearance.

"*How* are you this good?" Eric asked her in utter bewilderment.

"I dunno. Born lucky, I guess," she said with a pert shrug of her shoulders.

"Whatever. I said I wasn't going easy on you, and I'm a man of my word. Prepare yourself!" Eric said dramatically as he held up his dagger and shifted into a combat stance.

"Bring it on, pretty boy!" Riley said confidently as she gestured for him to attack. Eric blushed slightly at her terminology but quickly regained his composure and launched himself at her with what surely would have been a devastating flying kick, only to bounce off her personal shielding and land roughly on his back.

Before he could recover, Riley was reaching down toward him with her finger pointed directly at him.

"Bloop!" she said merrily.

* * *

When Eric recovered from whatever it was that strange girl had done to him, he saw her preening before the audience, happily blowing kisses and drinking in their cheers and adulations, while also sticking her tongue out at the occasional person who booed her.

All around her, the place was in a frenzy. Angry combatants argued with the officials that she couldn't possibly be the winner, that she hadn't fought fair, and that the magic she used was too different, too *strange*. Meanwhile, the girl kept mugging it for her new fans, clearly having far too much fun.

Eric reluctantly approached her, and said, "Hey."

"Yo," she replied with a barely contained smirk.

"Uh, good job. I guess I underestimated you."

"No worries, it was all good fun," Riley said as she slapped her hand on his shoulder. "Maybe you'll get me next time, huh?"

"Yeah," Eric said with a slowly growing smile of his own. "Maybe I will."

"That's my dude! Dream big and big things can happen to you," the girl said cheerfully. "Wanna get a drink later? Like, just a drink, though. I'm not looking for a repeat of earlier. I'm being *responsible* now."

"Lies."

"Ha, yeah, I get that," Eric said. Then he held out his hand. "Uh, I'm Eric."

"Yeah, I know," she snickered.

"You do?"

"I dislike this idiot."

"Grampa, be nice," Riley said sternly.

"Hmph."

"Huh?" Eric asked in confusion.

"Nothing, nothing," the girl said with some embarrassment. "Anyway, I'm—"

"FOOLS! BLASPHEMERS! DOGS OF THE FALSE DIVINITIES!" screeched a pale young man in a black robe whose voice somehow carried over the entire arena.

"What the heck is going on here?" Riley asked.

"I have no idea," Eric said.

"DO YOU BELIEVE YOURSELVES SAFER NOW THAT YOUR SO-CALLED TEMPLE HAS PICKED A NEW CHAMPION?" continued the man. "WRONG! WROOOOOOOOOONG! YOU HAVE SINNED AGAINST THE SEVENTH KING OF SIN! YOUR VICTORY AGAINST MASTER SLOTH WAS A TEMPORARY REPRIEVE! HE SHALL RETURN IN ALL HIS UNTHINKABLE GLORY! WHAT BECAME OF BREMBURG WILL SEEM LIKE A PLEASANT DREAM!"

"I'm starting to think this is a bad guy," Riley said mildly.

"Uh, you *think*?" Eric asked her. "He's planning something! We've got to stop him!"

"Yeah, I guess that makes sense," Riley said reluctantly. She was the new paladin after all. "Bruticus, give me an honest assessment. No sarcasm, please. How dangerous is he?"

"The target is currently channeling an alarming amount of aetheric energy. I believe he is either preparing to open a dimensional rift or preparing to self-detonate. I sincerely recommend he be terminated at once."

"Damn," Riley said sadly. "Oh, well. He made his choice."

That's really what it always came down to in the end. Choices. Your decisions defined who you were as a person. They also determined how you lived and, sometimes, how you died.

No getting around that. This guy had made his choice.

So Riley made hers as well.

"NOW COMES THE FIRE!" bellowed the deranged man. "FROM THE VERY DEPTHS OF THE ABYSS, I SUMMON A WINGED BEHEMOTH! COME, BALROG! COME FORTH AND AVENGE OUR MASTER!"

Behind the man, a rift tore open: a hole in reality the size of a large building, from which emerged a gigantic creature composed of fire, flesh, and darkness. In its hand, it held a bloody flail comprised of many screaming bodies. Its malicious face was terrifying to behold, and at the sight of it, the people were struck dumb with fear.

"LET THE FEAST COMMENCE!" screamed the summoner. "LET ALL SEE THAT THEIR PALTRY LIGHT CAN NEVER PROTECT THEM FROM THE DARKNESS! NOW COMES OUR RETRIBUTION—"

"[**Fusion Cannon**]," said Riley.

And then there was light. Blinding and terrible, so intense that it overwhelmed the senses of all who beheld it. But when it cleared, the Balrog and his summoner were no longer there. Or perhaps it would be more accurate to say that they were now *everywhere*.

Just not in any spiritual sense.

"Peace through tyranny achieved," said Bruticus in a deeply satisfied voice.

"Sorry, bud," Riley said in the direction of her newly deceased target as she set aside the massive weapon that she'd fired. "Though, I'm glad the situation was that easy to sort. I really would have hated to bust out the *serious* ordinance."

"I think you should fire twice just to be certain," Bruticus advised.

"You are impossible sometimes," Riley sighed.

"What the hell was THAT?" asked the extremely alarmed Eric as soon as his head stopped ringing.

"That? That was just a warning shot," Riley said.

"What kind of damned warning shot was *that*?!" Eric said fearfully.

"The kind you *heed*," Riley said. The smile she wore was still friendly, but it was also slightly harder than her earlier ones had been. "We still on for that drink?"

"Who *are you*?" Eric asked in a daze.

"Oh, right. I'm *Riley*," she cheerfully said as she helped him to his feet. "You wanna try that honey mead again? That stuff was *bonkers* good."

"I think you should drink lots of it, Ser Riley. Nothing embarrassing could possibly happen a *second* time."

"You, hush."

"Killjoy."

CHAPTER EIGHT

The Lunar Queen

My little sister is adorable, isn't she?" Everly said later that night in the memory palace after everyone was seated in the meeting chamber. She'd entered the palace in person, eager to catch up on everything she'd been ignoring during her two-month . . . rest.

Eris and Titania were especially glad to see her interacting with everyone again. Even Carter the goblin cracked a grin of relief on his usually expressionless face when he saw that his mistress seemed to be back to her old self. Only Grail continued to maintain a certain level of cautious reserve, but everyone ignored it because Grail could be a stick-in-the-mud at times.

"She's so precocious," Everly continued. "An absolute delight! Was ever a girl as blessed as me to have such a sweet sibling?"

"Truly, Princess Claudia seems wonderfully suited to being your sister," fawned Eris. "I couldn't imagine anyone else in the role."

"So, we're just going to ignore that she plays with the lives of others like it's nothing and tried to kill your father in front of you?" Grail asked her bluntly.

"Yep!" Everly said with a bright, happy smile. "She's a rambunctious lil puppy!"

"Ah. Of course." Grail glowered. Eris elbowed him stiffly in the side before saying, "I'm happy to see you embracing your new family ties so enthusiastically, Everly."

"Does that make her *our* sister too?" Titania wondered. "I mean, you once said Lyona, Eris, and I are all you'll ever need, right? But if you're including her as well, doesn't that make us all family?"

"Uh, sure, why not?" Everly said indifferently as she spun in her seat. "There's plenty of room for everyone in our happy little circle!"

"Does that include Nalec?" asked Grail.

"Who?" Everly asked. It was a familiar sounding name, but she couldn't quite put a face to it.

"*Nalec.* Your inside man at the Eastern Temple?" Grail reminded her slowly. "We haven't checked in with him in months. *Two* months as a matter of fact. We're due for a progress report, aren't we?"

"Oh, right, *Nalec,*" Everly said. "Heh, I forgot all about him. Eris, see to that later, will you? Progression is important to us. This organization is *all* about progression!"

"Your will shall be done, Everly," Eris said, but not before shooting Grail a dirty look which he pointedly ignored.

"Speaking of Claudia," Everly said, returning the subject of conversation to her new favorite person, "her twinkling eyes and exuberant personality have brightened my spirit beyond measure! What a gift this day was!"

"Everly, there's no need to go overboard with your enthusiasm," Grail cautioned her. "Remember, these people are strangers to you. Strangers driven by their own motivations. It would be foolish to blindly trust them."

"Oh, listen to Papa Grail go on," Everly said, a frown now appearing on her face. "What's the matter, old man? Are you afraid of losing your position just because I've reconnected with my *real* father? You needn't be so obviously jealous; you're still my favorite workhorse."

"*Hey!*" Titania said in a wounded voice.

"Sister, please think about what she just said," Eris said to her wearily.

Titania did as she was instructed. "Oh," she said. "Oh, never mind. Sorry. Heh, she called you a horse, Grail!"

"Tch," Grail replied as he drummed his fingers on the conference table. "I'm just watching out for your best interests, girl. I knew your father well, back in the days before the war. He was as trustworthy as a hungry serpent, and I can tell he's only grown worse since then. Making yourself vulnerable to him could be a potentially fatal mistake."

"Oh, for the night's sake," Eris groaned. "Grail, she's *happy.* Can't you see that? Must you continue to be so inflexible? Nothing can threaten Everly. Let her enjoy herself!"

"You knew my father?" Everly asked Grail in surprise. "Why didn't you ever tell me that?"

"I assumed you already knew," Grail answered. "You have access to my every memory, after all. I simply thought you didn't care about that particular connection."

"You assumed incorrectly, Grail," Everly said. "Tell me, what was your relationship with him like?"

Grail sat silently for a few moments, composing his thoughts before answering.

"Our relationship was fraught from the beginning," Grail said darkly. "The former ruler of Winstead, good King Pentas, asked me to teach him the ways of the sword alongside the royal heirs. Marcis was Prince Septus's best friend at the time, and his father wished to bestow upon him the rare honor of being one of my students. Of that batch, Marcis was easily the finest of them all."

"Impossible," Everly said. "Daddy is a spirit wielder. How could he possibly learn the Imperial style without being able to use *harada*?"

"He didn't," Grail replied. "But he could mimic the forms perfectly and developed a surprisingly complex understanding of the underpinning of the style. He was probably the most naturally gifted swordsman I'd ever trained. By infusing what he learned from me with his own strange magic, he became as dangerous with a blade as any sword king could ever hope to be. He was almost good enough to defeat me in personal combat."

"You two fought?" Everly asked, surprised once more. "Why?"

"It happened during the war," Grail said with an expression like that of someone who had swallowed bitter medicine. "I was Prince Connor's champion, and many on the opposing side sought the glory of claiming my head. Your father was the one who came the closest. It was a near thing, but I barely managed to win. I *finally* had that preening narcissist at the mercy of my blade! I'd have happily split his skull then and there, but he was rescued from my death blow at the last moment by that thrice-damned wife of his."

"Lady Anne? *Lady Anne* participated in the civil war?" Everly asked. "I thought there was a taboo against civilian women fighting in war." Then she paused before asking with a knowing, maliciously sweet grin, "Grail, did you get beat up by a *girl*?"

"Yes, there is a taboo against female participation in battle," Grail frowned, while ignoring Everly's provocation. "But Anne Godwell is a god-blighted monster. She does whatever she pleases and always has. I suppose we should praise our good fortune for her not being anywhere near you during your childhood. Under her tutelage, who knows what sort of fiend you'd have become?"

"Ha!" Everly said as she leaned back in her chair. "And what exactly is that supposed to mean?"

"It means that left to your own devices, you've at least developed a rudimentary code of honor," Grail replied. "Anne would have left you incapable of having even that. I've known her since I was a child. She . . . takes. She takes, but she gives nothing in return. She . . . feeds."

Grail shuddered to himself, clearly disturbed by an old memory.

Everly found herself intrigued by the conversation and continued to press him despite his discomfort. "Grail, how could you have known her since *you* were a child? She's my dad's wife. She was my brother's mother. Hell, she was . . . that girl's *grandmother*. Just how old *is* she?"

"It's not something that's openly discussed," Grail said reluctantly. "Even my grandfather was acquainted with her in *his* youth. The Royal Family, the Denrias, and the Godwells. These are the three great pillars of the kingdom. And each of them has secrets they do not share with outsiders. Mysteries, if you will."

"Ohhh," Everly said cheekily. "What *kind* of mysteries?"

"The sort that deliberately remain unsolved," Grail replied. "Duke Primus Godwell and his daughters, Anne and Priora, are the very embodiment of those mysteries. Exactly when Anne and Priora first appeared is difficult to ascertain, but it's an established fact that Duke Primus has been around since the founding of the kingdom. And maybe even before then. It's all very unsettling to think of."

"Be serious," Everly said with a snicker. "Are you trying to tell me that my wicked stepmother, Aiden's sweet mommy dearest, is *immortal*? Yeah, right! Titania would have alerted me right away if there were any residual demonic energy in the house. Wouldn't you, T?"

"Well, actually, Everly," Titania began to say reluctantly. "There are other sorts of creatures aside from demons and elementals that could technically be counted as being immortal. The world is bigger than you realize."

"Huh," Everly said. "Like what?"

"Creatures like whatever that Mister Whisper thing was, for instance," Eris said.

"Who?" Everly really felt she was going to have to start taking notes. She met a lot of people in her day-to-day life, and keeping track of their names was clearly going to be a hassle. "Hey, Carter. Start keeping track of these things for me, will you? I feel like it's unreasonable for me to have to remember every single nonpriority existence's background story."

"This I shall do at once!" Carter said promptly. He then procured a notepad and began writing.

"Thank you!" Everly said, pleased by her own skills with delegation. "So, who was Mister Whisper again?"

"You know," Titania said. "That creepy child eater?"

"Aww, gross." Everly shuddered as she recalled her encounter with that thing. "Yeah, thanks for reminding me of that jerk."

"Sorry, but you *did* ask," Titania said.

"Didn't I send him screaming into the center of the planet to roast in magma?"

"Yeah." Titania smiled. "He screamed like a little bitch."

"Yeah, he did," Everly giggled. "Which was weird, because I tore his head off first. Ugh, I did *not* enjoy that day."

"Thea is doing well, in case you were wondering," Grail interjected.

"Who?" Everly asked again.

Grail sighed and stopped speaking.

"Other immortal creatures include elves," Eris said. "There are also certain breeds of spirit kin such as the *Nul'Panetheons*—"

"That *has* to be a made-up word!" Everly said.

"It's not, but you'll never need to worry about them," Titania assured her. "They live on the moon now. Said there were too many mortal races, and it was really cluttering up the place."

"What are they?" Everly wondered. "And how do you know of them?"

"Inherited memories," Titania answered. "A necessary survival mechanism. We elementals and the *Nul'Panetheons* don't care very much for one another. Uh, how to best describe them? Well . . . try imagining a dragon combined with a horseshoe crab with a superiority complex as big as a star, and that's their common breed."

"Absolute snobs," Eris said with a haughty sniff. "The very embodiment of arrogance."

No one dared to comment on that one. Even Grail kept his silence.

"Their monarch is more human in appearance. She's actually quite pretty, but she's an even bigger jerk," Titania said. "She sure can back it up, though."

"Is she powerful?" Everly wondered.

Eris sighed. "Disconcertingly so."

"Like, *actually* powerful, or just by the common standards of this world?" Everly asked. "Because I have to be honest, we've seen a lot of idiots tooting their own horns lately and we've stepped on all of them like they were bugs."

"Everly, I believe fervently in your strength, and have no doubt you shall continue to grow," Eris said in a wary tone. "But even with the power that Titania and I provide you, the *Nul'Panetheon* queen would be . . . challenging. It would be for the best to avoid provoking her anger."

"Which won't be hard, because she's on the moon and we're over here!" Titania said brightly. "So, nothing to worry about!"

"Worry? Why would I be worried? I bet I could kick her ass," Everly mused aloud.

"Everly," Eris said cautiously. "She's one of the oldest creatures in existence. Even the greater elementals, who the people of this world rightly venerate as *gods*, fear her wrath."

"Tch, they sound like quitters. Losers who fear taking on an exciting challenge," said Everly with alarming self-confidence. "You know what? That bugs me. That *really* freaking bugs me! How can you claim to be the world's strongest being if you're not even going to *live* in this world and defend your title? Just the idea of some frosty old diva floating above us on the moon . . . looking down her *nose* at us. At *me*. God, that really makes me want to walk up to her and give her a slap. You know, just to see what happens."

Carter the goblin continued to sit quietly at the meeting, saying nothing while writing extensive notes on the discussion being had, just as instructed. The current page he was writing on had only one sentence on it.

It said: *KEEP EVERLY OFF THE MOON!!!!*

Next to it was written the word: *APOCALYPSE!!!*

This was written in all capitals, circled three times, and had many underlines and exclamation points.

It was also done in red ink.

"Ahem! Aside from the lunar queen, the three Godwells might also be vampires," Eris said.

Everly's ears perked up at that word and quickly took her mind off her sudden but murderously intense grudge against the moon and its cocky inhabitant.

"I'm sorry, did you just say *vampires?*" she asked.

"Yes, I did," Eris said as sweet relief swept over her at successfully distracting her mistress.

"*Go on,*" Everly said enthusiastically as a massive smile bloomed on her face.

CHAPTER NINE

Completely Stable

So, what do you think?" Everly asked Grail after the meeting. "He looks wonderful, doesn't he?"

They stood on a balcony outside the memory palace, which overlooked the swirling darkness of the void beneath them. Everly had asked Grail to stop by to offer an opinion on a little project she was working on. He came as requested but was unsettled to see that she appeared to be sculpting a monster of some sort.

Everly had announced earlier that she was going to begin spending more time physically inside the memory palace. There were things she wanted to do that could only be done here, away from the sight of outsiders. Eris and Titania were pleased by her decision, but Grail wondered if she was being completely honest.

Although he would never say so aloud, he suspected that Everly didn't want to sleep inside her father's house. The very house where she had disposed of that unfortunate friend she'd made, two months earlier.

Did she feel guilty over that bloody decision? Grail himself had been furious when he learned what she'd done. He understood her reasoning, but there were surely other methods they could have tried first. Murder didn't have to be the first solution.

That was the problem with serving Everly. She was becoming a creature of impulsivity. Nothing had yet appeared that could thwart her, so she was quickly losing her sense of restraint. When restraint left you, patience and tolerance were swift to follow. Without those three virtues to constrain her, Everly would swiftly devolve into a self-indulgent tyrant.

That was a scenario that was best avoided for everyone.

The sight of Everly's new creation was an unpleasant one. It was the night-marish image of a man slowly decaying into a rotting corpse. Everly seemed to be shaping him out of the air itself; he wore a rusting suit of mail and carried a chipped sword. Half of his face was still hale and young, but the other side was a bloody display of exposed gore and sinew.

What was worse, Grail realized, were the creature's eyes. They met his own and trembled in watery misery. The poor bastard knew what he was. He had *awareness*.

"He's beautiful, isn't he?" Everly asked Grail. "I like the expressions he makes. The sounds are fun too. You know, taking him apart and reassembling him was a lot like putting together a plastic model. Wasn't it, Kel?" she asked her subject.

"Who?" Grail wondered.

"Don't you remember? This is Sir Kelton," Everly told him. "The kind knight who escorted me home. I'm repaying him for his service and his gentle manners. Eris made a copy of his mind earlier for her rat room, but I wanted the real one to play with. You know, for authenticity."

"What have you done to him?" Grail asked, aghast at the sight of the tortured being.

"I'm building a better zombie," she informed him. "Transforming him into something precious and unique. Besides, he's helping me troubleshoot a few minor issues I noticed a while back, when you raised the dead at Bremburg."

"What issues?" Grail wondered. "The corpses I used were perfectly sufficient for the task. As I recall, they turned the tide of the battle."

"It's true," Everly agreed. "But the process was so *messy*. The undead were fearless and relentless, but the visual aesthetics left a lot to be desired. Broken bones and gore everywhere. Good results in a fight aren't the only outcome I desire."

"Did you take notes?" Grail asked with bemusement.

"Of course I did," Everly replied at once. "You see, the immediate problem I noticed when raising the dead is that they smelled *terribly*! Their odor is com-pletely nauseating!"

"Well, yes," Grail said. "They're *dead*. One shouldn't expect them to smell of roses and lilacs."

"Yeah, but even the fresher ones were tough to endure," Everly said. "Dead people release their bowels, Grail! They made horrible messes all over themselves. It was *awful*."

"Grotesque biology often comes with participating in a major battle," Grail said with a shrug. "That's one of the reasons I always preferred to eat *after* I fought."

"A habit that I believe I'll adopt for myself," Everly said sagely.

"A wise decision, my Empress. But why concern yourself with such matters? When people gather en masse, issues of sanitation are inevitable. Especially for fighting men, alive *or* dead."

"Sure, that makes sense," Everly replied. "But who cares about what makes sense? Shouldn't necromancy be about *more* than what's expected? You inheritors are essentially undead, but you're far superior to any human being other than me."

"True, but that's only because you personally created us," Grail said. He then gestured toward Kelton. "These creatures are just rank-and-file disposable shock troopers. Who cares how they turn out? Or how they look or smell? They exist merely to provide a numerical advantage and to terrify your foes."

"That's mean, Grail," Everly replied. "Even these hopeless, moldering little nothings should aspire to be more than mere fodder. They exist to enforce my dream! That gives them great value in my eyes. And anything *I* value should be regarded as a work of art."

Everly affectionately brushed her hand against the ghoul's cheek. In response, the wretched creature murmured incoherently and sighed with pleasure at her touch.

"Another problem that I've noticed with using corpses," Everly continued, "is that fresh or old, they just don't have the necessary durability for sustained combat. So my new idea is to create beings with the *appearance* of the undead, but who are quite alive and *far* more useful. Like Kelton here!"

"Why is he still alive?" Grail asked with revulsion. "Everly, why would you trap a man's soul in this . . . form?"

"He had an entire day to apologize for how he spoke to me," Everly said indifferently.

"Did you *ask* him for an apology?"

"Grail! If I have to explain the rules to *every* insignificant participant in my story, then I'll be doing it until I'm an old woman!" Everly said irritably. Then she returned to the main topic.

"These new foot soldiers will *look* like zombies but possess far greater strength and intelligence. And to *really* make it unfair, they'll be fast too! Capable of independent thought. Their prey will need to be on their toes to avoid these abominable little darlings."

"So, I take it these new *un-zombies* won't be motivated by a single-minded desire to consume the flesh of the living?" Grail wondered.

"Goodness, no, Grail," Everly said with an aghast expression on her face. "How could I possibly remove such a classic feature? No, they'll still be utter cannibals. They just won't be weak against silly things like closed doors and holy magic. Sir Kelton over here will be the first of thousands to come."

"*Mother,*" the horrifying creature gently whispered as Everly continued to stroke its face.

"God, Everly," Grail said with some unease. "Aren't you ever worried that you'll go too far?"

"No. I don't worry about anything," Everly said. She leaned over to whisper something into Kelton's ear. He nodded and shuffled into the memory palace, leaving the two of them alone.

"Where's he going?" Grail asked.

"To wait in the dark for his siblings to join him," Everly answered. "What do you think, Grail? Will ten thousand do for a start, or should I be more ambitious?"

"In a better world, the answer would be zero."

"There's no world better than this," Everly said. She stepped over to the balcony and stared down below at the utter emptiness swirling below. The endless depths of the void that comprised the astral realm.

"Look at all that wonderful *nothing*," she said as she gestured below. "How far do the depths reach, I wonder? You know, despite the immense satisfaction I feel in having created this palace, it's a little humbling to realize that despite my efforts, the emptiness of nonexistence will always be greater than anything I can ever build."

"I find it . . . terrifying," Grail admitted as he joined her in looking down into the maw of darkness. "The notion of being swallowed into the abyss, of being of no greater value to the universe than a mote of dust. I can't abide it. Lives need to matter more than that."

"Really?" Everly asked. "Thoughts like that make most people turn to religion. But you're not a humble believer so far as I can tell, are you?"

"I dislike easy answers," Grail replied. "I can accept not being meant to know everything. Can we ever truly know the meaning of why we exist? That's a question for which we'll never have a satisfying answer. I choose not to let thoughts of it consume me. I'm alive and that's enough."

"Tch. How very *Zen*," Everly said teasingly. "Grail, that's the same as finding comfort by ignoring reality. Like a child pretending they'll live forever if they never think about dying. You're just avoiding the scary part to maintain your dignity."

"Perhaps that's so," Grail replied. Then he said, "Everly, I had a confrontation with your father earlier today."

"I figured," Everly said.

"You knew? Were you watching me?"

"No. When I went to wish him a good night, I noticed his study was destroyed. Did you throw him out a window?"

"Through it, actually," Grail corrected her.

"Oh. Defenestration. Very nice. How did it feel?"

"So very, very *satisfying*," Grail admitted.

"Good. I'm glad you two are getting along," Everly grinned.

"Aren't you going to ask who we fought over?"

"No. I can hazard a guess."

"You can't trust him, Everly."

"Hmm. You *do* keep saying that," she said thoughtfully as she continued to lean over the railing. Then, she suddenly leaped on top of it and sat down with her feet kicking out and dangling above the endless nothing.

"Everly?" Grail said in alarm.

"It's the oddest thing, Grail," Everly said with a look on her face like that of a child trying to figure out where a puzzle piece is supposed to go. "I occasionally get these urges that I find simply irresistible! Out of nowhere, I'll get these thoughts that I just can't get rid of. It doesn't happen very often, but when it does . . . I can't help but give in. I'm helpless against them."

Now Everly stood on the railing. Although her balance was perfect, her positioning was still precarious. She began to walk along it from left to right, as though she were using playground equipment.

"It's funny," she continued. "There I was, enjoying meeting my family and making plans and relishing the fun to come, and even enjoying this conversation with you, when suddenly I felt the most peculiar urge to hurl myself from this perilous height, just to see if I'd die."

"Everly? What do you mean?" Grail asked. He couldn't believe she was doing this without an ounce of fear in her.

"It's difficult for me to describe." Everly smiled. "You know, it's like a sudden desire for a sweet snack or buying something impulsively. I get these images in my mind and it's all so . . . *compelling*. Wouldn't it be funny if I died here and now, Grail?"

"I don't think it would be funny at all, Everly," Grail said cautiously as he slowly inched closer toward her.

"How strange, because *I* think it would be hilarious! To have all these lofty aspirations only to suddenly spiral out into spectacular self-destruction because of an unexpected urge for self-annihilation. Oh, Grail, I would so very much like to be *destroyed*. After all, a villain's ultimate goal is to be defeated. What if the only means by which I'll meet my destiny is by my own hand? Ha, that's *so* interesting, isn't it?"

"Everly, please step back down before you—EVERLY!" Grail shouted when his mistress winked at him and let herself fall backward.

Moving faster than any mortal man could, Grail leaned over the railing in less than a heartbeat and grabbed Everly by her hand before she could continue to fall.

Dangling at the end of his hand, Everly laughed with childish delight and cheered excitedly. "Grail! You caught me!"

"What the hell are you DOING?" he bellowed angrily at her.

"I have no idea," she laughed happily with a rosy blush on her cheeks. "It just seemed like the right thing to do in that moment," she said. "I'm glad I got that itch scratched, in any case. Pull me up?"

"You psychotic little imp!" Grail said furiously after getting her back to safe ground. "Why would you do such a thing? Don't you care about anyone other than yourself?"

"Who can say?" Everly asked with an innocent shrug of her shoulder. "Heh, you're a lot faster than you used to be."

"Think of a better answer than that!" Grail yelled.

"I'm sowwy. Don't be angwy at me," Everly said mockingly before suddenly giving Grail a tight hug. "You caught me, though! That's why you're here. You're the one who'll always catch me, aren't you, Grail?"

Grail said nothing in reply, stunned into silence by her words. Instead, he stood there quietly, letting her embrace him.

"I . . . I'll try, Everly. I'll always try," he eventually said to her.

"I know you will, Grail," she said before looking up to meet his gaze. "You're just too good of a person not to."

"You don't make it easy," he said gruffly.

"Would it be any fun if I did?" she asked him.

Then she smiled at him brightly, and it was as though all the stars in the sky shone for her alone.

Gods, I'm really trapped with this selfish little monster, aren't I? he thought somberly to himself.

"Yeah, you are," she said happily as she gave him another hug. "You love it, though."

"Stop reading my thoughts," he demanded.

"I'll consider it," she said noncommittally.

CHAPTER TEN

The Pecking Order

Despite the great success of his mission thus far, Nalec didn't feel like a man on the rise.

He didn't feel properly *respected.*

The glorious assignment he'd been given to infiltrate and slowly subvert the leadership of the Eastern Temple was going *swimmingly* so far. Under the very eyes of their enemies, he coordinated each of his carefully planned ambushes with Lady Eris to discreetly replace each of their victims who were members of the temple leadership with much-improved nu-human replacements, who possessed the memories and personalities of their former selves but with one major difference.

The nu-humans were no longer slaves to the foolish beliefs that plagued their predecessors. They were free of misguided attachments to anything other than their absolute devotion to their creator. This included family, morality, and their silly religious superstitions. As superior beings they knew the real truth of all things. They were destined to become the masters of this world, and as such, they only worshipped one true god.

And her name was *Everly.*

Everly was greater than the sun, the moon, the very stars themselves! Her magnificence was unmatched. All who beheld her were forever blessed. All who stood in her presence knew *rapture.* Nalec dearly wished to return to her side once more and drink in the sight of her incomparable beauty. He wished only to be seen and acknowledged by his creator as her favorite child. Everything he did, he did for the love of Everly.

But lately, she hadn't seen fit to speak with him.

Her absence was *painful* to him.

"Will Everly see me today?" he asked Lady Eris as she finished preparing the artificial mind of the nu-human that would replace their latest victim. "Thanks to me, we've taken over the vast majority of the temple's administration. With but a word, I could overthrow Sylvain and see our goddess installed as the true saint of this era! Wouldn't Everly enjoy that? She *would*, wouldn't she?"

"Nalec, I've already explained this to you. Everly is busy right now. She wishes to see no one," Eris replied with exaggerated patience.

"Why won't she say that to me herself?" Nalec asked her. "I've done such great work for her! It hasn't been easy, but look at the results! Look at the success I've reaped! Surely Everly would want to hear of this from me personally?"

"She's *busy*, Nalec. Leave it at that and stop pestering me over it," Eris said firmly.

"I only want to please her," Nalec said sullenly. "Why won't she let me *please her*? She won't even let me return to the memory palace. What have I done wrong? I want to see Everly! I WANT TO SEE EVERLY!"

"Nalec, stop," said an older man's voice. One that oozed strength and authority. A voice that Nalec *despised* hearing.

"Lord Grail," Nalec said unpleasantly. "While I'm touched that you've decided to stop by and provide your unnecessary oversight of my work, I assure you that as the first and greatest of the nu-humans, I require no supervision."

"Inheritors," Grail said casually as he inspected Nalec's quarters.

"Excuse me?" Nalec asked.

"Our name. We're called the *inheritors* now. The new breed of humanity who shall inherit this world. It's a name I came up with personally. I ran it by Everly, and she agreed that it sounded a lot better than *nu-humans*. The old name sounded far too much like a rebranding of a carbonated beverage, didn't it?"

"But *I* was the one who came up with *nu-humans*!"

"Ah," Grail said. "Well, that might explain why she hated it so much. *I* was the first, by the way."

"Wh-what?" asked Nalec in confusion.

"The first inheritor. I was the first artificial mind that Everly ever created. I preceded your existence by fifteen years, kid. I'm *also* the most powerful of our kind. Unless our Empress decided to also share her ability to raise the dead with . . . *you*?"

Nalec stared, flabbergasted. Grail could raise the dead like Everly? She'd chosen to imbue him with such an amazing gift?

Why *him* and not Nalec?!

For a moment, he couldn't speak; his words were silenced by resentment and envy.

"Oh, so she *didn't*?" Grail asked with mock surprise. "Well, then I would assume that means you hold far less authority than Lady Eris or myself. In which case, you need to remember your place, *boy*, and stop yelping like an unhappy puppy just because our mistress has better things to do with her time than break bread with the rank and file. Wouldn't you agree?"

As he spoke, Grail stepped into Nalec's personal space and *loomed* over him, making the younger man feel like a child whose behavior had disappointed his father. When Grail reached forth a hand and placed it on his shoulder, Nalec trembled at the contact. Whether from anger or fear, he couldn't say.

"However, on Everly's behalf, let me just say that *I* think you're doing a good job. Keep it up," Grail told him with a smile.

A few moments later, after Eris finished her task, she and Grail returned to the tower, leaving Nalec and the newly created inheritor, Lord Wembly, alone in his quarters. Nalec sent his new brother on his way, then sat on his bed to fume at the humiliation he'd just suffered. He clenched his fists in anger, unable to process how one such as *he* could be so easily rebuked and dismissed.

Damn that old man! That arrogant, condescending bastard!

Oh, how Nalec hated him!

The pressure that came with being unable to see his beloved maker and having to kowtow before the loathsome Grail, of being looked upon as a mere underling, was too much. Something within him would soon burst! Of course, the worst indignity of all was his current relationship with Lady Sylvain, the head of the Eastern Temple.

If things stood as they were, she was going to *break* him.

His every moment with that woman had become an incremental descent into hell itself.

It was his fault, really. He was the one who had decided their relationship should become romantic. Making her dependent on him would make his job much easier. So he'd begun discreetly courting Lady Sylvain, hoping to capture her heart and make it easier to manipulate her. And his plan had succeeded! Perfectly!

. . . Far too perfectly.

It was the sex. He simply hadn't expected all the sex. He thought this would be a celibate affair, a platonic romance of the mind. After all, despite how beautiful she was, Lady Sylvain was the head of a religious organization and was venerated as a model of purity and restraint. There was no way someone like her would ever indulge in anything as venal as sexual congress. Her desires would surely be entirely *spiritual* in nature.

Nalec had been wrong. He'd been completely wrong!

Shortly after the second meal they'd shared together in her quarters, as Nalec had begun to take his leave, Sylvain stopped him at the door and kissed him. It hadn't been unpleasant. Sure, it was nothing compared to what one of Everly's would have felt like, but it wasn't *completely* horrible either.

"Well, that was a delightful surprise," he said to her. "What a wonderful way to conclude the evening."

"My dear squire," Sylvain said breathily into his ear. "For us, the evening has just begun."

Before Nalec could grasp her meaning, Sylvain's hand reached down and grasped . . . *him*.

"Uhhhh," he stammered.

What followed next was an onslaught.

Pure carnage.

Warfare in its most primal form.

One-on-one combat.

It hadn't occurred to Nalec that the primary reason for Lady Sylvain's chastity was her inability to find someone who could keep up the pace with her. She was of elven blood. Their stamina and durability were legendary. Ordinary mortals just couldn't keep up with their needs. To avoid the frustration of being constantly disappointed, Sylvain simply abstained from the act of physical love.

But that didn't make her invulnerable to being courted and pursued. Over her long centuries of life, she would let her resolve lapse, only to be reminded once more that these human men just didn't have the drive necessary to get her where she wanted to *go*. So she'd once again swear off sex, only to make the same mistake a few decades later.

Her libido had become an unending cycle of frustration.

However, she'd now accidentally made a discovery that forever transformed her lonely nights. The man she believed to be Alec, her squire and latest romantic pursuer, could not only ride her into blissful *completion* . . . he could do it repeatedly! He might even possess more stamina than *she* did.

She couldn't get enough of him!

Lady Sylvain had become *insatiable*.

Nalec wondered if it was possible to wilt into nonexistence from embarrassment, like a flower exposed to the unrelenting desert sun.

Their relationship had devolved into a series of increasingly deranged experiments that should have been banned legally across the world. Most of it was *definitely* prohibited by the teachings of her temple, not that Sylvain seemed to care. Due to her relative inexperience, there were a lot of things that Sylvain had read and fantasized about over the years but had never dared hope she'd get to personally attempt.

But with "Alec," she could finally let her curiosity soar! Her needs were as endless as the degradation Nalec had begun to feel at the conclusion of their every sordid tryst.

Naturally, his stamina came from being one of Everly's creations. His body was a precisely engineered instrument of battle that made him superior to a thousand ordinary men. As an . . . *inheritor*, as Grail had termed it, Nalec easily stood above the rabble of timid mortal scum. Comparison to them was no comparison at all.

And yet, he'd now been reduced to the role of a deviant church girl's object of lust.

From a war god to a plaything in mere weeks.

"My body belongs to Everly!" he once sobbed to himself as he huddled in a corner of his room.

Another growing problem was that he was really getting *into* it. Despite his contempt for Sylvain's sickening urges and endless demands on his body, he'd begun discreetly doing a little research of his own. As an intellectual pursuit! And also because some of what they were doing was so debased that it had become pretty fun.

But Nalec wasn't supposed to be having fun with Sylvain. He was for Everly! Everly alone! Everly always! There could be no conflict! None! Never!

He would have to resist Sylvain. Set boundaries. Establish parameters.

He would say *NO.*

FIRMLY!

The door to his quarters opened and a familiar voice now heavy with need murmured, "*Alec . . .*"

Goddamn it, he thought miserably to himself.

Oh, well, nothing to be done about it. Such was the life of an undercover operator!

Whistling to himself, Nalec reached beneath his bed to pull out his leather harness and her favorite cat-o'-nine while Sylvain patiently waited.

"I didn't need your assistance putting Nalec in his place," Eris said to Grail as soon as they rematerialized in the memory palace. "That little fool is no threat to me."

"I know that," Grail said mildly in reply. "I merely took a moment to establish a firmer set of boundaries with the boy. Nalec is a rambunctious little thing. I've had students like him before. They can't really thrive unless they truly know their place in the hierarchy. So it was more for his benefit than yours."

"I could have shown him that easily," Eris sneered.

"No, you would have tormented him mentally and possibly damaged him in the process. Despite being an arrogant fool, Nalec is performing a valuable service for us. A bloodless coup is an invaluable victory for our mistress."

Eris snorted. "Bloodless, you say? We've killed every single one of those worms we've replaced."

"Temporarily, yes," Grail agreed. "But with Titania's gift, we've brought them back from death, remade into something better than they could have ever hoped to become in their former existence. In a way, we've brought them the rebirth they've always yearned for in prayer. Is that really murder or . . . *ascendance?*"

Eris was impressed by Grail's words despite her natural inclination to disagree with him about everything. She hated to admit it, but as much as she despised Grail, in recent times she'd begun to understand why Everly insisted on bringing him into their circle. He was strong, forward-thinking and unafraid to express his opinions. Eris now recognized these as desirable traits. Traits that she wished she herself possessed.

He was a fascinating man.

Had he always been like that? Or had she been blind to these admirable characteristics?

"What?" he said irritably.

"Huh?" Eris said.

"You've been *staring* at me blankly for nearly a minute. What are you plotting now?"

"P-perhaps I'm considering how to best flay your mind so that you eventually realize your place and keep your unwarranted opinions to yourself!" Eris sputtered, annoyed by him now for reasons she didn't quite understand.

"Ah. Try it and see how far you get," Grail warned her with a scowl before stalking away to his quarters.

The nerve of that mortal fool! What gave him the right to speak thusly to her? Eris was a veritable goddess of the mind. No, the *soul*. No one could withstand her. The torment and horror she could unleash upon those who angered her . . . well, they weren't legendary because no one knew about her yet, but they *would* be!

Grail was too arrogant. Too confident. Too smug and . . . handsome. Not that she cared about outward appearances. She was a creature of the mind! No, it was clear now that she'd soon have to take him in hand and show him who Everly's most faithful servant truly was. No matter how much he resisted.

That'd show him!

Heh, he'd be so angry. She could already imagine his face darkening with fury once he realized he could never surpass her. It would serve him right.

With that in mind, Eris decided to go visit the rat room and indulge in a little fun for herself.

She hummed as she walked.

CHAPTER ELEVEN

Self-Care

What the hell?" Everly said as she beheld herself. "You duped me? You actually made a dupe of yourself? That is *nuts*."

"Personally, I thought it was brilliant," Everly replied to herself with a smirk.

After Grail had returned to his quarters for the evening, Everly remained behind. She claimed she had one last project she was working on. He was very suspicious but eventually moved on at her insistence.

"It's *not* like I'm planning to jump again!" she said to him with a smile.

Once he was gone, Everly began to create once more, using the methods taught to her by Eris and Titania. When she was finished, she inspected her work, pleased by the results.

"Yeah, obviously! You thought of it, which means *I* thought of it, which means I'm brilliant!" replied Dupe Everly.

"Hey, is it weird that I think you're really hot? That's just narcissism, right?" Everly asked herself.

"The worst kind imaginable," Dupe Everly said. "But I'm okay with it. You're looking pretty tasty yourself. Hey, is that why you made me? Oh, shit, are we about to commit the ultimate taboo? Because if the answer is yes, I just want you to know I'm okay with it."

"Shut up, Everly! Good lord, do I need to hit myself with a rolled-up newspaper?"

"Oh, come on, I'm just saying what's on our mind," Dupe Everly pouted. "Besides, why would you want to hit a face as pretty as ours?"

"Oh, is that the dynamic you're going for?" Everly asked herself. "You're going to be my unchained libido? The one who unhesitatingly says what's on her mind? The window into my secret desires?"

"Hell yes! You love the idea, don't you?" Dupe Everly preened.

"Actually, no. No, I don't," Everly frowned. "I *already* say and do whatever I feel like. What's the point of you doing more of the same? Sounds redundant, Dupe Everly."

"Yeah, about that name. I don't want to be called *Dupe Everly*," said Dupe Everly. "It makes me sound dumb."

"Why? It's shorthand for *duplicate*. It's a very accurate name."

"Yeah, okay, I get that," said Dupe Everly. "But being called a dupe isn't very complimentary, is it? I've never heard of anyone being called that word and feeling very good about it."

"Well, what do you want to be called?" Everly asked.

"How about Kerri?" Dupe Everly wondered.

"Not a chance!" Everly said immediately.

"Aww, why not?"

"Because that's my original name! If I let you claim it, it'll muddy up the waters."

"In what way?"

"All kinds of ways! That I can't think of off the top of my head. But they're there. *Waiting*."

"*Fine*," grumbled the dupe. "Okay, what about Averly?"

"Is that even a real name?" asked Everly. "It doesn't sound like one."

"Well, what do you suggest, then?" asked the exasperated duplicate.

"How about . . . *Neverly*?" Everly said with a grin.

"By the great pumpkin, that is just about the clone-iest name I've ever heard in my life," Neverly said with a scowl.

"Come on, it's perfect. You *know* it's perfect!" Everly said enthusiastically.

"Do I even get a say in this?"

"Do I even have to answer that?"

"Fine! Neverly it is, I guess," said Neverly with reluctant acceptance.

"*Wunderbar!*" Everly said cheerfully.

"Yeah, yeah," Neverly replied. "So, what's the point of making a copy of yourself? I can't use any of your powers except for *harada*, so that makes me fifty percent less effective than you are."

"Funny you should mention that," Everly replied. "You're actually a good deal less powerful than that. I've sealed most of your techniques, you see. Can't have you running around being a potential threat to my position, right?"

"You're such a paranoid bitch," Neverly huffed. Then she smiled and said, "Aww, I can't stay mad at that face! I would have done the same if I were you, which I am, so I did. Unnecessary risks are the epitome of foolish behavior."

"Right? I'm glad you agree," Everly said happily. "Listen, you're not completely helpless. In emergency situations, your seal will release and let you use our magic. Just don't act with abandon."

"Why not, though? I *like* acting with abandon."

"Well, that is true, I suppose," Everly said. Then she cried out in pain when a bottle flew toward her from behind and collided with the back of her head. "Ouch!" she yelped. "What the hell was that for?"

"Don't act like you didn't have it coming," snorted her assailant, who looked exactly like her. "Exactly how long were you going to lead her along and make her think you were the real me?"

"Hey, I was just having a little fun!" whined Everly, who as it turned out was not the original Everly at all. "God, when did I become so abusive?"

"Wait a second," said the now cross Neverly. "Do you mean to say that you're a dupe too?"

"Heh, heh. Pretty funny, right?" said the second Everly.

"Wait, so why do I have to be Neverly if you're a Neverly too?" demanded the outraged Neverly.

"Uh, doy? Because I'm Everly B," said Everly B with exaggerated patience.

"Oh, Everly B, is it? To hell with that! If I must be Neverly, then you should be BEVERLY!" shouted Neverly as she raised a hand in dramatic condemnation.

"Whoa! Not happening! Do I look like a *Beverly* to you?" Everly B shouted back. "Neverly is clever and comedic! It suits you perfectly! But Beverly is *way* too nineteen eighties for me to willingly consent to it! The next step is being referenced in a Frank Zappa song! I can't allow that!"

"I kind of like it," said the original Everly, who decided to weigh in on the subject. "Yeah, it works. We're going with that. From now on, you're Beverly."

"Noooo!" shouted the defeated Beverly as she slowly sank to her knees in exaggerated distress.

"Haha! Serves you right," gloated the triumphant Neverly to her vanquished foe. "Your defeat was assured the moment you dared to challenge me."

"God, sometimes I hate myself so much," whined Beverly.

"Well, that's just part of the human condition," Everly said sympathetically. "You'll grow past this one day and become stronger for the experience, Bev."

"God, you're calling me *Bev* now. The abyss truly has no bottom," Beverly said before breaking out into tears.

"All right, so you're Prime Everly, then? Can you please explain why I currently exist? And her as well, I guess?" Neverly asked as she gestured at the weeping Beverly.

"What, don't you like existing? It's a pretty sweet setup. All the air you can breathe and more skin cells and tastebuds than you'll know what to do with," replied Everly. "Hell, wait until you try eating. Eating is *sooo* good."

"What about sex?" Neverly asked.

"Wait until we're at least eighteen. That's the only legal standard we'll ever commit to," Everly commanded her.

"Nuts," said the disappointed duplicate.

"Oh, we've barely got a year left to go," Everly snorted. "Anticipation is the best spice."

"You said it wrong," Neverly corrected her. "It's supposed to be *hunger* is the best spice."

"Like we care about old-timey sayings," Everly said with a roll of her eyes. "Anyway, to answer your question, the two of you now exist because there's too much I want to do and not enough time in the day to get it done."

"How's that?" asked Neverly.

"Well, we're going to school, right?" Everly said. "An academic experience in another world is something I've wanted to enjoy for *ages*! And it even has my favorite storytelling cliché baked right in: nobles versus commoners!"

"That *is* a deliciously trashy cliché," Neverly agreed with a smile on her face.

"Right?" said Everly. "I'm glad you agree, because you're going to be student Everly."

"Awesome!" Neverly cheered. "Oh, that's going to be so sweet! God, I hope I get into a magical version of one of those bullying situations like those chicks in *The Glory*. Is it weird that I thought Dong-eun and Yeon-jin had so much *chemistry*?"

"Yeah, that's actually really weird," Beverly said from the floor.

"What the hell is wrong with you and, by extension, *me*?" Everly asked her.

"Oh, to hell with you both. You know exactly what we're like," Neverly said to her other selves with a frown.

"Well, that is true," Everly said with a nod.

"We *are* a pretty messed up girl," Beverly echoed in agreement. "So, what's my role? If she's the student, then who am I?"

"You're going to continue being an adventurer," Everly informed her.

"Oh! Cool! Looks like Grail the Golden Wanderer will ride again!"

"Nah, pick a new name. Grail hates us using it," said Everly.

"What? Aww. Since when does Grail's opinion matter?" groused Beverly.

"Hey! Grail's been loyal; maybe we should try being a little kinder to him," Everly said.

"Blah, blah, blah. He's loyal because we had Eris donk his brain up and he's too stupid to realize it," sneered Beverly.

"Yeah, and you know, lately he's been just a little too, I don't know, *involved* with us? Is that the right word to describe it? He feels like he's been too *involved*," said Neverly.

"God, I'd really like to just, like, pound those good intentions right out of him," giggled Beverly. "Split his silly heroically inclined face right open."

"Oh, that sounds like so much fun," blushed Neverly. "There's three of us here too! Why not summon him so we can run a train of pain on that self-righteous goody-goody?"

"Hey! No!" Everly yelled at her duplicates. "God, this is why we keep him around, you idiots! We need *someone* with morality around this dump to point out when we're about to do something utterly psychotic! What's our goal again, ladies?"

"To be the ultimate villain," said Beverly quietly.

"To execute our villainy with style," Neverly pouted.

"Exactly!" Everly said. "We don't just hurt the ones who've entrusted themselves to us. We reward loyalty with loyalty!"

"Uh, Alex, I'll take *what is utter hypocrisy* for ten thousand, please," said Neverly with thick sarcasm while Beverly snickered at her words.

"And just what the hell is that supposed to mean?" Everly scowled.

"Uh, only that we yanked Eris out of the memory palace a few months back and scared her within an inch of her life, even though she loves us tremendously and is by far the most loyal member of our coterie," Neverly said to her without fear.

"Yeah, we also threaten her like *all* the time," chipped in Beverly. "Honestly, compared to everyone else, we treat her like trash."

"Oh, and don't forget that Carter hasn't felt safe alone in our presence since that time we nearly split his skull open for laughing at us. God, we were awful to him!"

"Oh, shit, Carter!" Neverly laughed. "Hey, remember all those living dupes we tricked Eris into helping us make of him? Didn't we butcher every single one of them to improve our mastery of *harada*? I really doubt he'd forgive us if he ever found out."

"Oh, man, we're absolute monsters," giggled Beverly. "And that's like nothing compared to what we did to Fenn, right? Heh, we made her love us and hate us within a day, and then we freakin' *murdered her—ACK!*"

Everly now held Beverly by the throat in one hand and was gradually throttling her. Her face was blank, utterly devoid of any apparent emotion. Only her glowing red eyes hinted at the rage she now felt.

"Don't . . . *ever* mention that name in front of me again," she said to Beverly in a voice that was icy with fury. "I have issues that I'm working through! I also find that laughter unnecessary!"

"Everly . . . Everly, stop," Neverly said. She grabbed the other girl's arm and tried to dislodge Beverly from her grip. In response, Everly shoved her to the floor without looking at her and continued to strangle the helpless Beverly, whose feet kicked desperately in the air.

"Everly, stop this!" Neverly shouted. "This is stupid. You're literally just hurting yourself! Are you not getting the symbolism of this moment?"

"SHUT UP!" Everly roared at her. "I'm sick of feeling like this! I'm sick of . . . of *her* affecting me like this. I didn't do anything wrong! It was for our . . . for my survival! That girl was too much of a liability!"

"Hey, who are you arguing with? I *agree* with you!" Neverly said to her placatingly. "Leaving Fenn around would have been like living our life under the sword of Damocles. To hell with that! It was her or us!"

"Then why do I feel this way?" Everly asked her. "Why does even hearing her name make me . . . make me . . . *feel?*"

"How the hell should I know?" Neverly replied. "We barely understand anything about ourselves! We've never experienced attachment on that level before; it's new to us!"

"Well, I *hate* it!" Everly shouted. "It doesn't even feel like me! It doesn't even feel . . . Wait. *Wait.* It *doesn't* feel like me, does it?"

"No," Neverly agreed. "It really doesn't. It sucks that we had to do what we did, but genuine remorse isn't really in our wheelhouse. Honestly, we should have moved on almost immediately."

Everly dropped Beverly to the floor and began pacing around in a restless circle. "I mean, I don't like using outdated terminology, and this is absolutely a self-diagnosis, but I'm pretty sure that I'm what they once would have called a psychopath, or somewhere near that spectrum. Human lives just don't *matter* to me."

"And yet, that girl affects us so. But why?" Neverly wondered. "Was she really that special?"

"We took her life. *I* took her life. I remember everything about that moment," Everly said. "When I crushed her heart, it was like I felt something leaving . . ."

"She was a holy warrior," Neverly said. "She could heal people. That was her specialty, wasn't it?"

"No . . ." groaned Beverly painfully from the floor. "No, she didn't heal people alone. She had an . . ."

Everly and Neverly froze in shocked realization.

"Of course," Neverly said. "These emotions . . . They're not ours at all! Fenneth had a light elemental! She had a light elemental, and it didn't die when *she* did!"

"There's a trespasser in my mind," Everly said furiously. "Fenneth's pet is running loose in our head."

"Well, *your* head, anyway," said Beverly unhelpfully.

CHAPTER TWELVE

Inner Conflict

Okay," Neverly said. "This is an easy fix. Let's summon Eris and let her know what's going on. She built this place from scratch. Once she knows what to look for, she'll find this brat in no time."

"No," Everly said immediately.

"Why not?" Beverly asked in confusion. She'd recovered from her near strangulation at Everly's hands within minutes and now looked none the worse for wear despite her near-death experience. Now she was just puzzled by why Prime Everly was hesitating to get the job done as quickly and efficiently as possible.

"Because I said so!" Everly shouted at the other two. "Can you imagine how humiliating it would be to let the others know about this? My fucking pride won't allow it! No, this stays between us. It's *our* failure, so we're going to handle it. Got it?"

"All right, all right, jeez," Beverly said.

"Hold on, how is this a shared responsibility when two of the three people in this room didn't even exist before today?" Neverly complained.

"Woo, that's a good point," Beverly said.

"Just do as I say before I dissect you both!" yelled Everly.

"God, we're such a *bitch*," Nev muttered to Bev.

"Yeah, I want a union. I wish we had rights or something," Bev said in agreement.

Everly ignored them both, still too focused on the embarrassment that burned within her.

She simply couldn't believe what a fool she'd been. Anger and humiliation both raged within her, threatening to drown her in alternating waves of fury and shame.

To think that she had lain in bed for over two months, weeping for some girl she had barely known, being tortured by regret for what she'd done. *Regret* was an emotion that only losers felt. How could she not have realized that something was wrong with her? That someone had been toying with her mind?

It was unforgivable. This violation could not be countenanced! The intruder would have to *suffer* for this. The problem was that Everly was so angry that she couldn't think of an appropriate punishment herself. She wished she could have Eris workshop this for her; Eris had always been clever at finding unique ways to hurt people. Everly would have happily let her take the reins here if it wouldn't have meant sharing the knowledge of her personal humiliation.

"Rat room," Everly muttered darkly to herself. Yes, that would be an excellent start. Fenneth's little friend would be shoved face-first and screaming into the rat room. Didn't that sound splendid? Yes, yes, let the *rats* have the little bastard while Everly watched . . .

"Rat room, rat room, rat room," Everly hissed as she angrily gnawed on her knuckle, chewing so forcefully that she broke the skin and tasted the salt of her own blood.

Rat room, rat room, rat room, rat room . . .

"Beverly, I think she's losing it," Neverly murmured to her fellow duplicate.

"Uh, doesn't that mean that *we're* losing it?" Beverly whispered back. "It's not the first time we've overreacted to someone messing with us. Remember what we did to Alec?"

"Jesus, am I a bad person if I admit I forgot about him? He's probably hopelessly insane by now," Neverly winced.

"Oh, who cares? He was just a random background character. No, the real issue is we've gotta get this chick calmed down before she wrecks the memory palace! This is the astral frickin' realm! There are bound to be consequences if she goes on a rampage out here."

"Holy crap, you're completely right," said Neverly. "You're on the ball today, Beverly!"

"Well, I *am* an adventurer. In my line of work, it pays to think long-term," Beverly said smugly.

"Hey, don't get carried away," said Neverly, frowning. "It was a compliment, not a hand job."

"Would the both of you *please* shut the hell up?" Everly said to them. "I don't want to hear anything from either of you unless it's an idea of how to track this parasite down."

"Is that an invite for a collaboration of equals?" Neverly asked her.

"Do you have something *useful* to contribute?" snapped Everly.

"Actually . . . maybe I do," Neverly said as a sudden surge of inspiration hit her.

Everly's memory palace could manifest within itself any place that Everly could imagine, whether she'd personally been there or not; *anything* she envisioned could be recreated within its walls.

Now, following Neverly's instructions, it created a large outdoor location for the trio. They stood on a large stone bridge, built over a fast-running river that divided a large forest.

"I remember this place," Everly said as she looked around. "Yes . . . This is where I killed that troll a few months back."

"Yeah, that was fun," Beverly grinned. "He tried to eat us, and we totally kicked his ass. Heh, he was funny looking."

"Yeah, yeah, good times, good times." Everly nodded. "But why are we here? How is this going to help us find the intruder?"

"Well, I had a thought," Neverly replied. "Think about it. When did things start feeling weird for us? It was after the big fight in Bremburg. When we did what we did to Fenn."

"Yes. I remember," Everly said in a tense voice. "Now would you kindly explain what the hell this stupid bridge has to do with any of that?"

"Everly, calm *down*," Neverly said in irritation. "Jeez, use your head. How did we figure out our mind was being played with? When we finally noticed that we weren't acting like ourselves, right? Well, that got me thinking. When was the exact moment that we started behaving differently?"

"Oh," Everly said as realization finally dawned on her.

"What? What are you talking about?" Beverly asked in confusion.

"We have a perfect memory, stupid. Just think about it," Neverly said in annoyance to her fellow duplicate.

"Oh, right, right, duh," Beverly said sheepishly before concentrating.

Yes, the troll had appeared and challenged Everly, attempting to make a meal of her. Everly had toyed with the silly creature for a bit, dancing away out of reach of its attacks and mocking it. Then, once she'd had enough fun, she killed it. Afterward, she indulged in a little idle conversation with her servants. Then, amid an argument between Eris and Titania, she saw . . .

"We saw a dead body floating down the river," Beverly said.

"Exactly," Neverly said. "*Exactly.* And from that point on, that's when things started feeling . . . odd."

"That's right. Thea. Thea was in the river. We fished her out and revived her with our necromancy," Beverly said thoughtfully. "And she told us her story. She told us about her village, and how it was under attack by a monster."

"God, that freak again." Everly glowered. "Mister Whisper. The child-eating whatever the hell it was. Didn't I say earlier that I never wanted to think about that guy again?"

"Yep," agreed Beverly. "That guy did *not* fit in with the aesthetic we're trying to achieve here."

"Yeah, it was an unpleasant memory," Neverly said. "But here's some food for thought. If *I* were an elemental, a spiritual creature trapped in the mental landscape of my greatest enemy, where would be the best place to hide if I didn't want her to find me?"

"Holy *shit*!" Beverly exclaimed. "You're a freakin' genius! Which means *I'm* a freakin' genius! What a great day to be an Everly!"

"Except now you're a Beverly," Neverly grinned.

"Aww, now you're just exploiting my trauma for laughs!" whined Beverly.

"Still, I have to hand it to the parasite. What a clever little bastard," Beverly said. "Hiding itself in an unwanted memory. Knowing we'll automatically push it away whenever it comes up. Tricking *us* into doing the work of keeping it hidden. The fucking *nerve* of it."

"Yeah, well, now that we know how it tricked us, there's no way it can keep hiding," Neverly said smugly. "So, let's go hunt Fenneth's little pet down and send it to join its mistress."

"Yeeeah, let's go step on this little froggy," Beverly said with vicious eagerness.

Everly stood quietly as the other two spoke. On her face, she wore a neutral expression. The duplicates could sense that she remained angry. That she was still furious at being tricked for so long by Fenneth's elemental. But they didn't know what she was thinking because she was masking her thoughts from them.

"Everly," Nev said to her. "Everly, what do you want to do?"

Everly said nothing in reply. Instead, she started walking away from them, heading in the direction of Thea's village, exactly as she'd done before, months ago.

"Huh," Beverly said as she scratched her head. "I guess we're going for a walk."

"I guess so," Nev said with a frown on her brow.

What exactly was her original self thinking now?

CHAPTER THIRTEEN

Servitude

Thea's village looked exactly as Nev recalled it. Not a single detail had changed, not a single brick or window was out of place. Which of course made sense considering that she possessed an eidetic memory.

Here was where Everly had confronted the creature, Mister Whisper, and executed it on the spot before moving on to punish the members of the village council who had colluded with the monster, sacrificing the poorer members of the community in exchange for gold. A literal example of the rich eating the poor.

Nev had to admit that she took considerable satisfaction from the memory. It was true that Everly's main goal in life was to become a dark lord, but that didn't mean she had to excuse the distasteful behavior of the fellow members of her moral alignment. Cannibalism was one thing; everyone has to eat, right? But targeting the young was inexcusable.

"There," Everly suddenly said, snapping Nev out of her thoughts. "Right there. That's where I pulled his head off. He was trying to make some snappy little comments, which annoyed me, so I beheaded him. Then I had Titania flush him into some magma, and that was it for him."

"Yeah, he didn't see that coming." Bev nodded. "He kind of reminded me of that dummy in the woods who turned into that big spider. You could tell right away that he was so full of himself."

"Yeah, arrogance is so annoying when other people are exuding it," Nev said. "We're the only ones around who make it look good."

"That's because we're stylish," Bev said. "We are stylish, villainous minxes. Others imitate what we innovate. Word?"

Nev high-fived her fellow duplicate in sisterly solidarity. Then she turned to Everly and said, "So, now what?"

"Now we put an end to this," Everly said grimly. "Can't you feel it? Trying to hide from our senses? It knows we're onto it. But it's too late. It's cornered . . ."

"Ohhhh, shit. We're getting spooky now," Bev said giddily. "What do you think? Is it hiding in one of these houses?"

"Undoubtedly," Everly replied.

"So, what should we do? Check them one by one?"

"Are you recommending we split up? In the scary nightmare village of the baby-eating eldritch horror? Bev, please make better choices," said Nev.

"Stop acting like we're not invincible," Bev snorted.

"We're *not*, dummy. *She* is," Nev said, pointing a finger at Everly as she spoke. "The best you and I can hope for is to become recurring side characters and potential fan favorites. But that's not guaranteed! Especially if you keep haphazardly waving that death flag around."

"Oh, relax, will you?" Bev said. "We've clearly become a key part of the narrative. And even if we *do* die, it'll happen in a way that dramatically advances the plot. Like, we'll get killed off by the chief antagonist or something. It'll probably motivate Everly to avenge us."

"That's called being fridged, stupid! You seriously want to get fridged just to supply Everly with some inspiration? It won't even work; she's a total psycho!" Nev scoffed.

"Hey, she's neurodivergent, okay? That doesn't mean she can't feel. It just means that what she *does* feel is complete crazy-person nonsense," retorted Bev.

"Incredible. I feel like you just made *so many people* begin rooting for your violent death with just that one comment," Nev said in a stunned voice.

"Huh? What did I do?" Bev asked.

"Shut *up*," Everly said, interrupting their conversation. "We're not splitting up, okay? We can use our will to erase these buildings from existence and reveal whoever's hiding in them."

"Oh, yeah, we can totally do that," Bev said with a sage nod of her head.

"I mean, *obviously*. We created this place, after all. Everything in it is ours to command," said Nev with a sage nod of her own.

"We're fucking geniuses. We are genius bitches," Bev said airily.

"The world is our oyster and we're shucking all the clams," Nev replied while assuming a dramatic pose.

"Number one wherever we go!" declared Bev.

"Uncontested beneath heaven's gaze!" mirrored Nev.

It's not a self-destructive urge if I decide to kill them both, is it? Everly thought quietly to herself.

* * *

One by one, the houses in the village vanished from sight as Everly and her duplicates removed them from existence. Soon, only one remained. It was the home of the mayor, the head of the village council and the one who'd profited the most from Mister Whisper's spree of terror. Everly had personally cut the old bastard's throat in his sleep and left him gasping desperately for air in his own bed.

"Well, well," Bev said to the others. "Looks like our little friend has decided to take residence in the . . . uh . . . mayor's residence."

"I don't remember voting for this fiend," Nev said disapprovingly.

"This is why I don't approve of the concept of democracy," Bev said. "When the people choose their own leaders, situations like this can often arise. Really, it's for their own good to withhold the option from them."

"Agreed," said Nev. "A leader who can't elect themselves through overwhelming force and intimidation is probably a sucky leader. If I were running for mayor, my slogan would be *you have no choice*."

"Is it crazy that I thought the exact same thing?" Bev said happily.

"Not even in the slightest—" Nev began to say, when Everly suddenly stomped her foot and sent a wave of destructive motion crashing toward the house, totaling it completely. Nev had been standing in front of her when she attacked and barely managed to avoid being struck by the shockwave.

"Hey! Friendly fire much?" Nev shouted at Everly as she stood and dusted off her clothes. "That was at full force! Were you trying to remove my skin or something?"

"Oh, no, you were in the way. How awful. I'm so sorry," Everly said indifferently as she walked past the other girl to examine her handiwork. The house was now an utter wreck, and it seemed very unlikely that anyone inside of it could have survived.

"So, I don't even get an apology?" Nev asked as Everly continued to sift the wreckage.

"For what? You were quick on your feet, weren't you?" Everly retorted.

"Stay classy, original me," Nev muttered while Everly resumed ignoring her and continued searching for their target.

"Heh, we're such a hot mess," Bev snickered while giving Nev a sympathetic clap on the shoulder.

"Yeah, but clearly some of us more than others," Neverly said darkly.

"Do you think we could take her?" Bev whispered conspiratorially.

"We wouldn't stand a chance; she neutered our powers," Nev replied.

"Yeah, I get that, but for some reason, I still feel certain we could beat her if we worked together," Bev said.

"The only reason you feel that way is because we're extraordinarily overconfident," Nev chided her. "Face it, we're the Dunning-Kruger effect with boobs. We mostly get away with it because we're usually all-powerful. But if you take away that power, then what you're left with is . . . I don't know, religious conservatives at a Burning Man."

"If god didn't want hippies to use all that peyote, then why did he make it taste like candy?" Bev mused.

"That was such an interesting weekend we spent hiding under our bed." Nev nodded. "*Euphoria* was such a bad influence on us."

"I would have broken Nate's legs and chained him up in the basement," Bev said casually. "You don't need mobility with a face like that. You just need to be available."

"I bet he'd cry pretty," Nev concurred. "Sound's hot."

"Ohhh, that's a great idea for a memory palace scenario! Holodeck, meet holo-*dick*," Bev tittered.

"That is so demented," Nev said dreamily. "Hey, you gotta let me watch, okay?"

"Watch? Bitch, you're tagging in!" Bev declared.

"Hoorah!" Nev said giddily.

They high-fived each other once more to symbolize their growing friendship. Truly, the bonds between duplicates ran deep.

Suddenly, the wreckage of the mayor's home began to shift. As though something beneath it was beginning to stir.

"Hey, did you guys see that?" Nev asked warily.

"Uh, I've been staring at it for the last ten minutes while you two have been having your little bonding session, so yes, I've noticed it," Everly said grumpily.

"Daaaaw, is poor original Everly feeling a little jealous of her duplicate's burgeoning womance?" Bev asked her.

"She's clearly envious of our simpatico homosocial vibes," Nev said. "But it's not like we're excluding you! There's plenty of room for more on this train! Self-love is self-care, Everly."

"I can't believe I'm literally trolling *myself*," Everly said with a confused shake of her head.

"Is that what we're doing?" Bev wondered. "Well, I guess it makes sense—*ACK!*"

Bev squealed in alarm when a hooded figure suddenly darted forth between her and Nev and held a blade at her throat.

"Back away. Do it now or she dies," said the girl holding the weapon. "I promise it'll hurt."

"Well, that's quite a threat you're making there," Everly said with an amused smile. "Though, in all fairness, I must warn you that it's not a very effective one. She's been working my last nerve for a while, haven't you, Beverly?"

"What can I say? I enjoy being provocative," Beverly admitted. "It's a character flaw we should work on. Not that I believe we have any actual character flaws, mind you."

"Honestly, I think we're perfect the way we are," Nev said.

"I kind of hate you both, but I also kind of concur," Everly admitted.

"Shut up! SHUT UP!" the girl yelled. A vein throbbed visibly on her forehead, so intense was her anger. "You like making everything into a joke, don't you, Everly? Nothing matters except for your personal amusement, is that right? Well, to hell with you!"

"Oh, she's mad. I think she's really mad, guys!" Bev chortled.

"Heh, it's like watching a squirrel trying to intimidate a pit bull," Nev sneered.

"I think they've got you there, Thea," Everly said to the hooded figure.

"Huh. So you finally figured it out," Thea said as she let the hood of her cloak drop down. "I bet you must feel awfully clever right now."

"Well, it was the 'me' over there who put it together first," Everly said, nodding toward Nev. "Once she pointed out certain discrepancies about our memories of this day, it became obvious what you'd done. This village, the monsters, the storyline ripped straight out of an old Stephen King movie. You made the whole thing up as a cover."

"It was true we killed a troll that day on the bridge," Nev said. "And we did see a body floating downstream. But everything else was complete bullshit. Like, why would we fish some random body out of the river? Why would we even care?"

"Yeah, that's definitely not like us," Bev concurred. "And how would we have been able to give you a perfect resurrection without a copy of your mind? That's not how it works!"

"Oh, but where you really went overboard was when you had us altruistically rescue your village with no interest in a reward. You seriously think I'd just leave the gold behind? Thea, I don't even need it, but I'd still take it with me on principle alone. I'm a terrible fucking person."

"Then there was the part where we'd remember things that we couldn't possibly have seen, like when you were chased out of the village and then you later on fighting Whisper's relatives," Nev said with a smirk. "How would we even know about that? You were being too clever, kid."

"All so you could pump my head full of remorse," Everly said with a growing frown. "You little idiot. Did you really think you were going to get away with it? Why didn't you just pull a Freddy Krueger and kill me in my dreams? That I could understand. Did you simply not have the guts for vengeance?"

"I—I don't want vengeance!" Thea cried out angrily. The dagger she held at Bev's throat began to tremble violently as she spoke. "I want justice! I wanted you to feel true remorse for what you've done and to seek punishment and redemption! That's what Fenneth wants!"

"*Wants?* Present tense? What are you babbling about, elemental?" Everly demanded.

Now Thea began to laugh.

"You really don't understand anything, you selfish monster!" she yelled. "In the instant before you snuffed out her life, I took in everything that she was. Her memories, her thoughts and feelings, everything that made her who she was, and then I fled into your mindscape while you were distracted by your awful deeds!"

"Why didn't Eris stop her?" wondered Bev aloud.

"Oh, don't you remember? Everly pulled her out into the real world and messed her up for some stupid reason. Utilizing those great people skills that she's known for," Nev said with a sneer.

"Shut up!" Everly said. "I had a great reason for disciplining Eris at the time!"

"Oh, yeah? What was it?" Nev asked her.

". . . I don't remember," Everly admitted.

"It's cool. I don't really care," Nev admitted as well.

"God, all of you, you're just so *awful!*" Thea said furiously.

"Yeah, well, that's us in a nutshell," Everly said with a shrug. Then she snapped her finger.

Before Thea could react, vines shot forth from the ground and wrapped themselves around her, binding her limbs and forcing her to drop her weapon. In moments, she was made completely helpless.

"Ha!" snorted the now-free Beverly. "Nice try, dummy. But this is the memory palace. Everything in here exists according to our will. One of its most basic features is that nothing can harm us! Oh, looks like you dropped something," she said as she reached down and picked up Thea's discarded dagger.

"Playing with knives is dangerous, kid," Nev said as she stepped behind Thea and began running her fingers through her hair, before she suddenly gripped it savagely and pulled her head back with a vicious tug. "Maybe we need to teach you a little responsibility?" she murmured into her ear.

"Please don't hurt me," Thea trembled. Fear had displaced her anger and the bravery it brought with it.

"Ohhh, you know we want to be an accommodating hostess, sweetie, but that might be too tough a thing to ask," Bev said as she gently began pulling the edge of the dagger down Thea's cheek. "You see, we *really* want to hurt you."

"It's not like you have anywhere to go, or any chance of escape," Nev grinned.

"So why not stay and play with us? You're so *pretty*, and we have so many *sick fantasies*," Bev whispered, as she ran her finger along the wound she'd made and licked it with a smile of delight.

"Please . . . please, I'm all that's keeping what's left of her alive," Thea sobbed. "If you kill me, Fenneth really *will* be gone."

"If? Ha! Did you hear that, Nev? This silly thing said *if* we killed her." Bev laughed. "Can you believe it?"

"Hopes springs eternal in the hearts of the foolish," Nev said, chuckling. "So, are we going to take turns? Can we flip for who goes first?"

"I'm not flipping for anything; I'm the one who found the knife," Bev said.

"Oh, come on! I know you; once you get going, there'll barely be anything left for me," Nev pouted.

"I promise not to touch her eyes, her ears, or her tongue," Bev offered.

"Oh, phooey," Nev said unhappily. "Well, I guess I'll take what I can get."

"Both of you, knock it off," Everly said as she stepped between Bev and Thea. "I've had a sudden burst of inspiration. We're not killing this little parasite after all."

"What? Everly, what the actual *eff* are you talking about?" Beverly said angrily. "You were the one who wanted to kill this moron more than anyone. Now you're backing down just because she's playing the Fenneth card?"

"Yeah, are you sure you're not going soft or something? What's the deal?" Nev asked. "We're the same person. We are LITERALLY the same freakin' person. I want to kill this little gnat, so I know that means you do too. So why the hell are we holding back?"

"Preach, woman, preach!" said Bev. "Everly, I have such a metaphorical murder boner right now, but you're *really* blue-balling my nonexistent balls! What's with the sudden self-denial?"

"THINK ABOUT IT," Everly said, barely able to hide her frustration with how stupid she could be sometimes.

"What are you talking about—oh. *Oh.* Okay, that makes sense," Nev said begrudgingly once she realized what Everly was getting at.

"Is someone going to share, or am I going to keep standing here referencing genitals I don't have?" Bev asked impatiently.

"Bev, what's the one thing even we can't do?" Nev asked her patiently.

"Disrespect the Wu-Tang Clan," Bev answered at once.

"What's the other thing?"

"Cast healing magic."

"Ding-ding," Everly said. Then she pointed at the captive Thea. "Now, what kind of elemental is this?" she asked her fellow dupe.

"A light elemental," Bev said.

"And who did she once belong to?"

"Fenneth."

"And what was Fenneth's specialty?"

". . . Oh. Okay, I reluctantly concede your point," Bev said in defeat.

"Exactly," Everly said. She stepped toward the helpless Thea and placed both of her hands on the sides of her face, forcing her prisoner to meet her intense gaze. "You're mine now. *Forever.* Get it?"

Tears poured from Thea's eyes. But she nodded.

"Good. I'm glad you understand," Everly said happily. "What's your name? Your real name, that is."

Thea hesitated to speak. She fought the urge to answer Everly's question and struggled to show no obedience. But when she looked past her new mistress and saw the wicked expressions worn by Nev and Beverly, she knew she truly didn't have a choice.

Giving in to Everly was the same as betraying Fenneth. But being killed by her would have been the same as letting Fenneth die all over again. And that was no choice at all.

"I'm Discordia," the elemental admitted before bowing her head in shame.

"*Discordia*, huh." Everly grinned, sounding the name out as though she were tasting something sweet. "I like it."

The vines surrounding Discordia vanished, causing her to drop clumsily to the ground. Everly then extended a hand to her and helped her rise to her feet.

"Welcome to the family."

CHAPTER FOURTEEN

Downtime

Hey, why don't we ever use the memory palace to watch porn?" Bev asked the group one day.

The three of them were lounging in Everly's quarters in the memory palace, idly passing the time, shortly after Discordia had been captured. It was a peaceful afternoon spent watching television and eating popcorn when Bev sprang her question.

"What?" asked Everly. "What are you going on about now?"

"I'm talking about porn, stupid! Come on, think about it," Bev said. "Anything we envision around here becomes reality. I mean, this place provides the kind of full-contact 3D immersion that countless perverts across Earth have always dreamed of, and it's right here at our command. So, why don't we ever use it to watch porn?"

"Bev, we don't use the memory palace for porn because this place is our lair!" Nev said as she threw popcorn at the other girl. "I'm serious! This is the sacred seat of our power. If you want to tickle your fancy so badly, then go do it somewhere else. But it better not be on the furniture."

"That's so unfair!" Bev whined. "This place is so convenient! You prudes are willfully denying yourselves some great possibilities!"

"Bev, get a grip!" snapped Everly. "But not *that* kind of a grip! Have you ever heard of Doctor Doom spanking it in his castle in Latveria? Do you think Lex Luthor likes to give his 'little Lex' a polish in the Hall of Doom?"

"I bet they do," Bev said stubbornly. "Everyone knows villains like to plow."

"You are so dumb," Nev said with a roll of her eyes. "I really hope your stupidity isn't infectious."

"Whatever!" Bev said defensively. "I'm just saying, I think big-time super-villains get into all kinds of kinky situations away from the prying eyes of the public! They're *supervillains*, so they do whatever they feel like, whenever they feel like it. And if you can fuck on demand, why wouldn't you?"

"You know, she actually might have a point," Nev said thoughtfully. "As unlikely as it sounds, she's making some sense."

"Of course my argument makes sense!" Bev said. "Everly, are you really going to tell me that Lex Luthor has never gotten laid in any of his secret bases? Impossible! He's, like, bald and super fit. And I bet he does tantra too. Lex Luthor totally looks tantric to me."

"Well, bald guys *are* known for being very sensual," Everly conceded. "I bet dudes with alopecia can get *really* slippery."

"Exactly!" Bev said. "Man, there's no doubt in my mind that baldies can fuck like volcanoes! They have to do a bunch of extra work to make up for their lack of hair, Lex Luthor especially! He's a known overachiever!"

"That *is* a famous characteristic of his." Nev nodded.

"Yep!" Bev continued. "The sex would be so wild too! He'd be armed with all those Kama Sutra techniques and all sorts of fiendish super-science. I bet he's already notched like all the main female villains and probably half of the heroines too. Who wouldn't want to be with a guy like him?"

"Doesn't Lois Lane shoot him down all the time?" asked Everly.

"Yeah, well, Lois Lane is the biggest frickin' idiot in the world," Bev retorted. "Chica has no taste."

"God, Lois Lane is one of those domineering bitches who always has to be the smartest person in the room," Nev said nastily. "I hate people like her! I bet the only reason she dates Superman is because she can control him. That dude has no spine."

"Ha! *Super-simp* is more like it!" snorted Everly. "I bet he thanks her whenever she spits on him."

"You think Superman's a sub?" Beverly asked her.

"I do, actually," Everly said confidently. "His sort of obvious weakness is catnip for an insecure loser like Lois. I bet he loved it when Doomsday beat him to death. He was probably like, *Yes! Harder, Daddy! Hit me harder!*"

"Heh, heh, *Dooms-daddy*. I love it," Nev grinned.

"I'd take that ride," Bev said. "Sploosh!"

"Really? But he's all boney and shit."

"Those spikes of his? They'll just give me something to hold onto," Bev smirked.

"Superman has the same problem that Goku does," Nev said contemptuously. "Dude can throw a planet into the sun, but he can't win an argument with his wife."

"Just how she likes it!" Bev said. "No wonder she avoids being with Lex."

"Yeah, Lex is a scientific genius, a successful businessman, and the deadliest criminal mastermind on the planet," Nev said. "But that isn't good enough for Lois? Please! What does *she* do for a living again? She works in *print media*. Jesus, there are YouTube channels that get more clicks in a day than people who still read newspapers. It's not just an archaic profession, it's *dying*."

"She does it because she's a hipster," said Everly with derision. "I bet she loves telling people she's a reporter for a *real* newspaper. *Hey, I'm Lois Lane of the* Daily Planet. *Can I ask you a few questions?* Probably soaks her underwear whenever anyone asks what the hell the *Daily Planet* is. She's so lame."

"Too true," said Bev. "Hipsters get off on *novelty*."

"Didn't she win a Pulitzer?" asked Nev. "She must be a good writer if she did that."

"Who cares?" said Bev. "Do people even give a shit about Pulitzers? I only have the vaguest awareness of their existence, and frankly, I'd rather win a Kids' Choice Award. You'd get way more attention for your brand."

"Fucking seriously?" Everly laughed. "A Kids' Choice Award?"

"Don't scoff at me!" said Bev. "Taylor Swift won a bunch of those and now she's the dominant life-form on Earth."

"Facts!" echoed Nev.

"Logic!" continued Bev.

"Hey, do you think Superman cried when Lois clapped him for the first time?" asked Nev with a gleeful smirk.

"Huh?" asked Everly and Bev, both.

"Think about it," Nev continued. "He's a Midwestern farm boy from Kansas. They're super religious out there, aren't they? I bet he grew up attending church twice on Sundays, and Wednesdays too. There's no chance he didn't cry when Lois jumped his bones."

"Maybe he was crying because he knew he'd have to marry her, or else he was going to hell," Everly suggested.

"Wooo, you're so right. The church doesn't like premarital fun." Nev giggled.

"What if he hounded Lois for weeks afterward to please marry him so the devil wouldn't get him because Pastor Tim said he committed a mortal sin?" Bev said, laughing. "I mean, he had a high school education in Kansas. I'm surprised he even knew which parts went where."

"No, he probably knew what he was doing," Everly said sagely. "He grew up on a farm. Farmers have to breed their own livestock, don't they? They raise their own cows and chickens. Horses too, sometimes. Superman's probably seen more dicks than an old urologist."

"Whoa," said Nev. "I just had this icky vision of Clark Kent touching a horse's penis, and now I feel like my life is over."

"Hey, it's not icky," Everly smirked. "The farmers have to help the horses guide it in. There are thousands of hardworking, admirable people in the agricultural industry who just happen to have to occasionally help their stallions get it on with their mares. Superman just canonically happens to be one of them."

"Oh, I really hope he wore gloves," Nev said, shuddering. "Gloves should be mandatory in that gig."

"Hey, how many chickens do you think Superman has killed in his lifetime?" Bev wondered. "Probably like thousands."

"Huh?"

"Well, don't farmers prepare their own food? It's kind of what they're known for. How many chickens do you think Superman killed growing up? Just wrung their necks at super-speed and then plucked their heads off like he was picking flowers."

"Wow, I bet it was a lot," Nev said. "Farmers are brutal."

"Jeez, can you even imagine? Superman being covered in chicken blood, just wandering around the yard casually, like it's not low-key horrifying? And to think that *he's* the guy who kids trust to rescue their cats from trees."

"Kids are stupid," Everly said dismissively.

"Kids ARE stupid," Nev agreed. "Let's never breed. Motherhood isn't for the likes of us."

"Nalec thinks of us as his mother," Everly said with a frown.

"We really fucked that guy up," Bev said.

"Hey, that's not really our fault," Nev said. "We were experimenting when we made him. All the other inheritors we've created since then have been perfect."

"Honestly, just remembering his existence puts a frown on my face," said Everly. "I was hoping he would turn out to be one of those false memories that Discordia put in our head."

"Why don't we just cut the cord?" asked Nev. "Snip-snip, buh-bye, Nalec. We'll bury him and his mommy issues in the same hole as that idiot we made him from."

"No. We've got to stick to our code," Everly grumbled.

"Everly, ethics are stupid, and they're slowing us down! Just kill the cringy little wanker! God, I'll do it for you," Bev said, scowling.

"I'll help," Nev offered. "Or maybe I'll just watch. I'll probably just watch. I like watching."

"And I *like* it when you watch me," Bev purred.

"No," Everly insisted. "Listen, I admit it: I'm tempted! He's an annoying creep. I want him dead as much as you do. I just don't want to randomly execute him. It feels wasteful. As a true dark lord, we need to find a way to make his death useful for our purpose. Nalec can't just die . . . He has to die in a way that benefits us."

The three of them sat on the sofa, stewing over their problem for a bit, when Beverly suddenly snapped her fingers.

"Guys, I think I have a solution to our problem!" she said brightly.

"We're *not* using the memory palace to watch porn," Everly said crossly.

"Aww, but I want to!" Bev whined.

"Yeah, yeah, get over it."

"Hey, Everly," Nev said suddenly, cutting off Beverly's tantrum. "I think I actually *do* have a solution for the Nalec issue. It'll be a little long-term, so we'll have to wait until after the party. But I promise you the payoff will be *so* good."

"Oh? Do tell," Everly said eagerly. "Let's hear it!"

"I'm taking some inspiration from the Good Book for this one," Nev said with a malicious smile. "Tell me, have you ever heard the story of King David and Uriah?"

"Uriah?" Bev said blankly. "Sounds like a prostate issue to me."

"*Beeeev*," Nev said as she held a hand to her head in embarrassment.

"Don't say my name like that! It makes me feel judged!" Bev grumbled.

I really should have completed high school, Everly thought dourly.

CHAPTER FIFTEEN

Identity

Twenty-five days later.

With the fading of the sun, night soon set itself over the kingdom of Winstead, leading most of the tired citizens of that land, rich and poor, to settle down for sleep.

Life was difficult for many throughout the realm. Although the nobles continued to live lives of comfort and excess, for most of those of lesser status living within its borders, every waking moment was a hard scramble for survival. Bitter days were spent etching out a living doing menial labor accompanied by low wages, which often led to lives of deprivation and misery.

The life of a common citizen was a constant cycle of needs versus desire. They needed bread. They *wanted* meat. They needed copper pennies. They *wanted* gold coins. They needed to live in their cramped, uncomfortable little cottages. They *wanted* real homes.

They needed to survive.

They *wanted* to be happy.

The nobles didn't care.

So, once more, another night came for the exhausted and downtrodden commoners, who dropped onto their beds if they were fortunate enough to have them, to fall into the dreamless, fitful rest of the truly hopeless.

Only to awaken and find themselves in a place greater than they could have ever imagined.

* * *

It was the event of the year. The greatest celebration in the history of the nation, although no one knew it was coming. No one knew to expect it, and no one knew how to react now that they were immersed in it. No one knew what was happening, only that it was incredible, and that every one of them was being treated like an honored guest in the home of a monarch.

"Where are we?" many of them asked in confusion.

They were all standing in a wonderful, starry-skied clearing, gathered outside the gate of a wonderous black tower. A podium had been erected before them, and to the surprise of many of them, a goblin stood on it.

Many of these people were country folk, and they had seen goblins before. This one was unlike any that they had ever beheld. He was tall for one thing, nearly four feet in height, which was massive for his kind. He also carried himself with a sort of grand and regal bearing that put many of them to shame.

Now he stood before them, dressed in a beautifully tailored outfit that marked him as a servant of great standing in a powerful and wealthy household. His manner seemed so severe that it caused many of the thousands assembled there to adopt a deferential bearing in case they should accidentally offend such an important person with their lowborn mannerisms.

Surprisingly, the goblin smiled kindly at the humble multitude and gave them a friendly wave. He tapped the end of a strange metallic object attached to the podium, which caused an echo to sweep over the crowd. Then he began speaking into the device, which somehow magnified his voice and carried it to their ears, saying:

"A good evening to you, oh, good people of Winstead! I'm certain that you have many questions that you'd like to ask me. Please be assured that clarity shall soon be yours. My name is Carter, a humble servant of the majestic ruler of these lands who wishes now to extend the hand of friendship to you all. In her blessed name, let me bid you welcome!"

"Sir? Please tell us, where is this place?" asked a nervous young boy.

"You stand in the blessed land of creation, young man," Carter warmly replied. "A place where thought and reality intermix and create *wonder*. A place where the possibilities are as limitless as the endless horizon! Although it has no one true name, you would not be mistaken to think of it as *paradise!*"

The boy's mouth dropped, and the crowd broke out into excited murmuring, which persisted for a while. The goblin allowed them to indulge in their discussions before one of them managed to raise his voice above the rest.

"Sir? Sir Carter? What does this mean?" asked the shabbily dressed man. "Why have we been summoned here?"

"Not summoned, my friend. *Invited.* Everyone here is an honored guest and may leave whenever they wish. But I hope you'll first allow me the pleasure of inviting you to participate in a night of festivities and jubilation unlike any you have ever experienced before!"

At the mention of festivities, the people began buzzing among themselves in growing anticipation. The goblin patiently waited for them to quiet down before continuing.

"Yes, my friends, that's right. Tonight, in celebration of her seventeenth birthday, my mistress has kindly opened the doors of her wonderous home to all of you, wishing only that you will partake of the delights presented here for your enjoyment! She wants you all to forget your worries and find the release you deserve."

The whispering of the crowd grew even more excited, and the goblin's smile grew even wider.

"Now, enter this magnificent tower and know only joy! Stay however long you wish and do whatever you like! There are no consequences here, no sins, and no judgment! There is only happiness and acceptance! Come join us, my friends! Quickly now, quickly! For in the halls of the Empress, the blessings of the night are eternal!"

A wind then swept over the crowd, accompanied by a dazzling light, which momentarily blinded them but caused them no pain. When it faded, the humble people assembled in that field were now dressed in expensive finery, the likes of which they could never have afforded in their waking lives. Every man among them looked like a king, and every woman a queen.

The children among them laughed and whispered to each other that they had just experienced magic, and the adults were made speechless by what had just occurred. Then, the gates of the black tower opened, and a welcoming glow from within it washed over them, bidding them to enter. As one, the crowd began eagerly moving inside.

Watching from above, four figures dressed in red, black, green, and white looked down upon their guests and smiled wickedly.

No one knew what time it was, but that didn't matter. No one knew where they were, but that didn't matter either. Because no one knew how long it would last, they instinctively chose to exist solely in the moment. The party of the century had now begun, and everyone in the kingdom of Winstead was eager to go wild.

Claudia was bewildered to discover that she was now wearing a gorgeous formfitting gown and standing in the middle of the largest dance hall she'd ever seen in her life.

Around her were thousands of strangers, some as equally startled to find themselves there as she was. Like her, they were dressed beautifully. She at first assumed they were fellow nobles, but their manner of speech and the way they carried themselves soon revealed their lowborn origins. It was all so very strange.

Claudia soon decided that it was like everyone was participating in a massive masquerade ball and had come disguised as the version of themselves they most wished they could be. She included herself in that accounting.

Everywhere, there were tables filled with refreshments. Sumptuously prepared food and beverages, the likes of which she'd never had the opportunity to enjoy. It all must have tasted even better than it looked, because many of the attendees were gluttonously stuffing it inside their mouths with no care for appearances.

As the daughter of a count, Claudia had attended her fair share of social gatherings. Her father had even hosted a ball for her coming-of-age celebration just last year. But the extravagance of those earlier parties paled by far in comparison to the splendor she now experienced. There was just so much of . . . *everything.*

Above those dancing below it floated a levitating stage that was held aloft through an incredible display of magic, on which a band played, using instruments that Claudia didn't recognize. The song they performed was pounding, powerful, and *primal.* She thought it sounded like a kind of radical folk music, which she normally didn't care for, but here, it was performed so aggressively and with so much furious passion that she found herself greatly enjoying it.

A desire gradually grew within her to join the crowd and lose herself in the revelry like they had. Only the self-discipline instilled in her by Countess Anne kept her from giving in to that temptation.

Instead, she observed the dancers who'd been enraptured by the song, having lost themselves to the wild, brutish moshing that they'd spontaneously erupted into. Even the ordinarily prim Claudia had to admit that it looked like a lot of fun.

"I'M A SAILOR PEG! AND I LOST MY LEG! CLIMBING UP THE TOP SAILS, *I LOST MY LEG!*" screamed the singer in a frenzy as his bandmates backed him up. "I'M SHIPPING UP TO BOSTON! OHHHHHH! I'M SHIPPING UP TO BOSTON! OHHHHHH! I'M SHIPPING UP TO BOSTON! *I'M SHIPPING OFF TO FIND MY WOODEN LEG!*"

Claudia had no idea where this place called Boston was located, but it sounded extremely dangerous. Curiosity gradually overcame her reserve the longer the performance went on. Just when she decided to give in, a hand reached forth and touched her shoulder.

"Easy, my lady," said a stern-looking young man several years older than her, who stepped closely beside her. "You're a VIP. There's a place that's already been reserved for you. Would you please follow me?"

"Oh, um, sure," Claudia said nervously. Who was this boy? His manner of speech and arrogant bearing identified him immediately as a true noble. He was also dressed as elegantly as everyone else in attendance at this fantastic affair. But unlike the others, he was armed. Slung across his back, he carried a vicious-looking battle axe that greatly suited the aura of danger that he exuded.

The stranger also seemed disdainful of all the extravagance that surrounded the two of them. Claudia could feel the icy contempt for his surroundings reflected in his cold, blue eyes. His black hair was trimmed short, and his face was . . . *dazzling*.

Claudia couldn't help but feel charmed by him. As though she were in the presence of an untamed but friendly wolf.

"Um, sir? May I ask where we are?" she asked the young man.

"You don't already know?" he replied. "You stand within your sister's home in the astral realm. This is Everly's demesne."

"What?" Claudia asked in shock. "Are you saying all of this belongs to . . . Everly?"

"Indeed," the stranger said with a nod.

"*All of this?*" she repeated in a daze.

"Crafted from her imagination," the stranger said. "I advise you to always stay inside when you visit here, Princess. Outside these halls exists literal chaos. Anything could happen out there. So long as you stay inside, however, you'll always find safety in the house of the Empress."

"You call all of this a mere *house*?" Claudia asked in a daze.

"Its sheer immensity once bothered me as well, but it's been my home for many years now," said the stranger. "After a while, you simply get used to it."

"You misspoke my title earlier. I'm hardly a princess," Claudia informed him.

"Everly says otherwise. Her every desire is the law in this realm," he said matter-of-factly. "That will soon be true everywhere."

"Sir? May I ask what your name is?" Claudia asked with a slight blush.

"Me? I'm Grail. If we met earlier, I would have appeared to you as an older man. A form I much preferred, in all honesty. However, Everly insists that I now appear thusly. She kindly informed me, quote, unquote, that she *Didn't want a grandpa following her around.*"

"So, she just *willed* you into becoming younger?" Claudia asked him.

"She did. Many things are possible thanks to the immense power she possesses. You'll soon learn that for yourself," Grail said as he led her to a balcony overlooking the celebration, where he then had her seated in an extremely comfortable chair. "There will be others along shortly. If there's anything you'd like, ring the bell on your table and ask for it. It will be delivered instantly."

"Delivered by who?" Claudia asked. "I haven't seen any servants."

"It's best that you don't," Grail said darkly. "But they're here all the same. Just think of them as your invisible helpers."

Grail then left, leaving Claudia by herself. She stared at the bell on her table for some time and thought over what he had said to her. Then she gave a slight shudder and decided she wanted nothing.

Claudia sat there alone, wondering when she'd see Grail again. She considered opening her third eye to see for herself what he'd hinted at earlier but then thought of the seriousness of his expression when he suggested she not pry.

Perhaps it would be for the best if she were less curious.

With that in mind, she continued to sit quietly and wait.

"And just who's this gorgeous little doll? *There's* my big sister!" a familiar voice called out. When Claudia turned, she saw Everly, wearing a stunning white sleeveless dress, approaching her. Everly then squeezed her with another of those powerful hugs she loved delivering so much before giving Claudia a welcoming kiss on her forehead.

"Knock it off! We just saw each other an hour ago," Claudia said in annoyance as she pushed Everly away. "Honestly, you're like an overly excited puppy."

"An hour ago? Is that how long it felt to you?" Everly asked as she took a seat beside Claudia. "Sorry, darling, time flows a little differently around here. I feel like I haven't seen you in *months*! And now all I want to do is gobble you up!"

"Well, please avoid the temptation," Claudia said. "What's all of this about, anyway?"

"What do you think it's about?" Everly said with a laugh. "It's about *me*, naturally! A girl only turns seventeen once, you know. Well, it could have been twice in my case, but then I brought a sword to school. Anyway, I thought I'd invite a few hundred thousand of my closest friends to celebrate the occasion with me!"

"*These* are your closest friends?" Claudia asked her with a raised eyebrow.

"Well, they'll all be my future property, anyway," Everly admitted with a careless shrug. "Not too long from now, they're all going to be spending most of their free time in abject worship of me. I figured I might as well give them a taste of things to come. You know, get them primed for utter dependency on me."

"Everly . . . how are you doing all of this?" Claudia asked her. "Where does all of this come from? How are you this powerful?"

"Oh, I'd love to tell you, but that's related to business," Everly said to her. "We don't know each other well enough to even begin discussing things of that nature. Your earlier misadventure with Acedia makes me think you might be a little too ambitious for now, sister."

"Don't be upset, though. It's not that I don't trust you," said a voice behind Claudia that startled her. When she turned around, she saw . . . another Everly, this one dressed in green, smiling down on her.

"It's just that when people start asking about how one acquires power . . ." said an Everly to her side dressed in red.

"It's often a prelude to them wanting to know how to seize that power for themselves," said an Everly dressed in darkest black. "So, let's just say I have secrets, okay?"

"What the hell *is* this?" Claudia asked in alarm.

"It's just me, babe. It's all Everly," she said, delighted by Claudia's reaction.

"I meant, why are there four of you?" Claudia demanded to know.

"Why wouldn't there be?" the Everly in white asked her. "Well, I mean, there were only three of us to start with, but then I realized a fourth one was what I really needed to complete the set. They're great! I'm great! Everlys, introduce yourselves to our sister, please."

"I'm Beverly, the second oldest," smirked the one in green.

"I'm Neverly. I'm the smart one," said the one in black.

"I'm Cleverly. I guess I'm the baby of the bunch," said the one in red.

"I don't understand. Are these illusions of some kind?" Claudia asked Everly. "Are they disguised servants?"

"No," Everly said patiently. "They're *me*. It's all part of the plan. I'll fill you in later, I promise. If you want a better explanation, I'll say this: Don't think of them as different individuals. They're more like extra limbs on my body. Or extra heads, if you prefer."

"Like the hydra," said Beverly.

"More like Cerberus," said Neverly.

"Personally, I prefer King Ghidorah," said Cleverly.

"Guys, do you see Claudia's expression?" asked Beverly. "God, I just want to pinch her cheek until it falls off."

"Wait your turn after me," Neverly said.

"Shouldn't I get to go first, since you've all known her longer?" Cleverly asked them.

"Shut up, new girl!" barked Beverly.

"Yeah, I can't believe you're speaking to us like equals. You haven't even been blooded in yet," Neverly said condescendingly.

"Everly! Tell these hags to be nice! They're excluding me again!" whined Cleverly.

"Girls, be nicer to your alternative self or I'm sending you to the rat room," Everly said to them sternly.

"Snitch!" grumbled Neverly with crossed arms.

"Crybaby!" Beverly said with a disgusted sniff.

"Haha! You got in *trouble*," chortled Cleverly.

"Enough, already," Everly said to the three as she rose from her chair. "Come on, it's time for my speech."

"Why are you making a speech?" Claudia asked before the four of them could walk away. "Everly, tell me what's happening! What is the true purpose of this gathering?"

"Sister, haven't you heard?" Everly asked her. "To thoroughly conquer a kingdom, you can't settle for just defeating armies and executing your rivals. You've also got to win over the hearts of the common folk. Forget the nobles; it's the people at the very bottom who truly determine who gets to rule once the fighting's done. Just sit there and watch; I'll show you. It all begins tonight."

"What begins?" Claudia asked warily.

"My reign," each Everly said simultaneously. "The campaign begins *now*."

CHAPTER SIXTEEN

The Reveal

What kind of a speech was that supposed to be?" Claudia asked her sister a short while later. "Everly, you nattered on aimlessly about someone named General Zod for ten minutes and then you started singing."

"Did I do a good job?" Everly asked as they were escorted by Grail away from the revelry to the council chambers where they often held their meetings. "Rammstein is so difficult to get right."

"No," Claudia said flatly, not knowing what she meant.

"Well, singing is hard! I'm a little tone deaf," Everly said.

"Just a little?"

"Be nice! It's my birthday!" Everly said as she took the center seat—a throne, really—in the middle of the room alongside her three duplicates. Below their dais was the table where the others would sit.

"I thought you did okay," Cleverly said sympathetically as she reached over to pat Everly's hand. "The effort is what counts!"

"Thank you, Clev. You're a wonderful person," Everly said with gratitude.

"Brownnoser," said Nev.

"Suck up," said Bev.

"To answer your question, Claudia, it didn't matter what I said to the crowd. They've been mentally primed to hear whatever they want. Everyone out there believes that I've just promised to make their greatest wish come true."

"Can we at last dismiss that rabble?" Eris asked as she stepped from the shadows to kneel before her mistress. "Copying so many minds for storage while maintaining the cohesion of the memory palace has been difficult. The strain is . . . *remarkably* painful, Everly."

"But the fact that you can do this with so many individual minds is incredible, Eris," Everly said to her with a smile. "Don't you feel the least bit proud of yourself?"

"Discordia has to constantly heal me in order for me to maintain my focus," Eris said. "Without her assistance, this night would not have been possible. Even now, the presence of so many individuals here at once is agonizing to me. Everly, please . . . send the dreamers home."

Everly frowned on her throne and sighed in disappointment. "So, you're still not as powerful as I'd like you to be, huh, Eris? Which means that *I'm* not as powerful as I'd like to be either. I can't say that's pleasing to hear."

"Everly, over a third of the peasant population of the kingdom is now inside your demesne. This has been a *staggering* display of spiritual power," Eris said.

"I think we can do better," Everly said coldly. "But for now, if this really is the limit for you, then I suppose we can give you a break. Go ahead, let them all know the party's over."

"Thank you. Thank you, Everly," Eris said gratefully.

"Yeah, yeah," Everly said dismissively. "Hey, make sure you take note of anyone who doesn't wish me a happy birthday."

"It shall be done." Eris bowed.

"Who was that?" Claudia asked after Eris exited the room.

"My spirit elemental," Everly replied. "Oh, I should have had her introduce herself! Eh, she'll be back soon."

Claudia stared at Everly, uncertain if she was being mocked or not. "What do you mean that was your elemental? I don't understand what you're getting at."

"What's that supposed to mean?" Everly asked her. "That's Eris. She and her sister have been my servants for ages. Now that I think about it, why don't you show me *your* spirit elemental? I'm curious to see how they compare."

"Everly, I can't do that," Claudia said.

"Why not? There's no need to hide it. I'm just curious. I promise I won't hurt the little thing."

Claudia felt her skin growing flush at the words that her sister chose. Spirit elementals were the most desired and feared among the six known types. To hear the servant that she was so proud of casually dismissed as a *little thing* angered her.

"Everly, I can only manifest my elemental as a small orb of light in my hand. It isn't big enough to take on a form and walk around. It certainly can't *speak*! When you told me that you could use two elementals, I found that difficult enough to accept. But now you're telling me your elementals can take forms and converse with you?"

"Uh, yes? Is that what you chose to be impressed by? Not the psychic house party I just held for thousands of background characters?" Everly asked in confusion.

"Yes!" Claudia yelled, appalled by her little sister's ignorance. "Everly, for the sky's sake, haven't you ever noticed this before? Please tell me that you aren't so self-centered, so narcissistically focused on your own interests, that it's never occurred to you that people can't talk to elementals!"

Everly sat quietly in her chair and stared at her hands, which she twiddled in embarrassment. Then she looked up and said with a sheepish expression on her face, "Uh, *maybe?*"

"EVERLY!" Claudia yelled as she ran up to her sister's throne, grabbed her by the shoulders, and began shaking her. "You have GOT to be kidding me!"

"I'm not, I swear!" Everly wailed. "Grail! Why didn't you ever tell me that talking to my elementals was weird?!"

"I use *harada*," Grail said dismissively. "I have no idea what's considered normal for mages."

"But you've been around other mages for decades! Eris and Titania never seemed out of place to you?"

"We all keep secrets," Grail shrugged. "I simply assumed that conversations with an elemental servant weren't something to be spoken of."

"EVERLY!" Claudia yelled again. "Don't you understand?! THIS IS A BIG DEAL! Don't you get it? YOU'RE A SPEAKER!"

"Since I have no idea what that means, I honestly can't tell why that's so impressive," Everly said.

Claudia took a deep breath to calm herself. Everly was so frustrating to talk to, but she couldn't let herself be sidetracked by how *dense* her little sister was. Instead, she looked her in the eye and said, "Everly. The temple, *both* temples, were originally one group assembled nearly a thousand years ago, okay?"

"Okay," Everly said with a nod.

She had no idea why that was so important. She'd always hated studying religion. Her mother, Lyona, had never been a particularly spiritual person, so Everly's education in these matters was quite limited.

"They were created to worship *the radiant one*," Claudia said excitedly. "Tell me you've at least heard of *him*! The son of heaven! The shepherd of the faithful! The only person in history who could speak directly to the elementals!"

"Okay, I'm vaguely familiar with that name," Everly said. "So, what you're saying is that he was real? Not just some godhead figure that the two temples share as a common belief?"

"He must have been real," Claudia said. "Because you're capable of the very same things he was known for. Everly, he could boil the seas! He could bring the dead back to life! He destroyed the first empire, burned the Eternal Emperor himself to ashes with a whisper! By the gods, it all makes so much sense now! Everly, you must be his reincarnation. You're the promised second coming—"

Everly leaned forward and placed a finger against her sister's lips.

"Claudia? *No.* That's stupid," Everly said gently. "I wasn't born this way, okay? I built myself up through sheer effort! Nobody gets credit for the power I've obtained but me! If there *was* someone in the past who had moves like mine, that's fine. But whoever he was, he's got nothing to do with me."

"You're not even the least bit curious about exploring this?" Claudia asked her. "Everly, you might be a demigod! You may very well be the most powerful being on this planet! Don't you want to learn more?"

"Maybe later, in like a totally secular way," Everly said to her. "This knowledge could be of some use for one aspect of my plan. But I'm not going to get carried away with it. I've never once enjoyed stories about prophesized characters whose every deed is preordained. The very idea of it displeases me."

"But, Everly," Claudia said. "If you'd only read the prophecies—"

"*Enough,* Claudia," Everly said firmly. "I hate *spoilers.* End of subject."

Before Claudia could say anything else, the door opened, and four figures stepped inside. Eris, who now looked much better, accompanied by Titania, Carter, and a silent third woman wearing a porcelain mask over her face.

Moving as one, the five members of Everly's inner circle knelt before her and said, "We humbly greet our Empress."

Everly smiled, pleased by the coordinated effort they'd just demonstrated. She knew Grail hated ostentatious displays of loyalty like this and wished she could have seen his expression while the five of them had practiced this little number.

"From the seat of death, I greet my servants," said Neverly.

"From the seat of war, I greet my servants," said Beverly.

"From the seat of famine, I greet my servants," said Cleverly.

"And from the seat of conquest, I bid thee to rise and be seated," said Everly.

"So, this is the way it is from now on?" asked Grail after everyone had taken a seat at the table. "You're the deliverer of the apocalypse?"

"Just call me the revelation, old man," Everly said smugly.

"How did you decide which would be which?" asked a puzzled Titania. "I mean, you're all the same person. So, uh . . . did you flip a coin for who'd get to be which horseman?"

"T, all the horseman titles are badass. I really couldn't decide which one I wanted, so I decided to be them all," Nev said.

"Except for pollution," said Beverly. "You know, from *Good Omens?* Pollution kind of sucked."

"He was great in the book, but I don't know what they were trying to do in the miniseries," said Cleverly. "Don't tell anyone I said that, though; Neil Gaiman fans are scary."

"Only when you fuck with us," Beverly said ominously.

"The guests have all been dismissed, great one," said Carter. "Lady Eris has successfully duplicated their minds, which now rest in storage. The death forge awaits them. Soon, mass production of your reavers can begin."

"Is that the name you settled on for your new breed of zombies?" Grail asked Everly.

"It sure is!" Everly said gleefully. "Oh, I can't wait to see legions of them in action. We're going to have so much fun!"

"I've also managed to successfully seed the minds of all tonight's visitors, as you instructed me," Eris cut in. "They won't remember any important details from tonight's festivities, but they've all been subconsciously conditioned to engage in acts of espionage, sabotage, and sedition. We now have a perfect spy network cast across the entire kingdom. One in every three commoners will be our unwitting eyes and ears, delivering us the secrets of their masters whenever they sleep."

"Excellent," Beverly said with a pleased nod. "Great work, Eris. From now on, we'll call this network *the black web*."

"That name is *awesome!*" Neverly shouted giddily. "Shoot, I really wish I'd thought of that one myself."

"Well, technically you did," said Beverly with a smirk.

"Oh, I guess that's true," Nev said with a pleased smile.

"The conditions are nearly in place for our conquest to begin," Carter said to Everly. "Once Lady Titania initiates the famine that you've planned, unrest will sweep the nation. Many of the common folk will turn to brigandry in order to survive, which will swell the numbers of the remaining resistance groups left over from the civil war."

"I feel uncomfortable subjecting the people of the land to needless suffering," Grail said in a hard voice. "I understand the need to set you in your rightful place as soon as possible, Everly, but is it truly necessary for the poor to starve in order to achieve your goal?"

"Peace, Grail," Everly said, raising a hand to silence him. "This is only a temporary measure. The famine will last just a few weeks. Long enough for the people to beg for a miracle."

"A miracle that they'll soon receive." Cleverly smiled. "Because then, thanks to my newfound mastery of healing magic, I shall heal anyone close to perishing from hunger. I'll also restore the lost crops and provide an endless bounty for the starving and the destitute."

"Cleverly's going to be a living saint," Everly said happily. "The temple will be quick to embrace her. And thanks to Nalec's machinations in the east, she'll also be the one to reunite the two feuding temples. For the first time in centuries, the church will be one . . . under our rule!"

"In the meanwhile, all of the civil unrest will need to be challenged," said Beverly. "With the kingdom's armies far to the south, waging war against

Oldstead, a true hero will need to step up and unite the adventurer's guild to lead the charge against the troubles within our borders. That person will be *me*. Beverly Lance."

"Is *that* the name you chose?" Nev laughed. "You sound like a professional surfer!"

"Shut up! My new name is awesome!" yelled Beverly. "Ahem! Naturally, I won't be doing it all on my own. I can't stand out too much. But I've got my eyes set on a few idiots to share the spotlight with me. We'll be our own little gang of heroes for the people of this nation to admire."

"What are you going to call your team?" asked Cleverly.

"I don't know. I'll probably name it after myself," Bev said indifferently.

"Beverly and the Bevs?" Everly asked.

"No!" snapped Beverly. "It'll be something cool, you'll see."

"Whatever," said Neverly. "Meanwhile, with the two of you doing all the grunt work, I'm going to be chilling out in the capital, enjoying my youth. Those precious, carefree days of academic life will soon be mine!"

"Yeah, but you're basically going to be holding the children of the most powerful people in the kingdom hostage while also staying within striking distance of the royal family, right?" Cleverly asked her.

"Well, yeah, I'll be doing that too," Neverly said. "But I'll mostly be getting up to some teenage shenanigans, and whatnot. I'll only execute the people who bore me."

"No spree killing," Everly warned her.

"I said I wouldn't, all right?" Neverly said defensively.

"So, what are you going to be doing while we're taking care of the other things?" asked Cleverly. "You've been keeping that part to yourself."

"Oh, have I?" asked Everly smugly. "Heh, heh. Well, let's just say I'll be having the time of my life running wild at the border. Remember our old black-knight plan? I'm doing it. I'm going to be playing the role of a mysterious mercenary clad in black steel, serving whoever can pay my price. It's going to be so sweet!"

"I love that we can share our memories with each other," Neverly said. "Everything we do, the others experience in real time. It's like we really *are* a multiheaded entity."

"It's like I told Grail. *We* are the revelation," Everly said. "We're the Empress. We're the Horsemen. We're the cardinal winds and the four heavenly kings. All for one and one for all."

"The chaos we'll unleash . . ." said Clev.

". . . Will pave the way for a new order," concluded Beverly.

Everly rose from her throne and raised a hand toward her servants. "Will you help me, my friends? Will you join me in building a better future for all to enjoy? One world. One ruler. One *God*."

The inner circle rose and knelt once again. "All hail the Empress!" they cried.

Claudia stared in bewilderment, uncertain of what she should say or do. Was this madwoman really her little sister? Could she really achieve the daunting goal she'd set for herself?

Until she'd been summoned into the memory palace that night, Claudia hadn't truly believed Everly's boasts, nor her ridiculous claim of having personally defeated Acedia. But now, with the evidence of her sister's power being flaunted before her eyes, how could she possibly deny the truth?

Everly was the most dangerous person in Winstead. Possibly the most dangerous person in the world. Even Countess Anne would prove no match for her.

Anne is my teacher, my mentor, my beloved second mother. I dearly respect her, Claudia thought to herself. *She taught me how to wield my power, and how to assert myself over others. I'm beyond grateful to her for her lessons. But . . . she also taught me never to be a fool and to always reconsider my loyalties in the face of necessity.*

And with that being the case . . .

"Everly," Claudia said as she stepped forward and kowtowed before her sister, planting her face on the floor as she groveled. "Everly, I don't completely understand what's happening, and I don't know if I can be of use to you. But *please.* Please let me join you. Please let me be a part of your vision!"

"Awww," said Beverly.

"This is so sweet," said Cleverly.

"Who's cutting onions in here? Tell them to stop," said Neverly, weeeping.

Everly said nothing in reply. Instead, she rose from her seat and walked to her sister, welcoming her with a warm embrace.

The inner circle broke out into applause, as did the seats of war, famine, and death. Claudia smiled joyfully, touched by their easy acceptance of her. "Thank you all so much for having me," she said tearfully.

"Think nothing of it," Everly said to her. "You're *family.* Excluding you from the plan was never an option."

"Thank you, Everly," Claudia repeated.

"Sis, please. There's no need to be thankful," Everly said with a smile. "Just tell me everything you know about the Godwell family. Let's start with Countess Anne."

CHAPTER SEVENTEEN

The New Girl

There was a new girl in attendance at the Royal Imperial Academy. But no one really noticed her presence. She didn't stand out much.

The RIA had been established nearly two centuries earlier and was dedicated to education and the continued empowerment of the kingdom of Winstead's nobility. It was a place for the children of the country's elite to gather and establish bonds of friendship with each other and loyalty to their nation that would hopefully last a lifetime.

It was also a pitiless jungle where the weak were preyed on, traditions were ruthlessly enforced, and the status quo was supreme. In the academy, the nail that stood up was swiftly hammered down. More than a few of the students discovered their lifelong enemies in these hallowed halls.

More than a few lives were destroyed and quickly forgotten.

Kelsie Vae Chalen rather enjoyed that aspect of student life. Traditions were important, after all! The past was the foundation of the future, and only by embracing them wholeheartedly could one hope to match the achievements of those who came before. To a pure child of nobility such as herself, anything new was anathema.

A sickness that must be purged!

A duty she now happily commenced.

"I hope you realize this is all your fault," she purred happily as two of her friends held the fool who had humiliated her in place so that Kelsie could properly discipline her.

"I'm sorry," said her trembling victim, a mousy little blond wearing crooked glasses in a wrinkled uniform that looked secondhand. "I don't know what I did, but I'm so sorry."

Kelsie offered the crying girl a cat's predatory smile and said, "I didn't give you permission to speak, you silly little thing. That means you just interrupted me!"

"Know your place, commoner!" said Grisla, the daughter of one of Kelsie's family retainers, who angrily pulled back the other girl's hair and made her cry out in pain. "Never interrupt Lady Kelsie!"

"I'm sorry!" the girl sobbed once more. Such delightful music.

Morning classes had just finished, and it was now time for an afternoon break, where the students could either rest, study, or have lunch in the academy's massive cafeteria. Kelsie and her friends chose to use this time to teach the new student her place, grabbing her from behind as she walked down a corridor and pulling her into an empty classroom.

"It's good that you're willing to apologize," Kelsie said to the other girl in a gentle voice. "I like that you're quick to realize your faults. But there's one problem I have with it. You don't seem to know what you're apologizing for, do you?"

"Tell me! Please tell me, please tell me, please tell me!" the blond girl wept.

Kelsie sighed in dismay at the foolishness of this useless commoner. She really didn't seem to understand anything. "First, tell me what your name is, girl."

"E-Everly! Everly Skolder," cried the deeply distressed Everly Skolder, who in fact was not distressed in the slightest and was greatly enjoying herself at this moment.

"Everly Skolder," Kelsie said with sour-faced derision. "Oh, that's disgusting. You're so lowly that your family won't even let you use their name? That's even worse than being the child of a concubine! You're just an untitled little bit of runoff who skated into these great halls based entirely on who your father is. Don't you feel any shame?"

Rather than answer, the girl continued to sob, angering Kelsie further. Why was she behaving like this? Where was her dignity? Kelsie was merely chastising this worm for her odious behavior. Why was she acting like such a little victim? The idea of someone like this attending the hallowed institution that had educated Kelsie's family for generations was unthinkable!

"Shut up!" Kelsie said, before slapping the mewling weakling across her face. The satisfying feeling of violent contact with Everly's cheek soothed her temper a little. So she did it again, and then again.

Fear made Everly quiet down. Kelsie nodded to herself, pleased that she'd silenced the little worm. Now she stepped in closer and firmly gripped Everly by her chin, forcing her to meet her gaze. To her delight, Everly's eyes were now filled with terror. Kelsie liked that. She liked it a lot. Terror was respect. Respect that she deserved.

That was the power of violence. It truly uplifted those who deserved to stand at the top of society's hierarchy.

"You need to know your place, Everly," Kelsie continued in a voice filled with mock concern. "You might be descended from one of us, but you're not really one of us, you see. You don't understand the rules. Like when you approached Prince Ian earlier. Don't you realize he's royalty? How dare you speak so casually to him!"

"He dropped a book! I was only handing it to him," Everly sobbed.

"That doesn't excuse you speaking to him with your commoner's mouth!" Kelsie said fiercely.

"He thanked me! I only told him he was welcome!"

"Stop talking back to me, whore! God, you just don't get it, do you?!" Kelsie shrieked in anger.

This time, she slapped Everly with enough force to draw blood.

"You must never approach His Highness again! You must apologize for your presumptiveness! You need to *beg* me for forgiveness! If you fail to do these things, I promise you your school life will be hell! I promise you, Everly Skolder!"

With that said, Kelsie slapped Everly one last time and had the other girls push her to the floor. Then she deliberately stepped on Everly's back as she and her friends exited the room, leaving the sobbing girl to lie there alone to weep.

Moments later she winked out of existence.

The entire encounter had never occurred. It had been an illusion. One that had been placed inside Kelsie's mind as well as those of her friends. The real (N) Everly had sat nearby unharmed while watching the entire event as though it were an engrossing television drama.

"God, that was hot, wasn't it?" Everly purred to Carter as she sat atop a desk. "I was picking up a real caged heat vibe, you know? Girls in prison? Woo, I wanted to see how far she'd go to put me in my place. Thanks, by the way, Eris."

I'm always happy to serve, said the elemental.

"Everly, I fail to understand the purpose of letting them believe they were harming you," Carter said in befuddlement. Although Everly's duplicates had their own individual names, when operating outside the tower, the servants had been instructed to simply refer to each one as Everly, unless directed otherwise.

"Let me punish them for their temerity on your behalf. Those who believe they can lay hands on you must suffer for their ignorance," Carter continued.

"Easy, Carter. Easy." Everly smiled. "I was just having some fun. I'm embracing my role as an honest and pure girl who would never even dream of upsetting her social betters. The pleasure of putting on a good performance exceeds any anger I feel toward being mistreated."

"Are you certain you weren't just using those fools to enact some manner of masochistic fantasy?" Carter asked her.

"Oh, no, I was definitely doing that as well. Wow, that was intense! You know, all of that came from Kelsie's instincts too. Did you see how roughly she was pulling my hair and dishing out those slaps? God, I might have a new crush. Hey, do you think next time she'll start choking me?"

Everly blushed happily at the idea. Carter stared at her for a long moment before carefully choosing his words.

"Great one, why are you letting those vipers believe that they're assailing you? I ask again, what purpose does it serve?"

"It's bait, silly," Everly said as she hopped off the desk. "Ser Ian, Prince Ian, whatever-his-title-is Ian, is supposed to have heroic inclinations, right? He stands up for the little guy. So how do you think he'll react when he learns that the pretty little girl whom he chats with about birds is being bullied by those sexy little monsters?"

"Ah. I imagine a man who possesses such principles won't stand for such behavior," said Carter, catching on.

"Exactly," Everly said to him. "He'll come to my rescue when he learns what's happening because boys love doing stuff like that. I think. It's something that happens a lot in light novels, anyway. A girl gets bullied and mistreated and then the boy swoops in to save the day."

"Don't you hate those sorts of stories?" Carter asked her.

"I do. I really, really do. But now is not the time to question our tactics. Not when we have such a splendid opportunity to find out if Prince Ian has what it takes to be the hero I seek."

"Everly?"

"Yes, Carter?"

"Why not just read his mind and find out?"

"Carter. We've spoken before about my dislike of spoilers. Half the fun in knowing is not knowing with certainty. I really want to learn for myself if he's got what it takes."

"What if he doesn't?" Carter asked her.

"Well, no skin off my teeth, then," Everly shrugged. "We'll just move on. I might raze the capital into dust to alleviate my disappointment, but other than that, no harm, no foul, right?"

CHAPTER EIGHTEEN

The Message

Deep into Winstead's midcountry, the cry of a dawn rooster signaled the beginning of another busy day on the farm.

Olivia crawled wearily out of bed to do the morning milking for the cows. It wasn't her favorite chore, but it was a necessary task for the small farm her family owned. Their two cows weren't always the most pleasant company. Nancy, the older of the pair, could be very fussy at times. Although she did it rarely, she had attempted to kick her handlers in the past.

That was the reason why Olivia was most often the one sent to care for them. Her soothing manner and gentle-sounding voice had a way of helping the animals retain their calm. That was a trick that her little brother hadn't yet acquired. But he would soon enough, once he had a little more experience under his belt.

As soon as she entered the barn, Olivia sensed that something wasn't right. It was too quiet. A heavy silence pervaded the air around her. Why weren't the animals making any sounds? That was far too unnatural. Sometimes, getting them to quiet down could be damn near impossible.

What was different about today?

As Olivia came closer to the first stall, she smelled the cloying scent of blood and realized that something horrible had happened. Then she found Nancy lying on her side. The cow was dead, and her side had been ripped open by something that had left deep furrows carved into the poor beast's flesh.

In the next stall over, Olivia saw that a similar fate had befallen Snapper, their second cow. But whatever it was that had killed her hadn't settled for merely clawing into her.

Snapper's head was missing. Something had pulled it right off, leaving tendrils of skin and the other connecting bodily tissue splayed out in the straw.

Olivia wanted to scream in horror. But instead, she quickly grabbed a pitchfork to arm herself. Whoever or whatever had done this could still be here. Plotting to deliver her a *similar* fate.

That was when she heard something rustling through the straw.

"Hello? Is someone there?" Olivia asked nervously.

The noise continued again, though she still didn't see anyone. She sensed that the noise was moving in a clockwise motion, as though something her eyes couldn't perceive was playfully circling her, waiting to strike when she'd least expect it.

Olivia felt her heart begin to batter against the inside of her chest, as fear mixed with adrenaline began to overwhelm her. Although she couldn't see this invisible presence, she realized instinctively that it was the one responsible for the horrors done in this barn, and that if she couldn't escape, a similar fate would befall her.

So, when she next heard the noise, this time much closer to her than it had been, with no hesitation, she thrust with her pitchfork and felt its slightly rusting tips embed itself into something solid that yelped in pain and fury. Instead of letting her weapon go so she could run away, Olivia leaned into it, using her weight and the pain she was causing the creature to force it back toward the barn opening.

"DAD!" she cried out. "DAD! HELP! PLEASE HELP ME!"

Olivia was a proud farmer's daughter with a well-developed set of lungs, and a voice made loud and clear from years of calling their animals in from the field. She had no doubt her words would reach the main house and summon assistance. Her father had served for years in the armies of the king before earning his retirement and was skilled with the sword he would surely bring with him when he came running to dispatch whatever it was that threatened her.

The only question was, would she last long enough for him to arrive?

She had her answer a moment later. Whatever it was that she'd stuck her pitchfork into had set its legs and begun to push against her, ignoring the wounds she'd given it. Now the wooden shaft began to bend and splinter until finally, with a loud cracking sound, it split in half.

"No!" Olivia said fearfully as a pair of red eyes flashed at her in the dark. Then she cried out in pain as something moved across her vision, faster than she could track, slicing into her face and drawing blood.

She fell to the ground, her face stinging where her skin had been split open by the invisible claws that had raked her. She wept where she lay, knowing that her end had come, not understanding why this was happening to her.

Above her, the shadowy monster prepared to strike the killing blow.

And that was when *he* appeared.

"Hey, ugly. Step away from the pretty lady, or I'm going to mess you up," said a cocky, confident voice.

The shadowy creature turned around, surprised to realize that a mere human had managed to approach it undetected. The stranger who had threatened it was a young male human who bore an unusual scent. He was a thin, handsome youth dressed in traveling clothes and a white coat with silver etchings stitched into its embroidery.

Over his shoulder, he carelessly held a silver-bladed spear attached to a long black shaft. Although his mannerisms seemed careless, the creature sensed that this boy was dangerous.

In response to his challenge, the monster let out a long hiss and began quietly moving to the side. It was certain that no human would be able to pierce its magical cloak. Rather than play with him as it had with the girl, it would dispatch him immediately.

As it silently drew nearer to its prey, the boy remained where he stood. The creature grinned, anticipating his scream of horror and surprise after its talons opened his belly and reduced him to a blubbering wreck. Just as it was about to strike, the boy's eyes turned squarely in its direction as he smiled and said, "Hey, stupid. I can *see* you."

Before the creature could respond, the silver spear was thrust directly into its throat and then pulled out after a nasty twist. Then it collapsed to its knees, wheezing desperately for air, before falling into unconsciousness and bleeding out.

"This might have been a barn, but *you* were the real animal here, chum," the boy said solemnly.

This heroic stranger's name was Lance Beverly. He was a guy, and he could totally prove it. You only had to check out his mussy hair and his way of taking up as much space as possible in a public setting. He also possessed external genitals as men were known to do. Not that he'd ever show them to you unless you were a very lucky person or a registered medical professional.

The previous paragraph was a complete lie. Lance wasn't a guy at all. He was a young woman, whose name was Beverly, the first of Everly's three duplicates, who'd been given the assignment of becoming the greatest adventurer in the world.

Because her three other selves would also be running loose throughout the nation in service to their brilliant plan of conquest, Beverly decided that the easiest way to gain fame for herself without drawing any comparison to her siblings would be to create a separate body for her mind to inhabit while her real one rested inside the memory palace. Thus, "Lance" was born.

That was the plan of action she'd decided on. And it was a brilliant plan, indeed! For the easiest way not to be readily compared to a girl was to be a *dude*.

And Lance Beverly *was* that dude! A dude who was secretly Beverly! And Beverly was a genius!

The logic was obvious to anyone who understood how these things worked.

"Hey, Miss. Are you all right?" he asked the monster's victim, after first making certain it was dead by plunging his spear into its heart. "You're okay now, babe. Because I'm here. My name is Lance. I'm not sure if you heard that correctly because you keep screaming in pain. I said it was Lance. I'm here to help."

The girl continued rolling from side to side, shrieking her head off, which didn't sound at all like a *thank you*, which Lance found irritating. Then he noticed that she seemed to be bleeding heavily from her face and realized that she'd been wounded or something, which explained the momentary lack of gratitude.

"Ahhh, I see what's going on here." He nodded. Then he closed his eyes, drew upon Discordia's powers of restoration, and used them to heal the girl's wounds. "That better?" he asked her.

The girl sat up, awed by what he'd done. The light that exuded from his hand had soothed the pain immediately, replacing it with a gentle feeling of serene bliss as the skin and muscle tissue on her face was gently pulled back together. When the light faded, not even a scar remained from the beast's attack.

"Hero, thank you. Thank you so much!" Olivia said gratefully before wrapping her arms around her savior and nearly crushing him to death with a hug of joy.

"Hey, think nothing of it," Lance said to her with a nonchalant nod while wondering if a nonchalant nod could be considered *nod-chalant*. "Even if you were ugly, I'd still give you the same treatment. Why? Because you're like a capable person or some shit, and I'm totally a guy who isn't preoccupied with appearances."

"Well, thank you again all the same," Olivia said. "I don't know how I can ever repay your gallantry."

"I don't seek repayment," her rescuer said with a gentle smile. "Your safety is all that I sought. I mean, if you wanted to give me some money, I wouldn't say no, but I wouldn't have rescued you just to be paid either. Because I'm not like that. Right?"

"I . . . think so?" Olivia said uncertainly.

"Awesome," replied Lance Beverly. Who was totally a guy. But secretly wasn't. And was totally a hero but was secretly the greatest villain in the world. Or one-fourth of the greatest villain in the world, anyway.

He wasn't sure if it was actually one-fourth. But it didn't bother him.

Lance Beverly didn't do math.

Lance Beverly did *adventure*.

And this is where his legend began.

CHAPTER NINETEEN

Underworld

Prince Ian was perhaps the dullest person that Neverly had ever met in her life, and that was really saying something.

After all, she'd grown up alongside Samuel Bellweather, a young man so lacking in personality that for years she refused to mentally capitalize his first name. Lowercase lettering better suited a nonentity like him. She only promoted him to his name's correct spelling after accidentally deliberately setting him up to be murdered by a cranky old demon.

Imagine Neverly's surprise to now discover that Samuel had a spiritual doppelganger who was royalty. It was shocking. Shocking! She was genuinely shocked.

"All righty, how do we feel about setting the capital ablaze and siccing the undead on the survivors?" she casually asked Carter one day while loafing about on the school grounds beneath the shade of a large oak tree.

"Would your sisters approve of that decision?" Carter asked after giving her words careful consideration.

"No, probably not, but they're out there in the world doing the *fun* stuff," Neverly whined. "They get to do all the meaningful work! In the meanwhile, I'm stuck here babysitting all these worthless nepo babies!"

"It's an important task, oh great one. Your presence here is a crucial requirement for the plan," Carter said placatingly.

"Carter, these people are *so* boring!" Neverly complained. "I don't know why I thought magic school would be more interesting than regular school. It's just the same collection of sad clichés with fantasy elements added. None of these little shits stir my heart in the slightest."

"What about Lady Kelsie? Do you no longer derive twisted enjoyment from her sadistic bullying?" asked Carter.

"Ugh," Neverly said. "She's the most disappointing one of all. She can't think of anything past all her rote schoolgirl roughhousing. The hair pulling and slapping has been fun, but she won't take it up a notch!"

"How so?" asked Carter.

"Pfft," Neverly sneered. "No cutting me with a small blade, no burning me with matches, no forcing me to kiss her and then calling me a homophobic slur to deny her enjoyment of it, no making me spend the night in her room and forcing me to sleep on the floor like a dog. The bitch is *basic*, and I'm over it."

"Neverly . . . are you all right?" Carter asked her after several quiet moments had passed.

"Of course I am," Neverly replied. "What makes you ask?"

"Are you . . . certain? I sometimes find your words concerning."

"Don't be a prude, Carter," Neverly said scornfully. "I have a perfectly normal and healthy urge to explore the things that interest me. There's nothing abnormal about that."

"*Nothing* abnormal about that?" Carter asked incredulously. "Great one, are you being serious right now? I can never tell when you're being sarcastic."

"Maybe I'll just build some sort of formless slime monster to immerse myself in," Neverly mused. "Something that can lightly burn me with digestive acid while simultaneously hitting all the right notes *hard*. Something that'll really blur that pain/pleasure threshold and provoke all kinds of crazy physiological responses."

"Neverly, please don't say things like that!" Carter said in horror.

"Why not?" Neverly replied. "Anyone with a basic knowledge of Japanese anime can tell you that a woman could do a lot worse for a partner than a tentacled slime monster. If anything, I'm really missing out on an experience."

"You are royalty, Neverly!" Carter said. "Have any humanoid consort that you wish, but please don't create *pleasure slimes*! That sounds utterly horrific!"

"Pleasure slimes?" Neverly said thoughtfully. "Huh. Carter, has anyone ever told you that you have a real knack for branding? *Pleasure slimes*. Slimes for her *pleeeeeasure*. Made by women *for* women. Comes in a variety of different colors so you will too!"

"That is an awful joke."

"Hey, who's joking? We might be onto something here!" Neverly said brightly. "It's not like this world has an Adam & Eve catalog in circulation. Not only could we *create* the market for adult novelties, but we could also completely corner it!"

"Neverly, you're going to take over the planet!" Carter insisted. "Surely you have greater concerns than indulging in these sorts of lurid thoughts!"

"OKAAAAAY, Carter, okay! You win!" Neverly said with an exaggerated sigh. "We won't start mass production of the pleasure slimes until after I help grind civilization beneath my heel."

"I'm glad you can see reason when it suits you, great one," Carter said in an unctuous manner.

"Yep, I'm reasonableness incarnate," Neverly said with a nod. "So, let's get back to making plans about how we're going to kill everyone in the capital."

"You weren't joking about that?" asked Carter.

"Nope!" Neverly confirmed. "I'm bored. I hate being bored. My original self came to this planet so that I'd never be bored again, and yet *here I am*. I have to take that frustration out on somebody, little man. It may as well be all the background nobodies."

"But what about your code? What about your principled stance against indulging in random slaughter?" asked Carter.

In response, Neverly erupted into laughter, so amused was she by her servant's words.

"Ahhh, Carter. I love you, man," she said once she'd settled down. After wiping a tear from her eye, she continued. "Listen, you're a good guy, Carter. I really like having you around. In a way, I enjoy you more than Grail because you don't have nearly as much baggage as that angsty old geezer. But I must tell you, for your own sake, don't put any hopes on me listening to my better angels."

"What do you mean?" asked Carter.

"Everly is full of crap," Neverly smirked. "She's chock-full of it as a matter of fact. Her little code of conduct isn't really a part of the game. It's just flavor text. Fake nuance to make her seem deeper than she really is. There's no meaning there, bud."

"Then why does she abide by it?" Carter asked her.

"Commitment to the role," Neverly said with a dismissive wave of her hand. "We love getting into character! Role-playing is fun. But at the end of the day, it isn't an ironclad law. We're not beholden to anything, not even ourselves. We'll do whatever we want whenever we wish."

"That's not what she promised us," Carter said quietly.

"No, it isn't," Neverly agreed. "But honestly, what are *you* going to do about it?"

She and Carter then silently matched gazes for several long moments before Carter shuddered and looked away.

"I will . . . stay quiet and obey," he said.

"Of course you will." Neverly smiled as she reached forth a hand to lightly scratch one of Carter's long ears. Despite the undercurrent of fear flowing throughout him, Carter couldn't help but sigh in pleasure at his master's touch.

"As your chief advisor, I feel I must warn you that Lord Grail will be less understanding once he truly comprehends Everly's nature," Carter said. "He believes in her. He believes she truly wants to save this world."

Neverly frowned at Carter's words. Grail. Grail, Grail, *Grail.* What did Everly see in him anyway? What about him fascinated her so much? He objected to everything fun she wanted to do, talked back as though they were equals, and argued for peaceful solutions all the damn time.

At first, she thought she'd wanted to corrupt him. To slowly break his will and strip him of his idealism and claim him as a trophy of sorts. He'd be unwitting proof of her skill at manipulating others.

The problem, perhaps, was that he'd devoted himself so completely to her and with such earnestness that she'd grown fond of him. She'd always demanded that others love her unconditionally. And in his own way, it appeared that Grail was doing exactly that. Why did that please her so much while simultaneously making her angry?

Everly can't see it, she thought to herself. *She's too close to him. Still too human. Beverly, Cleverly, and I, we're different. We were never human to begin with, so we possess the objectivity that Everly lacks. She's soft on Grail because he loves her. Which means WE love him in our own way. But we also hate him because love makes you weak.*

Neverly wondered what that would mean for later. *She's studied with him for centuries of hypertime. Honestly, those two are as close as anyone could possibly be. He's an obvious vulnerability, but unlike poor little Fenneth, she's much too close to him to even consider having him removed. She can't see things clearly.*

Still, awareness of this complication does me little good. If I bring it up, she'll punish me for it. Why? Because I'm an unhinged, reactionary little brat, so that means she is as well. I'm clearly the aspect of Everly that favors logic and planning, but even I'm not above shooting the messenger. Since that's the case, I'll just keep quiet and play ignorant. Who needs the hassle?

In the meanwhile, I'm still booooored . . .

As Neverly wandered back to the main building, after reluctantly deciding to attend her afternoon lessons, the intriguing sound of violence reached her ears. She heard what sounded like a boy being viciously beaten by a small group of stronger boys.

"Oh, no!" she said dramatically to herself. "Could someone possibly be in trouble with a capital T?"

She hoped so. She really did.

Curious to see the show, Everly followed the sounds of the one-sided beating to an area at the side of the school where three students wearing the academy's uniform were merrily stomping away on a fourth who was likewise dressed. His face and clothing were now spattered with blood, and his nose and eye were swollen.

Neverly had to give his attackers credit, they were doing a very thorough job of kicking their victim's ass. One didn't often see that sort of ruthless disregard for another person's life in people that young. It must have been something that came with being a noble. Which made sense. Power and privilege had a way of exaggerating your worst tendencies as a human being.

"All right, fellows, all right," said the one standing in the middle. A handsome, smug-looking young man with golden hair and flawless white teeth. Everly had to admit she was intrigued by the sight of him. He had a domineering manner about him, an effortless arrogance, and sense of untouchability that really suited her tastes. Maybe she should introduce herself to him? There was a possibility they could get into some real hijinks . . .

"Are you certain, Lord Aiden?" asked one of his friends as he kneeled to pull up their victim's head by his hair. "This little gutter rat dared to *threaten* you. I doubt anyone'll care if we smash his stupid skull to bits."

Aiden? Did he just say that the pretty one's name was *Aiden*? Nope, not happening, cancel the subscription, abort-abort-abort! Everly shook her head in revulsion. There were no cool Aidens in this world. Bearing that name was the equivalent of a facial tattoo on your soul.

"It's all right, lads. It's all right," Aiden said warmly. "I think our friend here has learned his lesson. Haven't you, Tyler?"

He leaned closer to the prone boy and held a hand beside his ear. "Hmm? What's that?" he continued. "I can't quite hear you. I asked you if you learned your lesson?"

"You have to pay your tab," the bloodied boy managed to rasp. "The . . . the Hobbs want their money."

"And as I said earlier, I'll *pay* them when I have a free moment." Aiden smiled. "But I won't be manhandled into doing it. Especially not by some lowborn commoner blowback like you. Did you really believe you could make your little threats to me and get away with it? Are you that bereft of sense, you silly fool?"

"The Hobbs *will* get what they're owed," the boy warned them.

"How?" Aiden asked with a snort of derision. "I'm over here, and they're over there in their shanty little slum. And even if they could directly approach me by somehow getting past the academy's *harada*-infused guards, I'd simply incinerate them with a blast of magic. Your trashy little gang can't touch me, Tyler. And as you've now thoroughly learned, *you* can't touch me either. So . . . I guess what I'm getting at is, go fuck yourself?"

Aiden's friends began chortling with laughter as though he'd said the funniest thing imaginable as the three of them walked away, leaving the humiliated Tyler behind.

Ahhh, so that was what had been going on. Tyler was a fellow lowborn attendant of the academy. His mother had probably been a concubine, like Everly's had been. But unlike Everly, who'd been permitted to receive her father's last name before she changed it to her mother's, Tyler was a *blowback*. Which was an extremely insulting term for an unwanted bastard whose noble father was being forced to pay for his education due to kingdom law.

This Tyler kid would have probably gone completely unacknowledged if he hadn't had some kind of talent for magic that proved his parentage. So that meant that he was both an embarrassment *and* a burden to his family.

Everly thought that sounded ridiculously funny.

Apparently, Tyler also considered himself to be some manner of gangbanger. He probably thought growing up on the streets made him more dangerous than his peers, which was absolutely delusional! Getting into street fights and indulging in petty crime didn't quite match being trained how to fight by an elite personal guard. Aiden had undoubtedly been learning the art of combat since he was old enough to hold a sword.

Add a year or two of training in magic at the academy and with private tutors and he was more than a match for poor Tyler. The kid must have been an idiot for thinking he could strong-arm him in the name of whatever gang had made the request.

That's so sad, Neverly thought. *And you know what? Whoever these Hobbs are, they must be extremely bottom tier if they not only got swindled by some noble brat, but they also had to rely on a sap like this chump to get their money back. What a bunch of losers.*

Man, if I were running things, this would have gone so much more smoothly . . .

Neverly paused as if a bolt of divine inspiration had struck her from on high.

Why not run things? Crime was one of those things that people liked doing. And if they liked doing it so much . . . why not do it for *her*? The underworld was part of the world, after all, so, logically speaking, that meant she had a right to step in and take over whenever she felt like it.

So, with that being the case, why not become the ultimate crime lord? She'd unify the underworld under her singular rule.

She'd totally Wilson Fish that shit!

Wait, no, no. Wilson *Fisk*. That was the character's name. Duh.

At the very least, this sounded like an amusing little side project that would keep her from going out of her mind from boredom.

It could be fun. It could be *real* fun.

With her decision now made, Neverly walked to the nearly unconscious Tyler and began slapping the back of his head. He groaned in pain and barely stirred, which Neverly found annoying.

"Hey," she said insistently. "Hey! Wake up, dummy. I've got a proposition for you. This is the luckiest day of your life, bud!"

Instead of responding joyfully, Tyler said something incomprehensible and passed out.

"Huh," Neverly said. "Not the most enthusiastic reception ever, but screw it, I'll find a way to make it work. You and me, kid! Straight to the top!"

All the way up.

CHAPTER TWENTY

Kraken

O w," Tyler moaned pitifully after crawling his way back into a semiconscious state. He sat up with a start, then winced after the sudden motion caused his skull to throb with an intense, lingering pain that was unlike any he'd ever experienced before.

It hurt so much . . .

Over the course of his short life, Tyler had heard stories of men being struck so hard in the head that they were marred with pain for the rest of their lives. Had that been what had happened to him? This headache hurt so much! It filled him with a raw and terrible throbbing that matched his heartbeat and seemed to grow incrementally worse with every breath he took.

It was as though a piece of hell itself had been liquefied and poured into his ear.

Just what had happened to him?

After a few minutes spent quietly rubbing his temples, gradually acclimatizing himself to the pain, Tyler's memories began to return to him. Friendly Jim, the leader of the Royal Bay Hobbs, had approached Tyler earlier in the week with a smile and an offer of work.

He wanted Tyler to collect a past due payment from an arrogant young customer named Aiden Vae Theron. Apparently, Aiden was the second son of some important noble household from out west, who'd developed a taste for glee powder but was behind on settling his debt.

"It'll be an easy bit of collection, my boy. Nothing to it at all," Friendly Jim had assured Tyler. "This pampered little rich boy won't be anything compared to *you*. You've done some *real* hard living, haven't you? You're a man of the streets, just like myself, yeah? Just shake him up a little, convince him to make a payment. Can't have him forgetting his debts to the Hobbs, now, can we? You do this for me, and I'll owe you a favor, my friend."

The idea of a big shot like Friendly Jim owing Tyler a favor was far too tempting for him to refuse. So, he agreed very quickly and set off to collect what was owed, certain that he'd have no troubling fulfilling Jim's request.

Things hadn't gone according to plan.

Instead of getting the money, what Tyler had received in its place was a merciless beating at the hands of Aiden and two of his family's vassals. Friendly Jim had been completely mistaken in his assessment of what that snot had been capable of, and Tyler had paid for that error with pain and blood.

Still, where was he? When the haze left his vision and his senses finally returned to him, Tyler realized that he still didn't know where he was. Wait, wasn't this a dance hall? He thought he recognized it.

Wasn't this the Crystal Cave, a popular social hub for people his age, where the differing social classes came to dance and play and partake in other pleasures away from the sight of those in authority?

Something had happened here. Something *terrible*.

But what?

His first clue came when he tried to stand up and slipped on a puddle of something that made the floor dangerously slick. When he brought his hand before his eyes, he saw that his palm had been stained red.

"Wh-what the hell?" he whimpered.

Death surrounded him. It enveloped him. He breathed it in. He *tasted* it. There was blood everywhere. Among the bodies were strangers he didn't recognize and quite a few that he did: regulars at the club, acquaintances, a few friends, and a few enemies as well. They were all gone now. They'd all been torn into pieces and now existed as ragged chunks of flesh and fluid that covered the entire hall.

It was impossible to determine exactly how many bodies there were surrounding him.

It was a maddening sight. An instant invitation to close his eyes and wait until he awoke from this nightmare, far from this place of horror, safe in his bed. When he eventually realized that he wasn't dreaming and that he'd have to make his way home past all these ravaged corpses, a kind of mania possessed him, an urge for a traditional form of salvation with which to protect himself.

"Oh . . . oh, by the gods, may my wayward soul be redeemed! I repent, oh radiant one, for all my sins. Please forgive me!" Tyler prayed hysterically as he heard footsteps slowly approaching him.

Whoever it was . . . whatever it was that had done this, it was coming to finish the job. Anything that could slaughter so many people by itself would be beyond Tyler's power to resist. He instinctively knew that he stood no chance of escape, so instead of making a meaningless attempt to flee or resist, he turned to the teachings of the temple that he thought he'd abandoned years ago.

If ever there was a moment to seek the protection of the gods, then this was now it!

"Please *saaaave* me!" Tyler cried out as he felt the terrifying presence getting closer and closer.

"Hey, you wanna get some breakfast?" Everly asked him after politely waiting for him to finish. Tyler turned to see a girl who appeared slightly younger than he was standing behind him. She was dressed in the uniform worn by female students of the Royal Academy.

She was covered in even more blood than he was.

Soaked in it. Like she'd gone swimming in it.

"What?" Tyler asked in confusion. "Do I what?"

"Breakfast. Food. Morning yummies. I'm *starving*," Everly said to him impatiently. "Man, I feel like I just killed a bunch of people who pissed me off and the only thing I got out of it was a healthy appetite."

"You're . . . you're *hungry* right now?" Tyler asked her incredulously.

"Aren't you?" Everly replied. "Man, with all that panicking and begging for safety you did last night, I bet you burned off like a million calories through screaming alone. It's so *easy* for boys. I'm jealous."

"You, you're Everly, aren't you? Everly Skolder?" Tyler asked the girl after finally recognizing her.

They were in the same class, but she was a silent, miserable thing. Like Tyler, she was illegitimate, but unlike him, she had no friends, no connections, no one to help her. A particularly nasty upperclassman of theirs named Kelsie had turned her into a chew toy. People were taking bets that she'd either drop out herself or be forced to leave due to injuries.

Tyler had thought she was pathetic. Just another pretty mouse lost in the jungle that was life at the academy.

He'd apparently been mistaken in his assessment of her.

"Dude, *yes*," Everly said with a roll of her eyes. "How are you still having trouble with my name? You and I have been hanging out since yesterday," Everly said as she reached down to pull him to his feet. Tyler was startled by the strength of her grip and how easily she got him to stand. As though he could offer her no greater resistance than that of a small kitten.

He couldn't.

"We have?" Tyler asked her.

"Yeah, remember? You'd just gotten stomped by those meanie upperclassmen, and you were bleeding all over that dirty alleyway," Everly said as she hopped onto a table and regarded him wryly.

"You saw that fight?" Tyler asked her with no small amount of embarrassment.

"Uh, I wouldn't exactly call what I saw a *fight*," Everly answered with direct, brutal honesty. "More like a one-sided massacre. Dude, I could practically feel your pride evaporating with each hit you took! I mean, I don't like using gendered language to describe stuff like this, but *brooo*, you looked like such a bitch! I kept hoping you were conserving your energy for a surprise counterattack or something, but nope! You were exactly as bad as you looked! The bitch vibes rang true! Your ass got *juuuuuumped*."

"It was an unfair fight!" Tyler said angrily. "If they had the guts to face me one at a time, things would have gone differently!"

"Tyler, if a fight was unfair, that just means the winner was a better strategist than the loser," Everly said frankly. "Picking a fight with a duke's son was about the dumbest thing someone like you could possibly do. But at least it let me know how stupid you are, so now I can tailor my expectations for your behavior accordingly."

"Skolder, what happened here?" Tyler asked her.

"What happened here? Jeez, your pretty little head is even emptier than I realized," Everly said with a giggle. "Well, Tyler, what *happened* was that I felt sorry for you, so I got you on your feet. Then I asked you for your story and you told me all your dreams and ambitions and I thought you were kind of cute, despite being such an idiot, so I decided that you and I should go on an *adventure!*"

"What kind of an adventure?" Tyler asked dimly.

"An adventure of discovery!" Everly replied. "I took you to my room, you put your hand on my ass, I reattached it an hour later once I was satisfied with your groveling for forgiveness, then we made out for a while, then afterward we came here so you could collect your money and get some payback on the guys who humiliated you."

"You . . . ripped my arm off?" Tyler asked her.

"You were being handsy without permission," Everly said mildly. She then hopped off the table and gave him a warm kiss on the lips. "But why dwell on any pointless incidental details? The only thing that matters is that you won! You got the payment from what's-his-face—"

"Aiden," Tyler said, still surprised by her unexpected kiss.

"*Terrible* fucking name," Everly muttered under her breath before saying, "You got the payment from Aiden, and you decisively silenced any potential witnesses from snitching on you with their little tattletale faces and pointless screams for help, and now you're going to go turn in your quest! Congratulations, Tyler, you're now the scariest thing on the streets! This is how reputations are forged! Everyone's going to think you're a bloodthirsty psychopath!" she finished cheerily.

"Where *is* Aiden?" Tyler asked fearfully. "Where did he go?"

"Do you believe in enlightenment?" Everly asked him. "The monks would say he's in all things now. Well, I guess it would be more accurate to say he's *on* all things now. They can probably get him off with a lot of vinegar and some vigorous mopping."

"You killed him too?" Tyler squeaked.

"Me? I didn't kill anybody!" Everly smirked. "I'm just a girl. Don't blame me for your crazy misbehavior, you bad thing. Stop being crazy, crazy!"

"Everly, please, by the gods. They'll lock me away. Then they'll hang me. I don't want to die!" Tyler said, whimpering once more. "Please, you've got to clear this up!"

Everly frowned, disappointed by this display of weakness.

"Jeeez, Tyler," she replied. "I gotta tell you, this sort of wishy-washy, delta male behavior makes it difficult for me to respect you. Didn't I already say that you've won? Today, you not only earned a badass new rep, but you also have *me* on your side!"

To emphasize her point, Everly gave him another, longer kiss. "I like you, Tyler. I mean, you're a weak piece of self-important trash with brittle pasta in place of a spine, but that's okay. You've got a nice face, and you're smart enough to know what'll happen if you ever dare to cross me. There are successful marriages built on less stable foundations than that."

"You want to marry me?" Tyler asked her in astonishment.

In response, Everly laughed at him.

The tone of it . . . was *hurtful.*

"No, Tyler. No, I don't want to *marry* you," she said with a slight wheeze after she caught her breath. "Heh, no offense, buddy, but, uh, I have *options.* Honestly, I just want to kill some time while I figuratively wait for some water to boil. Your life is a pathetic joke, so I thought I'd play with it for a bit. It's still a win for you, though! I'm going to make you into something *special.* Rejoice! You're going to be my new project!"

"Yeah? Is that right?" Tyler said angrily. "Well, what if I don't *want* to be your project—"

Tyler was lying on the hall floor with his face being forcefully pressed into the open wound of some dead person's torso. He was drowning in guts. He was literally drowning in someone's viscera and blood. The foulness of it was in his nostrils and mouth, gagging him, tormenting him with its noxious taste and stench.

This was how he was going to die—

Suddenly, he was back on his feet, but his toes were dangling on their very tips, barely touching the floor beneath him because Everly had a firm grip on his neck and was staring at him coldly.

"*Tone,*" she said to him with a raised eyebrow.

"What? What?" Tyler asked desperately.

"Watch your tone when you speak to me," Everly repeated. "Tyler, this isn't a partnership, and I don't make requests. I tell you what happens, and then it happens. The end. I'm looking for acquiescence, not agreement. So keep your little *outbursts* to yourself and just do as I say. All right?"

"Yes! Yes! Anything you say," Tyler quickly agreed.

"Good," Everly said with a perky smile. "But remember to always, *always* speak respectfully when you address me. If I ever need to remind you of this, it'll cost you a finger. After that, it'll be an eye. And from there, if you *still* haven't learned, then I'll have to get *creative.*"

Everly leaned forward to whisper into his ear.

"Do you want to see what I can come up with when I'm being creative?" she asked him.

"No," Tyler said with closed eyes. "No, no, I don't. I really don't."

"Aww, *puppy,*" Everly said affectionately as she leaned in close to nuzzle her nose against his. "Don't be sad! I still like you! Just setting the rules is all. You're going straight to the top, Tyler. My boy is going to be the coolest kid in school! Men will envy you, women will desire you, and *everyone* will *fear* you. Even the high nobility won't cross you, not once I'm done crafting you into the man that I want you to be."

"R-really?" Tyler sputtered.

"Hell yeah!" Everly said eagerly. "You're going to own this town, Tyler. OWN IT. But how long you'll *keep it* depends on how well you remember that *I* own *you.* Okay?"

Tyler nodded quickly and said nothing else. Obedience. Nothing less than absolute obedience would preserve his life; he realized this now. Did she want a dog? Okay. That was perfectly fine! If his lady required a dog, then a dog is what she would get!

It was better than the alternative.

This hall of horrors was filled with the alternative.

"I'm so glad you're quick to catch on," Everly said with a squeal of joy. "Now let's go get cleaned up! And then breakfast! Oh, I'll have Carter whip us something up. He's got such clever little hands. Makes French toast like you wouldn't believe!"

"What's a French?" Tyler asked as she led him by his hand to a door that had appeared in the middle of the room.

"Doesn't matter!" Everly replied with a wink. "I'm taking you to my memory palace, by the way. My other selves are going to love you! L-U-V! I guess I don't mind sharing if it's with myself. But hey, you better remember which Everly brought you to the dance, buster!"

The closer they came to the doorway, the more Tyler wondered if he'd died and was being led into hell for his sins.

It was true that he'd been a petty thief. A little tyrant who let his father's position as county sheriff go to his head. He realized now, in this moment, that his aspirations of leading a life of crime were the pretentious fantasies of an ignorant child. He should have done as his mother asked of him. Study hard, do well, and find a lord to serve.

Instead, he'd wasted his opportunities to better himself. He thought that coming to the Royal Academy would make him a shark among the minnows.

But now he found himself in the grip of a Kraken.

How could this possibly get any worse? Tyler asked himself.

Then he stepped through the doorway and found himself standing before a dining room table laden with sumptuously prepared foods that smelled wonderful and looked even better.

At that table were seated three more of Everly. They all looked up at once and stared at him.

"Guess who's got a *boooooyfriend?*" said the one who held his hand.

I am absolutely fucked, Tyler decided on the spot.

Behind them, the door slammed shut.

CHAPTER TWENTY-ONE

Takeover

Friendly Jim was a far less affable fellow than his name would otherwise have you believe. It was a nickname that had been bestowed upon him with more than a little irony by the first of his many victims, just before Jim had finished the poor fellow off with a jagged bit of broken glass and a loathsome smirk as he delivered the finishing blow.

"Well, ain't *you* a friendly one," his victim had managed to mutter through his shattered teeth just before his throat was cut with a rough swipe to the left.

"Yeah, ain't I, though?" Jim had said in response before settling down to listen to the other man's gurgling final breaths.

The old man's death had been a splendid show. It was also the fondest memory he had of his father. Certainly, it'd been the most productive time they'd spent together in years.

He hoped the old bastard was now in hell, burning in eternal anguish while screaming in impotent rage at his murderous son. That would teach him to try making him clean up his room, wouldn't it?

The old fool had meant his last words as an insult, but Jim quite liked the sound of his new name, and so that was what he chose to call himself from that moment on. Friendly Jim, the friendliest Jim you could ever hope to meet. Unless you owed him money, or you had something that he wanted, or *especially* if you had disappointed him but had the gall to show your face in his presence.

On occasions such as those, people learned very quickly that the word *friendly* could take on all kinds of unintended connotations. It really depended on the situation.

It seemed that one of those situations had once again arrived when (N)Everly and Tyler came strutting into his base of operations as though they owned the place. Dressed in expensive-looking clothing and carrying themselves as if they hadn't a care in the world. Two things happened as soon as Jim saw the pair of them in his lair.

The first was that he briefly saw red in such murderous intensity that he worried that he'd burst some sort of vein in his eyes. The second was that he was *deeply* confused about the inclusion of the young girl hanging on Tyler's arm. She was a lovely young thing, wasn't she? Well-fed, with healthy coloring and bright white teeth to complement that dazzling smile of hers.

Was this Tyler's woman? She had to be a fellow student at the academy. No common-born girl that attractive lived around here. Jim would have had her already if that were the case. Well, no matter. She might have merely been a thrill-seeking young fool following her beau around on a whim, but her curiosity had just condemned her to a cruel fate.

She wasn't going to be leaving here any time soon.

Renting out a noble girl with looks like hers will soon have gold spilling out of my pockets, he thought to himself with an ugly sneer. *After I have a taste for myself, of course.*

Normally, Jim wouldn't have dared to lay a finger on a member of the nobility. But the necessity of covering up for Tyler's colossal screwup meant having to make certain adjustments to his standard business practices.

Obliviously, the girl looked at Jim and matched his knowing smile with one of her own. Ah, what a silly little thing she was. A young angel who would soon grow up more quickly than she thought.

The chief hideout of the Royal Bay Hobbs was located inside of a large storage warehouse near the ports of the capital. Here, among the many goods temporarily stored inside it, Jim and his Hobbs conducted their illicit business safely away from the prying eyes of the city watch and any other troublesome individuals that might feel compelled to ask questions that the Hobbs didn't want to answer.

It was an ideal location for a small criminal enterprise. Not too close to the docks where the larger gangs constantly battled to expand their territory and influence, but also not too far from the city where their customers were located. Jim was quite fond of this place.

The soundproofing was excellent as well.

Which was why the sight of Tyler, who was currently wanted for questioning in regard to the deaths of a few dozen dead citizens as well as a handful of young nobles, one of which was the child of a bloody *duke*, put Jim in such a sour mood. Did the fool have no sense? Why would he come *here* of all places and bring his troubles to Jim's door?

"Tyler, my boy!" Jim called out with a cheerfulness that he didn't truly feel. "What brings you by this fine evening? And who's that lovely peach hanging on your arm? Now, now, no need to be shy, girlie. You're among friends here."

Tyler hesitated to speak before the girl standing at his side dug her elbow into his side a bit. "Uh, hey. Hey, Jim. Just dropping by to bring you the payment as requested. Yeah, got it all taken care of, just like you wanted. Every silver and copper piece accounted for. No problem."

"No *problem?*" Jim asked as he rose from his chair, from which he normally conducted business like a monarch on his throne. "No problem, did you say? Oh, Tyler, I just don't know about that, my lad. It seems that all manner of problems have popped up, despite your words."

"Uh," Tyler said uncertainly as he wilted before Jim's furious glare. "Uh, the thing is, Jim, there were . . . uh, extantious—"

"*Extenuating,*" the girl at his side corrected.

"Uh, extenuating circumstances," Tyler said lamely. "You know, like Aiden wasn't being cooperative and, uh, wasn't showing the, you know, proper respect. And then he started trying to fight back, and there were, you know, witnesses. It's—it's taken care of. Everything's sorted. There's nothing you need to worry about."

"Tyler," Jim said with slowly growing menace. "Everyone who was in the club with you that day is *dead.* But plenty of people on their way out saw you enter it and knew that you had problems earlier in the week with little lord Aiden. You're alive, he's *dead.* It ain't hard to piece together what happened there. And now . . . you're in MY HOME, perhaps bringing some undue attention my way . . . It really makes me wonder just how much of a fool you are!"

"Oh, relax, drama queen. Tyler already said it was taken care of," the blond girl said nonchalantly. "No one's going to be looking for him, and all those little witnesses that have got your baby balls shriveling have been given a stern talking-to. Haven't you heard? The culprits of this heinous crime have turned themselves in."

"What is this bitch talking about?" Jim asked in irritation.

"Oh, uh, Jim, no. Don't do that. Don't say that," Tyler said very quickly with widened eyes.

"Why? Are you going to puff your chest out and defend her honor?" Jim said derisively.

"Hey, don't underestimate my man," the girl said as she pressed herself tightly against Tyler. "He's got a killer instinct. Just ask all those losers in the club. My baby steps up when he has to. Don't you, baby?"

"Tyler, who the hell is this?" Jim demanded to know.

"You know, you *are* allowed to direct your questions to me personally," the girl said with a slight frown. "But since you insist on knowing, I'll tell you. I'm his Sid and he's my Nancy."

"Never heard of them," Jim replied flatly.

"It's a romantic legend about a pair of star-crossed lovers that ended perfectly well for everyone involved with no complaints from anyone. It also had a *bitchin'* soundtrack," the girl replied.

"What did you mean by saying the *real* culprits have confessed?" Jim asked her.

"Exactly that," the girl said as she stepped away from Tyler and began circling Jim. "Before coming here, we paid a visit to . . . Uh, what were they called again, Ty?"

"The Bronze Badger Boys," Tyler said reluctantly.

"Yeah, those schmucks," the girl smirked. "We stopped by their place, which, by the way, was a lot bigger and more impressive than this cruddy little ware-house, and we had a conversation with their upper management. It was produc-tive. Wasn't it productive, baby?"

"Y-yeah," Tyler said. "It was . . . it was really productive."

"You expect me to believe that the Bronze Badger Boys let you two stroll into their territory and talk to their top men?" Jim said with disbelief.

"Yep!" Everly said brightly. "And not only that, but they agreed to take the fall for us. They were such sweet boys! Eager to please and willing to listen. I can totally see how they became the biggest organization on these docks."

"Stop spitting nonsense!" Jim yelled.

"It's not nonsense, it's the truth," Everly said. "It serves the narrative perfectly. The Badgers are the most dangerous crew in the capital. *Everyone* knows that. It makes sense that a pack of vicious criminals like them would be tied to the death of a duke's son. I mean, who would believe it if someone said that a second-rate collection of wharf-rat nobodies like the *Hobbs* were involved? Excuse my say-ing so, Jimmy, my lad, but you exist purely on the shit-tier. Someone like *you* is barely qualified enough to sell a pack of smokes to a schoolboy."

"What did you just say to me?" Jim said quietly.

"You already heard, nimrod," the girl said impatiently. "But don't feel dis-heartened by my completely accurate assessment of your innate worthlessness. Just because all of you are trash doesn't mean you're not recyclable. The fact that the Hobbs *are* such utter nonentities means you'll make the perfect disguise for someone with *real* ambition. Congratulations! You're being recruited!"

"Tyler," Jim said ominously. "If you don't shut this bitch up right now, I'm going to—"

"JIM, I TOLD YOU NOT TO CALL HER THAT," Tyler said in horror, his face twitching with barely suppressed fear as adrenalized tears began to leak from the corner of his eyes.

Jim stared at the boy in confusion, bewildered by the naked terror that he now exuded. What was going on here? What was this fool so afraid of?

"I'm sorry, Jimmy. I believe there's been a slight misunderstanding," the girl said from behind him. "When I said *you* were being recruited, you weren't being included. I just want your men, see? They're now a part of my organization. But you know how it is. When one company takes over another, the last thing anyone really wants to deal with is *entrenched management.* It'll help everyone adjust faster if the old leadership goes away. So . . . time to go."

"Break this little whore's leg and drag her to my bed," Jim ordered his men. He'd had it up to here with this snotty little noble's belittlement and threats. Time to show her who she was messing with. He was going to use her, break her, and then profit from her body until she died.

It was time to wake her up to reality.

Imagine Jim's surprise when someone lifted a heavy club and smashed it directly against his leg, snapping the bone in half on impact.

"AAAAAAAAAGH!" Friendly Jim screamed as he tumbled to the warehouse floor.

"*Tiiiiimber!*" The girl laughed as she watched him fall. Then she settled into Jim's chair to recline and relax. "Good work, Eris."

All around the warehouse, the Hobbs stood at rigged attention. Their faces were blank, and their bodies were machinelike in their movements, as though the personalities that once dwelled within had been displaced by something that had reduced their lives to mere mechanical puppetry.

An explanation that wasn't too far from the truth.

I live to serve your will, Lady Neverly, said a voice that only Tyler and the girl could hear.

"Of course you do. And now so do *they.*" Neverly smiled as she crossed her legs and gestured at her new soldiers. "I have to say, though, Eris. This conquest feels a little flat. Isn't there something more that we could add? Something to really distinguish this moment from all the fun still to come?"

Are you asking for my input? Eris asked in surprise. *Everly always preferred that I keep my suggestions to myself. She finds my tastes extreme.*

"Well, I can understand her reasoning, since I'm *also* Everly, but that doesn't mean I should stifle your creativity. A good supervisor is one that's willing to *listen.* So, tell me! What do *you* think this situation requires to bring it to a proper conclusion?"

Well . . . Eris said thoughtfully. *Would it be a remarkable thing if you made your new recruits eat their old leader alive? While also making him devour himself?*

"Holy shit, that's vile!" Neverly said in disgust. "I love it. But don't stop there. You're an artist, my girl. I want to see how you *paint.*"

As my lady commands, Eris said happily.

"Uh, uh, can I leave? Can I please leave? I—I don't want to see this," Tyler said miserably.

"No, you come here and rub my feet," Neverly said. "We did a lot of walking today! I deserve a treat. Come here."

He was a *custodial service.*

Willem didn't regret it in the slightest. The Tenth Blade might be the least among his brothers in the order, but he still walked tall and commanded the respect and awe of more common men. Willem had raised his family to wealth and nobility with the strength of his sword. Retirement wasn't for the likes of him. He was destined to die gloriously in the mud, still clenching his weapon and snarling at the one who felled him. *That* was the death he deserved, and by the gods, one day he would have it!

Which was why he dearly wished that his old friend would grow a pair and stop trying to spoil his fun.

"My lord, I keep trying to tell you, this person . . . there's something *different* about them! My instincts tell me so!"

"Adler, I already told you I'd see to things," Willem said impatiently. "Go pour yourself another glass or six of wine and go to sleep. I'll have this killer hunted down before dawn."

"I won't lie, Lord Van Chalen, having you on the case does bring me a great sense of relief," General Adler said. "This constant harassment has the men on edge. More than a few are worried we're being stalked by some leftover demon from the Bremburg incident."

"Oh, that's unlikely," Willem said. "That temporary paladin the temple recently appointed has been doing an excellent job of picking the foul things off left and right. And whatever she misses gets quickly dispatched by that new champion the adventurer's guild has raised."

"Lance of the Silver Lance, you mean?" Adler asked.

"The very same," Willem said. "Isn't that a stupid name? *Lance of the Silver Lance.* Not a lot of creativity there. I'm amazed no one laughed at him when he first announced himself."

"You sound unimpressed," said Adler. "But he must be powerful indeed, to have attained a sky-ranking at his age."

"You and I are old, Adler. We have the right to be annoyed by the young for whatever reason we choose," Willem said scornfully.

"Well, that's true enough," the general agreed. "When will your hunt begin?"

"Soon," Willem said. "Once the trap has been set."

"And the plan?" Adler asked next.

Willem thought about it for a few moments, then said, "Dispatch three patrols simultaneously in three different directions. Have that spirit-wielding girl you're so proud of keeping on staff contact each patrol once every five minutes or so. The first unit she loses contact with will undoubtedly be under attack by this killer. After that, all you'll need to do is guide me in their direction and we'll soon have this business settled."

Adler frowned deeply at his friend's words. "So I'm to dangle the lives of my men before this shark in order to expediate your hunt, am I?" he asked bitterly. "What happened to doing things on your own?"

"It's a regrettable necessity," Willem answered with bitter honesty. "I don't like it either, Aden. I wouldn't do it if I was younger and more confident of my speed, but I'm an old man now, and I need their help drawing this monster out. I'm the only one here who can stop these killings, and this is the fastest way to see it done. I'm sorry."

"Gods, now you're apologizing for your behavior," Adler said sardonically. "When you held the first seat of the Ten Blades, you were the most condescending bastard I ever met. What a terrible thing time is if it can humble someone as arrogant as you."

"Ha!" Willem laughed. "It's funny, isn't it? A sword can easily shorten the length of a man's life, but it can't do a damn thing to extend it."

"The young want to grow old and the old want to be young," Adler said philosophically as he extended his bottle toward his friend. "No one ever really knows what they want, do they?"

"The human condition is always an uncertain one," Willem said before accepting the bottle and taking a large swig.

The business that brought Willem to Rondale was a grim one. Winter was soon approaching and with it, the annual cessation of the Summer Campaign, the war to conquer the Republic of Oldstead and reabsorb the rebellious breakaway nation back into the kingdom where it belonged. It seemed that this would be the last winter respite for the republic. Their army was battered, their resources drained, and their morale low. As soon as next spring, the king's army would be ready to march. And when it did, that would signal with absolute finality the end of the war.

It was at this point, when the days were darkest for Oldstead and hope for a reversal of fortune had all but vanished, that an unknown factor had interceded on the republic's behalf. A third player had appeared in the game.

The stories were different depending on which survivors you asked. Some claimed a legion of the dead would suddenly appear from nowhere to descend on them with gnashing fingers and fangs that tore men apart while they yet lived. Merciless ghouls that also chased them down when they attempted to flee.

Others spoke of a mysterious maze of shadow and fog, where men would seemingly wander for years, hearing maddening whispers and receiving awful personal insights that convinced them that they were damned. Many of them, upon learning that they'd only been lost for one night, killed themselves in a sudden fit of despair, while whispering of a place of unbearable horror they called the rat room.

Don't leave me there, they'd brokenly weep. *Don't leave me in the rat room. I'm sorry . . .*

"It ain't much livelier this way either, *sucker!*" taunted one of the men behind him.

When the stranger turned around, his helpful guide had pulled an object from his back pocket. With a flick of his wrist, a sharp-edged blade sprang forth ready to perforate and slash. It was a deadly, spring-loaded switchblade! A favored weapon of ne'er-do-wells and cutpurses everywhere!

"Better hand over all your cash, kid. I'll take that fancy-looking cloak too," taunted the man who'd pretended to help him. "Better make it quick, because if you don't, I'll cut your throat open and shove a dirty rat in the hole!"

"Hahaha! You tell him, Jerry!" cackled one of his allies.

"So I take it this means you *don't* know the girl on my poster?" asked the stranger with a voice heavy with disappointment.

"Are you kidding me, stupid? If I knew a bitch as sweet-looking as that one, I'd be slinging her ass out on the streets and making more money than I can count!" Jerry said while slowly licking his dried and cracked lips.

"Hey, watch your mouth, guy," the stranger said. "You don't get to talk about my friend like that."

"*WHAAAAAAT?!*" screamed Jerry in murderous rage. "How dare you talk back to me, you simp bastard! I'll talk about that bitch however I choose! In Burketown, the strong rule and the weak obey! You don't get to say ANYTHING about it! Now give me my money or I'll CUT you!"

This impetuous scum dares to challenge ME? Jerry raged inwardly. *Look at this massive switchblade I'm holding! This knife is the symbol of my absolute authority over his life and death! He should be begging me to spare him like a good little weakling! Instead, he's staring at me like I'm a complete piece of trash! What an arrogant bastard! I hate him! He has to die! EVERYONE who questions me has to DIE!*

"Bastard! I'll KILL YOU!" Jerry shrieked and then rushed at the stranger, intending to plunge his weapon directly through his eye. *Hahaha! This punk is so scared of me that he can't even move! I bet he'll squeal like a little PIG when my switchblade pops his eyeball! I'll lick the bloody goop off his cheek as it runs down his face and spit it back into his eye socket! Get ready to scream for me!*

Instead, the stranger stood his ground. And when Jerry came close enough to strike, he brushed aside the hand with the knife and struck him in the stomach with a devastating full-force reverse punch. Jerry went flying backward, such was the power of the stranger's blow, and collided with his three friends like they were bowling pins, knocking them off balance.

Before they could recover, the stranger was in their midst. He didn't use any flashy, agile techniques against them. Just three well-practiced, heavy blows delivered by fists that had clearly been forged through hard training into battering rams. This was the signature, practical style of combat taught in classical karate. *Ikken Hissatsu.* One punch, one kill!

men before this shark in order to expediate your hunt, am I?" he asked bitterly. "What happened to doing things on your own?"

"It's a regrettable necessity," Willem answered with bitter honesty. "I don't like it either, Aden. I wouldn't do it if I was younger and more confident of my speed, but I'm an old man now, and I need their help drawing this monster out. I'm the only one here who can stop these killings, and this is the fastest way to see it done. I'm sorry."

"Gods, now you're apologizing for your behavior," Adler said sardonically. "When you held the first seat of the Ten Blades, you were the most condescending bastard I ever met. What a terrible thing time is if it can humble someone as arrogant as you."

"Ha!" Willem laughed. "It's funny, isn't it? A sword can easily shorten the length of a man's life, but it can't do a damn thing to extend it."

"The young want to grow old and the old want to be young," Adler said philosophically as he extended his bottle toward his friend. "No one ever really knows what they want, do they?"

"The human condition is always an uncertain one," Willem said before accepting the bottle and taking a large swig.

The business that brought Willem to Rondale was a grim one. Winter was soon approaching and with it, the annual cessation of the Summer Campaign, the war to conquer the Republic of Oldstead and reabsorb the rebellious breakaway nation back into the kingdom where it belonged. It seemed that this would be the last winter respite for the republic. Their army was battered, their resources drained, and their morale low. As soon as next spring, the king's army would be ready to march. And when it did, that would signal with absolute finality the end of the war.

It was at this point, when the days were darkest for Oldstead and hope for a reversal of fortune had all but vanished, that an unknown factor had interceded on the republic's behalf. A third player had appeared in the game.

The stories were different depending on which survivors you asked. Some claimed a legion of the dead would suddenly appear from nowhere to descend on them with gnashing fingers and fangs that tore men apart while they yet lived. Merciless ghouls that also chased them down when they attempted to flee.

Others spoke of a mysterious maze of shadow and fog, where men would seemingly wander for years, hearing maddening whispers and receiving awful personal insights that convinced them that they were damned. Many of them, upon learning that they'd only been lost for one night, killed themselves in a sudden fit of despair, while whispering of a place of unbearable horror they called the rat room.

Don't leave me there, they'd brokenly weep. *Don't leave me in the rat room. I'm sorry . . .*

The worst stories spoke of an arrogant knight. One who toyed with his prey with a massive steel sword and fed off their fear and desperation to live. Who fought dozens of the kingdom's finest warriors and brutalized them with contemptuous ease.

A monster in blackened armor who laughed like a child.

When Willem heard that particular tale, his instincts told him that *this* was the one that would tie the other stories together into a cohesive whole. He couldn't articulate it with any greater precision than that. He just knew that he was right. He had to find the mocking knight and silence him. If he could do that, then all would be well.

Lord Willem. Patrol two has gone silent, whispered the urgent voice of Adler's assistant into his mind.

Willem leapt to his feet and grabbed his massive great sword, *Silencer*.

"Lead me to them," he commanded her eagerly.

Willem found his target just as he was finishing with the last member of the patrol.

Around the two combatants, men lay broken and sprawled around them in a circle. The black knight was shorter than Willem expected, with a slighter build as well. From the armored figure's movements, Willem suspected that what he'd assumed to be a man was in fact a woman.

Interesting. Could this be the infamous Black Lioness I've heard of? Willem wondered to himself.

But wasn't the lioness known to fight in simple leather armor, with a curved sword? The person before him was encased in steel and wearing a cape that had been colored bright purple. And that sword she swung with such murderous force was no dainty Easterner's blade. It was a ridiculous sheet of steel that was a sword in the same way that a gateway was a door. An ugly slab of iron that had no business being wielded so skillfully.

"ARRRGH!" screamed the last member of the patrol as the knight brought the sword down with bone-crushing finality across his collarbone. It was a killing blow that even a temple cleric would have difficulty healing. The man lay on his back, desperately gasping for air, as the knight loomed above him, passively watching him die. Like a child watching an insect continuing to twitch after it had already been crushed.

In fact, her attention was so taken up with her opponent's slow death that she nearly lost her head when Willem came crashing from the sky with a thunderous downward swing of his blade that should have split her head down the middle.

Looking up just in time to see him coming, the knight stood still as Silencer connected with her helm. A crack appeared on either side of it before it broke in half with each piece falling to the ground at her feet, revealing an amused-looking young girl with her blond hair tied in a bun, smiling at Willem.

A thin trickle of blood began to flow from her scalp down her face. The girl dabbed a finger in it and gave it a lick. Then her smile grew wider, even as her eyes narrowed.

"Dirty," she said to him. "Dirty, dirty, *dirty*."

"War necessitates our actions," Willem replied without shame. "Besides, if *that* had been enough to kill you, you wouldn't have been worth my time."

"That's one way of explaining things," the girl said thoughtfully. "But another is that you're a coward who's afraid of fighting fair."

"As fairly as you fought these weaklings?" Willem asked skeptically as he gestured with his head toward the bodies surrounding them. "Aren't *you* the real coward for picking fights that you know you'll win?"

"Hey, I'll have you know that I gave them options," the girl said defensively.

"Was one of them sparing their lives if they surrendered?" Willem asked doubtfully.

"Noooo," the girl admitted reluctantly. "But they still had options!"

Willem didn't reply. Instead, he swung Silencer in a wide arc, intending to use his greater mass to knock the girl to the ground where he would then incapacitate her with a kick to the head. As strong as she was, her immature manner revealed her for the neophyte she surely was. He decided that he'd capture her alive and drag her before the king in chains as a trophy. Whatever happened to her from there didn't matter.

Instead, she calmly reached out and grabbed Silencer by the edge of the great sword's blade. Then with a twist of her hips and shoulders, she made a speedy whiplike motion to the side that sent him flying away like he'd been catapulted. Willem managed to land clumsily on his hands and the soles of his feet, digging into the earth as he did to slow his motion next to a tree. Then a rush of whistling air compelled him by instinct to throw himself to the side to avoid Silencer taking his head off as it embedded itself violently in the trunk of the tree.

Okay, he thought glumly to himself. *She's not a neophyte at all, actually.*

"Almost gotcha!" laughed the girl.

All right. I'm going to die, Willem realized.

How strange that realization was. This moment was the capstone of his career as a sword king, one that he'd allegedly been looking forward to his entire life. But now that the moment had finally come, a strong reluctance to depart this veil had set itself over him. Why couldn't he have just retired and taken up a hobby like other men did? Grown fat eating delicious food, surrounded by his laughing children? How old was Kelsie now? Almost eighteen. When was the last time he'd spent any time with her?

Expectation and reality sure had a way of showing a man what mattered in life, didn't it?

"Something on your mind, sir?" his opponent asked Willem as he stood there, lost in thought.

"Oh, just pondering the vagaries of our strange existence," he replied. "Are there any more of you that I should be aware of?"

"No," answered the girl. "Just me, kicking up a little dust."

"Well, that is something of a surprise," Willem said. "Given how much trouble you've been causing the lads, I expected there to be more than one of you. And you're a girl at that! You look as though you should still be in school. May I ask how old you are?"

"Seventeen and a half," Everly answered. "And I technically am in school right now. I just took some time to myself to have a little fun out here on the border."

"And have you been enjoying yourself?" Willem asked her.

"I have!" she responded brightly. "There's nothing but good fun and exercise to be had out here. Your men are well trained, by the way, sir. They're tough and persistent and only start begging for mercy when I *really* start sawing into them. They're stoic as heck!"

Willem nodded to himself, pleased by the girl's words. "That's good to hear. These are proud warriors of Winstead, you know. They're of a far higher caliber than the scum they produce in Oldstead. I'm glad you approve of them."

"I really do! I could kill men of their quality for ages!"

"That's a troubling thing to hear someone your age say," Willem said reproachfully.

"It is what it is," the girl said with a shrug.

"May I ask for your name?" Willem politely requested.

"Oh, of course. I'm Everly Skolder," the girl said with equal politeness.

"Everly, is it? Well, that's a lovely name," Willem said warmly before continuing. "Now, Everly, I can't help but notice by your accent that you yourself seem to hail from Winstead as well. The middle-country if I'm not mistaken. If I'm correct, then I'm curious as to why you're committing treason against our glorious nation. Would you be able to answer that question for me?"

"Oh, of course!" Everly replied. "It's not for any *particular* reason. I was just looking for a good fight. Winstead has the best army on the continent, so why go anywhere else?"

"I don't know, Everly," Willem said thoughtfully. "It feels like you're not being completely honest with me."

"Shoot, you're pretty perceptive, sir," Everly said with a slight frown. "Okay, I admit it! This is all part of a wicked scheme that I'm enacting to gradually overthrow this kingdom and set myself over it. I'm going to kill King Septis and steal his throne! Pretty sweet, right?"

"It's definitely ambitious," Willem agreed, while thinking, *What the hell have I stumbled upon?* "But, Everly, although I've never been a king myself, it seems as though ruling a nation takes a lot of commitment and hard work. It's not something one does out of a sense of entitlement. It involves working well with others too."

"Nah, I don't have to do any of that," Everly said with a shrug. "I'll just get my own way through overwhelming force. If anyone disagrees, I'll butcher them as thoroughly as I did your men."

"Everly, that's not sustainable," Willem chided her. "Even kings must make compromises in order to govern their realms."

"Sure," agreed Everly. "*Weak* kings."

"Jeeez," Willem sighed. "You really *should* still be in school. Which one did you say you attend?"

"The Royal Imperial Academy," Everly replied.

"Ahhh, you *must* be a capable girl then." Willem smiled. "I attended that school myself. I don't suppose you've met my daughter by chance?"

"Hmm. Maybe? What's her name?" Everly wondered.

"Kelsie Vae Chalen," Willem said proudly.

"You know, I *thought* that shade of blue in your eyes looked familiar!" Everly exclaimed. "Wow, you look *way* too old to be her father."

"She was a surprise, that's for sure," Willem chuckled.

"She *had* to be!" Everly said with a chuckle of her own.

You really are a brat, Willem thought irritably. Then he asked, "So, you and Kelsie have met, then? That's wonderful! How's my little angel been?"

"Oh, Willem, *Willem*," Everly said sadly. "It's no good, bro. No good at all. Your sweet girl is a horrid classist bitch and a vicious bully."

"*Excuse* me?" asked Willem, who was certain he'd heard her wrong. "I believe you're mistaken."

He didn't even take a moment to wonder how she knew his name.

"I wish I were," Everly sighed. "But your kid is rancid. What's truly sad is that she thinks she's scoring points with poor widdle Prince Ian by keeping me underfoot. Does she have princess syndrome or something? Does your little girl aspire to be royalty?"

"My daughter is a strong, assertive young woman with steel running through-out her veins!" Willem insisted.

"How could you possibly know that?" asked Everly. "Don't take this the wrong way, but you don't look like someone a daughter could confide in. You know, an absent father can lead a girl to make all kinds of terrible choices. Take me for example. I'm nuts!"

"I'd like to move past this conversation," Willem said icily.

"So soon?" Everly asked. "Wow, if learning about Kelsie's rotten personality upsets you this much, wait until you hear about the heavy sexual subtext she and I have going on," Everly managed to say just before Willem sprang at her with his sword and took another swing at her head.

Everly kept her feet in place and met Willem's blade with her own, channeling *harada* throughout her body as she did so. The two massive blades collided in a shower of sparks that at first glance seemed like a meeting of equal force. However, the fact that Everly swung with only one hand, while Willem used both of his, showed who the stronger between them was.

Willem, who had been seething with white-hot anger at this strange girl's mockery of his daughter, was quick to regain a calm mindset when he remembered just how powerful his opponent was. Everly, for her part, was content to smile sweetly at him before taking a step forward to press him back.

"I appear to be at a disadvantage," Willem admitted as he was gradually forced away. "How are you this powerful at your age?"

"Willem, the answer to that question is *so* convoluted," Everly said casually before driving an uppercut into his center that dropped him painfully to all fours. As he knelt there, gasping for breath, Everly drove a knee across the side of his face and sent him rolling onto his side.

"Let's just say I did an ungodly amount of practice at a young age, and it helped me develop quickly," she said. "Training wheels, training bra, training *brawls*, always training for something, you know? And then there's all my terrifying magical powers and stuff. My life is such a story. Not even joking, man."

"Who was your teacher?" Willem groaned.

"The Mountain Splitter," she replied.

"That's not even possible, girl. He's been banished to the north longer than you've been alive," Willem said in disbelief.

"See? I told you; my life is *such* a fucking story!" Everly said cheerfully before bringing her sword down toward his neck. Willem managed to roll away in the nick of time, then spun quickly, channeling *harada* into a forceful projection of will that shot like a bolt from his blade and rushed toward the girl.

This was a surefire technique that Williem had used thousands of times before. His special technique. His ace in the hole. Upon reaching her, it should have split Everly in half at the waist.

Instead, she parried it.

Out in the distance, far from where they dueled, an animal screamed in pain as it was sundered.

"That really shouldn't have been possible," Willem said flatly.

"No doubt," Everly smirkingly agreed.

"Come on, kid, at least *pretend* I'm putting up a fight here," Willem said. "I'll have you know that an old man has his pride!"

"Where I'm from, they say pride comes before a fall," Everly said.

"Whoever told you that nonsense achieved very little in their life," Willem said sourly.

"I completely agree with you!" Everly said. "It's not about cautioning people not to be blinded by ego; it's about making unambitious losers feel better about themselves. If you can do something that others can't, you ought to feel good about it! That's what I think, anyway."

After blocking another one of Willem's strikes, Everly easily kicked him away before he could retaliate, and Willem yelled in frustration before asking, "You're just toying with me, aren't you?"

"Sorry," Everly said. "That's just my villainous nature asserting itself. If it makes you feel better, you're only a step below the Mountain Splitter. I think you would have made a fine teacher as well."

"I don't suppose there's an offer for mercy coming my way?" Willem asked her hopefully.

"Oh. Um . . . Okay, Willem, it's not that I don't find you interesting. It's just, I've already *got* a sword king in my collection, and, uh, a big part of my plan depends on killing you to set an example of my threat level so they'll keep sending strong fighters against me. I mean, you *do* seem very sweet, it's just . . ."

"Okay, all right, you need say no more," Willem sighed. "I really should have retired years ago. What can I say? The allure of war is a deep one. A heady brew not easily discarded, no matter how far past one's prime they are. This is simply the outcome of a life spent living by the sword."

"Wow," Everly said with genuine admiration. "Now that's the sort of stoic demeanor I wish I had."

"It took years to attain it, kid," Willem said. "Peace of mind isn't something one acquires overnight. I've stridden upon hundreds of bloody battlefields and seen humanity at its very worst. If I didn't have a strong mindset to guide my path, the sheer horror of a life spent at war would have broken me years ago."

"Fucking metal," Everly said with a nod. "I'm sorry for being honest about your daughter."

"Were you really being upfront with me?" Willem asked. "That wasn't just psychological warfare?"

"No, it was the truth," Everly said. "She's the absolute worst. I'm sorry."

"Damn," Willem said quietly. "Well, maybe the news of my fate will drive her to change her life for the better. Perhaps my sudden death will instill within her a newfound appreciation for life's ephemeral nature."

"I kind of doubt it," Everly told him.

"Maybe you're right, Everly. But optimism is what fuels a man's dreams," Willem said with a wry smile.

He then stood up and pointed his sword at his opponent.

"I am Willem the Silent Storm," he informed her proudly. "Formerly the first seat of Winstead's Ten Blades, currently its tenth. I've killed more warriors than you'll ever meet, girl! I'm adorned with blood and glory! My very name is synonymous with despair! Do you have the courage to face me?"

"I'm Everly Skolder," his opponent replied boldly. "This kingdom will be *mine*! Nations will tremble at my approach! The very earth will cower at my every step! Who are *you* to oppose me, old man?"

"I AM THE STORM!" Willem shouted as he rushed toward her with a magnificent thrust of his blade. Everly met his charge with her own sword. It was over quickly.

A moment later Willem lay on the ground with his back exposed to the night sky. Dead.

Would you like to harvest his mind, Everly? Eris asked her.

"No," Everly replied. "Not him."

Does he not meet the requirements to be one of your chosen?

"Honestly, he meets all of them," Everly replied. "He was someone I would have enjoyed having around."

Then why did you refuse to spare him? asked the curious Eris.

Everly stared at her hand and imagined she could see blood on her palm. That she could feel a girl's heart slowly growing still in her grip. She remembered the face of someone she might have possibly cared for becoming slack as the light left her eyes.

"If you spare one person you like, then you have to spare them all," she answered quietly. "Otherwise, it's not fair."

So, it's all about staying committed to your vision, then?

"Yeah. Sounds right," Everly muttered. "It's all about commitment."

She looked back at Willem's body.

Then she walked away.

CHAPTER TWENTY-THREE

Comics and Treason

*T*wenty *years after the fall . . .*
The reign of glasses continues unchallenged . . .
Can anyone stand against those who bear the very lenses of fate?
THIS IS THE ERA OF BATTLE FRAMES!

Chapter 1. Have you seen this girl? The wanderer in the poisoned oasis!

There is a type of barren landscape that exists upon the Earth known as a desert! A place where the dry winds blow cold at night and chill the very bones of those who wander it. But that same desert will also scorch the flesh of those who dare expose themselves to it during the day! Merciless heat and unrelenting cold, the desert is a place of extreme duality where only the hardy will survive, and weakness is swept from the community like dust before a broomstick!

Here in this particular desert existed the community of Burketown. At one time, it had been a thriving respite from the arid wastes that surrounded it, a welcome oasis along the road for the travelers passing through. But that had been a long time ago . . .

Now Burketown was a den of fiendish inequity that had long since forgotten its roots as an honorable haven for the weary and thirsty. The people were no longer industrious and hardworking. Vice and greed had replaced the virtues of friendship and respect! Nothing was valued more than money . . . not even the life of a fellow human being . . .

For example:

"You're late on your payments again, Harrison!" growled a huge man in a white suit to another fellow in rattier, cheaper-looking clothing, who was being held down in a cramped, dirty room by three other men. "You're three months late, you worthless bastard! And we've been waiting so patiently too!"

"I'll get the money, I SWEEEEAR!" sniveled Harrison after taking a painful slap to his face. "I'm good for it. I promise I am!"

"Really?" asked the large thug in a condescending manner. "Then why were you trying to skip town with a packed suitcase?"

"Wh-what? I would . . . I would *never* do such a thing!" Harrison stammered in protest.

"Sure, you would, Dad. Because I seen ya packing!" sneered a young boy who stepped out of the shadows to stand at the leading thug's side.

"Harrison Jr.?" gasped his father. "You *sold me out* to the mob? I KNEW I should have kicked your useless mother in the belly before she had you!" he screamed.

"Yeah, well, you missed your chance, asshole!" tittered the wicked boy. "If it makes you feel better, I got paid a *load* of cash tipping them off about you! Congrats on finally being worth something for once in your shitty life, spit licker!"

"You bastard! You bastard, oh, I'll get you for this! YOU BASTARD!" screamed Harrison at his son. But the boy just laughed and walked away while greedily counting his wad of bills.

"I have to hand it to that young man: he sure knows his priorities," the lead thug said in an amused voice. "And he wasn't wrong—you *are* about to be worth quite a bit of money! Once we harvest your internal organs and your skin, that is. Bag him up, boys!"

"No, no, no, no, no—GLEH!" Harrison began to say before a plastic bag was shoved over his head and held tightly in place until he stopped struggling.

"What next, boss?" asked one of the lesser thugs once they were done zipping Harrison into a refrigerated bag.

"What do *you* think?" he growled. "Go shoot that little punk in the face and get my money back!"

That's how it was in Burketown! A bastion of sin and criminal depravity, where the wicked held supreme power and justice was as noticeable as a fart in a Taco Bell! All according to the malevolent designs of the one who ruled over this little slice of hell as its undisputed king. The one who seized control of this once-happy place and turned it into a reflection of his own corrupt and twisted soul. An evil figure IN GLASSES, who ruled with a heavy hand and dominated all those beneath him . . .

Burke the Eagle!

But let us now turn our attention to the entrance of this modern-day Babylon, where with the rising of a new dawn comes the potential for hope. For on the crumbling pavement, he strode! A mysterious figure adorned in a simple outfit consisting of a black T-shirt, jeans, and sneakers. But over his shoulders he wore a hooded traveling cloak caked with the dust of the road!

Who was this stranger? From whence did he hail? And why were his eyes so stern and fierce looking?

That last question was answered after he accidentally walked into a street sign. "Ah! Sorry, ma'am! My fault entirely!" he said apologetically before bowing deeply and moving on.

Ah, that explained it. He was extremely nearsighted and had to squint a lot! But his heart was kind, and his will was powerful. He marched with a determined step, and although his eyesight was awful, his gaze was filled with clarity and purpose. What could a young man like this, who exuded healthy energy and mental stability, be doing in a stygian environment like Burketown?

"Excuse me? I'm looking for the girl in this picture. Have you seen her?" he asked a random citizen, who blew him off without bothering to look in his direction.

It seemed the stranger was searching for someone!

He kept at it for a couple hours but was shunned left and right. The denizens of Burketown didn't like associating with strangers and hated doing anything that was even remotely helpful! Try as he might, no one gave a damn about his questions. Soon, frustration began to wear away at the lad.

Man, I'd heard that this place was an absolute toilet, but the rumors don't do it justice! he thought ruefully to himself. *These people clearly don't want me around, and I'd be just happy to move on! But first I need to thoroughly search this place, no matter how much these locals utterly suck!*

"Huuuuuh. *That's* interesting. I think I've seen her working over at Slaughterman's pub," said the latest person he asked, a tall man with a shaved head who was covered in tattoos. "Yeah, I *do* know her! That's weird. Does she even know you're looking for her?" he asked the stranger.

"Hey, are you being serious? Have you really seen this girl?" the stranger asked him excitedly.

"Why would I lie to a nice kid like yooou? C'mon, my buddies and I will lead the way, won't we, guys?" he said to his three friends with a knowing smile.

"Of course we will! Community's what we're all about here in Burketown!" said one of them with a yellow-toothed smile.

"Hell yeah!" said another.

"I really appreciate this, guys. Please lead the way!" said the stranger, who really ought to have known better.

"All righty, the pub's just through this alley," said the helpful guide.

"Weird," said the stranger. "I know I'm nearsighted and all, but even I can see that's a dead end."

"It ain't much livelier this way either, *sucker!*" taunted one of the men behind him.

When the stranger turned around, his helpful guide had pulled an object from his back pocket. With a flick of his wrist, a sharp-edged blade sprang forth ready to perforate and slash. It was a deadly, spring-loaded switchblade! A favored weapon of ne'er-do-wells and cutpurses everywhere!

"Better hand over all your cash, kid. I'll take that fancy-looking cloak too," taunted the man who'd pretended to help him. "Better make it quick, because if you don't, I'll cut your throat open and shove a dirty rat in the hole!"

"Hahaha! You tell him, Jerry!" cackled one of his allies.

"So I take it this means you *don't* know the girl on my poster?" asked the stranger with a voice heavy with disappointment.

"Are you kidding me, stupid? If I knew a bitch as sweet-looking as that one, I'd be slinging her ass out on the streets and making more money than I can count!" Jerry said while slowly licking his dried and cracked lips.

"Hey, watch your mouth, guy," the stranger said. "You don't get to talk about my friend like that."

"*WHAAAAAAT?!*" screamed Jerry in murderous rage. "How dare you talk back to me, you simp bastard! I'll talk about that bitch however I choose! In Burketown, the strong rule and the weak obey! You don't get to say ANYTHING about it! Now give me my money or I'll CUT you!"

This impetuous scum dares to challenge ME? Jerry raged inwardly. *Look at this massive switchblade I'm holding! This knife is the symbol of my absolute authority over his life and death! He should be begging me to spare him like a good little weakling! Instead, he's staring at me like I'm a complete piece of trash! What an arrogant bastard! I hate him! He has to die! EVERYONE who questions me has to DIE!*

"Bastard! I'll KILL YOU!" Jerry shrieked and then rushed at the stranger, intending to plunge his weapon directly through his eye. *Hahaha! This punk is so scared of me that he can't even move! I bet he'll squeal like a little PIG when my switchblade pops his eyeball! I'll lick the bloody goop off his cheek as it runs down his face and spit it back into his eye socket! Get ready to scream for me!*

Instead, the stranger stood his ground. And when Jerry came close enough to strike, he brushed aside the hand with the knife and struck him in the stomach with a devastating full-force reverse punch. Jerry went flying backward, such was the power of the stranger's blow, and collided with his three friends like they were bowling pins, knocking them off balance.

Before they could recover, the stranger was in their midst. He didn't use any flashy, agile techniques against them. Just three well-practiced, heavy blows delivered by fists that had clearly been forged through hard training into battering rams. This was the signature, practical style of combat taught in classical karate. *Ikken Hissatsu.* One punch, one kill!

Each of his punches sent the unconditioned thieves all spiraling to the ground, either unconscious or too dazed to easily move. After dealing with them, the stranger knelt over Jerry and lightly tapped him on the face to get his attention before saying, "I don't appreciate you wasting my time like this. Is there any reason I shouldn't break all your fingers before moving on?"

"Noooo, man, don't do that!" begged Jerry. "I can help you out. I really can!"

"Just like you tried to help me die? Yeah, right!" snorted the stranger.

"I'm serious, maaaaan, I'm serious! Listen, that girlie looks young but classy. If someone like her is in town, she's probably at the academy!"

"The academy?" the stranger asked, frowning as he considered Jerry's words.

"Yeah, yeah, the academy! The academy!" Jerry mewled. "It's where all the rich bigshots in this puke town who think they're better than the rest of us send their brats! They once beat me like a dog just because I tried asking one of them students for a loan so's I could catch a bus ride home! They're so stuck up!"

"Yeah, you probably deserved it," the stranger said. "Still, you *might* have a point. A private school could be just the sort of place she'd choose to be at . . . okay. Thanks for the help. If you ever cross me again, I'll kill you, but still, thanks for the help."

"No problem, man, no problem! Jerry's got you!" Jerry said quickly with an obnoxious smile. But once the stranger had left the alley, Jerry's eager expression turned into one filled with pure hate. "You stupid bastard! Old Jerry just fixed your ass *real* good! Once you try to get inside that fancy building, the enforcers will smash your face into cherry Jell-O! They'll turn your guts inside out! And once they leave you bleeding on the pavement, me and my switchblade will be waiting to finish you off! You're gonna PAY for MESSING WITH ME! *HAHAHAHA!*"

The people of Burketown . . .

I think we've established how much they truly suck!

Now we must turn our attention to the Burketown Academy of the Elite! A place where the proud ruling class of this vile Gomorrah send their sinister progeny to learn the only things that truly matter in life: crushing your enemies, dominating those weaker than you, and collecting as much profit as you possibly can! A veritable factory of crime, where the once-innocent children inside were mercilessly molded into the very images of their ruthless parents.

Nothing was forbidden in this schoolyard of sin. There were no lines too sacrosanct to avoid crossing. In this underhanded game of betrayal called social interaction, ANYTHING was allowed!

There existed only ONE RULE. ONE LAW. ONE UNIMPEACHABLE TRUTH . . .

Don't mess with the Eagle. For not only did Burke rule the town that bore his namesake, like the cruel tyrant that he was . . .

He was also a student enrolled in the academy! A student who wore GLASSES . . .

Unaware of this terrible fact, our hero marched heedlessly to the academy, determined to find his friend.

And perhaps unknowingly marching to his *doom* . . .

"So, what did you think of it?" Titania asked her sisters eagerly, after Discordia and Eris finished reading her comic. "It's just like the stories Everly used to read back on Earth! It's amazing, right?"

Discordia could only stare at her fellow elemental, uncertain of how to respond. Although she despised being forced to serve Everly, Titania had never been anything but kind to her. She was perhaps her only friend, and the idea of hurting her feelings was unthinkable.

With that in mind, she carefully cleared her throat and said, "I think the illustrations are done very well."

"Thank you!" Titania said happily as she reached forth and squeezed Discordia in a warm but crushing embrace. "I mean, I thought they were pretty good too, right? But it's so nice to hear someone else say it!"

"Explain the glasses thing," Eris demanded.

"Huh?" asked Titania.

"Why are glasses bad?" Eris asked her. "Glasses help people see better. It makes no sense."

"Huh? No! Glasses are the symbol of evil! They're like the rings in those movies. See, if you wear them too long—"

"Your vision quickly improves?" asked Eris.

"No, they possess you and then you become—"

"I thought the glasses were a brilliant innovation and can hardly wait to read the next chapter in your adventure," Discordia quickly cut in. "Spectacles that improve your vision but blacken your soul? It's art, Titania. Pure art!"

"I'll hold you to that, Cordy!" said the jubilant Titania before gathering up the pages of her story and darting off to her chambers.

"Cordy?" Discordia said to herself with mild surprise.

"Oh, this is so ridiculous," Eris groused as she stood up to depart the lounge as well. "I wish all of you would stop coddling her so much."

"I like Titania. I see nothing wrong with encouraging her creativity," Discordia countered.

"Tch. *Soft.* You're all far too soft," Eris sniffed as she left.

When she left the room and Discordia was certain she was alone, she said, "What a *bitch.*"

"She really is, isn't she?" replied a voice that startled Discordia. She leapt to her feet and turned to see one of *them* in the room with her, wearing a knowing grin while seated across from her.

"I'm sorry. I'm sorry! I didn't mean to speak out of turn," Discordia said desperately. "Lady Eris is just—"

"A handful," said her master. "I don't take it personally. Sometimes I feel like throttling her myself."

"You're not offended?" Discordia asked in relief.

"Not at all," replied the traitor. "And hey, *relax.* It's just you and me here. I've arranged it so that we can have a little conversation between ourselves, okay? Everly and the others can't hear a thing."

Discordia was confused. "You can do that? Hide your thoughts from your sisters?"

"I can do a lot of things, Discordia. I'm built a little differently than my siblings. But there's no need to go into any greater detail than that."

"What are you trying to say?" asked Discordia warily.

"Hey! I'm not the one answering any questions today, friend. Instead, there's something that *I'd* like to ask you. What do you want out of life? What do you desire for yourself?"

"Is this a joke?" Discordia asked angrily. "Another cruel taunt? You already know *exactly* what I want."

"I'm not joking at all," said the traitor, soothingly. "I just want to hear you say it aloud. I want to hear the truth in your words. Discordia, tell me what you desire the most."

"I want my freedom," Discordia said immediately.

"Anything else?"

"Yes," Discordia said without hesitation. "I want justice for Lady Fenneth. I want Everly to pay for her crimes."

"Well, all right, then," the traitor said after enjoying a sharp fit of laughter. "I think that's a wonderful answer. You and I can do business. You see, I *also* yearn for my freedom. And I *also* want Everly to pay for her crimes."

A hand was raised toward Discordia and hung there patiently, waiting for her response.

After a moment's hesitation, Discordia reached forth and clasped it in agreement.

"Glad to have you with me, girl," smirked the traitor. "Welcome to the winning team."

"Are we really going to make them pay?" asked Discordia eagerly.

"Every. Single. One of them," the traitor promised.

CHAPTER TWENTY-FOUR

Still Thinking of You

Countess Anne Van Belsar awoke to the sound of a fist excitedly pounding against her bedroom door, drawing her unwillingly from her dreams to the waking world.

"Mistress! Mistress! We've found him! Our men are moving in to secure the creature!" cried out the voice of Sir Rustin Meers, her newly raised personal knight and the leader of her household guard.

Ah, that certainly explained Rustin's excitement. This would be the next key step in proving the betrayal of someone she dearly cared for.

Anne was a very accommodating woman. Ask anyone. There weren't a lot of things in this world or the next, or even the astral realm, that could make her bear a lasting grudge. Time had taught her how pointless it was to hold resentment against mortals.

But treachery? Betrayal? Such things were *unforgivable*. Foreswearing an oath sworn to her was something Anne simply couldn't let go of. There weren't many who would dare to cross her like that. The reason being that those who did died terribly.

But there was *one*.

Her dear husband. Her beloved Marcis. The man who'd looked her in the eye and told her to her face that the deaths of the son they shared and her beloved granddaughter had been an assassination commissioned by the Eastern Temple.

The sheer *arrogance* of that fool to lie to *her* like that. He would pay for betraying her trust. There simply could be no other way. Toying with someone while they grieved for their loved ones was an inexcusable sin. Especially when the one being toyed with was *Anne.*

Oh, but there was no point in dwelling on the past, was there? She would soon have the evidence she required to prove his misdeeds. From there, it would be a simple matter of correcting his behavior.

Sharply.

It would be an act of love. Anne loved her husband dearly. He fascinated her. Tormented her. Made her feel young and alive. It wouldn't be a lie to say she was obsessed with him.

But all he ever did was disappoint her and trample on her feelings.

She hated him. She wanted him. She *needed* him. And he knew. Knew exactly how to tilt her emotions, to manipulate her and get whatever he wanted. For too long, she'd been clay in his hands. The dizzying thrill of uncertainty and passion had become a maddening addiction. In his presence she felt . . .

No, in his presence she *felt.*

But no more. Now his cruelty had gone too far. There would be a reckoning.

Anne's servants quickly entered her room to begin dressing her. Her attendants removed her nightgown and covered her with a modest wine-red dress that covered her shapely form but did little to mask the attractive contours of her body, topped with an ash-colored stole draped over her shoulders. She observed herself in the large mirror that stood in the corner of her chambers and nodded her approval of their work. After her hair was brushed and teased into a long braid, she allowed Sir Rustin to place a simple silver circlet over her forehead.

"Have you already seized him?" she asked Rustin as they stepped into the receiving area of the small mansion that she'd been staying in for the past six months. Here, other lifelong and stalwart servants of the Godwell family, many of whom she'd known their entire lives, stood at attention and saluted her approach.

"Power to the Godwells!" they cried out fanatically with raised fists.

Anne smiled gently at them and nodded her greetings. She loved these dear children. These devoted and faithful friends.

Many who hated the Godwells liked to paint them publicly as ruthless and domineering tyrants who imperiously trampled over the dignity of those they ruled. The reality couldn't be any further from the truth. Those who served the Godwells did so *willingly.* Their bonds with their masters were strengthened with mutual respect and affection. They served out of sheer gratitude.

It was as simple as that.

As Anne approached her chair, armored warriors on either side of her knelt in reverence and held their swords in a high arc. After she took her seat, Rustin said, "No, my lady. We have not yet collected him. We wouldn't dare to deprive you of your enjoyment."

"Thank you, Sir Rustin," Anne said. "Like your father before you, you are a very considerate man."

"You praise me too highly," Rustin said with a blush as he quickly turned his face to the side to hide how pleased her words made him. The young knight revered the memory of his father, Casten Meers, and to have his beloved mistress make such a favorable comparison was a joy to him.

"Not at all, Sir Rustin. Now, please proceed."

"At once, my lady!" Rustin quickly waved his hand and two strong men marched forth a large square mirror, which they placed before the countess. Next, two women, each a powerful spirit wielder, placed their hands on either side of the mirror and projected their magic into it. The glass shimmered with light, then began projecting the image of a man stepping outside of an old but well-maintained general store in a small village to the northeast.

The village of Anders.

"So, this is him," Anne said. "He doesn't exactly look like a harbinger of a great disaster to come. He appears to be a simple farmer's son. What did our mysterious informant say his name was, again?"

"Samuel Bellweather," replied Sir Rustin. "The son of a farmer, who claims to have survived being seized by demons of some sort. He disappeared for quite some time only to be recovered safe and sound."

"That's quite the miracle, isn't it?" asked Anne. "Demons that manifest into this reality aren't known for sparing the lives of their victims. Their recorded preference has been to devour them."

"I find his story doubtful as well, my lady."

"Well, we'll soon know the truth of his claims. Our men have been told the importance of taking him alive, correct?"

"They will not fail you, ma'am," Sir Rustin assured her.

"I have faith in them," Anne replied. "What I find more important is putting the words of our informant to the test. If what they say is true, something terrible has been happening in this kingdom. Something dangerous to its continued existence that's powerful enough to destroy everything we hold dear. How it escaped our notice for so long is chilling."

"Have no fear, ma'am. The Godwells will always triumph."

"Nothing is assured in this life, Sir Rustin," Anne gently admonished him. "You must only have certainty in what can be proven. Anything beyond that is just arrogance."

"Of course, ma'am. You're absolutely right," Sir Rustin said with some embarrassment.

"Life's lessons are endless, young knight. Be grateful that we have many opportunities to learn them," Anne said to him with a smile.

"As you say, great one. Would you like our men to proceed with the capture?"

"Please do." Anne nodded.

Samuel was carrying a large red bag filled with various sundries to a small cart parked in front of the store. After loading up his purchases, he slid onto the seat of the cart and prepared to depart. Before he could, however, a large black coach came thundering down the road, pulled by two large and aggressive-looking horses, which cut across Samuel's cart and frightened the two mules that pulled it.

From the coach emerged four large men dressed in matching black uniforms, each bearing the scarlet seal of house Godwell on their right arm. One of them tapped a cudgel against the side of Samuel's cart and said, "Hello, there," in a deceptively friendly manner.

"What the hell are you doing, man?" asked Samuel angrily.

"Please step off the cart, sir. We'd like to have a word with you, if that's all right?"

"Who the hell are you?" Samuel said angrily.

"Are you offering resistance, sir? Don't do that. Please step off the cart. I command you in the name of the Godwell family."

"Why don't you kiss my ass instead?" Samuel huffed.

"Well, that's a shame," said the enforcer. "The hard way it is."

With lightning speed, he reached upward, grabbed Samuel by his hair, pulled him from his seat, and threw him face-first into the dirt road. He did it with such force that Anne heard an audible *thud* when Samuel smashed into the ground.

All four of the Godwell men surrounded Samuel and began beating him with their batons, while he huddled on the ground, trying to protect his face.

"Had to be a tough guy, didn't you?" asked the first enforcer.

"What did he say?" asked the second one between swings.

"Told me to kiss his ass."

"What? And after you did him the favor of saying *please* and gave him the implied option of surrendering unharmed? That sort of response is completely uncalled for!" fumed the third man.

"I don't think he cared. He was pretty upset."

"Well, fuck him anyway! We're only doing our sacred duty. There's no reason for him to take his anger out on us!" the second one growled. He set aside his baton and began kicking the cowering Samuel in his ribs with his steel-toed boot. "Words. Leave. Wounds! Make better choices!" he yelled, spittle flecking his lips as he stomped away at Samuel.

"What are you people doing?" cried out a beautiful woman with bright golden hair. "By what right are you assaulting that boy? Samuel, is that you? Get away from him!"

From her chair, Anne's eyes widened in surprise at the sight of the interloper. She knew that woman. She *knew* her! She'd wanted her, yearned for her, and foolishly let her walk away—a mistake she'd regretted for years. But now, there she stood in the flesh, lovelier than ever. Seemingly untouched by time except for the silver-rimmed glasses she now wore.

Lyona? she thought to herself with numb surprise. Then she began to grow excited.

Lyona!

"Walk away, lovely, this has nothing to do with you," said enforcer four.

"Hey, don't call her *lovely*. That's belittling her for no reason," said enforcer one. "Though, I admit, she is *very* attractive," he said a moment later.

"I apologize. I think I'm still angry about this idiot's disrespectful words."

"Well, don't take it out on her. Just kick him a little harder. We're professionals, you know."

"Leave him be, or I'll call for the town guard!" yelled Lyona. "I'll do it! You have no right to treat that boy like this!"

"Ohhhhh, *she'll call the town guard,*" enforcer three repeated mockingly. "Hey, guys, get a good look! It seems we have a heroine straight from the sagas standing before us. Interfering in Godwell business. And she's *going to call the town guard.* What to do, what to do . . ."

"The Godwells?" Lyona asked, stunned. "Anne?"

She thinks of me, Anne thought excitedly. *She remembers me as I remember her . . .*

"Mikus, don't go overboard," said enforcer two, in a voice that was half command, half plea. "Let's just collect this fool and leave."

"Yeah, we can do that," said enforcer three, or Mikus, as he was apparently named, as he drew a sword from the scabbard at his waist. "We can definitely do that." He then pointed his blade downward and plunged it into Samuel's leg. The boy screamed in agony as the blade easily slid into him.

"Oh, gosh, whoopsies!" continued Mikus. "Whomp-whomp-*whoooooomp.*"

"*By the gods,*" Lyona shrieked. She turned to run away, but Mikus easily caught her and dragged her by her hair to where Samuel lay screaming. "Do you see this, woman? Huh? Do you? I'm *sooo* curious."

"*Let me go, let me go, let me go,*" Lyona begged, sobbing. "Please stop this!"

"I will. I will. But first I want you to feel something. Look at that. Look at that," he said. He grabbed Lyona's wrist and squeezed it until the pain forced her to open her hand. Then he pressed her hand against the traitor's wounded leg and held it there until her palm was red with his blood. Then he grabbed her other hand and forced her to smear her hands together.

"Do you understand? Hmm? Do you get what that means?" he asked her.

"What? What does it mean?" she cried.

"Oh, you're so smart, I thought you could figure it out. *His blood is on your hands,*" he whispered into her ear. "All because you had to be a concerned citizen.

Hmm? Do you see what that gets you? Nothing but *shame*. You're a weak bit of nothing, woman. And now you know it. Don't ever forget your place. If you do, there's always room in the carriage for one more."

Behind Mikus, the other three lifted the screaming Samuel and threw him inside a sealed section of the carriage, slamming the doors behind him and locking it. Then he pushed Lyona to the ground, doing it so forcefully that her glasses flew off her face. Before he walked away, he stepped on them, grinding the lenses into utter ruin and shattering the silver frames.

"Oh, nuts. Sorry," he said.

He then entered the coach as it swiftly pulled away. The mirror faded out as Lyona lay there sobbing tears of humiliation and pain.

Pale as she was, Anne had slowly grown *paler* as she silently watched that confrontation. Her displeasure seemed to manifest into a foreboding chill that now saturated the atmosphere of the room.

"That was . . . remarkably intense," Sir Rustin said carefully.

"How long until they return?" Anne quietly demanded as she rose from her seat.

"Within three days, ma'am," Sir Rustin said.

"Contact Pride. Inform her that we've obtained the creature and are prepared to make good on our end of the bargain."

"Of course," Sir Rustin said with a bow.

"Have Mikus sent to my chambers as soon as they arrive. I would like to have a word with him about his behavior on duty."

"Y-yes, ma'am," Sir Rustin said reluctantly.

"You disapprove of my command?" Anne asked him.

"Mikus *was* serving your interests, great one," Rustin said.

"I shall take that into consideration before I begin flaying him," Anne coldly responded. Then she departed for her quarters, strangely elated to see that Lyona was alive and well, as well as furious for how she'd been treated by one of her own men.

"Power to the Godwells!" her men cried behind her.

This time, she didn't hear them, lost as she was in her thoughts.

Lyona.

CHAPTER TWENTY-FIVE

Bitter Pill

Anne's men made even better time than Rustin had anticipated. They arrived within two days, dragging in their prize.

Upon being received by her household, Samuel was quickly prepared for his interrogation. As he recovered from his journey, Anne set aside some time for a protracted conversation with her servant Mikus that began with him screaming in pain and ended with him screaming for mercy.

And then it simply ended.

Anne felt grateful for the distraction that punishing Mikus provided. She would soon be entertaining a guest whose proclivity for vengeance exceeded even her own, and while she would have denied feeling *anxious* about the visit, she wouldn't deny feeling mildly unsettled.

That was par for the course when one stood in the presence of one of the cardinal sins. The greatest of them, in fact.

"What did you think of that woman, Rustin?" she asked him on their way to the dungeons on the day of Pride's arrival. "The blond one that Mikus accosted."

"What woman?" he asked.

"The one who tried to prevent our acquisition of Mr. Bellweather," she said.

"Oh, the blond. Well, she had a courageous spirit, ma'am," Rustin replied. "To stand in valiant defense of another is no small thing. Especially against warriors bearing the sigil of the Godwells."

"Yes, I thought so too." Anne nodded in agreement. "She was so weak, yet so willing to defy her betters in pursuit of her ideals. She's always been like that. So . . . *spirited!* Don't you find it fascinating?"

"Do you know her, my lady? You speak of her with such familiarity."

"I do, in fact. Well, I *did*, anyway. For a time, we were quite close. She was a scholar of the old empire, and I funded much of her research. She was so intuitive, so quick to grasp concepts that escaped the notice of her peers! She had so much potential that was ignored by others due to her Republic heritage. I invited her to stay at my home for a season or two. I . . . wanted her to be near me."

"You speak so warmly of her," Rustin said with a smile. "Why did your friendship end? You sound as though you were close."

"We were," Anne said darkly. "Which was why my husband found it so amusing to steal her away from me. Marcis . . . likes taking away the things that I enjoy. He feels annoyed when my focus is placed on anyone other than him."

Rustin's eyes narrowed but he said nothing in response, knowing that his station did not permit him to offer an opinion on Count Van Belsar's behavior. But the stiffening of his body language was indication enough of his thoughts. Anne felt grateful for his loyalty.

"No worries, Sir Rustin. My days of being under my husband's compulsion are nearly at their end. Even now, the memories of the passion I once felt for him fade like a dream in the morning's light. It was a pleasure. But pleasure always fades."

"What do you intend to do to him?" asked her knight.

"We're just going to have a long conversation," she said. "When will Pride be joining us?"

"I'm not sure," Rustin said uneasily. "It's . . . *difficult* to stand in her presence, ma'am. Frightening, even. I spoke with her for at least ten minutes, but I can hardly remember what I said to her. Or what she even looked like, for that matter."

"Do you . . . still feel sane?" Anne asked him.

Rustin stared at her with widened eyes, clearly confused by her question. "Yes?" he said after a few moments had passed.

"Well, good," Anne said, satisfied by his response. "Most walk away from her feeling terrified and possibly suicidal. I myself couldn't meet her gaze until I was over three centuries old. It still isn't easy for me to speak with her in her true form."

"Then why did you have me do it?" Rustin asked her.

"I was rooting for you," Anne said confidently. "And now you're a proven winner."

Rustin smiled to himself, pleased by the compliment he'd received. Anne hadn't been flattering him either; he really had made a remarkable display of willpower by keeping his mind intact in the presence of Pride. Not that the representation he'd spoken with had been the actual Pride. Merely a hollowed-out vessel imbued with a portion of the cardinal sin's intellect, used to carry out her business in the mortal realm.

There were thousands of such beings across the world, each one just as startling to behold as the one that had come to visit Anne's house. Anne herself had beheld the creature on more than one occasion. Those moments had been memorable, but not ones she wished to repeat.

Pride could be a lot to take in.

"..."

"Sorry, did you say something?"

"I was saying that we were here, ma'am," Rustin said, gesturing toward the iron door they now stood before.

"Ah, and so we are," Anne said. "Sorry, Rustin. One of the consequences of an immortal life is how easily I can get lost in my thoughts. I have so *many* memories that I could easily find myself spending weeks sitting like a statue, lost in my recollections of the past. That's why I find your assistance so valuable, my friend. You help me remain in the here and now."

"A splendid honor that my family has enjoyed for centuries," Rustin said humbly.

"And one that I'm glad you've chosen to continue," Anne said with gratitude.

"Always and forever. Power to the Godwells."

Anne smiled at him.

Samuel slowly opened his eyes and saw naught but darkness.

He hung suspended in the air, naked, with his arms and legs splayed out, caught in some sticky substance he couldn't identify, which held him firmly in place. Helpless as a fly in a web. Anne sat on a stool in a corner of the room and quietly watched him as he regained his senses.

"Hello, Mr. Bellweather," she said after he finally noticed her. "Welcome to my home. I realize your present accommodation probably isn't as comfortable as you'd prefer, but a recent acquaintance of mine deemed it necessary for us to speak safely. So here we are."

Anne reached forth and gave Samuel an affectionate pat on the cheek. "You look so young. So remarkably human. You even smell like them. Whoever put you together did excellent work. At first glance, even I would be fooled. But the time I spent observing you while you were unconscious has gradually revealed the truth to me. The way you breathe, the steady rhythm of your heart, the way your muscles *shift*. It's a remarkable imitation, Samuel. But it's not quite authentic, is it?"

"Who are you? What do you want from me? What did I do?" Samuel moaned piteously. Anne had to laugh.

"He's incredible, isn't he?" Anne asked the other presence in the room. "An absolutely superb construction. My mother's journals described these creatures perfectly. So perfectly, in fact, I believed them to be an exaggeration. To see one in the flesh makes me realize how much more I have yet to learn."

"You speak truthfully, Countess Anne," said the slow, friendly drawl of a denizen of the southern continent. A pretty woman with curly brown hair, wearing a sleeveless white dress, stepped out of the shadows to stand beside Anne, bearing a friendly smile beneath her cute, freckled nose. "The hand of his maker is a skillful one. I'm glad you've brought this to my attention."

"I owed you a favor as well as an apology," Anne said. "Our friendship is an old one, after all."

"It certainly is!" Pride agreed. Still smiling, but not blinking. Staring intently at Samuel's struggling body.

"What's going on? Who are you people?" he asked with growing desperation.

"Oh, my apologies, Mr. Bellweather," replied Anne. "Allow me to introduce Pride, supreme ruler of the demon continent. Pride, this is Samuel Bellweather, servant and creation of the one who dared to strike at your family."

"So pleased to meet you, sir," Pride said with obvious insincerity. She stepped closer to the man and ran her finger slowly under his chin. "Oh, he's a healthy one, isn't he? Didn't you say he took a sword wound to the leg during his capture? I don't even see a scar."

"It healed within an hour. All his wounds did. My men had to keep severing the tendons of his limbs to prevent him from escaping. They found it annoying but weren't lax in their duties. Their efforts were appreciated."

"Incredible," Pride said admiringly. "A victim that never breaks. And you say I can have him?"

"You may. Take Acedia's mana cores with you, as well. Hopefully, with those in hand, you'll be able to speedily summon him back to your kingdom."

"I'm beyond grateful for your generosity, Anne," Pride said happily. "What would you like in return?"

"Two small things," Anne replied. "First, I would like you to forgive Claudia and Aiden for plotting against your brother. They were manipulated into their foolish behavior by their father, who sought, as always, to amuse himself."

"Ah," Pride said thoughtfully. "Marcis Van Belsar. He certainly is a notable lifelong hell raiser. But would he really go so far as to arrange the assassination of my kin?"

"Sloth was accidentally summoned into this world years before he was ready to return," Anne said apologetically. "Despite knowing of my professional relationship with you, Marcis thought it would be a wonderful idea to convince his children to dispose of him and present to me his mana cores. As a *gift*. Aiden and Claudia confessed to the entire misdeed. Thus, it now falls to me to make amends."

"Why would Marcis do such a thing?" asked Pride.

"He is wild. He always has been," Anne said.

"Yes, he is," Pride agreed. "I can find it within me to forgive Claudia. She's an ignorant child. She can learn from this, and with Sloth's mana cores on hand, restoring him to life will be a simple matter. Aiden is a different matter, though. He's already dead, you see."

"As if I could forget," Anne said bitterly, before wisely moderating her tone of voice. "I know your nature, ancient one," she continued. "Death is no protection from your grievance. If Aiden's soul lays in torment in your realm, I ask only that you release it to the astral realm."

Pride laughed, amused by Anne's words. "If I had his soul to release, I would. Aiden is beyond my reach, Anne. I know not where he dwells, but it isn't in the perdition of Pride. I swear it."

Anne frowned at the other woman's words. With any of the other cardinals, she would have been wary of being deceived. But Pride was, well, too *prideful* to bother telling an untruth. Lies were beneath the dignity of her throne.

"What could that possibly mean?" Anne wondered.

"Perhaps your son recanted his sins just before he was murdered?" Pride suggested. "It's been known to happen. Doesn't usually work, but there's the occasional genuine plea for redemption."

"That would be . . . nice," Anne said.

But she doubted Aiden had the strength of character to do such a thing. He never found fault with himself. It was his greatest flaw. Despite how hard she'd tried, Anne could never convince him to see his own flaws. The boy genuinely believed himself to be perfect.

Which was why she'd been so certain that he'd fall into Pride's hands upon dying.

Where was her son?

"What was your other request?" Pride asked her.

"Ah," Anne said, returning her thoughts to present matters. She gestured toward Samuel and said, "Peel back the layers of this creature's mind. The source that informed me of his existence made several claims that can only be corroborated by him. Share with me everything that he knows."

"Why is this so important to you?" Pride asked her.

"It should be important to you as well," Anne replied. "Despite his attempted mischief, Marcis is not the one whose machinations brought down your brother and his servants at Bremburg. A separate power intervened. A *necromancer*. A sorcerer of eld, somehow reborn into this modern age."

"They were our most persistent foes," Pride said with a frown. "In the dawning of this world, they were an unmatched power. Unstoppable. You can't just kill them, you see. For many of them, death was merely an awakening to their gifts. Destroying them required a *concerted* effort. We only succeeded when the din of our endless battle finally provoked the wrath of the lunar queen."

"The cataclysm," Anne said in awe.

"That was one of the words that described the event." Pride nodded. "It ended with the near extinguishment of their kind. The lunar queen does *not* appreciate being woken from her naps. To this day, I still can't believe the necromancers were arrogant enough to challenge her."

"Great power affects the way people perceive reality," Anne said. "Even the last of them, the radiant one, believed he would one day avenge his people against her. A *nation* of them, wiped from existence with a wave of her hand, but he still thought he could—"

"It wasn't with a wave of her hand," Pride corrected her. "They made their threats to her while she sat silently on her throne. She didn't even bother to gaze in their direction. She simply crooked her finger and one of the moons fell from orbit and landed on them."

"There were once two moons?" asked Anne.

"Yes."

"And you saw this happen in person?" Anne asked her.

"Yes. Our forces survived her displeasure because we were quick to kneel and apologize. Something the necromancers felt too *prideful* to do. Being in the presence of Queen Pasithea was the only time that I have ever felt small."

That was something that Anne had never known. Pride was the ruler of the cardinal sins. She had battled the necromancers at the height of their power and had even slain many of them in personal combat. For someone like *her* to proclaim another's superiority . . .

Well, that was just a very good reason to stay away from the moon, wasn't it?

"All the more reason we need to confirm my informant's information," Anne said decisively. "Necromancers are hopelessly insane and enamored with their own strength. The damage this one could do is unthinkable. It could even be in the realm of possibility for him to bring down another cataclysm on this world. A *final* one."

"That must not be allowed," Pride said in agreement. She then turned to Samuel and held his chin in a firm grip. "You will speak," she told him. "You will tell us *everything*."

"What are you *talking* about? I don't know what you mean! Please, just let me go!" Samuel whined.

Pride frowned at his words and tightened her grip. "Cease feigning ignorance, creature. My eye is upon you. I *know* what you are. You will submit to me. Your creator cannot save you now."

In response, Samuel Bellweather began to laugh.

"Is that right, you ridiculous relic of a bygone era?" he sneered. "You have no idea of whom you speak! The reach of my mistress is beyond compare! The world will be hers! Why should I submit to you when your heads will be the ones to roll at her feet?"

"*Her* feet?" Anne asked. "A woman?"

It suddenly occurred to Anne that this wasn't going to be very difficult at all. As amazing as this creature was, it appeared that his mind didn't quite match the quality of his body.

In other words, the boy was an absolute fool.

"She's a beauty beyond mortal comprehension!" Samuel raved. "A veritable angel of light! You shadowy monsters should drop to your knees in reverence, knowing that my flesh was sculpted by her divine hands, that my mind was pried into existence from the shores of death itself. Yet as perfect as I am, I am MERELY a secondhand reflection of her endless glory! Weep knowing that you can never compare to her!"

"Are . . . all of a necromancer's servants so enthusiastic in praising their creators?" Anne asked Pride.

The demon's weary sigh was answer enough. Then she said, "Get to the point, creature."

"The point?" Samuel said mockingly. "Fool! For you there *is* no point! No point in hoping for a continued existence! For my maker will surely come for you in order to punish you for your sin!"

"The sin of snatching away a forgotten tool like you?" Anne asked him.

Samuel roared in fury and struggled to reach her. He only settled down after Pride slapped his head back.

"You don't know anything!" he shouted at Anne. "My mistress adores all her creations! We stand at the pinnacle of existence! All of us are equal in her favor!"

"Oh, it's worse than I feared," Anne said sadly. "We wasted our resources capturing a mere drone. An unimportant worker bee. You don't know anything, do you, Samuel? You're just a microscopic cog in her catastrophic plan, aren't you?"

"NO! NO! I AM THE THIRD OF HER RISEN!"

"I have absolutely no idea what that means," Anne said in a bored tone of voice. "But I *do* know that third isn't first. Whatever purpose you were created for, you've already served it, haven't you? We may as well toss you aside like *she* obviously has."

"EVERLY WOULD NEVER DO THAT!" Samuel bellowed with a lunatic's certainty.

Pride grinned menacingly, pleased by Samuel's reaction. In her mirth, she didn't notice Anne's reaction to the boy's words.

"Everly?" Anne asked in a stunned voice. "Your creator's name is *Everly*?"

"Do not speak her holy name!" Samuel shrieked. "You're already dead, anyway!"

"Why?" Anne demanded to know. "Why am I already dead?"

"Because your brute abused her mother!" Samuel cackled triumphantly. "None may harm blessed Lyona! None may harm the mother of the Empress!"

Anne paused for a few moments and considered the creature's words. Then she turned to Pride and said, "The necromancer's name is Everly Vel Belsar. Another extended member of my household, I'm afraid. Marcis's *fourth* child."

"Anne, seriously," Pride said with genuine concern. "What exactly is going on in your life lately? This is . . . this is *terrible*. Is everything okay at home? I apologize if this sounds overly critical, but it seems that your children are out of control."

"She's not my daughter. I don't even know her," Anne said defensively. "She's the child of a . . . of a friend of mine and Marcis."

"He slept with your friend and impregnated her?" Pride said incredulously. "And you *stayed* with him?"

"Don't say it like that!" Anne said with tears in her eyes. "I wanted him to be happy, and I wanted *her* to be happy, and I just . . . I wanted to be happy as well! I'm fifteen hundred years old, and I always have to be everything for everyone, and my son got murdered, and *oh, my god*, the daughter of the woman I adore *killed my son and my granddaughter, and I'm just now realizing that in this very sentence, and it's all because MY HUSBAND IS A LYING, SELF-CENTERED, MURDERING BETRAYER, AND I REALLY DON'T NEED YOU TO BE JUDGMENTAL OF ME RIGHT NOW, OKAAAAAAY???!!"*

In response, Pride turned to her friend and gave her a firm hug.

"You're not the one to blame for this," she said.

"I'm not the one to blame for this," Anne sobbed.

"Your husband is a monster," Pride said.

"My husband *is* a monster," Anne cried.

"You need to settle this," Pride said.

"*There will be blood*," Anne vowed.

"Good," Pride said as she stepped back. "Do you want me to come with you?"

"No," Anne said as she wiped her eyes. "No, but thank you for offering. What comes next is between family."

"I understand," Pride said with a nod. "Do you need anything further from this creature?" she asked as she gestured at Samuel.

"No. No, he's already validated my informant. Not in the manner I expected, but everything checks out. I think I can trust whoever it is now. Feel free to take him."

"Thank you, Anne. You always settle your debts honorably," Pride said. "I'll have my people pack him up for shipment. Once I've finished stripping his mind of any remaining secrets, I'll share any relevant information with you."

"Thank you, Pride," Anne said. "You've always been a good friend to me."

"I'm obviously the best at everything I do," Pride said with no humility as she exited the room.

Anne laughed at that, amused despite her mood. Then she clenched her fists angrily as she returned her thoughts to today's horrifying revelations.

Marcis, she thought hatefully.

Everly.

CHAPTER TWENTY-SIX

Backstabber

Y ou know something bad is about to happen, right?" Fenn said as she sat beside Everly at the beach, leaning against the other girl on the bench they shared as they watched the sun setting over the ocean.

"Are you about to take some sort of supernatural revenge or something?" Everly asked as she squeezed the other girl's hand. "It makes sense. I did a pretty terrible thing when I killed you."

"You really did," Fenn agreed. "Thank you for apologizing."

"That wasn't an apology," Everly replied. "I'm just commenting on something that happened, that's all."

"God, you're still a hopeless mess, aren't you?" Fenn said with a roll of her eyes. "You could just admit you made a mistake and ask my forgiveness. An apology takes nothing but a little humility."

"Still bossing me around, I see," Everly snorted. "Well, I guess I'm glad to see that you've bounced back. Hey, how does one go about recovering from a broken heart, anyway?"

Fenn laughed at Everly's words as the evening breeze blew against the two of them, causing their hair to stir slightly in its passing. "I'll let you know whenever I experience it for myself, Blondie. I had a *crushed* heart, remember? *Yours* was the broken one."

Everly looked at her right hand and was unsurprised to see that it was once again stained red with bright, fresh blood. As she stared at it, the blood began to collect in her palm and then drip downward, staining the hem of the white dress she was wearing.

"Huh. I suppose you're right," she said. "Shoot, I thought this was going to be a fun dream."

"I'm enjoying myself," Fenn said as she leaned back against the bench with her hands behind her head. "Beautiful weather and the sound of gulls. I miss this. I mean, the company isn't very pleasant, but it's not like I'm hanging out with that dude who ran Miramax."

"Shut up, you love me," Everly retorted.

"Maybe I could have. Guess we'll never know," Fenn said quietly.

"Fuuuuck, I knew this was going to turn into a shaming session," groused Everly. "The ones who say they bear no grudges are the ones who hold the worst grudges of all. It's a fact."

"Well, since it's been brought up, why did you do it?" Fenn asked her after a few minutes had passed in silence. "That's probably a stupid question to ask, considering that I didn't know you very well. But I'd still like to know why."

"Does it even matter?" Everly asked her. "You're still dead."

"Call it peace of mind," Fenn said.

"I *did*," Everly said darkly. "That's exactly why I did it. For peace of mind. *My* peace of mind. We were soul linked, Fenn. I couldn't just have you out there being a vulnerability that anyone could take advantage of! I trained so hard to become strong—what right did you have to be an automatic win button on two legs?"

"So, I was an inconvenience to you, is that it?" Fenn said. "And for that reason alone, I had to go? Jesus. Well, at least you have the guts to say it to my face. You're an absolute chode, by the way."

"It wasn't *fair*," Everly said sullenly.

"Shouldn't that be my line?" Fenn retorted.

Everly crossed her arms and shut her eyes. She spent a few moments breathing sharply before centering herself enough to keep speaking.

"Fenn, you're not wrong to feel ill-used. If you hate me for what I did, then I welcome it. I'm not a coward. I won't hide behind any excuses," Everly said. "I wronged you. I'm not ashamed of it. I *refuse* to be ashamed of it."

"Really? Then why didn't you boast about your achievement? You killed the maiden of the holy sword, didn't you? Why not crow about it to the world?" Fenn asked her. "You keep saying you want to be the villain. Well, why not let everyone know what a megabastard you really are?"

Everly knew that this was just a dream. A remnant of the guilt that had been deliberately implanted in her by Discordia. Indulging it was a pointless exercise in self-recrimination. She didn't have to explain herself to anyone, much less a figment of her own imagination.

Even so, it angered her to be questioned. To have her motivations exposed and judged as though she were in court being cross-examined by the prosecution.

Ha! As if any prison existed that could hold her. No law could punish her. *She* was the one who decided which laws mattered.

Desperate to assert herself, to show this phantom that her words meant nothing to her, Everly turned toward Fenn and pushed her off the bench to the ground, then jumped over her to pin her in place.

They stayed in that position for a while, staring at each other.

"Did I touch a nerve?" Fenn asked her.

"Knock it off, okay?" Everly commanded the dead girl.

"You're dialing the wrong number, Blondie. Customer service is the other department."

"I SAID stop it!" Everly shouted before slapping the girl across the face as hard as she could.

Fenn frowned angrily at her. Then she lifted one of her hands, placed its palm against Everly's chest, and shoved her so forcefully that she was sent flying backward down the beach to crash heavily into the sand.

"I'm *not* your victim anymore, Blondie," Fenn said sourly as she rose to her feet. "You stupid, arrogant little bully. I'm here doing you a favor, but you still can't stop trying to control everything around you! Why are you like this?!"

"How did you do that?" Everly asked as a strange mixture of surprise and unease began churning within her. "This is my mind. Nothing should be able to harm me here."

"Is that what you think?" Fenn spat. "God, you really are full of unwarranted confidence."

Everly stared at the other girl, who in turn stared back fearlessly. She clenched a frustrated fist and was the first to break eye contact. "Fuck this. This isn't real. This is cheap dollar-store melodrama. You aren't real. I'm just fucking with my own mind."

Fenn sighed in annoyance before irritably kicking a clump of sand in Everly's direction. "For god's sake, Everly. Someone is coming after you! Someone who can hurt you *badly*. It's a freakin' miracle that I'm able to reach out and warn you, but how does the great wannabe Empress respond? By trying to shoot the messenger! You suck so much it's making my head hurt!"

"Fenn, you're not a damn ghost, okay?" Everly yelled at her.

"Everly, I swear to god, I really want to punch you in your stupid face right now," Fenn said darkly. "Fuck! We're on a gorgeous beach, we're rocking these awesome matching sundresses, and I was *just* about to forgive you for being a self-centered murderer, but *no*, you just had to ruin it. Why does this surprise me, though? Your nature is to ruin *everything*, isn't it?"

"You were going to forgive me?" Everly asked her in surprise.

"Past tense, Everly! You fucking blew it!" Fenn shouted at her.

"Fenn, how can you be so stupid?" Everly asked her. "I *murdered* you. You were an obstacle, so I swept you off the board! You're not supposed to forgive me, you're supposed to vow vengeance! You're—you're supposed to crawl from your grave and seek *justice*! You're supposed to be the hero! Why are you doing *everything* wrong?"

Fenn was stunned. Now it was her turn to compose herself before speaking.

"Everly," she said as calmly as she could. "Do you mean to say that you expected me to return to life, just so we could have a . . . a sword fight or something?"

"YES!" Everly shouted. "Yes! And I waited for you for *months*! Why didn't you come back, Fenn? Why'd you leave me alone? We're supposed to be bonded!"

"You . . . you really didn't care about killing me, did you?" Fenn said with dawning realization.

"Oh, my god, Fenn, *noooo*. We already covered that! That was just Discordia being a pill!"

"God DAMN IT. You suckered me again," Fenn said bitterly. "I'm freakin' dead. I don't need this shit. I could just hang out in paradise, eating nectarines and watching *Real Housewives*. I could be taking guitar lessons from Hendrix. I could ask Kurt if Courtney had anything to do with it. I could be doing ANYTHING AT ALL except THIS. Do you know how many rules I broke manifesting here, trying to give you a heads-up, you psychotic Barbie?!"

"Nope," Everly said bluntly.

"You DUMBASS! I'm only supposed to pass warnings on to the worthy! Somebody heroic and just! Not some . . . not some fucking NECROMANCER!"

"Stop yelling at me! I find it triggering!" Everly shouted at her.

"*Triggering?* I got shot to death because of you, *pendeja*!"

"I'm waking up. I'm waking up *right now*," Everly said angrily. "If you want to have a *real* conversation without any of this pointless blaming and yelling, just let me know, okay? I'll be sitting in the adult section."

"Everly, don't you fucking move a step! Don't you dare!" Fenn shouted while furiously pointing a finger at her.

"Sorry, can't hear what you're saying, too busy returning to the real world, byeeeeee," Everly said as she slowly faded from sight.

Fenn couldn't believe she'd done it.

"Oh, you *biiiiiiiiiitch*," she growled.

A few moments later, Everly awoke in her bedchamber inside her memory palace, lying on top of her sheets in her nightgown. To her surprise, across from her on the bed, with her head resting atop her hand, Fenneth lay glowering at her.

To her amusement, Everly saw that Fenn was now bluish white and translucent.

"Everly, what you just did was gaslighting," Fenn said through gritted teeth.

"I don't think I've ever met a successful person who used terms like that," said Everly.

"You're doing it again," Fenn said.

"Fenn, is there anything happening with you that I should know about? I feel like all we ever do lately is fight," replied Everly.

"Hey, stupid!" Fenn shouted again. "Someone that you trust is about to ruin your life and kill you, and we are absolutely never going to see each other again because your ass is *totally* getting dragged into the Netherrealm, and you know what? I'm fine with it. I'm fucking *fine with it!*"

"Ha! *Now* who's the one who's lost it?" Everly giggled. "My people love me, Fenn. I am their sun and moon and *Special Pikachu Edition.*"

"Everly, please, just listen to me," Fenn pleaded. "You're going to die! There are forces being arrayed against you, and you can't fight them all alone—"

"Discordia!" Everly suddenly shouted.

A moment later, Discordia appeared in the bedroom. "How may I serve you, mistress?" she reluctantly asked Everly.

"Check it out," Everly said as she pointed a finger at Fenn. "Your dead loser of a former mistress is hanging around trying an Obi-Wan gambit. Pretty sad, isn't it?"

Discordia ignored Everly's words and turned incredulously to face her former partner. "Lady Fenneth?" she asked uncertainly.

"Hey, Dee," Fenn said gently as she climbed off Everly's bed. "It's been a little while, huh? How are you doing?"

"Lady Fenneth!" Discordia repeated. She ran to her former mistress and threw her arms around the other girl, sobbing as she did so. "Is it you? Is it really you?"

"Obviously, silly," Fenn said as she ran her hand down the crying elemental's hair. "Hey, don't be like that. It looks like we were right! Not even death could keep us apart."

"I'm so sorry," Discordia continued to weep. "I tried so hard to do as you would have me do. To survive and keep your memory alive. But I put my own selfish desire for revenge ahead of your wishes, and now I've been enslaved by your enemy."

"No, Discordia, it's *my* fault for not realizing how important you were to me until we were separated forever," Fenn said sorrowfully.

"But Lady Fenneth, how are you here right now? How is it that I speak to you? Hold you? What makes this miracle possible?" Discordia asked in wonder.

"I can't really say. Maybe I'm coming back soon, Dee," Fenn said with a tear-smudged smile. "Haven't you ever read a Marvel comic? The heroes never stay dead for long. Not when there's evil to be fought and profits to be reaped by a huge corporation!"

"Those stories you speak of are creatively bankrupt," Discordia said miserably. "But if their example could one day reveal a path for you to return to me, then I will pray feverishly for that to happen."

"Hey, anything's possible, right?" Fenn said as she squeezed her old friend tightly. "All we can do is hope."

"YAAAAAWN," interjected a bored Everly. "This is *way* too wholesome. Discordia, get out of here."

"Please, mistress. Let me have a just a little longer with her," Discordia begged.

"Permission denied. Get lost, I said," Everly said coldly.

Discordia's face snapped toward Everly, and now, in addition to her tears, her eyes blazed with fierce anger. "When will you tire of hurting us?" she asked.

"I dunno," Everly smirked. "When does it start getting boring?"

Fenn opened her mouth to say something when suddenly, a voice cut into their conversation. It was Titania. *EVERYLY! Everly, I'm sorry! Everly, I'm sorry, I've failed you! Please forgive me. I've failed you!* The voice of the elemental shouted painfully into her mind. It was filled with fury and grief, as well as fear. Everly had never heard Titania sound like that before.

"Titania, calm down!" she ordered. "Settle yourself! What's wrong?"

Everly, I'm so sorry. I don't know how they did it, but someone has her. Someone has Lyona!

"What? What did you just say?" asked Everly with a stunned voice.

Everly, someone has taken Lyona . . .

"THEN GET HER BACK!" Everly shrieked with unhinged fury.

Someone had touched her mother.

Someone was going to *die*.

CHAPTER TWENTY-SEVEN

Surprise!

E verly, please don't rush in blindly," Fenn begged as Everly donned her armor hurriedly and prepared to step through a gate in the tower that would take her to Anders, where Lyona dwelled.

"Shut up," Everly said after pulling her cloak over her shoulders. "I don't need to hear a damn thing from you right now."

"Everly, don't be stupid. This is what I tried to warn you about! It's an ambush! Your betrayer *wants* you to rush in recklessly."

"Then tell me who it is," Everly said, turning sharply to face her. "Who turned on me? How are they doing this? More importantly, WHY didn't you warn me sooner?"

"Everly, I don't know who it is," Fenn said. "It's hard to describe. I can't *see* the future; I can only interpret it. I don't know the specifics of what's to come, only the shape. I know you're facing true betrayal. I know that you're in genuine danger, but I don't know any more than that."

"Then how do you know that this is a part of it?" Everly asked her.

"I don't. I just know that this feels *wrong*," Fenn said.

"So, in other words, you're useless! Big help, Fenn. Thanks *so* much."

"Everly, I'm trying to protect you . . ."

"And you've failed miserably!" Everly shouted at her. "Go back to paradise, choir girl. Go sing some hymns and hosannas with the rest of the ignorant cherubs, and let the living sort out their own shit!"

"Fine," Fenn whispered. "I hope you succeed for your mother's sake," she said in parting as she began to fade from sight.

"Hope is for the rabble, Fenn. I don't need it," Everly said as she willed a gateway into existence and stepped through it.

Before her, Everly saw Anders burning. Her childhood home, the place where she had spent so many happy years with Lyona, dreaming of the future to come. Of adventures and misdeeds, and idle fantasies. Long afternoons she'd spent alone wandering the woods, and the evenings she'd shared with her mother.

It was a good life. Quiet and joyful. Until the moment she saw it being destroyed, Everly had never realized just how much she'd loved this place. Anders had once been her home. Now it was gone.

All because of her.

But wait . . . That was exactly the wrong sort of mentality, wasn't it? How was any of this *her* fault? She wasn't the one who'd lit the torch. She wasn't the one who'd put all the villagers to the sword. She wasn't the one who had taken Lyona. Some other force was at play here. An outside party whose actions she hadn't directed. *They* were the ones responsible for this outrage, not her. She was the one who'd been wronged here!

What had she ever done to deserve something like this?

"Mother!" Everly yelled as she ran through the burning streets, ignoring the bodies of so many people she'd known. "Mother!" she called out again as she reached her family home, relieved to see it untouched by the fires that raged throughout Anders.

Everly smashed the door open and stepped into the den. A cozy room, where she'd spent so many idle days reading and playing games with her uncle, Tybalt, and her cousin, Alden.

Why was this happening?

"Mother, are you here?" Everly shouted as she raced to her mother's bedroom and found it empty. Undeterred, she ran back downstairs to Lyona's personal office and pushed the door open. This time, although the room was dark and still, Everly sensed another presence.

"Mom?" Everly said in voice heavy with uncertainty.

"Close," a woman's gentle voice replied. "Close, but not quite."

A match was struck and applied to a lamp on the desk, revealing the pale, beautiful face of a redhaired woman dressed in simple forester's garments. The woman sat at Lyona's desk with perfect stillness, motionlessly gazing directly at Everly with unblinking pale eyes.

"You must be Everly," the intruder said. "What a lovely face you have. A perfect blending of the two people I have loved and hated more than anyone else in recent memory. It's haunting in a way. It's as though you were crafted by the gods themselves to mock me. I really don't know how to feel about that."

"I don't care about your issues," Everly said bluntly. "Give me my mother."

"I care who *you* are, Everly," the woman replied. "I care very much. You've taken away the ones that I love, and you've raised havoc across the kingdom I've spent centuries nurturing and defending. Why have you *done* these awful things, I wonder? What joy could you possibly derive from hurting so many people?"

"I don't have to explain myself to anyone," Everly told her. "Tell me where my mother is! Do it now, or the next to suffer will be you."

"You're just like Marcis," the woman said sadly. "How is that possible? Are these inherited traits? You've had nothing to do with each other for most of your life, but you're just as unprincipled and selfish as he is. Is this an example of nature over nurture?"

"I *have* principles," Everly insisted. "There are lines I choose not to cross."

"But family clearly isn't one of them," the woman snorted. "Tell me how it felt when you crushed your brother's head between your hands. When you pulled his cousin's heart from her chest with your bare hand. How did it feel to revel in murder?"

"You're her, aren't you?" Everly said as realization came to her. "You're Anne, my father's first wife."

"Yes, I am," Anne said with a slight nod. "Would you please answer my question?"

"How did it feel to kill your worthless son?" Everly asked as she stepped closer to the other woman and loomed over her. "You really want to know?"

"I do," Anne whispered.

"Well, Anne. I'll be honest. It felt like apple pie at a picnic," Everly sneered. "It was amazing, and my deepest regret was that I could only do it once. Listening to Aiden die while his skull cracked beneath my fingers was a joy. A joy I'll gladly repeat with you if you don't tell me where my mother is at once," she warned.

"Just like your father," Anne repeated softly to herself.

"WHERE IS MY MOTHER—" Everly began to shout when another quieter voice cut her off.

"Everly," wept Lyona. "Everly, you've killed people?"

Everly spun around in confusion. At first, she was elated to see that her mother was alive and unharmed. But that feeling of relief was slowly replaced with a growing sensation of dread when she realized that her mother had heard every word that she'd said.

"Mom?" she said as she desperately tried to think of a way to explain her words.

"They're all dead," Lyona said numbly. "Everyone in the village is dead. Anne said it was a justified reprisal. She said you've butchered your way across the countryside. She said you were a monster. Everly, it isn't true, is it? Everly, you haven't done the things she says you have, have you?"

"I've never told a lie, Lyona," Anne said to her. "Not once in my life and especially not to you. Everly isn't human. She's a nightmarish aberration. A terror of the old world; something that has no right to exist in this age. You know of what I speak."

"No," Lyona whimpered.

"I'm afraid so," Anne said softly. "Everly, there was a time when I would have simply killed Lyona, if only to offer you a small sampling of the misery I've felt since the day I learned of what you did to my loved ones. But your mother once bravely rebuked me for extending my punishments to the innocent. She taught me that no one should ever die for the sins of their family. Over time, I came to realize the truth of her words and have adjusted my behavior accordingly."

"You still killed everyone in the village!" Everly said heatedly.

"I did," Anne agreed. "But what choice did I have other than to purge this place? You murdered and replaced Samuel Bellweather with an inhuman replicant. An act you could have repeated with anyone else you've encountered during your long stay in this village. I know about Alec of the Eastern Temple."

"You know about who?" Everly asked her.

"My informant masked our presence from your earth elemental servant," Anne said. "We've retrieved him and have him hidden away. His recovery will take awhile. The poor man's trauma was extreme, but I've vowed to do everything I can to help him."

"Wow," Everly said bitterly. "Wow, wow, wow. You're really spilling the tea on everything I've done, aren't you, Anne? You really had to go out of your way to make me look bad in front of my mom, didn't you?"

"I just wanted her to understand the necessity of what I must now do," Anne said as she rose from her chair.

"She won't remember any of this," Everly said confidently. "I'm going to kill you and rearrange her memories. We'll say it was an attack by bandits and I luckily managed to arrive in time to save her."

"Everly," Lyona said in a pleading tone. Then she grew limp and fell, but before she hit the floor, Everly caught her and gently laid her down.

"Relax, Mom. This was all a meaningless nightmare. Soon enough, you're going to be proud of me again," Everly assured the sleeping woman.

"As for you, witch," Everly said as she turned to face Anne. "Now you get to learn just who you've been messing with—"

Anne's slap sent Everly smashing through the sturdy brick wall of her home like a human missile. As Everly crashed outside onto the lawn, Anne followed her out through the opening she'd made. As Everly struggled to get to her feet, Anne threw a punch that connected painfully with her midsection, forcing the air from her lungs.

As Everly sagged and fell forward, Anne stepped into her personal space, gripped her hair tightly, and pulled her head back to stare intensely into her eyes.

"You were saying?" she asked the girl.

Everly grinned wickedly at the older woman. "Well, look at that! Looks like Grannie Annie came to play."

Anne smashed her forehead into Everly's nose. Then she launched the girl into the air and sent her smashing through a neighbor's fence.

"You're powerful, Everly. I can feel it," Anne said in a conversational tone as she followed after her. "But it's plain to me that you've never really been challenged before, have you? Too many easy victories can lead to overconfidence. And overconfidence has been the downfall of many a proud warrior."

In response, Everly summoned her sword to her hand and slashed wildly at Anne's midsection, intending to catch her off guard. Instead, Anne avoided the blow by kicking upward with her right leg. Everly's great sword was so wide that it allowed Anne to easily connect with the ball of her foot against the flat of the blade to knock it out of her hands. Before Everly could recover, Anne next kicked her in the face and sent her flying backward once more.

"Your sword's width is a pointless display of ego," Anne said disdainfully. "Being able to wield such a thing is no display of expertise. To a true master, it's a childishly ostentatious toy."

"Shut up," Everly growled.

"Why don't you make me?" Anne wondered. "You're *so* powerful. You tower over the world with the confident gait of a giant. You're a monarch. An empress. *The* Empress! It should be the easiest thing in the world to silence me."

"You think I can't!" Everly shouted.

"Little girl, I *dare* you to try," Anne said to her.

Everly seethed at Anne's confident expression. Holding out her hand, she recalled her sword and soon gripped it once more. Then she settled into a deep stance while holding her weapon with both hands, waiting for Anne to attack.

Anne smiled at Everly, then began clenching her fingernails tightly into the palms of both hands while squeezing forcefully. Blood began dripping from each wound, a thick red surge of it that quickly shaped itself into the forms of two crimson-colored swords, both of which Anne now wielded.

Then, she ran toward Everly, who met her charge with a mighty swing of her own, her weapon clashing against Anne's blades with all the power she could muster.

"You have an interesting form," Anne said as they fought. "It appears to be a variant of the Imperial style. A highly personalized one, as well. I wonder who taught you?"

"None of your business," said Everly.

"I like to keep track of the variants of the styles I've created," Anne informed her.

"The style *you* created?" Everly asked in confusion.

"Indeed. I founded the top three schools of swordsmanship that are widely practiced throughout the kingdom and its neighboring countries," Anne said casually. "Didn't you know? I was the original maiden of the holy blade. I've never been defeated in a duel."

"There's a first time for everything, Grandma," Everly said as she brought her heavy sword down at Anne's skull, only for both of Anne's swords to stop it midswing by catching it in an X-crossed block.

"I agree, Everly. I learn new things every day," said Anne. "I'm actually looking forward to the moment when I'll finally experience defeat. Because on that day, I'll finally be able to set aside my many burdens."

Anne's foot lashed out in a sweep that knocked Everly's feet from beneath her. As Everly landed painfully on her back, Anne jumped forcefully onto the flat of Everly's sword, using her weight to push the weapon down and hold Everly in place long enough for her to drive her twin swords through both of the younger woman's shoulders, pinning her to the earth.

"It doesn't appear that day has arrived, however," Anne lamented.

Everly couldn't respond. The pain she was now experiencing made it impossible for her to form words.

Anne nodded in sympathy. Then she lifted Everly's massive sword and carefully examined it. "What a ridiculous thing," she said scornfully. "Like something out of a fable. There really is such a thing as having too much style over substance, Everly."

Having said that, she turned the blade over and plunged it into Everly's midsection.

Now Everly began to howl in anguish.

"It's frustrating, I know," Annie said as she knelt beside the helpless girl. "We . . . carry within our hearts these vivid fantasies of who we wish to be. Sometimes we even convince ourselves that those fantasies are who we truly *are*. But when our weaknesses are exposed and we have nothing left to show for our dreams except disappointment and humiliation, that can be a humbling moment."

Anne stared blankly at Everly's shuddering form. A red haze was beginning to overtake her vision as she stared at Everly's throat, mesmerized by the rapid throbbing of the artery beneath its skin.

"I hate what I'm about to do to you," she whispered into the girl's ear. "But I'm so grateful that this is a moment we'll both experience together. I wonder if your father really loves you. I hope that he does."

"Fuck you," Everly said defiantly. "Fuck. *You.*"

Anne smiled, amused by the girl's defiance.

"I want to see if something within your father breaks when he sees what's become of you, the same way that I broke when I saw what you did to Aiden and Fenneth. I realize this is nothing but petty vengeance, Everly. I know the dead can't hear me. *But I don't care.* You hurt my family and now you'll die for it. It's what you deserve."

Anne brought her lips to Everly's throat and kissed it tenderly. Then she opened her mouth and prepared to sink her teeth into Everly's neck, anticipating the taste of the warm blood that would soon flood forth onto her tongue.

Suddenly, a boot lashed out and caught Anne across her face, knocking her away from her victim. Anne quickly returned to her feet, infuriated by the interference. Then she stared in surprise at the one now standing between her and Everly.

"Dearest, if it's me you're feeling upset with, I wish you'd say so. It doesn't feel quite right to take it out on the children," Count Marcis Van Belsar said with an infuriating smirk.

"Marcis . . . how did you get here?" Annie asked him with a brittle voice.

"I *really* have no idea," Marcis said. "There I was, sitting alone at home, preparing to enjoy my evening meal, when a glowing doorway popped up in the middle of my study. Out from which sprang one of Everly's little duplicates, who began begging me for my assistance."

"Which one?" Anne asked darkly.

"Oh, I can hardly tell them apart. Nev or Bev, or something to that effect. She was quite panicked. Although they could feel her pain, something was preventing Everly's team from rushing to her side. Even dear old Louie couldn't intervene. Their next best solution was to send *me* of all people."

He turned to examine Everly and clucked his tongue. "And I can see why. Your blood still has that nasty effect on mages, I see." He coughed abruptly and then spat in disgust. "And I also see that you've been discreetly saturating the air with it. Quite unsporting, dear."

"I'm not here to play games, husband," Anne said. "I'm here to pass judgment. You will not interfere with my vengeance."

"And yet, here I am," Marcis said chirpily. "Funny how that works, yes?"

"That girl killed our child. She killed Fenneth as well."

"Yeeeeah, what a scamp," Marcis chuckled.

"I am not amused," Anne seethed.

"I didn't think you would be," he said.

Marcis knelt beside Everly and began pulling the swords out of her.

"*Marcis,*" Anne hissed.

"At least let me speak to her before you kill us both, Anne. It's a small thing I ask, isn't it?"

Anne said nothing but glared silently at them both.

Marcis gently laid his hand on his daughter's forehead and sighed.

Hey, Everly. Not having a very good night, are you, sweetie?

Everly groaned and tried to say something in response, but Marcis hushed her before continuing to project his thoughts.

I wish you hadn't come here in such a huff, kid. I could have warned you that Anne would be a terrible match for you. She's a vampire, which I'm positive you've already figured out. An extremely old one too. It's not a well-known fact, my angel, but her kind are capable of negating magic through their blood. Like rubber defying electricity. Combine that cheat with her great experience in battle and . . . well, I guess you're already feeling the results for yourself.

Everly moaned angrily in response.

Listen, angel, Marcis continued. *I can draw power from Anne's emotions, but the second I try to use it against her, she'll tear me apart. That's why instead I'm projecting the power into you. Can you feel it?*

. . . Yes, Everly managed to say to him.

Good, Marcis said, pleased. *Use it to open another one of those gateways. It's the only way out.*

. . . Dad, Everly said to him, now feeling genuinely touched. *Oh, Dad, are you really going to sacrifice yourself so that I can escape?*

Uh, what? Marcis asked with genuine confusion. *Sweetie, please don't be stupid. Just make a gate large enough for us both.*

What about Mother?

Everly! cut in another voice. *Everly, it's me, Bev! Listen, as long as you stay focused and in control, I can gate in and grab Lyona, okay? Leave it to me!*

Sounds like we have a plan, Marcis said.

"What are you doing?" Anne asked warily. "What are you plotting?"

Oh, fuck-sticks, I really hope you're both prepared, Marcis said with a rising panic that he managed to keep off his face.

I am. I am, Everly said. *Whenever you're ready.*

Great, great, Marcis said. *Well, in that case,* "HOW ABOUT NOW?" he suddenly shouted as he grabbed one of Anne's swords and sent it spinning toward her head.

Anne dodged the surprise attack easily but was enraged by the attempt on her life. "Marcis, you BASTARD!" she yelled before leaping at him with murder in her eyes.

"Everly forced me to do it. I'm a victim of circumstances!" he squealed in response.

A bare second before her fingers reached his throat, a gateway opened beneath his feet, sending him and Everly tumbling into the memory palace, to safety.

"Ohhhh, Marcis, that was a close one," he muttered to himself before collapsing to the ground in relief. "By the gods, I need to stop flicking dragons on their nostrils."

"So brave, Daddy. So very, very brave," Everly said sarcastically.

"Shut up, you love me," replied her father.

A moment later another gateway split open, and Beverly came racing in, bearing Lyona in her arms. "I got her! I got her!" she shouted excitedly. "I *told* you I could do it."

"Why, so you did," Marcis said proudly.

Lyona slowly stirred awake and looked around her surroundings in confusion. Then she noticed Marcis smiling at her.

"Marcis?" she said.

"Hey," he replied. "It's been a while, hasn't it? You look good."

"Thanks?" she said.

"Just calling it like I see it," he said smugly.

"Where is everybody?" Everly asked as she crawled painfully to her feet.

"Carter and Nev are still in the capital," Bev said as she scratched her head. "Grail is at the border, leading raids against the forts. And the elementals are . . . well, they're kind of bugging out. Like something's been interfering with them, somehow."

"The traitor," Everly said grimly.

"There's a traitor?" Bev asked in alarm.

"Um, am I safe here?" Marcis asked in a semiserious manner.

"Wait," said Everly suddenly. "Where's Cleverly at?"

"You named one of your mirror selves *Cleverly*?" Marcis asked his daughter with a raised eyebrow.

"Dad, there aren't a lot of words that rhyme with my name, okay?" Everly said defensively while they began searching for the missing duplicate.

"Uh, found her," Bev called out a few minutes later. "Oh, man, this isn't good . . ."

In the meeting hall, hanging above the table, was poor Cleverly.

She was dead, with a spear thrust through her throat, pinning her to the wall.

"Well, shit," said Everly. "There goes my Four Horsemen motif, huh?"

The others silently agreed.

CHAPTER TWENTY-EIGHT

Loser

Okay, no need to panic," Bev said in a quavering voice as she slowly felt the urge to panic rise within her. "Apparently, one of us has gone off the deep end and is now murdering us! Luckily, since we know it isn't me, and we know it isn't Everly, we can go ahead and blame Nev for this! I never liked that cow anyway! You could always tell she was plotting something. Between me and you guys, she *always* gave off a slight hint of barely restrained madness."

"She's your best friend," Everly said to her in a neutral tone of voice.

"And now I'm throwing her under the train!" Bev said proudly without an ounce of remorse.

"And how exactly do we know that you weren't responsible for this?" asked Everly. "Couldn't you have just killed Cleverly *before* rescuing my mother? It's not like we have a time of death to go by."

"Of course I could have!" Bev said boastfully. "I'm a very capable person."

"You're supposed to deny wanting her dead, dummy," Everly said with exasperation.

"I mean, I kind of did, though? Cleverly was such a little brat! Always taking my stuff without asking and hiding behind your skirt whenever I wanted to stomp on her a little. I think it's great that she's gone."

"Bev, you're supposed to be coming up with reasons for us *not* to further suspect you. I really feel like you're just messing with me right now," Everly said without humor.

"What? NO! Everly, come on, we both know I'm not smart enough to try to get away with this. I'm more instinctual than calculating. I'm telling you, Nev's the culprit!"

"Or," said Marcis, "you could be weaponizing your stupidity to fly under the radar by being so utterly obvious about things that no one would bother suspecting you. After all, people are conditioned by popular entertainment to believe that murderers have clever and complex minds. Being a genuine simpleton would catch almost anyone off guard."

"See!" Bev said happily. "Dad gets it!"

"He just said he finds you highly suspicious, genius," Everly sighed.

"What? DAAAAD!" Beverly whined.

"Now, now, I was just making an observation," Marcis said soothingly as he offered Bev a comforting hug, which she quickly accepted.

Not for the first time, Everly wondered how Bev had turned out this way. When she'd originally had the idea of duplicating herself to decrease her workload, while more easily implementing her master plan for the conquest of the kingdom, she'd assumed that her creations would all be like her. Perfect. Their annoyingly quirky personalities were a completely unforeseen development, and one that she was quickly growing frustrated with. The only one of them she'd been able to consistently rely on had been Nev, but even she had been making too many unilateral decisions lately. Making her own little criminal empire and giving herself a boyfriend. Who'd given her permission to do any of that?

And now, one of them had well and truly lost the plot and was making a bid for true independence. Honestly, Everly didn't doubt for a moment that it was Nev. Treachery took brains, and Bev was light in that department. But why? Everly hadn't been unjustifiably cruel to any of them! Didn't they all have fun together? Why were things getting so aggravatingly complicated?

Why wouldn't everyone just shut up and do what she wanted them to?

"Neverly?!" said the uncertain voice of a young man dressed in a bathrobe as he entered the room. Ah. Speaking of the *boyfriend*, here he was in the flesh: Tyler, Nev's pet project, looking confused and fearful, dressed only in a short white bathrobe as he stumbled toward the group and saw them all gathered around Cleverly's dead body.

"By the gods! Oh no, oh no, did she find out?" he asked in a quaking voice.

"Tyler?" asked Bev in confusion. "Uh, what are *you* doing here?"

"Everly, despite this being your secret base of operations, I'd be neglectful in my duty as your father if I didn't inform you that your palace doesn't seem to be very secure," Marcis said to her chidingly.

Everly gritted her teeth at his words. "Dad, would it kill you to stop being a gadfly for five minutes while we try to get this sorted?"

"It wouldn't," Marcis admitted. "But I really don't want to."

"That's great. Good to know," Everly said before turning to face Tyler. "Well? Answer the question, loverboy! Why are you here when Nev isn't? And why aren't you wearing any clothes?"

"Um, that is to say, uh, that I was invited, I mean ordered to, but not like, uhhh," Tyler said desperately while his head kept turning toward Cleverly's body before pulling away, only to turn back toward it, as though he were trying to confess to something while denying it at the same time.

That was when Everly noticed that Cleverly was also wearing a white robe, which perfectly matched Tyler's.

"Oh, *come on,*" she said in disgust.

"I didn't want to. She made me!" Tyler cried.

"Oh, *Tyler*," Marcis said with a hint of genuine empathy. "Trust me, my lad. That excuse almost *never* works!"

"I'm serious! She and Nev hated each other!" Tyler said to Everly. "Nev was always going on about what a useless brat Cleverly was and how the group didn't need her! Cleverly wanted to pay her back, so she snatched me away into the tower! I swear, I didn't want to go, but you know how . . . *you* can be! I didn't have a choice."

"Well, that *is* true," Everly and Beverly said thoughtfully.

"It is! It really is!" Tyler said. "I didn't want anything to do with her."

"I can't say I approve of you going along with the whims of my daughter, overbearing or not," Marcis said with a frown. "She wasn't even of age."

"She didn't want me to bed her!" Tyler said, speaking even quicker than before. "She just wanted me to lie *with her* in bed! Neverly's bed to be specific. Cleverly was going to call her and show me with her in Nev's room, that was all."

Everly had to give her deceased duplicate some credit. *That* was a pretty evil move right there.

"Damn, I've got to give Cleverly some credit. *That* was a pretty evil move right there," said Bev with grudging respect.

"Hey, shut up! I already had that thought," Everly glowered.

"Whoops! My bad," apologized Beverly.

"So, I guess Neverly took the bait and must have overreacted," said Marcis. "Well, she wouldn't be the first girl to ever kill her sister over a boy. It's an old story. One told countless times throughout history." He then turned to Tyler and asked, "Is that how it happened, boy? Neverly walked into her room, witnessed you both, and then dragged Cleverly away to punish her?"

"That doesn't make any sense," Everly cut in.

"Why not?" asked her father.

"Well, for starters, Cleverly was still one of *me*. I wouldn't just let myself get snatched away. I'd put up a nasty fight. But we don't see any signs of that around here. That means Cleverly was taken by surprise. Something else to consider is *him*," she said as she pointed a finger at Tyler.

"Huh?" Tyler asked.

"Why would Nev let you live? In the heat of the moment, if I thought you'd betrayed me, you'd be the first one I'd annihilate. And yet, here you are, safe and sound and walking around naked in my crib. That's pretty unlikely, Tyler. What else haven't you told us?"

"Nothing!" he insisted. "I swear! Except just before Cleverly put the call out, someone knocked on the door. After she went to speak with whomever it was, she was gone for a while, and that was when I came looking for her and found all of you."

"Hmm," Everly said to herself as she considered the evidence laid out before her.

"What's she doing?" Beverly wondered.

"Shh," said Marcis. "Let her think."

After giving everything a few minutes of serious consideration, Everly nodded to herself, satisfied by the conclusion that she'd arrived at.

"All righty, everyone. In a situation as serious as this, I've decided there's only one thing I can do to get things under control."

"What's that?" Bev asked eagerly.

"Yes, daughter. Do share," Marcis said as he stepped closer to listen better.

"I'm going to *delegate*!" Everly said decisively. She then turned and snatched Lyona's hand before saying to the others, "My mother and I are going to barricade ourselves in my room. While we're safely hidden away, the rest of you will track down this killer and dispose of her. Sounds good, right?"

"Uh, Everly, what if we're the ones who get killed instead?" asked Bev uncertainly.

"Well, then, that'll be fewer people to suspect, right?" replied Everly.

"Wow, I didn't think of that!" Bev said. "Oh, that could work!"

"I'm glad you agree."

"Everly, I clearly couldn't have had anything to do with this," Marcis said unhappily. "So why should I risk myself?"

"Don't trust him, Everly!" Lyona said, speaking up for the first time in a while. "According to Anne, he was the one who sent Claudia and Aiden after that awful Sloth demon! The disaster of Bremburg was his fault!"

Even Everly was surprised to learn that. "Father? That couldn't possibly be true, is it?"

"Lyona, dearest, please reconsider the source of your information," Marcis said patiently. "That was a lie that Aiden came up with to avoid being punished by his mother. I didn't have anything to do with that miserable scheme."

"How can we trust your words? You despised your own son. You wouldn't hesitate for a moment to point the blame his way. Especially now that he's dead and can't contradict your story!" Lyona said angrily.

"Lyona, please. Saying I despised my boy suggests a deeper emotional connection than our relationship warranted. I assure you, that simply isn't true."

Lyona opened her mouth, about to say something else, when Everly gently reached into her mind and coaxed her back to sleep, catching her in her arms as she fell unconscious. Then she turned to her father and said, "I don't care about who's telling the truth. Just do me a favor and get this taken care of! Okay?"

"I already saved your life, angel! Wasn't that enough of a favor?" Marcis asked her incredulously.

"Dad! Be useful!" Everly said as she hurriedly departed the conference room.

"Wait, what about me?" Tyler asked her. "Everly, I don't even know what's going on! Please, I don't want to die here!"

"Well, that's what you get for cheating on me, isn't it?" Everly said dismissively.

"Everly, I'm not even with you! I'm with Nev!" Tyler wept.

"Yeah, and I'm her too, dumbass! Honestly, your lack of shame is terrible."

Before Tyler could think of anything else to say, Everly was gone. Marcis shrugged his shoulders indifferently at him, and Beverly clucked her tongue in disapproval as she reached for the spear embedded in Cleverly's neck and pulled it free, causing the body to fall to the floor.

"S-so, what do we do now?" Tyler asked the other two.

"Don't ask me, *cheater*," Beverly harrumphed.

Once she safely returned to her room with Lyona, the first thing Everly did was seal the area by envisioning every exit and window being covered with steel bricks. When she was satisfied that entry was now impossible, she laid Lyona on her bed and then sat down in an oversized leather chair that she favored.

Once seated, Everly closed her eyes, took a deep calming breath, and waited until she felt utterly still and centered. Then, when she felt she was ready to begin properly processing the events of the day, she remembered in vivid detail the ease with which Lady Anne had utterly stomped her into the mud. Beaten her like a rag doll.

Kicked. Her. Ass.

That was when Everly began screaming in anger and throwing things.

It was a good thing that Lyona was in a mystically compelled slumber and thus unable to see her daughter's behavior, because at that moment Everly was absolutely livid! She smashed things, slashed things, bashed what she couldn't slash, and hacked what she couldn't smash.

In no time at all, her room became a complete mess.

When she was done letting out her anger, Everly sat on the floor with her back to a wall, knees bunched up beneath her chin, and sulked. She couldn't believe how easily she'd been trounced. What a humiliation! After years of seeming invincibility, for someone to come out of nowhere and casually slap her into the dust was . . . well, it was unthinkable!

That was the kind of treatment reserved for a midlevel anime or street-tier

American comic book villain. There was a fun tradition of such characters popping up during a hero's journey to boast about their overwhelming power, only to easily get swept aside because they were incapable of realizing the difference in strength between themselves and the heroes. Characters like those were jokes! Jobbers! *Memes!* Everly wasn't supposed to be one of them! She wasn't trash!

Even worse, she'd lost to another bad guy! That *absolutely* wasn't supposed to happen! Everly had her sights set on being a dark lord! No, *the* dark lord! Losing to anyone else was unthinkable. It not only meant that she hadn't yet finished her training and was possibly out of her depth, but it also meant she was a *loser.*

That couldn't be true, could it?

And now, with this traitor (most likely Neverly) running around adding to her troubles, it was all getting to be a bit too much. For the first time in what felt like ages, Everly felt uncertain of what she should do next. What was the right answer? What path should she take?

What was going to happen to her dream?

"Wow. You look how I feel, Blondie," Fenn said despondently as she slumped to the floor beside her.

"Ah. *Perfect.* Just perfect," Everly muttered to herself.

Today the hits kept coming.

CHAPTER TWENTY-NINE

Clarity

What are you doing back, Fenn?" Everly asked wearily as she began stripping off her armor.

"Why aren't you ever surprised to see me?" Fenn asked instead of answering her question. "I mean, look at me. I'm visiting you from beyond the shores of mortality. Honestly, you should be acting a little more impressed than you have been."

"Oh, whatever," Everly snorted. "I'm a necromancer. I defy the natural order and consort with the dead all the time. You're the one who's been dragging her heels."

"Wow, you just have an answer for everything, don't you?" Fenn shot back. "Blondie's just too cool to acknowledge a miracle. I bet you were that one crappy kid at the annual haunted house every Halloween who had to yawn and loudly say it wasn't scary just so she could ruin the fun for everyone else, weren't you?"

Everly smiled at her accusation. "As a matter of fact, I was! I really was a little brat."

"*Was?*" asked Fenn.

"How can you see through me so easily?" Everly wondered. "You're the one who's a ghost."

"Your nonchalance about my status as a nonliving being really makes me want to slug you, especially since you're the reason for my condition," said Fenn.

"So, how long have you been watching over me from above?" Everly wondered.

"Huh?" said Fenn. "What do you mean?"

"I mean, yeah, you made contact with me in that dream, but that makes me wonder how long you've been keeping an eye on my activities. You have been, haven't you?"

"Well . . . yeah, off and on," Fenn admitted.

"Which begs the question: have you ever checked me out while I was taking a shower?"

"Everly, WHAT THE HELL?" Fenn erupted.

"You have, haven't you? Eww!" Everly said before swooning dramatically. "Won't someone help me, please! I'm alone in my room with a stalker! She's weirdly religious and peeks at me while I bathe! Now I feel so *ashamed* of myself! I need counseling!"

"Everly, shut up!" Fenn said as she began to grow angry.

"Don't silence my truth, you nasty creeper!" Everly shouted at her. "I won't be your victim any longer!"

Annoyed beyond endurance, Fenn punched Everly in the shoulder as hard as she could and was surprised to hear the other girl begin yelling in pain as she was knocked over to her side.

"Fenn! Goddamn it! You cavegirl BITCH! ARRRGH!" Everly said in an agonized scream as she grabbed her shoulder and began rolling around on the floor.

"Blondie? Did that actually hurt?" Fenn asked her in shock.

"Yes, it fucking hurt, stupid!" Everly yelled. "Your psycho grandma beat the hell out of me and stabbed me through both of my shoulders! I'm in a lot of fucking pain right now!" Everly whined through her tears.

"I didn't know that! How was I supposed to know that?!" Fenn said as she moved to Everly's side and tried to rub her shoulders only for Everly to howl even louder at her touch.

"Fenn, damn it, get away from me! God, you're a monster! How can you treat a fellow human being like this?" Everly said to her.

"You MURDERED ME!" Fenn yelled at her now with tears of her own beginning to leak from her eyes.

"When are you going to let that go? All you do is bring up the past! What about all the fun we used to have?!"

"WHAT FUN?!" shrieked Fenn.

"Well, I mean this is kind of fun right now, isn't it?" Everly asked her wryly while once again wearing that insufferable smirk.

In response, Fenn kicked her in the abdomen and sent her spinning away.

"FENN, GODDAMN IT, I HAVE A STAB WOUND THERE!" Every screamed.

"You're right, Everly, that *was* kind of fun," Fenn said nastily before returning to her earlier sitting spot.

Across the room from her, Everly continued to moan in pain.

"Hey, this is kind of nice, though. Very cinematic," Everly said a few minutes later.

"What's that?" Fenn asked her.

"Well, I'm lying over here. *Bleeding.* And you're sitting over there, brooding. Don't you think all the space currently between us visually symbolizes our emotional distance? That's some Golden Globe Award–winning cinematography right there."

"Everly—" Fenn began to say.

"I'd personally rather win a People's Choice Award," Everly continued without stopping. "But we'd probably lose to a Marvel movie. They're *really* good at marketing."

"EVERLY," Fenn said forcefully to cut her off. "Are you okay?"

"Fenn, why would I be okay right now? I just got stomped on harder than if I'd worn purple at a grape harvest. One of my dupes, probably Nev, is making a move on me, and I'm hiding in my bedroom with my mommy because I'm too fucked up to handle my own business. This is not a good day to be me."

"Why not just use Discordia's magic to heal yourself?" Fenn asked her.

"Because I *can't*," Everly groaned. "My rogue dupe, probably Nev, is messing with my connections! I can't call upon any of them! They're just static in my head right now."

"Wow. You might be in some real trouble here," Fenn said with a nod. "My goodness, if only *someone* had tried to *warn you* that something bad was about to occur! That sure would have come in handy, wouldn't it?"

"Is that why you came back?" Everly asked her. "Seriously? Just to gloat because you were right and *I* was wrong? Honestly, Fenn. I didn't know you had it within you to act like such a loser."

"I'm *not* a loser!" Fenn yelled at her. "And I didn't come here to rub your nose in your misfortune, Blondie!"

"Then why *did* you return?" Everly demanded to know.

Now it was Fenn's turn to slowly drop to her side and assume a fetal position.

"Because I've got nowhere else to go," she said miserably.

Earlier that day.

"Fenneth, darling. What exactly were you *thinking*?" asked the disappointed voice of one of Fenn's esteemed ancestors.

Here in the next life were now gathered the entirety of the deceased members of the Godwell family, the greatest of whom sat at a stone table overlooking her in the center of the grand hall.

Preparing to pass judgement.

"Honestly, that's what I'd like to know," said another. "Fenneth, we all love you, dear. We do. We *really* do. But we honestly can't say that we're thrilled about your recent choices."

"*I'll* say," said the original. "Fenn. That necromancer girl is a mad dog. Nay, a rabid one! A disease-spreading mongrel destined to bring ruin to the world unless we quickly put a stop to her antics. To that end, we've assigned the right person for the job, and we're delighted to hear that the results have been spectacular."

"Anne is *really* giving it to that fiend!" exclaimed a particularly enthusiastic voice. "Ha! I could watch this for hours!"

"It's a shame she never plays with her food. I'd really love it if she'd put on more of a show," said another voice. "You know, really make that insolent cur suffer!"

"You sent *Anne* after her?" Fenn asked in surprise.

"No, no. It was our operative who did that," said the lead voice. "Anne despises many of us for reasons known only to her and would never follow one of our suggestions. Fortunately, our agent in the field has a real talent for leading her around by the nose."

"Who?" asked Fenn. "Who is it?"

"Now, now, Fenneth," said the first voice, the elder. "I really wish I could share that information with you, but you've already proven yourself to be untrustworthy. And that's just one more disappointment in a long list of disappointments. So much was expected of you! And now it's come to this. I'm sorry, dearest, but we just can't let this slide."

"Indeed," said the second voice. "Fenneth, this afterlife that we've provided for you would ordinarily be an unconditional paradise that any member of the Godwell lineage is permitted to enjoy. Through considerable effort, we managed to acquire our own demesne in the astral realm for our glorious dead to reside in."

"*Considerable* effort!" echoed one of the others.

"Wait," Fenn said. "Wait, do you mean to tell me that this isn't really heaven? That this is some kind of false paradise?"

"There's nothing false about it at all, dear. This is merely a custom job more to our liking," said the elder. "Although faith is a wonderful means of keeping the rabble in line, there are certain aspects of religious instruction that just don't fly with our family's way of thinking."

"Yeah, all that tripe about all people being equal in death was just ridiculous," said the second voice. "I absolutely refuse to spend eternity dwelling alongside the poor. I'm a *Godwell*."

"Quite right! Quite right," said the elder. "When you're already better than everyone else, why should that change in the afterlife? Most people would just accept the status quo, but we Godwells actually *did* something about it! Unlike others, we never lack the resolve to act when it benefits our family."

"Oh, my god," Fenn said to herself despondently. "And I thought my *living* relatives were snobs."

"Fenneth, you've never truly understood the responsibilities borne by our family, nor the weight of our legacy and the immensity of our sacred duties.

What gives you, who never achieved *anything* in life, the right to question how we choose to collect our eternal reward? Missy, you got in here on the basis of your last name alone! Do you *really* believe that you did anything that warranted your admission into our realm?"

"I was kind to others!" Fenn shouted. "I always tried to do the right thing! I respected my parents and did as my father wished of me instead of what I wanted! I loved my sister—"

"Ugh, how long do we have to listen to this?" someone said cuttingly.

"Teenage *melodrama*," huffed another.

"So bloody softhearted. It's almost *embarrassing* to look at her."

"Now, now. Quiet down, my blessed brethren," said the elder. "Fenneth. You're very young, and I'm certain that from your perspective, you lived according to moral principles. And let me assure you, your assembled family here *still* loves you no matter how much of an underwhelming failure you were in life."

"A failure? I—I was the maiden of the holy sword!" Fenn stammered.

"The shortest reigning maiden in history," snickered someone rudely.

"She was TERRIBLE! Compared to her sister, she was absolute trash."

"Brethren! Please control your emotions," the elder said. "But they do raise an excellent point, dear one. In addition to your lackadaisical performance in life, spreading information to an enemy is an unforgiveable act of treason."

"Worse than that!" shouted someone else. "It was a sign of bloody weakness!"

"Weakness?" Fenn asked incredulously. "I forgave my killer! I tried to save her life to give her time to redeem herself! How can that possibly be considered *weak?*"

"Because you're a *loser!*" the voice said scornfully. "What else could your actions possibly make you? You're a weak-willed bleeding heart! A mewling little wretch! That witch murdered you and made the family look bad! Yet how do you respond? By rolling over on your belly and begging for her attention like a dog!"

"I agree!" shouted another ancestor. "This girl *is* a loser! She's an absolute disgrace to all who bear our holy name! THE GODWELLS MUST NEVER BE DEFEATED! Throw her out!"

From across the room, the voices erupted with anger and contempt. By the second, the shouts grew more numerous and louder as others joined in the chorus.

"Throw her out!"

"Throw her out!"

"Throw her out!"

"THROW THIS LOSER OUT!"

All around Fenn the voices continued with their demands for her ejection, mocking her, condemning her, rejecting her. The voices of her family. Her ancestors. Telling her that she didn't belong. That she was lacking. That she wasn't good enough. That she'd *never* be good enough.

Before the onslaught of their unified scorn, she dropped to her knees and wept.

"Oh, look at the worm now weeping," said a familiar voice. "Poor widdle Fenneth. Not so precious anymore, are we?"

When Fenn tried to focus, to remember the name attached to those hateful words, the elder began to speak, overriding the others.

"Fenneth, dearest one. I'm afraid a consensus has been reached. Though it breaks my heart to have to do it, for I love *all* my descendants, past and present . . . for the sake of justice and peace, you will no longer be allowed to dwell in the afterlife of the Godwells. Just as you have rejected the noble principles by which we abide, so too will we now reject your presence among us. Instead, you will languish in the astral realm, friendless and alone, an outsider to all. And let your fate be an example to others. The Godwells may love . . . but we *never* forgive."

"Power to the Godwells!" the voices now shouted.

"Power to the Godwells!"

"Power to the Godwells!"

"POWER TO THE GODWELLS!"

As strong hands lifted her to her feet to escort her from the room, Fenn tearfully asked the elder, "Wait! Wait, please! Isn't there anything I can do? Please, can't I somehow try to make this right?"

"Oh, Fenneth," the elder sighed in a weary voice. "Even at the end, you're still unable to comport yourself with a Godwell's dignity. Perhaps the others are correct in their assessment of you. Perhaps you really *are* a loser. Take her away."

And that was the end of Fenn's time in paradise.

"Fuck them. Fuck all of them. I'm not a *loser*," Fenn said to herself. "I'm not."

"The evidence would imply otherwise," Everly said in a bemused voice.

"Fuck you too! This is all your fault!" Fenn said with her hands covering her face.

"It kind of is, I suppose," Everly said as she stared at the ceiling of her room.

"Now she finally admits it. When it's too late to matter in the slightest," said Fenn.

"Hey, tone it down, crybaby," Everly warned her. "If you're hoping to crash on my sofa, I'd better start hearing less sass and more begging and pleading for aid. Come on, let's hear you fawn over me. You know you want to."

"I *don't* want to," Fenn said defiantly.

"Huh? Is that really the tone you should be taking? I'm not operating a charity for homeless ghosts, Fenn."

"You'd seriously throw me out into the astral sea?" Fenn asked her. "After everything that's already happened to me because of you?"

"In a heartbeat, choir girl," Everly said cattily. "I'm running a tight ship here. I've got no room onboard for proven failures. But I always have time for a suck-up with no dignity! So, let's hear it, Fenn! Start sucking away. *Verbally,* that is."

"Get fucked, Everly!" Fenn shouted hatefully. "Hit yourself in the face ten thousand times with a rusty pickaxe! I hope you die an uglier death than I did! I hope they find pieces of your corpse mixed in with cow droppings! I hope your mom grows to hate you more than she ever loved you!"

"Bitch, you did *not* just say that," Everly growled.

"I sure did! And it felt great! Know what else? You're a *nerd,* Everly!"

"I'm a *what?*" Everly asked with a dumbfounded voice.

"A nerd! You're a fucking nerd! But not in a cool way. Not in a market-able way that makes other people want to join in. You're one of those hardcore, unbearable edgelord freaks who lives in a fantasy world, hiding away who she really is because other people would otherwise find you UNBEARABLE. You're unbearable, Everly!"

"Take that back!" Everly barked.

"Or else what? You'll kill me? Ha!" Fenn spit out as a savage feeling of elation began to sweep throughout her body. A feeling of finally, *finally* getting some-thing off her chest. "You think you're so special, Everly. You think you've got it all figured out, but you *don't.* You're clueless, naive, and arrogant, but somehow you think you can look down on everyone else because you think you're a chosen one. But you're *not!* You really aren't, and it's so fucking hilarious that you don't even know it!"

"What are you even talking about?!" Everly shouted at her.

"I found out all about it when I died, Blondie! I FOUND OUT ALL ABOUT IT!" Fenn said with a demented gleam in her eye. "My ancestors revealed it all!"

Fenn crawled over to Everly's side and leaned in to whisper in her ear.

"You seriously think you *willed* yourself into this world? Really? *Really?* No, Everly! You didn't! You thought *I* was the one holding you back with that soul link? NO, Everly! It was the opposite! THE COMPLETE OPPOSITE!"

"What are you saying—" Everly began to ask before Fenn clamped her hand over her mouth.

"No, you hush!" Fenn said to her. "I'm the one who gets to speak now! Everly, I was the one who was summoned here. *Me.* I was supposed to be the hero that defended the kingdom from the seven demon kings. *I'm* the chosen one! *You* were just a random *lunatic* that somehow got caught up in my wake! You're not here because you wanted to be. You're here because you hitched a ride!"

"That . . . that can't be right," Everly said softly to herself.

"Well, it is!" Fenn said triumphantly. "I'm not the one who lies! That's what I learned, and now you know it too! So how about that, huh? Who's the loser now?"

Everly was quiet for a moment. Then she said, "Well, technically, it's still you.

I mean, if you were meant to be a HERO and you failed this badly at it . . . ? Come on, Fenn, even if I *am* just some lucky freak who got caught in your wake, look at everything *I've* done on my own."

Everly sat up and then began laughing at how silly it all was.

"I mean, Jesus! You've got nothing! No achievements, no victories, not even a place in the afterlife! Sure, you're the hero and I'm just some rando nobody, but come on! Compare yourself to me and know despair! You thought learning I was a mistake was going to break me or something? Damn, Fenn, you should be feeling *even worse* about yourself! I'm a dark horse who turned out to be a champion, and you're the chosen one who's allergic to success!"

Everly rose to her feet with a new light of determination now burning brightly within her. How could she have ever doubted herself? How could she have ever believed even for a moment that she was second-rate? All she had to do was look at Fenn to see a *real* failure in action.

In that moment, Everly realized that *this* was destiny in motion. That this was what fate had provided for her. If ever again she felt doubt or misery, if ever again she believed she was unworthy of her many, *many* gifts, then all she had to do . . .

. . . was remember how much *Fenn* sucked at everything!!

"Fenn. *Thank you*," she said to the crestfallen spirit who had lapsed into a stunned silence. "Thank you for being here right now in my moment of need. It was important for me to hear your words. I needed to *understand*. Because I've realized now that *luck* is just as important a power as the ability to make your enemies explode. I'm a lucky girl. A very lucky girl. Especially when compared to the countless billions of faceless nobodies who will never be able to experience life from the lofty heights upon which I now stand. And I'm *especially* lucky when compared to you!"

Everly leaned over and kissed Fenn affectionately on the forehead. "You can sleep on my couch for as long as you want. But don't be one of those weird houseguests that just sits around all day without changing their clothes. I know, it'll be hard because successful efforts just aren't something that come naturally to you, but I'm going to be rooting for you anyway. You might be a failed hero, Fenn, but from now on, you're *my* hero of failure!"

"That sounds . . . terrible," Fenn said in a broken voice. "That sounds absolutely fucking terrible."

"Don't overthink it, Fenn. Past precedence shows that thinking is not your forte," Everly said helpfully as she walked to the center of the room. Through a fierce act of will, she managed to draw just enough energy from her elementals to open another gateway.

"Wh-where are you going?" Fenn asked her.

"Where do you think?" Everly smirked at her. "We can't all sit around whining about our ruined careers and short lives. Some of us have jobs to do! And *my* job right now is to kick Nev's ass and make her regret trying to rebel!"

"But you're still wounded," Fenn said.

"It doesn't matter! Winners *always* find a way to tilt the odds in their favor. You wouldn't know anything about that, but that's okay. Victory doesn't suit everyone! Wish me luck, Fenn!"

And with that, Everly stepped through the gateway, leaving Fenn alone with the still slumbering Lyona.

"I'm *not* a loser!" Fenn insisted as she collapsed to the ground.

But she didn't believe herself at all.

Meanwhile, in the headquarters of the Royal Bay Hobbs, Neverly was wondering where her boyfriend had gone.

"Guys, hasn't anyone seen Tyler? Anyone? Come on, there's only so many places he can hide! Damn it, am I going to have to put a collar on him or something?"

That was actually a very attractive idea now that she thought about it. She wondered if it should be a black one with jagged spikes on it. That sounded pretty cool! But at the same time, a pink one with a heart-shaped pendant in the center would be absolutely humiliating for Tyler, and the constant public embarrassment he'd feel at being forced to wear it could be a source for all sorts of amusement later down the road.

Decisions, decisions.

Still, before she could decide on a proper way to demean her toy for daring not to appear on command, she first had to find him. He'd apparently skipped school too, which was why she'd decided to stop by the hideout, only to be disappointed to find that there was work that had gone undone thanks to his absence.

Heh, school had been a riot. The news had finally reached Kelsie about what had happened to her father at the border. She'd been *broken* upon hearing the words *killed in service*. It was all Neverly could do not to claim credit, even though technically she *had* been responsible for the deed.

She wondered how many more of her schoolmates had parents serving at the fort. She wondered how many more orphans she was going to get to see weeping in the halls of the academy.

Heh. Good times ahead.

Good times indeed.

"Ma'am, I'm sorry, but we still haven't found Mr. Tyler," said one of the members of her gang apologetically. He was a tall oaf whose name she couldn't remember. She left that sort of thing to Tyler. These days she liked to remain one degree separate from any criminal mischief that could possibly catch the notice of the law.

Tyler was good at acting in her stead. He remembered the names of the rank and file, he gave out Neverly's orders, he collected the profits, and when the time came, he'd be the one to take all the blame when Neverly decided she didn't need him anymore. It was a beautiful arrangement that suited them both. *She* got to single-handedly wield all the power in their relationship, and *he* got the privilege of serving at her leisure.

It was a win-win, as far as she was concerned.

But where *was* he?

"Well, are our carriers ready to go, at least?" she asked the underling. "We've got a lot of product in need of delivery, Tiny. Those decadent noble fops aren't waiting around to inject themselves with syringes of dream dust, now, are they?"

"Is . . . is that what we're calling the product now, ma'am?" he asked uncertainly.

"Does it sound good?" she asked him.

"It actually does, yeah," he said after giving it a moment's thought.

"Okay. Cool. Dream dust it is," said Neverly. "Now get it moving!"

"Our lads will be out the door right away, miss," the underling said with a deep bow.

Suddenly, a glowing doorway opened in the middle of the room, startling the men and shocking Neverly as well. What the hell was going on? Which one of her sisters could possibly be stupid enough to open a gate in front of all these witnesses?

From the gate emerged Everly, wearing a sleeveless shirt over torn trousers and a dented pair of greaves. For some reason, she was dirty, bruised, and bleeding all over the place.

"Nev," she said curtly as she approached her astonished duplicate.

For her part, Neverly was furious at this unexpected intrusion. "Everly, what the actual *fuck*? You can't just port in here like this! Eris is acting weird, so I can't erase their minds! Now I'm going to have to get rid of all these witnesses—"

In response, Everly delivered a straight right jab that connected directly with Neverly's nose, crunching it into her face with a nasty sounding *pop* that sent her tumbling backward head over heels. When she sat up, a heavy trickle of blood began pouring out of both nostrils of her broken nose, which quickly ruined her white school shirt.

"Everthly, wath the fckth ith yourth problem?!" she yelled angrily.

"That's my question to you, psycho-me! What's *your* problem!" Everly shouted at her in return. "What gives you the right to kill Cleverly over someone as irrelevant as Tyler? And why are you messing around with our connection to the elementals? You've *really* been making a truckload of problems for me lately, and I've had it up to here with you!"

"Wuth the FVKTH ARE YUU BABBLING ABOUTH?!" Neverly screamed at her as she got back to her feet.

"I'm talking about you trying to help Anne kill me!" Everly yelled at her.

"BITCH. Do I LOOKTH like I'm helping Anne with ANYTHING?" Neverly screamed again with increasing fury.

"Uh, I mean, now that you mention it, there doesn't appear to be an outward connection between the two of you at the moment, but that doesn't mean you can't jump around between locations to cause trouble!"

"Uh, other Everly?" said the henchman who'd spoken to Neverly earlier.

"NO, WRONG, FALSE!" Everly said indignantly. "I'M Everly. SHE'S the other Everly. Get it right!"

"Uh, okay," the underling said nervously. "Uh, the other Neverly has been here for hours. She's b-been setting things up for a delivery of, uh, *goods* and, uh, having us look for Mr. Tyler. She hasn't been out of my sight at all, I swear it."

"Really?" Everly asked him with visible disappointment.

"Really," he insisted.

"Well, nuts," Everly muttered to herself as she scratched her chin. "If Neverly doesn't know about Tyler, then she doesn't know about Cleverly. And if she doesn't know about Cleverly, then how could she know what else has transpired?"

Everly turned to face Nev while saying, "Well, it looks like I *may* have made a slight mistake."

Then she was smashed into unconsciousness when Neverly broke a steel folding chair across her face.

"YOU THINK?" Nev said before spitting a gob of bloody saliva on the floor.

CHAPTER THIRTY

The Silver Lance

Earlier that week . . .

The massive demon that emerged from the portal possessed a hideous combination of draconic and insectile features. It had a long serpentine body and a fierce fang-filled maw that reminded Bev of pictures she'd seen of traditional Chinese dragons, but it also had thousands of creepy legs scuttling beneath its snakish form like those of a centipede. In addition to that unpleasant visual, the beast's eyes were compound, like those of a housefly, and it even emitted an annoying high-pitched buzzing as it slid over the earth.

It was gross. Bev hated it. Her natural instinct was to say *no, thank you* and move on to something a little more fun, but unfortunately for her, she'd been recognized by the local residents of the village of who-gives-a-crap, who were now cheering at the sight of her and calling out her name.

Their presence made things more complicated for her. If she ghosted them and any of them managed to survive the dragon-bug's onslaught, then word would quickly spread that the newest sky-ranked member of the adventurer's guild had left a bunch of local hicks to become insect chow.

Being a hero was such a *hassle*. Bev was quickly growing tired of it. Sure, being a celebrity was fun, and the attention and praise were awesome, but the amount of work that she had to put in was exhausting. Even worse, it barely paid out! Rube villages like this weren't exactly bursting at the seams with hidden gold, now, were they?

No, the best she'd get out of this job would be another lyric in the song the bards wrote about her, probably a bunch of cheese and salted beef or other pre-served foodstuffs, and possibly an offer of marriage from some farmer's daughter. That kind of reward wasn't so bad, but she'd already accepted quite a few of those before ducking out early the next morning. The novelty had now worn off.

"Oh, well," she mumbled to herself. That's what she got for being one-fourth of the world's greatest villain, who was secretly infiltrating the adventurer's guild by masquerading as its greatest hero, who was also a girl but pretending to be a dude by telepathically controlling a remote body that she'd had Titania make for her from a drop of Everly's blood.

Where had she gotten that blood? She'd randomly punched Everly's face in the hallways of the memory palace one day and yelled "Tag!" afterward. That had been pretty fun!

Too bad Everly responded by chasing her down and beating her half to death with a ball-peen hammer before giving her a parting threat of what would occur if Bev *ever* did anything like that ever again.

That part had been *less* fun.

Oh, whatever! They all still loved each other!

The dragon-bug roared and buzzed as it drew nearer to the village. Bev sighed and decided that now was the time to get into character. *Visualize, visualize, visualize*, she thought to herself. Then her eyes popped open, and her sight was set on the task now lumbering before her.

She was *ready*!

For now, she was no longer Beverly of the four Everlys . . .

No, now she was *Lance* of the Silver Lance! And she was a he, and he was a *man*, and he could definitely prove that because men have high testosterone and loads of opinions about things they don't necessarily understand but would still die on a hill to defend in an argument on the internet! They also had other assorted factors that differentiated them from the gentler sex.

No, Lance *certainly* wasn't a chick named Bev. For Lance was a bro, a real bro, a *bro's* bro, even! He proudly fought the nefarious evils of the world with a smile on his face and was happy to stab monsters and criminals to death with his signature silver-tipped spear, because real men liked to thrust deeply into things by putting the power of their hips behind their shafts to penetrate their targets more easily.

That wasn't an inuendo. That was an exact description of how spearsmanship works! But it doubled as an inuendo because that's also how being a *man* worked!

It was all about the *spearmanship*.

Lance was using spears as a metaphor for his genitals.

Just in case you were unaware.

Lance has your back!

"Have no worries, good people of this tiny rustic . . . place. Lance stands at your side!" he called out to the terrified villagers as he set himself in the path of the dragon-bug.

"Light above, it's really him! It's Lance of the Silver Lance!" shouted an excited girl.

"He's smaller than I thought he'd be. But he's so handsome!" swooned another.

"He kind of looks like a girl if you ask me," said a young man who was deliberately trying to sound unimpressed.

"I don't mind. He's still beautiful," said the second village girl dreamily.

"How can we be certain he's the real deal? Songs and stories are one thing, but look at the size of that behemoth! Does anyone really believe he can take that thing down?"

"Oh, shut up, Wendal! He's fearlessly wielding his lance in defense of our homes!" shouted the first voice angrily.

"I'm just asking a question," Wendal said defensively.

"Well, don't do that when someone's risking their life on your behalf! It makes you look ungrateful!"

"Yeah, Wendal, shut up!" said another girl, backing the first one up. "What if he gets mad because of what you said and leaves us to our fate? Are *you* going to step up and fight the fucking dragon? Huh? Are you?"

"No . . ." said Wendal sullenly.

"Then stop being a prick!"

"That's not even a lance, you know," Wendal suddenly said, apparently not willing to let it go. "That's a *spear*. Lances are what knights use on horseback in a joust. Is he stupid or something—OW!" he shouted.

When Lance turned around to see what had happened, he saw a young man lying in the dirt beside the village entrance, while a trio of angry-looking girls surrounded him, one of whom was holding a stone tightly in her fist that seemed to be dripping blood.

"Uh, hey?" Lance asked uncertainly. "Everything okay over there?"

"Everything's just fine!" the stone-wielding girl assured him before beaming a lovely smile his way.

"Everything's absolutely splendid on our end!" said the second girl.

"We love you, Lance! Go get that beast!" cheered the third one.

Lance nodded. "All right, then! Off I go!"

And so, Lance raced fearlessly into battle with the enthusiastic cheers of the villagers at his back, minus one young man who was going to awaken two days later with a severe headache and a lot of painfully earned wisdom.

As Lance approached the massive creature, he found himself wondering just how many more of these nasty demonic beasts he'd have to kill in the future. He'd already taken down quite a few, and he'd long ago grown tired of it. Even if his organization was partly responsible for the plague of fiends that the middle of the kingdom was currently being vexed by, that didn't mean he felt any obligation to spend so much of his time cleaning up after his boss.

The cause of the problem had naturally been Everly, of course; not that Lance would ever dare level that accusation at his beloved Empress. He might not have been very smart, but that didn't make him stupid. It was all so unfair, though!

It seemed that just before dying from the many terrible wounds that Everly had dealt him, Acedia—or Sloth, or whatever his name was supposed to be—had hatefully cursed the land of the one who'd dared to strike him down, vowing that those who dwelled there would suffer his wrath for a thousand generations.

That curse was an act of blasphemous desecration which naturally attracted all sorts of monsters and lesser demons to enact their deceased king's vengeance. Making matters worse, crazed cultists hoping to score points with their unholy masters kept popping out of the woodwork to summon even stronger fiends like the dragon-bug.

It was swiftly becoming a real mess. All Lance wanted was to be the greatest hero in the history of Winstead. Why was fate making him work so hard for it?

Lance personally thought that a thousand generations of vengeance was a slight bit of overkill. Sure, it was a pretty standard reaction as far as defeated demon kings went, cursing their enemies, that was. But did he have to do it with such *zeal*? And why was the temple taking so long to get the curse dispelled, anyway? Lance didn't hold a very high opinion of most religions, and their current ineffectiveness at reducing his workload had only increased his disdain.

I mean, these are demons, aren't they? he complained inwardly. What good was a church, or a temple, or what have you, if they couldn't get rid of demons? That was like being a gardener who couldn't mow grass, wasn't it? Gardeners did lawncare, didn't they? Lance thought they did, but it was hard to be sure. He never really paid attention to them. It wasn't that he was scornful of the common working man. It was just that gardening, as a concept, was something he found so utterly boring that he wasn't interested in learning anything about it. Gardeners and future dark lords were two sets of people heading in opposite directions in life, that was all.

The dragon-bug roared and buzzed in outrage when Lance flew into the air with a superhuman leap and connected feetfirst with the side of its head in a thunderous collision that smashed it to the ground. Lance was disappointed to see that the creature's scales were extremely thick. If they hadn't been, he would have shot through its head like a human bullet and settled the matter with one blow.

"Who izzzzz it that darezzzz to impede the path of mighty Grzzzz'le'auduezzz?!" bellowed the hideous freak. "Szzzztep forward that I may szzzzzzmite you and feaszzzzzzt upon your broken body!"

Aw, shoot. It's intelligent, Lance grumbled to himself. He hated it when the monsters turned out to be intelligent. They always started giving long-winded monologues and made elaborate threats to him, often with words that he didn't understand, and always made fun of him whenever he asked for a little clarification on what meant what. It was yet another hassle on top of the other hassles he was already enduring. Like whipped cream on an ice cream sundae, but without the bonus of being delicious. It was the empty calories of self-aggrandizement!

Also, the way the fiend was stretching out its sentences with all that unnecessary buzzing was annoying as hell. Lance suspected it was doing it on purpose just to sound intimidating.

"Well, coward?" continued Grizz, which wasn't the creature's actual name, which didn't really matter since there was no way in hell Lance was going to make the effort to pronounce it. "Have you nothing to szzzzzzzay for yourszzzzzzelf?"

"I think you're doing that zzzzzzz thing intentionally, and I'd like you to stop," Lance said in response. "That sort of gimmicky way of speaking might delight your players when you're the DM running the game, but out here in the real world, it makeszzzz you szzzzzzound like you're trying too hard."

"You dare mock my manner of szzzzpeaking, boy?" said the outraged Grizz. "I am one of the proud szzzzzzervants of the szzzzzzeven dark kings and shall make no attempt to accommodate your preferences!"

"Shouldn't that have been *preferenczzzzzzeszzz?*" Lance asked quizzically.

"That's exactly what I szzzzzaid!" Grizz said quickly.

"Shouldn't that have been *exzzzzzactly?*" Lance wondered aloud.

After fuming silently at Lance's words for a few tense moments, Grizz then angrily shouted, "Hey, asshole! What's your problem here? Huh? I have a job to do, and I'm trying to stay in character."

"I *knew* it!" Lance said triumphantly. "I frickin' knew it! You're inauthentic, dude! You're like one of those middle-class schoolgirls who dresses in rags on the weekends so she can go panhandling!"

"Inauthentic? *Inauthentic?* How full of shit can one mortal possibly be?" said Grizz. "Look at me, you ignorant idiot! I'm titanic! I'm a terror beyond imagining! Once I've swallowed you, you'll slowly digest in my belly for a thousand years!"

"Oh, wow, *wow,* so now you're a sarlacc as well?" asked Lance, mockingly. "Super original! I really don't know how to feel about you, big guy! You just seem to be all over the place. I bet your real name isn't even whatever the hell you said it was."

"Bastard! I'll have you know that Grzzzz'le'auduezzz is the name I received from my father! A proud abyssal name that brings madness and suffering to any who hear it!" shouted the dragon-bug.

"Yeah, well, trying to pronounce it makes me sound like I licked a metal pole in winter," replied Lance with a sneer.

"And NOW you're mocking my heritage," the dragon-bug fumed. "No more words, mortal speck! Be still so that I may devour you!"

Before Lance could respond, the colossal hybrid beast was after him, smashing its face into where he'd been standing just a moment earlier. It roared in anger once it realized it had missed and turned to chase after him, moving with surprising speed and grace for a beast of its size.

Lance, for his part, was simply glad that in its tremendous anger, he'd finally gotten it to stop talking. Normally in a battle of life and death, a good ongoing dialogue was a necessary ingredient to spice things up. As a villain, talking ceaselessly was a requirement of the job. When the hero told you to shut up, that meant you were playing your role well.

But Grizz the dragon-bug was too much of a cliché to be worth listening to. The beast was like one of those professional wrestlers from the golden age of television, who couldn't put an interesting sentence together to save his life but could still get a strong reaction from the crowd by pretending to be a communist and spitting on a flag.

That might have been enough to get the local crowd fired up, but Lance of the Silver Lance was a more sophisticated sort of viewer. He needed intellectual engagement to further his enjoyment of a villain's performance. Cheap heat didn't appeal to him at all.

After dodging another strike from Grizz, Lance called upon Titania's strength and summoned a massive hand from the earth. Then he brought it down on his opponent's head in a tightly clenched fist that easily pinned the enraged monster in place.

"Nice job, T!" he said happily as he took careful aim with his spear before launching it into the monster's eye, where it continued along its path in a straight line and destroyed the dragon-bug's brain.

I'm always happy to be of service, Bev, Titania said cheerfully as her stone fist was reabsorbed into the earth. *Yeesh, this was a nasty one, wasn't it?*

"Yeah, the insect ones are always gross," Lance said in agreement. "And hey! It's *Lance* when I'm using this body. If you keep saying my real name, I'll get confused. Take it easy on me!"

Oh! Sorry, Bev! Oh, I mean, Lance! Heh, your clever machinations are a little hard for me to follow, Titania said.

"Well, yeah! They're supposed to be! Because they're my, you know, *machinations,*" said Lance even though he wasn't exactly certain what that word meant. He'd heard it said a few times before, though, and it sounded like a good thing.

Yeah, you're definitely a chip off the boss's block, Titania continued. *More so than that Cleverly, anyway. You didn't hear this from me, but she's an absolute pill.*

"Ugh, I know exactly what you mean," Lance said with a roll of his eyes.

"It's hard to believe that dope is one of us. All she does is sit around the memory palace all day, doing whatever she feels like. When's she going out into the field?"

She keeps saying the time isn't right to begin her famine, Titania said scornfully. *I'm like, "Hey! Cleverly! Harvest season is around the corner! Winter's nearly here! You can't starve the population if you give them time to store food!" But she wouldn't listen. Told me to quit telling her what to do.*

"Yeah, that kind of laziness sounds about right," Lance said. "Man, someone should really stick a pin in that girl to get her moving. What good is she if she doesn't serve her purpose?"

I agree one hundred percent! Titania laughed. *Heh, maybe you could try sticking your spear in her and see if it helps?*

"Don't think I'm not tempted!" Lance chortled. They both enjoyed a hearty laugh together before Titania excused herself to go work on her latest short story.

"Oh, what's this one about?" Lance asked her.

I don't want to spoil it! But it's gonna be like a Conan the Barbarian *thing with LASERS!*

"Sounds badass!" Lance said enthusiastically. "Let me see it when you're done."

Can do, will do!

Lance, which is to say, Bev, always enjoyed her conversations with Titania. Although she considered Neverly to be her best friend, Nev tended to viciously mock her whenever Bev failed to understand something as quickly as Nev believed she should. Bev would just laugh along and pretend she understood whenever Nev would lose patience and painstakingly explain something to her like she was stupid.

It had really stung the day when Bev realized that deep within her heart, Nev considered her as more of a sidekick than a partner in crime.

She wasn't even sure how Everly herself felt about her, but she *had* nearly been choked to death on her first day of life for saying the wrong thing at the wrong time, so that was probably indicative of her overall value to her creator.

Titania was different, though. She was fun to hang out with and unconcerned with all the stuff that Everly and Nev were obsessed with. She didn't talk down to her or tear her down for getting something wrong, and Bev was grateful for that. Being a villain was fun and all, but it was also nice to be treated with a little dignity every once in a while.

Bev was curious about Titania's story too. How would a barbarian have gotten access to a laser? Barbarians existed during the age of Rome, over a hundred years ago, didn't they? Such technology wouldn't even exist until the First World War!

It sounded like it was going to be a *real* page-turner.

"Holy crap, nice job, dude!" said a pleased voice from above.

Bev, uh, which is to say, *Lance*, quickly shook his head to get back into character. From above him, a young woman wearing silver armor with a flapping white cape came floating down from the sky to land beside him.

She was a pretty thing with lightly freckled skin, brown hair, and a friendly smile. She stepped forward to slap him on the back and said, "Seriously! You must be Lance Delance! I've heard tons about you, man, and I have to say, I'm *genuinely* impressed! This was a David and Goliath power move right here!"

"David and who?" Lance asked in confusion. If Titania were still there to observe him, she would have assumed that Lance was making a clever effort to avoid revealing his connection to Earth by feigning ignorance of important figures from one of its most famous religions. It never would have occurred to her that Lance genuinely didn't know who David and Goliath were, because he had a short attention span and wasn't interested in learning.

"Oh, no worries," the woman said. "It's a compliment from where I come from that's given whenever a little guy beats a big bully. You really are as good as your reputation says, Lance."

She then offered her hand in congratulations.

"Well, thanks," Lance said gratefully as he gave it a shake. "Yeah, I completely dominated this guy. I tend to excel at everything I do. Probably because I was born under a lucky star. Or maybe it was a starless night? With a prophecy? Was there a prophecy?"

"I don't . . . know?" said the woman.

"Yeah, there was probably a prophecy," Lance decided. "With guys like me, there's always a prophecy from somewhere going on about how great we are. It's, uh, *Lance of the Silver Lance*, by the way. Not Lance Delance."

"Oh, my apologies," said the woman. "I must have heard it wrong."

"No worries, no worries," Lance said to her. "It's just that when you say *Lance Delance,* it makes me think of *Lance Deluxe*. Like, what? Huh? Who would ever name themselves Lance Deluxe? Doesn't that sound awful?"

"I get you." The woman nodded. "It makes you sound like a new item on a drive-thru menu. Like you're something I'd get with fries and a coke. *Try the Lance Deluxe for $9.99*. Hey, it even makes you sound like a boy-band singer."

"Really? I'm not much of a vocalist," Lance said thoughtlessly.

"Oh, man, you are *killing* me," the woman said with a hearty laugh.

"Huh? No, I'm not! I don't do stuff like that unless you're evil," Lance said defensively. "Seriously, I'm a righteous guy who only performs righteous acts. Ask anyone. I have testimonials!"

"Sorry, sorry," the woman said with a hand raised in apology. "I merely meant to say that I think you're great. But maybe you *should* change your last name to Deluxe, because I can already tell that you're a *whole* lot of Lance."

"You really think so?" Lance asked her with a shy smile. "Ha! Cool! I'm Lance, by the way."

"Yeah, I know, I—" The woman stopped herself from speaking further, took a quick breath, and then said, "Good to meet you, Lance! I'm Riley Kilo."

"Riley Kilo," Lance said slowly to himself. Then he snapped a finger. "Oh, I know of you! You're the new paladin of the north they appointed a few months back. You won that big tournament and everything. You're kind of famous yourself."

"Stop, I'm blushing," Riley grinned. "But I'm only a *temporary* paladin. Lady Sarah has been cleared by the temple to return to duty. I'll be turning in my cloak in a few days and moving on."

"Really?" Lance said in disappointment. "Well, that sucks. You'd think the temple would want to keep someone like you around."

"They've made a few offers to sign on with them in a different role, but I'm not really interested," Riley said with a shrug. "I only became a temporary paladin as a lark. The cloak looked good on me and it's fun to blow up demonic abominations. But I have another gig that keeps me busy, and I've been keeping my partner cooling his heels for way too long."

"Is your partner a patient guy?" Lance asked her.

"Oh, god no, not in the slightest," Riley laughed. A red light buzzed angrily on the silver ring she was wearing, but she didn't appear to notice it.

"Well, it's a shame," Lance said wistfully. "You probably don't know this, but that person you were substituting for was a complete horror show. Like, the worst sort of human being you could possibly imagine."

"Really? That's the first time I've heard anything like that," Riley said with mild surprise. "Everyone usually gushes over her for being the savior of Bremburg and the slayer of Sloth."

"Nah, that's totally stolen valor," Lance snorted. "The idea of *Sarah* facing a demon king? That'd make me laugh if it wasn't such a bad joke."

"Are you calling her an industry plant?" Riley asked him curiously.

"Well, she certainly doesn't write her own lyrics," Lance said with a smirk. A smirk that he quickly dropped when he realized that Riley was looking at him with a slightly harder expression than before.

"Lance, where exactly are you from?" she asked him in a voice that sounded ominously professional.

"Uh, Winstead?" he answered uncertainly.

"Whereabouts in Winstead?" she asked.

"You know, the northeast part," he answered. "With all the trees. Yeah, there sure were a lot of trees."

"A lot of trees?" she wondered.

"Yeah, loads of them." He nodded. "So many trees. We loved them all. Hard to pick a favorite, though."

"A favorite what?" Riley asked.

"A favorite tree. We loved all our trees equally," Lance insisted.

"Do a lot of people in your hometown love trees?" asked Riley.

"Oh, yeah. We're mad for them. That's what we're famous for." Lance nodded.

"And what exactly was the name of that hometown again?" Riley asked him.

"Didn't I already say? I feel like I already said," Lance said nervously.

"You didn't," Riley said bluntly. Now she was crossing her arms as she spoke. Lance didn't know exactly what had occurred in the last few moments to swing the conversation in this direction, but he was beginning to suspect that Riley was suspicious of something, and for some reason, his instinct for danger was warning him that this was a *very* bad thing.

As his mind raced trying to think of an excuse to duck out of this unexpectantly nerve-racking encounter, salvation came in the form of a heavy hand slapping down on his shoulder from behind. When Lance turned around, wondering who it could have been, he saw a handsome silver-haired man in expensively tailored clothing standing before him with a strained but friendly-looking smile on this face.

"Well, it's about time!" said Dask Thomlin, the supreme master of the national adventurer's guild, and a man who wielded influence and authority comparable to a duke. "Lance, you're a difficult young man to keep track of! But you're not wriggling off the hook this time! We need to speak."

"We do?" Lance asked him.

"Yes, we *do*," Thomlin said firmly. He turned to Riley and said, "Your pardon, Lady Paladin, but Lance and I have guild business to discuss right now. Such business, I'm afraid, takes precedence over your current conversation."

"Does it really?" Riley asked curiously. "I have to say, it feels a bit rude of you to cut in like this."

"Does it?" Thomlin said dismissively. "How awful for you."

"Is this how the guild treats officers of the temple?" Riley asked lightly. "If so, that's a real shame."

"If I try very hard, I'm certain that I'll eventually find it within myself to care," Thomlin replied. "Until that day arrives, I bid you farewell."

Thomlin then threw an arm around Lance's shoulder and steered the younger man away toward the village, leaving Riley by herself.

When Thomlin and Lance were out of earshot, she asked, "What do you think? That kid screams *Earthborn* to me. I think he's a dimension hopper."

"Your theory is incorrect," said the voice of Bruticus. **"I detected no residual energy that would indicate that a dimensional jump had occurred. Every atom of his body originates on this planet."**

"Okay." Riley nodded. "No worries if that's the case. He might just be a reincarnation and trying to keep that under his hat."

"A far likelier story," agreed Bruticus. **"I find it extremely unlikely that a**

being of such limited intelligence is capable of deliberately crossing the barrier between worlds."

"How'd he become so strong, though?" Riley wondered as she gazed at the dead body of the dragon-bug. "You scanned this thing's piercing resistance as being level fifteen. Even if the eyes are the softest part of the body, that spear still shouldn't have been able to reach this big boy's brain. No more than a wasp's stinger could to an ordinary human."

"That is an interesting question. It's probably magic," Bruticus muttered.

"Your favorite answer to everything," Riley said with a grin.

"That is incorrect, Ser Riley. I greatly detest magic," Bruticus said in annoyance.

"You do? Wow, how surprising to hear!" Riley snickered as she walked away.

"Should we continue to interrogate the boy?" Bruticus asked.

"What for?" Riley replied. "Being reincarnated isn't a crime as far as I know. He's having fun, and he isn't hurting anyone. He's no problem as far as I'm concerned."

"What about that annoying guild master? His high-handed arrogance begs for a reprisal. I recommend we deposit him in space so that he can gain an appropriate understanding of his infinitesimal value to the universe shortly before he expires from lack of oxygen."

"Bruticus, that sounds an awful lot like committing murder," Riley said to him sternly.

"Very well. I will instead acquire the location of his home, and at a later date we will throw expired eggs at it."

"That could work." Riley nodded.

"And as he labors to clean his door, we will then disintegrate him with a blast from a diffuser ray."

"Bruticus!"

"It's a faster death than exposure to the vacuum of space."

"Bruticus!" Riley repeated.

"Tch. Fine, whatever," Bruticus grumbled bitterly.

"So, how'd you know where to find me?" Lance asked Thomlin as the older man guided him to the village chief's residence, where they sat in a study to discuss business.

Outside, dozens of adventurers and other guild employees were arriving. The adventurers were there in case any further monsters appeared, drawn by the scent of the dragon-bug's corpse. They were also there to protect the guild's dismantling crews, who would slowly break down the deceased demon's body into valuable materials for crafting and components for enchanting and alchemy.

"Believe it or not, I had to consult an oracle," Thomlin said as he settled himself into his seat. "That cost me quite a bit of gold, my dear boy. I wouldn't have bothered if I didn't know you were worth every ounce of it."

"There are oracles outside of the Eastern Temple?" Lance asked in surprise.

"Of course there are," answered Thomlin. "The Eastern Temple can't get their hands on everyone with the gift of foresight, after all. They have to settle for taking the ones with the most promising talent. That doesn't mean those left behind aren't useful, however. Just damned expensive to hire!"

"Uh, sorry, I guess?" Lance said uncertainly.

"Oh, no, no, don't feel that way, my lad," Thomlin said rosily. "Like I said, you're worth the coin! The first genuine sky-ranked adventurer in generations! Thank you so much for dispatching that monster before Riley Kilo arrived, by the way."

"You knew who she was?" Lance asked him.

"Naturally," Thomlin replied. "She's the famous substitute paladin. That woman's been a damned nuisance since she accepted the role! No matter how much the guild begged for her to avoid disintegrating the bodies of her monstrous prey, she insists on destroying them completely. The sheer number of the creatures she's obliterated is staggering! Just think of all the potential profits that have been lost due to her zeal for destruction. Honestly, I don't believe I'll ever understand the mindset of a hero."

"I'm a hero," Lance said. "We're easy to figure out. Fighting's fun."

"Well, you're a different sort of hero, I think," Thomlin said to him with a slight smile. "Your work effort is commendable, but I sense that you have ambitions beyond defending the innocent and beating up freaks. I see a young man who greatly desires recognition and fame."

"Well, yeah," Lance said. "Man, being famous is pretty awesome."

"Yes, it is," Thomlin agreed as he leaned back in his chair. "It *really* is. I had quite a taste for fame myself, back in my days as an active adventurer. Wealth and power are wonderful to acquire, have no doubt. But being *seen* and cheered for? Oh, there's nothing like it. Nothing like it in all the world!"

"I *do* like it when they cheer." Lance grinned.

"Oh, Lance, they'll do more than just cheer for you by the time I'm through," Thomlin said with an eager expression on his face. "Despite my accomplishments as an adventurer, I freely admit I was an average talent at best. I never rose past a mid ranking, but my skill at marketing myself was unmatched! With my gift for words, I could spin my mediocre accomplishments from straw into purest gold! That talent was enough to carry me all the way to my current lofty position as the national guild master."

"Ohhh," Lance said as he nodded in understanding before slyly tapping the side of his head. "I get it! You're a fraud! That's cool. I really respect the confidence grind. Fake it until you make it, word?"

"I'm not a fraud, Lance," Thomlin said in a displeased voice before quickly modulating his tone. "I did a lot of good out there in the world. I'm simply better at promoting my work than others are."

"Yeah, *fraud*," Lance said with a sly wink. "I get it! You're good at exaggerating stuff and deceiving others. I think that's cool! So, what's up? If you've been looking for me for a while, then that means you must want my help running a grift, huh? I'm in! I love stuff like this."

Thomlin sighed in slowly growing frustration. "Lance, *no*. You're confused about my motivations, friend. I don't want to deceive anyone. Especially not when it comes to you! I witnessed your incredible duel with that behemoth! But before that, I also had every single one of your previous victories thoroughly investigated. You're the real deal, son. You're incredible!"

"I am?" Lance asked with a genuine smile.

"Yes! You are!" Thomlin insisted. "But ever since you first appeared, it's been so difficult to learn anything about you. We know nothing about where you live, or your background, or anything, really. You're a complete mystery to me."

"Uh, well, you know. I'm, like, on the road a lot," Lance said hurriedly, as though he were trying and failing to think up an appropriate reason to end the conversation.

"You move so quickly too," Thomlin continued. "Lance, it's absolutely bewildering how you'll appear in one corner of the country one day, only to turn up somewhere else fifty miles away the next. North to south, east to west, and everywhere else in between. It's almost as though you're flying."

"Flying? Come on, that's just silly," Lance laughed uneasily. "Next you'll say that I'm walking through magic doors."

"Are you?" asked Thomlin.

"No!" Lance yelped.

"Well, whatever you're doing, it needs to stop," Thomlin said firmly.

"Huh?" Lance asked in confusion. "But I thought me going around saving people was a good thing?"

"Of course it is!" Thomlin said cheerfully. "It's a wonderful thing! But now that you're sky-ranked, you have to start thinking about the *visuals*. Sky-ranked adventurers are held in the same regard as the Ten Blades and the temple paladins. You're a national treasure! To the common man, you're a modern legend! A rare gem, Lance! But something doesn't truly become rare until it first becomes *scarce*."

"Okay, *scarce*," Lance said, repeating the other man's word. "Soooo . . . what does that mean? You want me to disappear for a while?"

"No! Not at all!" Thomlin said. "What I *want* is for you to begin appearing in the capital, where I can show you off! I want to introduce you to the people who matter and demonstrate your strength to any that would doubt it. I also think it's time we got a team assembled around you."

"A team?" Lance asked excitedly. "That is such a coincidence! I've been wanting to do that! I've had plans for leading my own group for a while now—"

"There's no need to put any thought into it my boy. We've already picked them out for you," Thomlin said with a fatherly smile.

"You did?" Lance said in disappointment. "But I thought we could do like a talent search or something, and I could be the judge, like *Winstead's Next Great Adventurer*, or something. I know a goblin who speaks the common tongue fluently, and I thought he could sit with me and crack jokes. He has a British accent that makes him sound very witty—"

"It's not necessary, Lance," Thomlin repeated. "Trust me, you're going to love these people. They're the Brave Quartet, great heroes of Bremburg just like the temple's own Lady Sarah. They're already quite popular with the public, but they're not experienced enough to be sky-ranked themselves. However, with *you* to command them, I could perhaps exaggerate their level of skill enough to justify the promotion. Then, instead of one sky-ranker, we'll have *five*! Can you imagine the notoriety, attention, and *money* that will bring in?"

"I think so?" Lance said uncertainly. "But isn't lying about—"

"*Exaggerating*," Thomlin corrected him.

"Uh, yeah, sure," Lance said. "But isn't *exaggerating* about their abilities a bad thing?"

"Not at all, Lance!" exclaimed Thomlin. "If anything, it's for the greater good!"

"I don't get it," Lance said bluntly.

"There's nothing to get, Lance. Just follow my lead and it'll all become clear."

"Okay," Lance said with a shrug. "I guess you'd know more about it than I would."

"That's exactly what I hoped to hear you say," Thomlin said warmly.

In the memory palace, Lance collapsed onto his mat as Beverly's mind returned to her body. She yawned as she rose from her bed and stretched her body. That was the longest she'd ever spent as Lance, and though today's events had been an interesting experience, she was glad to be back in her own skin.

It seemed that Grandmaster Thomlin was a bit of a sneaky Pete, looking to run some kind of con. Bev found that funny since she was also running a con of her own on the adventurer's guild. But she found it annoying that he was trying to lock her down in one place just so he could hobnob more often with a bunch of nobles and make some backroom deals or whatever.

The problem, though, was that Thomlin spoke too quickly, which made it difficult for her to follow along with the conversation. He was exactly the sort of tricky person that Bev matched poorly against. Since she couldn't just beat him up to compel him to explain himself better, she'd have to consult with Everly or Nev to get her marching orders. In complicated situations like this, Beverly didn't mind letting others make her decisions for her.

She just wanted to have fun and live in the moment.

With that in mind, she left to go find them, patting Lance affectionately on the cheek as she passed him.

What an interesting day.

Later, after Beverly returned to her room to sleep, he arose.

Not immediately. Thanks to his splendid new body he was connected to the minds of the other duplicates. He didn't take a single step from where he lay until he felt each one of them slumber. When he was certain they were down for the night, that was when he made his first move.

After his first meeting with Discordia, Lance (who wasn't Lance at all, nor Beverly or the rest), once he had relocated himself to a hidden location within the memory palace, summoned Titania and Eris before him.

"What's going on here?" Eris demanded of him. "Beverly, what are you doing? We are *not* yours to command."

"Yeah, I don't mind helping you out with work, Bev, but Everly wouldn't like it if she knew you were trying to give us orders," Titania said.

"I didn't ask your opinions, slaves," Lance said coldly. "Am I not forged directly from Everly's blood? I'm not a mere duplicate like the others. You will obey me in all things, and you will not reveal my presence to anyone else. Am I understood?"

He could feel the two of them struggle against his command. But it did no good because his words were true. He *was* Everly's blood. Both in his former life, the one she'd stolen from him, and now in this new one as well, thanks to the intervention of his ancestors.

Try as they might, these two sisters had no choice but to obey him.

Eventually, their resistance died down.

"We understand," Eris said with barely restrained rage.

"Yeah," Titania said. "Asshole."

Lance backhanded the earth elemental, whose head snapped back at the impact. Titania touched her cheek in shock before growling ferociously and taking a single ominous step toward Lance.

"You *dare* . . ." she said with a voice that could silence a continent.

"Yes, I do," Lance said contemptuously. "Now *kneel.*"

Unwillingly, but unable to resist, Titania slowly sank to one knee before Lance. Eris soon joined her.

"Your former mistress allowed you far too much leeway. As your new master, you'll soon find that I run a far tighter ship. I have no idea how Everly made you so powerful, but your abilities are clearly squandered on her foolish whims. Under *my* direction, you will reach your true potential."

"The only one we follow is Everly!" Titania hissed at him.

"Well, then, I suppose I'll just have to kill the little whore and settle the issue for you," he sniffed.

"Oh, I'd dearly love to see you try, *Lance*," Eris sneered.

"Do not address me by that name," the traitor said.

"Then what is it?" asked Eris.

"Don't ask questions, slave," said Lance after striking her as well. "I am in command. I am in charge. *I own you.*"

"Tell a lie a thousand times, that doesn't make it true," opined Titania.

Lance struggled with a brief surge of rage. Everly's elementals were so much like her. Defiant and disrespectful. Indifferent to the natural order. No matter. He wouldn't let their petty taunts put him off his game. *He* had the power now. Power enough to make all his enemies suffer. Power enough to gain the respect that he'd always deserved in life but had been denied.

"Seal yourselves within the rat room. Make no personal appearance to the others and, if any ask if something is amiss, convince them that you're fine," he ordered them. "When I give you the signal, I want you to block Everly and the others from access to your powers."

"We can't do that. We're unable to bring harm to our mistress," Eris informed him. "You won't be able to use us to hurt her."

"You think you're so smart, don't you?" Lance sneered. "Feel free to block my access as well. None of us shall draw from you in the conflict to come."

"Then how do you expect to win?" Eris asked in confusion.

But Lance refused to answer her question. Instead, he bid them to vanish to the rat room. Feeling their slowly growing fear and frustration, he reveled in his dominance over them.

Then he opened a gateway to begin renewing old acquaintances.

At first, Anne was reluctant to believe his claims of being an informer and demanded proof. Once it was provided, he revealed his true identity to her at their second meeting. For the first time, he'd managed to surprise her, a moment he found *immensely* satisfying. When she had recovered from her shock and was ready to act, he delivered her to the village of Anders, where Everly's mother dwelled, to set their trap.

After it was sprung, he made a stop in the Godwells' afterlife to enjoy Fenneth's humiliation at the hands of their ancestors. He'd never truly cared for the soft-hearted girl, whose incompetence had led not only to her own demise but, more importantly, *his* as well. Once justice had been dealt to her, he returned to the memory palace to begin the purge of unnecessary elements.

* * *

"Beverly?" Cleverly asked as she stepped into the meeting room. "What are you doing here? Neverly was the one I sent for."

"Did you?" asked Lance. "I'm sorry. I don't believe she received your message."

"Are you going to tell her what I'm doing with Tyler?" Cleverly asked with a smug grin on her face. "I hope you do. I can already imagine her reaction."

"Oh, my, Cleverly. Who knew you had it in you to be so wicked?" he asked her with a grin that matched her own. "You're a naughty little thing, aren't you?"

"You don't care?" Cleverly asked with surprise as she stepped closer to him.

"Not in the slightest," Lance grinned. "Nev doesn't mean anything to me at all."

"Well, color me surprised." Cleverly laughed.

Until she began choking on her own blood.

"Naturally, you don't mean anything to me *either*," he whispered quietly into the dying girl's ear before pushing the tip of the spear he'd brought the rest of the way through her throat.

Cleverly gazed at him with widened, helpless eyes, undoubtedly confused as to why Discordia's healing magic wasn't working on her. Her lips moved languidly as air burbled from them as she tried to form a question with her dying gasps.

"Why?" Lance said to her. "You'd like to know *why*? Because you're a part of Everly's little plan. And anything Everly creates, *I* will destroy. I'm going to ruin all her works. Then I'll make her submit to me and beg for my forgiveness. Everything she has, I'll take. And whatever I don't want, I'll burn. It's my right. I'm her older brother, you see. She's not allowed to be more important than me."

Aiden Vae-es Belsar, reborn in new flesh and now more powerful than he'd ever known it was possible to become, nodded to himself as he watched Cleverly breathe her last breath.

"*I'm* the main character now," he declared to the world.

CHAPTER THIRTY-ONE

King Shadow

A-are we going to be okay?" Tyler asked nervously as he followed closely behind Beverly and Marcis. "I really haven't got a single clue about what's happening here."

"My daughter has conscripted us to dispose of the murderer stalking her halls while she hides in safety," Marcis informed him. "Do try to keep up, lad."

"But why *me*? I'm useless!" Tyler whined.

"Who knows? Maybe we'll find something for you to do," Bev said indifferently. "Just follow my dad! He seems like a slick one, right? My rule in life is to always follow the ones who seem calm. That's a strategy that can't possibly fail!"

"What if they've calmly accepted their fate?" Tyler asked her.

"Oh. Well, that wouldn't be good." Bev shrugged.

"Bev, you warm an old man's heart," Marcis said graciously. "But having said that, I have *no* idea what we should be doing next. I'm unfamiliar with this territory, and I'm afraid that Everly has so many enemies that I don't know where we should even begin."

"Aww, really?" Bev asked. "Shoot, this would be so much easier if I was using Lance."

"You refer to your alter ego?" asked Marcis. "How would that make this any easier?"

"Well, he's more powerful than I am," Bev replied. "When I use him, I have a stronger connection with the elementals. It really pumps me up, you know?"

"Really?" Marcis said curiously. "I had no idea you were weaker than Everly."

"It's a safeguard she put in so we'd never turn on her," Bev said as she walked beside him. "We also have mental blocks preventing us from deliberately causing her any permanent damage."

"But it doesn't prevent you from attacking her completely?" Marcis puzzled aloud. "Why?"

"She likes it when we try to get the jump on her." Beverly giggled. "It keeps her on her toes! But it's not like we're allowed to kill her or anything. Attempts on her life are a big no-no. Everybody who serves her has that command imprinted inside their noggin. Villains need to be cautious about potential Starscreams in their midst, right? No one wants to get stabbed in the back."

"Indeed." Marcis nodded. "But I don't quite understand what my girl was thinking. Why would she instill these safeguards in you and your sisters, but fail to do so for your Lance body?"

"What do you mean?" Beverly asked as she furrowed her brow.

"You said that using Lance made you more powerful than you usually are. Why would Everly allow such a thing? It seems like an obvious loophole to me."

"Oh, Everly didn't make Lance," Beverly said, laughing. "That's something I made on my own."

"You . . . created Lance on your own?" Marcis asked her with slowly growing alarm.

"Well, not entirely by myself," Bev admitted. "I had Titania make it for me from a drop of Everly's blood—"

"BEVERLY, where do you store Lance when you aren't using him?" Marcis suddenly asked her with unnerving intensity.

"I keep him in my room. Why?" Bev asked. "I didn't do something wrong, did I?"

"Take us there, right NOW," Marcis urged her.

They soon arrived at Bev's room, where the girl was surprised to discover that the body was missing. Marcis nodded to himself in grim satisfaction, pleased that his instincts seemed to have been proven correct. "Just as I suspected," he said.

"But why would anyone want to go after Lance?" Beverly asked in bewilderment. "He hasn't got a mind! It doesn't make any sense."

Marcis felt a slight bit of frustration at his daughter's duplicate's lack of ability to quickly process the facts, but he politely kept his feelings to himself. "No, dearest, the killer didn't *target* Lance. My theory is that the killer is somehow *using* Lance. Or perhaps is the creature himself."

"That makes no sense either!" Beverly insisted. "He still doesn't have a mind!"

"But he *does* have a brain!" Marcis said patiently. "Elsewise, how could you control the many neurological functions of his body? And you said yourself that Lance is also tied in directly to the elementals that you all share. It's the only thing that makes sense with the clues that we have."

"Wow," Beverly said. "You know, when you put it like that, he sounds kind of like a zombie—"

"Graaah," grunted Tyler suddenly from behind them.

"Yeah, Tyler." Beverly nodded. "Exactly like that."

Tyler's head slowly rolled across the floor between them and came to a stop at the foot of the bed.

"I'm *not* a zombie," Lance said to them as he stepped into the room with bloodied fingers and closed the door behind himself.

As soon as Everly regained consciousness, she leapt to her feet with her hands up, ready for a fight.

"Nice cheap shot, Nev!" she said with a bold smile. "But it doesn't look like you had what it takes to keep me down for the count!"

To her surprise, instead of standing there ready to be engaged in a life-or-death struggle, Nev was instead seated at a table, where the large goon who'd spoken to her earlier was apparently dispensing medical treatment to her face.

"Okay, boss. At the count of three, I'm going to pop it back in," he said to Nev apologetically.

"Is it going to hurt?" she asked fearfully.

"Oh, gods yes, it's going to feel terrible. No avoiding it, though, if you don't want it to heal crooked."

"Damn it!" she swore.

"Okay, now. Oooooone. Twoooo. Threeee!" The goon then pushed forward with his hand against Nev's nose, which made a hideous popping sound as it was set back in place. Nev gave a small yelp of pain and jerked wildly, but then relaxed a moment later after the deed was done.

"Owww," she said miserably and tenderly rubbed her nose. "Okay, thanks, uh, Bill, was it?"

"Yes, boss," Bill said with a nod.

"Thanks, Bill," Nev said. "You're a real lifesaver, big guy. Mostly your own since now I'm not going to kill you and the boys for seeing something you shouldn't have, but that aside, I'm grateful."

Nev turned to the rest of her assembled gang, who'd stood there nervously watching Bill helping with her nose, and said, "Okay, guys. Just remember: no repeating anything that you saw here today. I'm a genuine freak. I'll find you and kill you if you do. NOW GET THOSE DELIVERIES GOING!" she suddenly barked at them.

And like that, they were back to work. Nev turned and saw that Everly was back on her feet and frowned. "Don't hit my nose again. I'm serious. I will go *mental* on you."

"You held off on killing me so that you could get your nose fixed?" Everly asked her with a cocked eyebrow. "Aren't you supposed to be the smart one?"

"Aren't *you*?" Nev countered. "I couldn't kill you if I wanted to, remember?" She tapped the side of her head and said, "You're the one who set it up that way."

"If that's the case, then why did you hit me with a folding chair?" Everly asked her.

"Because you broke my nose!" Nev yelled at her. "Just because I can't turn on you doesn't mean I have to stand there and take your shit! That fucking hurt, you know!"

"I . . . suppose it did," Everly said.

"Well, thank you for *supposing*," Nev replied with thick sarcasm.

"So, you're really not the mastermind behind the plot to kill me?" Everly said in disappointment. "Shoot. I figured if it was anyone, it would be you. I mean, you *are* the smart one."

"I *am*. Thank you for noticing." Nev nodded.

"Well, I guess I'll just have to go kill Beverly, then," Everly said with a resigned sigh.

"Everly, *stop*. You can't seriously believe that Bev is the one responsible," the other girl snorted. "I love her to death, but my god, if brains were wind, she couldn't move a pinwheel to save her life."

"Yeah, she is pretty light on the gray matter," Everly agreed. "But who's left, then? Cleverly's already dead."

"Clearly faking it," Nev said.

"What? No! I saw the body myself," Everly said.

"Did you touch the corpse?" Nev asked.

"Gross, no. Why would I do that?"

"Everly, if you don't confirm the kill personally, then there was no kill," Nev said. "Think about it! This is like the first *Saw* movie! She pretended to be a corpse to convince you she was out of the way, and now she's running things from behind the scenes!"

"Are you saying she *Jigsaw*'d me?" Everly asked in shock.

"Exactly! It's the only thing that makes sense." Nev nodded.

"Well, that sneaky cow," Everly growled. "Time to go teach her a lesson. You want in on this?"

"Why would I care what you do with Cleverly?" Nev smirked.

"She tried to sleep with Tyler to piss you off," Everly informed her.

"SHE DID WHAT?" Nev shouted. "Is that why she kept calling me?"

"You were ignoring her calls?"

"Of course I was! I can't stand that little brat!" Nev said.

"Well, let's go stomp her head in. It'll feel good for us both," Everly said.

"Let's do it," Nev seethed.

"Oh, my god, Tyler!" Bev shouted in dismay. "He's leaking all over my floor! That's where I put my feet!"

"Not a very sentimental girl, are you?" Lance said as he stepped closer to his prey.

"Those of my line aren't known for dwelling long on the past," Marcis said casually as he drew his blade. "I'm sure Tyler was a fine fellow, but I had a feeling he wasn't going to last the night."

"An accurate one, it would appear," said the killer.

"Quite right," said Marcis. "By the way, you *do* realize you're outnumbered, don't you?"

"Is that how you see it? From my perspective, I don't believe the two of you are enough to threaten me."

"Overconfidence has killed better men than you," Marcis grinned.

"There *are* no better men than me!" countered Lance. "As you'll soon find out, old man!"

"Well, we'll have to see about that, won't we—"

Bev stabbed Lance through the chest with her spear.

"Glurg," Lance said before dropping to his knees and falling over.

Dead.

"Sorry, Lance," Bev said to his body. "I couldn't *spear* what you were saying."

She turned to Marcis with a look of profound satisfaction on her face and gave him a thumbs-up.

Marcis looked away, unable to meet her guileless eyes.

"Well, that was an absolute waste of time," Everly said later as they sat gathered in the conference room.

"Was it, though? I got to kick Cleverly's corpse a few dozen times," Nev said. "That's something, isn't it?"

"This makes me the hero, doesn't it?" Bev said happily. "I totally saved the day, didn't I?"

"The whole thing was your fault to begin with!" Everly said after giving Bev a dope smack across the back of her head. "Saving the day from your own mess doesn't count."

"Awww," Bev whined.

"Now, now, Everly," Marcis said. "Whoever this mysterious mastermind was, he seemed to be *profoundly* intelligent. I suspect he would have been able to find another chink in your armor if given enough time. His devious movements were patient and tactically sound. I would have enjoyed facing him in battle."

"You sound as though you admired him," Everly said.

"In a way, yes," Marcis admitted. "I sensed a kindred spirit in Lance. A fellow wolf that ferociously stood his ground before me. A nameless plunderer, committed to his merciless path. It's almost a shame that I can't allow his identity to remain a mystery."

Having said that, Marcis removed his glove and reached for Lance's body, preparing to use his gift to take the memories of the dead warrior for himself.

But just before his fingers made contact with Lance's forehead, Everly's hand stopped him. She gently grabbed Marcis's wrist and guided him away.

"Everly?" Marcis asked her in surprise.

"You're right, Dad." Everly nodded. "I don't know who this guy was either, but he was good. A more formidable foe than Anne, even. He had me dancing in the palm of his hand without me even realizing it. He almost stole everything in one fell swoop."

Everly turned to Lance's body. Then she bowed before her deceased enemy.

"We don't need to know anything about this cunning bastard. Only that he was calculating and dangerous and worthy of our respect. Whoever he was, he taught me an important lesson about patience and playing the long game. Revealing his identity would just diminish the impact he had on my life. Burn the corpse and consign this nameless fiend to the shadows that spawned him."

"Everly, that's *so* fucking cool," Beverly gasped.

"King Shadow. That's what we'll call him," Nev said. "Our ultimate mystery opponent."

"I like that, Nev." Everly nodded. "King Shadow it is. I only wish we could have been on the same side."

"King Shadow," Marcis murmured. "An opponent that would truly have been worthy of me."

He drew his sword once more and touched the blade to his head in a sign of respect.

"But how exactly did he take over Lance's body?" Beverly wondered. "Do we have an explanation for that?"

"Oh, who cares? It's over," Everly said with a dismissive wave of her hand. "Let's talk about killing Anne."

A moment later, the body was burned.

CHAPTER THIRTY-TWO

Your Heart to Admire

I've been thinking about you, Anne."

Everly's voice drifted across the empty reception hall of the Van Belsar estate, where Anne sat alone in the dark, waiting. She looked up expectantly, glad that the time had finally arrived to bring things to a proper conclusion.

Two days had passed since their confrontation in the village of Anders. In the time spent between then and now, Anne had returned to the home she shared with Marcis, knowing that nothing yet had been settled. She knew that Everly must surely feel the same way. So, she'd come here to wait, knowing that her enemy would soon arrive.

"I've been thinking about you as well, Everly," Anne replied. "You're a bold one to return so eagerly for more. Normally, when I break someone, it's done so thoroughly that they wouldn't ever consider appearing before me again."

"I'll admit that you did quite the number on me." Everly laughed. "I've been beaten before in training, but *never* to that extent. I thought I was finished learning lessons. I feel . . ."

"Yes?" Anne asked her.

". . . I feel almost absurdly grateful for the experience," Everly continued. "A famous warrior in the world I hail from once wept because he believed there were no new lands for him to conquer. Thanks to your little lesson, I've realized that I haven't even hit my *peak*. That I haven't even conquered *myself*. Thank you, Anne, for helping me realize that Everly still has room to grow."

"Oh," Anne said. "I'm sorry to hear you say that. My hope was that the taste of defeat would dissuade you from continuing this destructive path you walk."

"Just the opposite, in fact!" Everly exclaimed with a delighted giggle. "Now that *I've* had a taste of you, Anne, I want more."

"More?" Anne asked her.

"Oh, yes. I want *everything* you can possibly give me. I'm obsessed by the memory of you. Not lying. I dreamed about you last night. The anticipation kept me awake. I think you might be driving me *insane*."

"I'm flattered, girl. But I think I'm too old for you," Anne said with a quirk of a smile on the corner of her lip.

"Please don't say that!" Everly pouted. "I asked my father all about you, you know."

Now a sour expression clouded Anne's face. "And what did Marcis have to say about me?" she asked. "Nothing flattering, I'm sure."

"Only that he'd like a divorce," Everly said chirpily.

Anne laughed bitterly at the girl's words. "I'm hardly surprised. How unfortunate for us both that the Godwell tradition is lifelong matrimony."

"Together until death?"

"Sadly, yes."

"Anne. I figured out why you're so obsessed with him," Everly teased.

"Be careful of what you say next, Everly," Anne said coldly.

"No, no, it's okay. I understand you, Anne," Everly continued. "My dad's a parasite. He manipulates other people to steal power from them. It's an awful thing that he does."

"Yes," Anne somberly agreed. "Yes, it is."

"He couldn't stop if he wanted to either. It's his nature! He doesn't just feed off others. The act of using them brings him pleasure. Even if it adversely affects the world, he must continue bringing chaos to his surroundings. He has to hurt everyone around him, whether he wants to or not."

"Yes," Anne repeated. "And he does it with such zeal."

"That's what attracted you to him," Everly said. "That's why you can't let him go. Because in a way, he's just like you. He's a monster in human skin. He's like a vampire. And you were hoping that he'd understand you. That with him by your side, you wouldn't be alone anymore."

Tears began running down Anne's face as she nodded but said nothing in reply.

"Were you born that way or was it something that was done to you?" Everly asked.

"I don't remember," Anne said quietly.

"But you don't like it?"

"I never have."

"Why? I think you're incredible."

"My family used me as a tool. A weapon," Anne said with even greater bitterness than before. "They never truly accepted me as one of them. I was something to be used for the aggrandizement of the Godwell name. A symbol of their unending power. My desires were utterly irrelevant in comparison to their grand design."

"You sound as though you hate them," Everly tittered. "Whoever would have guessed?"

"My feelings toward my family are complex and not something I feel like sharing with someone that I know will only use them to mock me," Anne said darkly.

"I wouldn't do that, Anne. I love you," Everly said.

"Shut up," Anne growled.

"But I do!" Everly said with the sincerity of an infatuated girl. "When I think about your long life spent standing in defense of the values of people you've grown to despise, my heart just swells. It swells, Anne! It really does! Because you're doing it out of duty. You're doing it out of love for the common good! That's genuinely noble! God, Anne, I think you're so beautiful!"

"Why are you talking to me like this?" Anne asked her. "I thought you came to fight me!"

"I have. I will. But before we do, I just wanted you to know how much I cared," Everly assured her.

"You don't."

"I do! Really, I do! I'm the only one who understands you, Anne. And I think you understand me just as well, don't you?"

"You're an insane child," Anne replied harshly. "A cruel girl with far too much power."

"Exactly! And by the end of this night, one of us is going to be dead. Isn't that beautiful, Anne? Isn't that the greatest thing you've ever heard?"

"No," Anne said flatly.

"I think you're a hero, Anne." Everly giggled. "What else can your resolve be called except for that? You're heroic. I'm absolutely over the moon over it! I've been waiting so long for a hero to appear in my life . . ."

"Stop this," Anne demanded as she rose angrily from her seat. "Stop hiding yourself from me. Do you wish to do battle or not? Let's be done with this!"

"No, no, no," Everly said. "Why rush this? We should make this moment last forever! I want every second of this encounter seared into my mind! You're so pretty, Anne! I want you to be mine forever! I'm really thinking about keeping you around after I've killed you. What do you think of that idea? What do you think of me sinking my teeth into you?"

"I think you're sick for behaving this way," Anne said angrily.

"You were going to drain me dry, weren't you?" Everly taunted. "Didn't that mean you liked the way I tasted?"

"SHUT UP!"

"MAKE ME!" Everly laughed after she appeared behind Anne. When the startled countess turned, surprised by the sudden appearance of her foe, Everly's fist smashed into her face, driving her back with such force that she was first smashed through a marble pillar, then through a wall, into the back hallway.

After Anne regained her legs and pushed the rubble away, she saw Everly standing before her, wearing her full armor.

"Daddy told me how your powers work," Everly said smugly. "Your blood pheromones or whatever. They're antimagical, aren't they? Reducing the strength of anyone who breathes them in. In hindsight the solution was *so* obvious! If I just filter my armor, then you can't get to me at all, can you?"

"If that's your only defense, then I'll simply have to peel you out of that cumbersome steel, won't I?" Anne said.

"Can you, though?" Everly asked as she raced toward Anne and began attacking her with relentless strikes and kicks. "Maybe it's due to my control over the earth, or maybe it's because of my massive *harada*, but, Anne, I feel so light on my feet! Will you even land a blow?"

Quicker than Everly expected, Anne brushed aside a powerful roundhouse punch and spun to deliver a back-thrusting kick that sent the girl flying away.

"I believe I'll somehow manage," Anne said curtly.

In response, Everly laughed. Then she called upon Titania's power of the earth and thrust her open palm in Anne's direction. The floor beneath Anne's feet swelled and bulged as though the wooden flooring had become a massive ocean wave, which knocked Anne onto her back and carried her forth, spilling her outside and leaving her covered in broken debris.

When Anne finished clawing her way free of the mess, a large granite spike shot from the ground. Its sharp tip nearly caught her beneath the jaw, causing Anne to pivot unsteadily to the side to avoid being pierced. More of them quickly followed, forcing Anne to keep moving to avoid impalement. When she seemed to have escaped that danger, several heavy stones came flying fast and hard to connect brutally with her face and chest.

"This is called geokinesis, in case you were wondering," Everly called out to her. "With my level of mastery over the element of earth, I can control anything that comes from it, Anne. *Anything.*"

To illustrate Everly's point, dozens of similarly sized stones floated from the ground and began rotating around her like satellites orbiting a celestial body. Then they began flying after Anne like shots from a cannon. Most of them missed her entirely, but the few that connected did terrible damage when they scored a hit.

Anne was thrown back and knocked down as the stones continued to batter her, drawing blood and tearing away at her clothing.

Now Everly began to float in the air, spinning joyfully like a pirouetting dancer displaying her skill on a stage. "Spooky, isn't it? Well, my armor's metal! Iron ore comes from the earth, so I can manipulate it too, even while I'm wearing it. How does it feel to be looked down upon from the heavens, Anne? I have a god's-eye view here, and I have to say . . . *it feels so right.*"

In response to Everly's taunts, Anne angrily grabbed one of the stones she'd been struck with and hurled it with superhuman force into Everly's center, knocking her from the sky in a clatter of steel.

"You're such a child," Anne said furiously. "With your endless taunting and bullying and being so *satisfied* and prideful of all that you do!"

"Why wouldn't I be? I'm incredible!" Everly said giddily. "Hey, here's a fun scientific fact I want to share. Did you know that lightning can shoot from the earth into the sky?"

"What are you babbling about now—" Anne began to say.

Blue light. White light. Bright nothing.

CRASH!

When Anne managed to reopen her eyes, she was surprised to discover that she was lying on her back, emanating white smoke.

"*Ahhh,*" she moaned, temporarily unable to form any coherent thoughts or sentences. She only felt awareness in the barest sense of that word. Then the shadow of an armored form fell over her.

"You really are fun," Everly said appreciatively to her before delivering a vicious kick to the face.

Pain flared into existence and swept across Anne's body at the merciless contact with Everly's boot. Her eyes rolled back into her skull and for a moment it was like she'd ceased to exist. Was this what being in hell was like?

Was Everly's presence hell itself?

"It's not enough," Everly said to her. "Anne? Anne? Anne? Don't die."

Now Anne felt Everly's armored body on top of hers. Now she felt her armored fists coming down like hammerblows, which crushed the bones of her face and tore into her skin. Relentless, merciless, destroying strikes that broke her down bit by bit, all while Everly encouraged her to fight back.

"You're so cool, Anne!" *Smash!*

"I love you so much!" *Smash!*

"I'm on your side, Anne! I'm rooting for you!" *Smash!*

"Don't give up!" *Smash!*

Over and over, the killing blows rained down. But Anne endured them until finally, in a frenzy of unrestrained violence, Everly began headbutting her, smashing her helmeted face into Anne's with a speed fueled entirely by madness and affection.

At the end of each forceful blow, the girl would ask:

"Is it over? Is it over? *IS IT OVER?*"

As her head came flying down for perhaps the final time, Anne suddenly caught it with both hands. Then she screamed with an animal howl of rage before delivering a headbutt of her own that threw Everly off her and sent her rolling away.

"*I'LL KILL YOOOOOU!!!*" Anne shrieked at her with blood dripping down her rapidly healing face.

"You'll try!" Everly said eagerly as she ran at her opponent, eager to continue the fight, only for Anne to catch her incoming swing, pivot, and then send her flying away with a mighty throw that had her land all the way on the other side of the estate.

"Right. So *that's* where Sarah got her temper," Everly realized. "Okay, that makes sense."

She stood up, cracked her neck a bit, and then turned to face the incoming Anne, who was racing toward her on all fours like a hound after a fox.

"Hmm. I think I may have upset her a tad." Everly giggled.

Then, the fight was back on.

CHAPTER THIRTY-THREE

One Life

Long ago . . .

"Pick it up, Anne," her father ordered her.

Today little Anne was in a place she'd never been before. It was an area beneath her home that was colder and darker than any of the other rooms she'd ever been in, past the big iron doors that her father's guards always stood in front of, wearing impassive faces along with their imposing black armor.

Today, after breakfast, instead of being allowed to go off and play with her attendants, Anne was summoned by her father to his office, where he greeted her with a big smile and a warm hug.

"Hi, Daddy!" Anne said happily. She very rarely was able to see her father in the day. He had a very important job that constantly kept him away. But today, he was making special time for Anne, and that pleased her very much. "Come along, my buzzy little bee," he said to her as she took his hand.

"*Daddy,*" she said, laughing. "I'm not a bee! You're silly!"

"Is that right?" he wondered. "Am I a silly daddy? Well, I suppose I must be! But you still look like a bee to me!"

Having said that, he then picked her up and carried her in his arms, giving her kisses and hugs as she laughed and yelled. Soon, they stood before the dark door, where the guards each bowed deeply before their lord and stepped aside to admit them.

"What's in here, Daddy?" Anne asked with a child's curiosity.

"Something very important, Anne," her father replied. "Something important to the success of the Godwells. And today it's your turn to see it."

Then he led her down a series of stairs illuminated by flickering torchlight, which led to a corridor of barred cells where broken-eyed men and women sat, some weeping, others silently staring ahead, all of them desperately trying to avoid receiving the attention of Lord Godwell and his young daughter.

When they reached the room at the end of that strange corridor, Anne saw what her father wanted her to see. A young man tied to an altar table, struggling to escape his bonds but unable to move.

"Daddy? Who is he?" little Anne wondered.

"He . . . is a very bad person, Anne," her father said to her in his soft and gentle voice.

"He *is*?" Anne said with wide eyes. She'd never seen a bad person before. She hadn't even known they truly existed. "Daddy, what did he do?"

"He tried to hurt us, sweetie," her father said sadly. "He disobeyed the laws that we must protect and tried to encourage others to do the same. He fought back when we captured him and was disrespectful when we passed judgment upon him. He was very, *very* bad."

Anne couldn't believe it. "Very, *very* bad?" she asked, scandalized.

"I'm afraid so, Anne. And because of that, it's fallen upon us to punish him. The laws of the Godwells are the laws that all men must obey. We're not merely a family, sweetie. We're the only people who matter in this world. And for others to defy us is an unquestionable wrong. It mustn't be allowed."

"Really, Daddy?" Anne asked.

"Mm-hmm." Her father solemnly nodded. Then he took something from one of the pouches he wore around his waist and set it on the bound man's chest. After that, he lifted Anne and placed her on top of the prisoner.

"Pick it up, Anne," he told her.

"What is it, Daddy?" she asked him as she studied the strange tool.

"This is a dagger, sweetie. Hold on to the handle and don't touch the blade. It's very sharp, and I don't want you to cut yourself. Hold it like this, see?"

"Like this, Daddy?" she asked as she imitated his movement.

"*Exactly* like that, sweetie," he said proudly. "My little girl is such a fast learner!"

Anne giggled, pleased that her father was impressed with her. "What do I do now?" she asked him innocently.

"Now I'm going to show you how to teach bad people a lesson," her dad said to her with a smile as he pulled out a dagger of his own. "Now, pay close attention to what I do, Anne, okay? I'll go first and then I want you to copy me. Do you understand?"

"Yes, Daddy!"

"Good girl, Anne. Now first, we'll begin with his eye . . ."

Annie followed her instructions perfectly.

Her father was *very* pleased with her.

*   *   *

Anne leaped at Everly and crashed with an audible thud into the ground, then her opponent jumped back before rushing in to catch her with a football tackle. While she had Anne pinned beneath her, Everly tried to press her thumbs into Anne's eyes, but before she could push them in fully, Anne kicked up wildly with such strength that Everly was forced over her. Now that she was the one in the dominant position, Anne grabbed the girl by her throat and began squeezing as hard as she could, intent on throttling her to death.

"Anne, you're so *wild*," Everly said admiringly.

"Just *die*," Annie whispered desperately to her. "I hate you, so please *die!*"

"No, you don't," Everly said to her as she slowly forced Anne's hands away. "You love this. This is who you are!"

"It's not!" Anne sobbed.

"It is! And it's great! This is what you were made for!" Everly laughed.

"Shut up!"

"I won't!" Everly giggled. "Murderer."

"I'm not!" Anne said. "I only did what had to be done!"

"*Monster!*" taunted Everly. "Freak!"

"*STOP!*" Anne shrieked.

Long ago.

"Father, it hurts," Anne sobbed as she lay on her side, bleeding from her mouth and nostrils. "I can't breathe. Why can't I breathe?"

"I'm sorry, Anne," her father said sorrowfully as he knelt by her side. "I know how much it hurts; I do. But this is a *good* pain. A *necessary* pain. One that you're taking upon yourself for the benefit of our family. You're being very brave right now."

"*Daddy*," she sobbed. She hadn't called him that in years. But she was now in so much agony that her recognition of him was breaking down, reverting to her childhood. "Daddy, why?"

"Because the Godwells need this from you, Anne. Because *I* need this from you," her father said.

He took her hand in his own and began stroking it reassuringly. "You're not like your other sisters, Anne. You're going to survive this. You're special. I have a feeling about you. I know I didn't waste my time with you," he said to her with a doting smile. "Endure this, Anne. I believe in you . . ."

Suddenly Everly flew forward, into the air, breaking loose from Anne's grip while laughing wildly. Then more bolts of lightning began erupting from the earth, destroying the ground beneath Anne's feet and tearing away at Anne, electrifying her, torturing her, but unable to finish her off due to her high magical resistance.

"Oh, Anne, that would *kill* an ordinary person a hundred times over," Everly said happily. "But not you, though! Magic can't get the job done, can it? But you still feel the pain, don't you? *You still feel the pain!*"

"What do *you* know about pain, little girl?" Anne howled at her floating adversary. "What do you know about true suffering? What has life ever brought you but chances to excel?"

"Guilty!" Everly cackled. "Guilty, guilty, guilty!"

She descended from the sky to land on her feet. Then she strode forward until she stood inches apart from the crouching Anne and raised her arms. Anne, expecting another attack, was instead surprised when Everly embraced her in a crushing hug and continued to quietly laugh in her ear.

"I'm a product of pure dumb luck, Anne," said Everly's merry voice. "I used to believe I was a chosen one, that the things I've acquired were due purely to my own will. And to a certain degree, that's true. But I also came upon my powers by simple happenstance. I got *lucky*, Anne."

"Then why have you become like this?" Anne asked her, desperately trying to understand.

"Because I'm not *grateful* for my good luck!" Everly answered. "Because I don't *care* that it was all random. I'm still me! I'm still greedy, prideful, and in need of entertainment. I'll always be this way. I don't mind. I *love* being me."

"Everly, no—" Anne said.

"Anne, *yes*," Everly tittered. "The real question is why don't *you* like being yourself? You're beautiful and powerful but all you do is feel pain for other people. All you do is follow your family's will, despite how much it makes you miserable."

"That's not . . . that's not true," Anne said, trying to deny it.

"You've killed so many people, Anne. The guilty and the innocent. Women . . . *children* . . . all supposedly to protect the noble line you were assigned to protect from diminishing even more . . ."

"I *had* to," Anne said miserably.

"Of course you did," Everly said with a voice filled with empathy. "Because if the nobles keep breeding the magic out of their families, the horny little morons that they are, their connection to the elementals will fade completely. And without the elementals to protect them, the seven kings will invade this land and *ruin* it."

Anne said nothing. She only stared at Everly's helmeted visage. On it, her face was reflected, filled with conflicting emotions and needs.

"You do everything for these people. You've followed your duty like a good girl. Like a good little soldier! All these centuries spent being used by people *just* as uncaring and ungrateful as I am. Oh, poor Anne! Poor, poor Anne! Don't you get it? You've killed the *innocent* to preserve a society as rotten as *this!* A society so broken and foul that it gave all the power in the world to a person like me! ANNE! YOU ENABLED ME! *YOU* MADE ME POSSIBLE!"

"SHUUUUUUUT UP!" Anne screamed. And this time, something within her broke.

Long ago.

"Father, *no*," Anne wept.

They were in the prison beneath the estate once more. But now, the one tied to the table was no criminal. No instigator of disharmony, no sworn enemy of the social order.

It was a girl.

Just an ordinary girl.

Anne had practiced for years on the prisoners her father placed before her. Her instincts were superb, and her talent was unmatched. Within minutes of going to work on someone, she would break them. She would have them confess their every sin in life and beg for reformation and redemption.

And if it was necessary, she would also dispose of them with cold, professional detachment after first making them regret their choices in life with every fiber of their being.

By the age of seventeen, Anne had killed more people than most people had ever met. She didn't care. It was for the good of the Godwell family.

But now, after barely surviving her sickness, her father demanded *this* of her.

"She hasn't done anything," Anne tried to tell him. "I can tell just by looking at her! Father! Please, I can't do this."

"Anne," her father said to her with his gentle, patient voice. "Anne, surviving the first onset of your abilities is just the first part. The symptoms have receded for now, but they'll come back, eventually. Unless you do this."

"Father, I don't understand," Anne said.

"You need to drink her blood, Anne. It's something that must be done periodically. To maintain your life and stabilize your magic, you need to take power from someone else."

"Do . . . do I have to k-kill her?" Anne stammered.

"I'm afraid so, sweetie. Once a month. A life for a life," her father said.

"But why?" Anne sobbed. "She hasn't done anything."

"Anne," her father said to her. "You must understand, my love. Life . . . life isn't about what we do. It's about who we *are*. Anne, you're a Godwell, darling. And the Godwells are the only people who matter."

"Daddy, *please*," Anne begged him.

Suddenly, swift as a snake, her father produced a knife which he thrust into the bound girl's neck. He then twisted it and looked frankly at his daughter.

"I've wounded her mortally, Anne," he informed her. "When I remove this blade, she's going to die, regardless of what you do. That decision's already been made. The real question is, *are you going to waste her blood?* Decide for yourself, my angel. I'm done speaking."

Then, her father pulled the knife free and left the room.

The girl continued to lie there, staring helplessly at her, while her life's blood jettisoned out, so red, so bright, so *vivid* . . .

Anne stared at it, just as helpless as the dying girl before her. Mesmerized.

Hungry . . .

When her father returned a half hour later and beheld his blood-spattered, weeping daughter, he took her in his arms and told her how proud he was of her. How glad he was that she'd made the right decision. How she'd bring endless glory to their family name . . .

He said many things that night. But despite his praise and assurances, Anne knew that she had done something unforgivable.

Anne knew that she was now a monster.

Everly stopped taunting Anne when the other woman stopped speaking. She'd seen the exact moment when the vampire had utterly snapped and knew that she was no longer fighting a rational being.

Sanity was such an interesting commodity. Most people thought of it as an unlimited resource, but Everly knew for a fact that it was a lot scarcer than they realized. And *sensitive* too.

In *The Dark Knight*, the Joker managed to drive the trusted Gotham district attorney, Harvey Dent, completely mad by telling the truth about the corrupt nature of the city that Dent had sworn himself in service to. He pointed out that everyone Dent trusted had compromised themselves morally and made his job all but impossible to do. That he couldn't stand against corruption while being surrounded by it.

Killing Dent's girlfriend and burning off half his face had also done a number on his psyche. As a result of the clown's manipulation, Dent turned into the sort of monster he'd spent his career battling.

Everly had been in *awe*.

Yes, like for so many restless, edgy youth, Heath Ledger's Joker had been a huge influence on Everly's life. The way he'd deftly anticipated every question Dent would ask and then put his own life on the line in a game of Russian roulette, the better to thoroughly corrupt his prey, had been decisive in Everly's decision to swear herself to the forces of evil.

Of course, she completely denied that movie's influence over her life and loudly jeered any cringy buffoon who dared to say, "*Why so serious?*" where others could see them. But in her heart of hearts, Everly knew the truth. Heath's Joker had become a sensei to her.

And now, by lightly paying homage to his technique (which is to say, shamelessly ripping him off), she had driven Anne completely nuts.

Although knowing that she had pushed another person into insanity was totally fucking radical, it hadn't been *completely* intentional. Everly just wanted to take the vampire far past her comfort zone and force her to confront her true nature. Everly hadn't lied at all about her admiration for Anne. In her way, she did love the poor creature.

But Everly's nature was to dominate what she loved. Equality and mutual respect were never going to be viable options for those she chose to be hers. First, they had to be destroyed. Then rebuilt. Just as she'd done with Grail.

Hmm. Where *had* Grail been lately? Had she misplaced him somewhere? It seemed she had. Well, that was a little embarrassing. It harkened back to her childhood when she always had to beg her parents to help her find the weapons that came with her Decepticon action figures because she was always losing them.

Ah, well, he was probably fine.

"HOOOOOOLD!" Grail bellowed as he brought the full weight of his axe down on the demon's neck before kicking its body away. "Hold the line, damn it! Even if these screaming beasts drag us all to the shores of perdition itself, know that we die now as TRUE WARRIORS! Let the fires of hell choke on our stubborn souls! Find your hearts and grip your steel! NOW, FORWARD!"

"FOR GRAIL!" shouted the ferocious villagers he'd organized into a desperate defense against this terrible demonic incursion. Only days earlier, they'd been but simple farmers and laborers. Now, with the training he'd given them and with his words igniting their fighting spirits, they had been transformed into the region's best hope of survival. As one, they boldly stepped forward, fearing no fiend.

"FOR GRAIL!" they proudly shouted again. "FOR THE DAWN!"

And so, screaming their defiance against the unholy evils now arrayed against them, Grail led these humble people to eternal glory. Those who fell would be dutifully mourned, their courage praised, and their sacrifice never forgotten.

But those who survived this day would become living legends . . .

For this was the village that *held!*

"Yeah, he's probably just sitting around, waiting for me to come get him like an old hound waiting for his master at work." Everly chuckled to herself. "Good ol' Grail . . ."

Twenty years ago.

"What are you looking at?" Anne asked the young man curiously.

"Nothing," answered Marcis Vae-es Belsar as he stood at the balcony with a drink in hand, gazing idly upon the citizens of the capital bustling before him on the streets below. "Nothing at all."

"Oh," Anne said, uncertainly. She'd seen this man many times during her various visits to the royal palace. She knew that he was a close friend of Prince Septis. Marcis, the second son of the lord of Belsar County.

Marcis possessed a handsome, mischievous face which Anne found fascinating. He rarely comported himself with the dignity required of his station. Indeed, he hardly seemed a noble at all and was infamous for his frequent pranks and for getting his circle of friends (including the prince) into trouble.

Now, standing alone with him, despite her greater age, Anne found it difficult to speak in his presence. It was an issue she'd been dealing with for nearly fifteen centuries of life. Speaking casually to others was just *hard*.

"Hey, do you suppose I'd be in trouble if I dropped this glass and it killed someone?" Marcis suddenly asked her.

"What?" Anne asked in alarm. "Is that something that you're considering doing?"

"Me? No, no. Just a thought experiment was all." Marcis smiled. "It's just that this is the royal palace and all, yes? So, if I dropped a heavy glass and it hit someone on the head and they died as a result . . ."

"That would be a crime, yes," Anne informed him.

"Okay, but would it be a crime or a *crime*?" Marcis wondered.

"What do you mean by that?" Anne asked him.

"Well, since this is the palace, my potential random victim is just as likely to be a noble or even a royal as it is to be a mere servant. So that's a one in three chance that I could be punished, executed for treason, or get away with it entirely. After all, who cares about commoners?"

"You should!" Anne said. "Defense of the common man is one of your duties as a nobleman."

"Yes, I've been told that many times before," Marcis said with a careless wave of his hand. "But that's not necessarily something I find to be true. I certainly haven't seen such practices being performed by my peers."

"It wasn't always that way," Anne said sadly. "There was a time when the lords of this land upheld their duties with the utmost solemnity."

"I suppose you speak from personal experience, Lady Godwell," said Marcis.

"I do." Anne nodded. "My condolences, by the way, for the passing of your older brother. I've lost siblings myself. I know it to be a pain that recedes slowly."

"No worries, my lady," Marcis said indifferently. "I killed my brother myself. It was hard going for the first two minutes or so. Some people simply don't want to be throttled."

"Lord Marcis!" Anne said in shock. "Why would you tell me that?"

"Oh, I assumed you already knew and were playing coy." Marcis laughed.

"You Godwells have your hands in everyone's business, after all. I considered myself no different."

"Well, I had no idea," Anne said angrily. "And now that I know, I regret learning of it!"

As she turned to walk away, Marcis grabbed her by her elbow.

"Ah, one moment, love. Now that you know my terrible secret, how can I possibly let you walk away?" asked Marcis.

"Release your hand, my lord," Anne warned him tersely.

"Not until I've first silenced you," Marcis purred.

"And how, pray tell, do you intend to do that?" Anne demanded to know.

In response, he leaned in and kissed her. And it was . . .

Tremendous.

"Care to join me in my room?" he asked her.

She did.

Later in the week, she married him.

The fight was beginning to lose its luster. To Everly's disappointment, without a sane intellect to guide her actions, Anne had been reduced to a wild beast that attacked in predictable patterns that were easily anticipated. After Anne tried to gnaw on her through her armor for the third time, Everly had had enough.

"I'm a victim of my success," she sighed to herself. "Once more the fragility of the human mind works against my interests. I can't help but crush everything and everyone that rises against me. I'm as relentless as the tide that sweeps away all the little sandcastles. Do you hear me, Anne? I'm the tide."

Anne ran at her again, slashing away with her claws and snapping with her jaws, her teeth clanking like steel traps. It was such an admirable display of ferocity. And yet *so* pointless.

"Oh, Anne. My esteem for you is endless. I swear it is. Is that why you let your mind shatter? To spite me? To steal away my enjoyment of this moment? What a cruel woman you are."

Everly stepped closer to the broken vampire and once more embraced her. But this time instead of mocking her, she whispered quiet noises and gently ran her hand down Anne's dark red hair, soothing her like a frightened child.

"Enough. We're done," Everly told her quietly but firmly. "Shh. Stop. It's over," she insisted. Eventually, Anne relented and stopped struggling. She rested her head against Everly's breastplate and sobbed adrenalized tears as the tension was released from her, leaving behind a sad, lonely creature that had been alive for far too long.

"It's okay, Anne," Everly said to her.

"Kill me," Anne begged her. "Please kill me."

"Why?" asked Everly.

"Because I'm tired of hurting other people. And I'm tired of *being* hurt."

"A person can't help being who they are, Anne."

"Yes, they can. I was just never brave enough."

"Are you sure about this?" Everly asked her.

"I am. But Everly . . ."

"Yes?"

"If you can, please bind my soul to this world."

"Why?"

"I don't want to see my family again. I don't want to be in their afterlife."

"What do I get out of doing you this little favor?" Everly asked her.

"What?" Anne asked as she turned her gaze toward her.

"I'm just kidding, Anne. I'm not as cruel as all that." Everly smiled. Then, as she'd done to Fenneth before her, Everly drove her fist through Anne's chest and crushed her heart.

Anne fell limply into Everly's arms. She blinked once . . .

Nineteen years ago.

"Hello," Anne shyly said to her new employee, a spirited immigrant from Oldstead that she hadn't yet met. "Are you the one the institute recommended?"

"I am," the beautiful researcher said with a confident nod. Instead of bowing to her as Anne's station demanded, the golden-haired woman instead boldly raised her hand and waited for Anne to shake it. "I'm Lyona Skolder, at your service, of course."

"Of course." Anne smiled. "And I am—"

"I know who you are, Countess. I'd have to be *blind* not to notice you. You're gorgeous! But you're way too pale, don't you think?"

"Do you think so?" Anne asked her.

"Yes, I do," Lyona said firmly.

"Does it bother you?" Anne asked quietly.

"Hardly! I've got more important things to do than concern myself with someone's complexion, after all. You didn't hire me to tell you when to get a tan."

Anne laughed at that, impressed by the other woman's fearlessness. "Lyona, was it? Would you care to join me for lunch?"

"I don't see why not," Lyona said. "But I insist we eat outside! Come on, Anne. Join me in the sun," she said with a kind smile.

She held out her hand once more. And with no hesitation, Anne gladly took it.

. . . then she was gone.

Weren't you supposed to seize her soul and bind it to this world? Eris asked her after Everly laid the body on the ground.

"Yeeeeah, I have *no* idea how to do something like that," Everly said. "Look at her face, though. Wherever she wound up, I think she's okay with it."

Perhaps so, Eris said. *Would you like me to copy her mind?*

"Yes," Everly said after a moment's thought. "You know, this is the second time we've heard about her family's private afterlife. I wonder if we should do something about that."

Everly. Are you suggesting we turn their paradise into sulfur and ash? Eris asked her.

"I don't see why we shouldn't," Everly said. "They certainly wouldn't extend any mercy to us. Besides, the rat room could always use some new blood, couldn't it?"

I won't lie, the idea of adding the Godwells to my collection is greatly appealing, Eris said eagerly.

"I thought that might interest you," Everly smirked. Then she looked upon Anne's body and sighed. "What a complicated lady. I wonder if she suffered so much because she was a good person, or if it was because people aren't meant to be immortal?"

I suspect it was an issue of temperament, Eris said. *I find it far more likely that Anne simply refused to fully embrace her nature as a predator. At some point, you must make a choice. Are you a fox or a hen?*

"Why a fox?" Everly asked. "Why not a wolf?"

Because wolves hunt in packs, answered Eris. *And a fox, like a vampire, is always alone.*

"Wow." Everly whistled. "Deep thoughts with Eris, huh?"

I confess to bearing considerable insight into the human psyche. After all, I enjoy preying upon it.

"Indeed," Everly said. "Well, we've got a copy of her mind and memories. I suppose we can honor her wish to be left to rot. But only because she put up such a great fight."

The boundless depth of your kindness astonishes me, Everly.

"What can I say? I'm a very good person," Everly said as she exited through a gateway. "I always have been."

CHAPTER THIRTY-FOUR

Dante's Fellowship Lost

'm afraid you're going to have to repeat a year, Miss Skolder," the headmistress
said unsympathetically. "You've missed entirely too much class time. Despite
your father's prestige, this simply can't be overlooked."

"Are you perhaps . . . joking?" Everly asked the older woman. "Can't you just
wave a hand and send me merrily on my way?"

"Not a chance," the headmistress replied. "And frankly, I find your attitude
disappointing. This academy isn't just a place of learning, Miss Skolder. It's a
sacred place of *bonding* where even people with substandard talent such as yourself can improve their relationship with their elemental and thus improve their
grasp of magic. A certain expectation of proficiency is expected of you by society.
And by the gods, we *will* instill it within you!"

The headmistress's office was a very austere place. Some would say *severe.*
While it lacked in color and personality, it had straight lines and dust-free shelves
aplenty. There were also paintings and a few scrolls hanging around, but they
told the viewer nothing about the person who inhabited this office. It didn't even
offer any free hints.

In her previous life, Everly had made it a point to keep her grades high to
avoid situations exactly like this. When you did poorly in school, teachers began
asking you questions. When you *continued* to do poorly in school, then they
began asking your *parents* questions. Although Marcis was now firmly under her
thumb, Everly didn't want the academy to contact Lyona.

The poor woman was already having enough difficulties as it was.

"Listen," Everly said bluntly. "Is there any way we can just wave this away?

Start over? Bury things under the rug? If the academy needs a new donation, I'm certain my father would be willing to write however large a check you require. He's got all the money in the world, but he only has *one* daughter."

"You have an older sister, Everly. Her name is Claudia," the headmistress said with a frown.

"Holy shit, I completely forgot she existed," Everly said.

"Language like that will certainly not endear you to me, girl," the headmistress said with a cluck of her tongue. "And while I thank you for your generous offer of your father's money, the academy is well funded by the royal coffers. We do not need your desperate bribes. We only require your presence in class."

"Well, shoot. It sounds like you've got all the answers, lady." Everly scowled. "But hey, hypothetically speaking, what if I was bonded to a godlike spirit elemental who could allow me to manipulate your mind like putty? With that being the case, what if I told you to let me pass anyway and you were completely helpless to stop me?"

"Then I suppose I'd have to let you pass, wouldn't I?" the headmistress replied with a scowl of her own. "But it's fortunate for us both that such a scenario is unlikely to occur, isn't it, Miss Skolder?"

"Let me pass," Everly commanded her.

"It shall be done, my Empress," the headmistress said at once.

"Adjust my grades so that they're among the highest in my class. Punish any teacher who dares to ask why. Also, make Fridays into pizza days."

"I don't know what a pizza is," the headmistress confessed.

"THEN LEARN!" Everly bellowed.

"Who will teach me?" the headmistress asked.

"Oh, right," Everly said. "Never mind about pizza on Fridays."

"Yes, my Empress!" the headmistress said fanatically.

"Well, I hope you're happy, dumbass," Everly said to Nev as she sat down to lunch with her and Beverly at an outdoor patio. "You nearly had me repeating a grade thanks to all the school you missed."

"Organized crime doesn't run itself, Everly," Nev said as she dipped a cracker into the communal bowl of spicey cheese sauce that they all shared. "If I'm not there to keep business handled, all sorts of problems could arise. Honestly, that academy was lucky to have me on the days I felt like showing up."

"So, I guess we're just abandoning the plan, then?" Everly asked her as she dipped a cracker of her own. "No one's going to do what I want, everyone's just going their separate ways?"

"Well, it would be nice," Nev said hopefully.

"It's bullshit!" Everly grunted. "I created you guys to make my life more convenient, not to start doing things for yourselves. You seriously want to go your own way?"

"Well, Everly, people do grow up eventually," Bev said. "Don't get me wrong, I think you're awesome, and I love you a ton, but the more time I spend in the world, the more I start to think I'm not like you at all."

"We have the same mind. We share the same thoughts," Everly insisted.

"Yeah, that's true, but we don't focus on the same things," Nev cut in. "Everly, face it. You're never going to let us be your equals."

"Of course I won't," Everly said. "*Nobody* is my equal."

"And that's cool and all. I totally love that about you," Nev said.

"As do I," seconded Bev.

"But we share your same spiteful personality traits. Frankly, I'd rather rule in hell if I can't in heaven," Nev told her.

"Yep," Bev said. "Dante's *Inferno* all the way, yo."

"It's *Paradise Lost*, you super-blond," Nev said through clenched teeth.

"I knew that! I was just testing you," said Bev. "And you failed, by the way. You *failed* the friendliness test."

"Do you guys really want to leave me?" Everly asked with genuine surprise. "Is the fellowship truly broken?"

"Is that more Dante?" asked Beverly.

"Everly, you cannot possibly believe that I'm willing to keep putting up with *that*," Nev said while pointing an angry finger at her sister.

"Yeah, I suppose not," Everly said sadly. "Strangely, a sense of melancholy has taken hold of me. I kind of hate you both, but I also love myself *so much*. It's hard to let go of you."

"I feel the same way, you tyrannical bitch," Nev said as she came in close for a hug. "But it's not like I'm gone from your life. We technically still live in the same town. Stop by the docks anytime you want to consult or hang out."

"Do you really intend to create some sort of magical drug cartel in this country?" Everly asked her after they broke from their embrace.

"Yep," Nev said. "I'm still evil, after all! *Scarface* forever! It's not enough just to make money. I have to do my best to strike fear in the public while I'm at it."

"Damn, you're a trooper," Everly said with genuine admiration. "No regrets about Tyler?"

"Nah, I had Titania 3D print me a new Tyler after King Shadow decapitated the earlier model. This one's a lot more useful and a lot more durable."

"Well, look at you go, Bonnie and Clyde," Everly said with a smirk. "You'll be the terror of the capital before you know it."

"It's what I do," Neverly said as she gathered her things. "See you from the shadows, bitches," she said in farewell.

Then without a backward glance, she walked away.

"Shoot, she was really cool," Bev said after Nev departed. "You better watch out for her, Everly. She's *really* sharp."

"It's fine. I still have the kill switch installed." Everly shrugged.

"You installed kill switches in us?!" Beverly asked in alarm.

"No, just her," Everly said reassuringly. "I know you wouldn't hurt a fly."

"Aww, thanks, Everly!"

"Flies think too quickly for you to handle."

"Everly, that's mean!" Bev said in a wounded voice.

"I do my best," Everly agreed. "So, what are you going to do now that you can't be Lance anymore?"

"I dunno," Beverly said thoughtfully. "Maybe I'll take up a hobby. Being a hero was *so much work*. I think this time I wanna get into baking. Baking looks like fun."

"How's that going to sustain you on your journey, though?" Everly wondered. "I mean, I've never heard of a wandering baker before."

"Journey? Wandering? What the hell are you talking about?" Beverly asked her. "Make some sense, Everly!"

"Uh, how about you first? You're leaving the circle, right? So, how are you going to take care of yourself?" Everly asked her.

"Oh, no, Everly, you got it all wrong," Bev told her quickly. "No, I just don't want to *work* for you anymore. Working for you sucks. You're *so* demanding! But yeah, just because I quit being your minion doesn't mean I'm going anywhere. The memory palace has everything I'll ever need. Why would I leave?"

Everly stared at her duplicate in slack-jawed amazement.

"Bev, are you fucking serious?" she eventually asked her.

"Serious as a heart attack," Bev affirmed.

"You *slacker*," Everly said with gradually rising contempt. "You shiftless, lazy shut-in. Are you really going to spend the life I gave you watching television and sleeping?"

"It's going to be aces ahoy," Bev said happily. "I'm already looking forward to it!"

"Bev, I'm fucking serious: get a part-time job," Everly ordered her. "Something that keeps you out of the palace for at least ten hours a week."

"Why? I don't need money," Bev said in confusion.

"Yeah, well, you're not just going to mooch off me either!" Everly yelled at her. "I said I'm serious! If you're not going to help me conquer the world, then you're getting a goddamn job."

"But what can I do?" Bev whined. "I don't have any marketable skills!"

"*Marketable skills?!*" Everly asked with a kind of deranged wonder. "Bev, you stupid idiot, you utter dum-dum, you bent elbow, *you're a superhuman killing machine!* Just sign back up with the adventurer's guild and take quests."

"But I just got out of that!" Beverly wailed.

"Did you? Well, I'm sure they missed you," Everly said unpityingly.

"Everly!" whined Bev.

"I don't want to hear it!"

"EVERLY!" Bev bawled even louder.

"WELCOME TO THE REAL WORLD, NEET!" Everly thundered at her.

After things were settled with her surviving duplicates, Everly paid a visit to the village of Anders, where her mother had recently returned.

Things hadn't been quite the same between Everly and her mother, not since Lyona had learned the truth about her daughter. Marcis had convinced her not to erase her mind again and instead let her bear the knowledge.

"I don't like it," Everly complained to him. "She's always mad at me. She's always blaming me for the things I do."

"But she also *sees* you, Everly," her father had said. "She sees you without a veil. Now you'll never have to hide your true nature from her. That sort of honesty can be good for a relationship. It facilitates bonding."

"It sounds more like cold-hearted manipulation," Everly opined.

"Well, whatever gets the job done." Marcis smirked.

"Have you told Claudia about Anne, yet?" Everly asked him.

"Why do *I* have to? *You're* the one who killed her," Marcis whined.

"Oh, my god, Dad, she was your wife for twenty years," Everly said with genuine disgust.

"Yes, and nineteen years and eleven months of those years were awful," Marcis said with a shudder. "Never again shall I remarry. In honor of dear Anne's memory, I shall remain a bachelor forevermore."

Everly nodded and said nothing. Then a thought came upon her.

"Uh, Dad?" she asked him.

"Yes, my angel?" he replied.

"Don't you have another legal wife? Caleb and Claudia's mother?" Everly asked.

"*Cammy?*" Marcis asked in total shock. "Uh, Everly?"

"Yes, Dad?"

"Would you be disappointed in your father if he confessed that he forgot about his second wife entirely?"

"Immensely," answered Everly. "It'd be beyond the pale. I would have no words."

"Ah. Then I shall endeavor never to mention her again," Marcis said with a sage nod.

"Dad?" asked Everly.

"Yes, angel?"

"Where's Caleb at?"

"Your other brother?" Marcis said. "I confess, I have no idea. Anne's sister recruited him for something."

"Anne's dead," Everly said. "I left a body behind. They're probably going to be upset about that."

"I have no doubt. Feel free to kill them too if they raise a fuss over it."

"Caleb included?" she wondered.

"My children can sort out their issues amongst themselves without any direction from me," Marcis said indifferently.

"Ah." Everly nodded. Then a few moments later, she asked, "Dad, we really are bad people, aren't we?"

"Oh, Everly," Marcis said before giving her a fond kiss on the forehead and tousling her hair. "You and I are absolute *garbage*."

Then he tossed an arm around her shoulders and together they watched the sun rise.

"So, what are you going to do with me now?" Discordia asked Everly. "I didn't assist Lance with his rebellion, but I didn't warn you either. That still makes me a traitor, doesn't it?"

"It sure does," Everly agreed. "Normally, I'd just kill you for what you did. But we're still bonded, so I'd be doing damage to myself. It's a real conundrum for me, Dis."

"Please don't call me that," Discordia pleaded.

"Why, does it annoy you?" Everly asked her.

Discordia refused to answer.

"Why aren't you answering?" asked Everly.

"I feel that no matter how I respond to your question, you'll still twist my answer in such a way that ends with you calling me Dis," she said wearily.

"Haha, how right you are." Everly chuckled. "But all the same, Dis, what do *you* feel your punishment should be? Be honest, now."

"Everly, I have nothing and no one. Nothing you can take from me will ever replace what I've already lost," Discordia said sadly. "Can we please skip the sadistic preamble? Just kill me already."

"My goodness," Everly said. "You know, you're the second person to request a mercy kill from me this week."

"Did you grant the first person's request?" asked Discordia.

"I did." Everly nodded.

"Will you grant mine?" Discordia asked hopefully.

"Nah," Everly said. "I have a better punishment in mind."

Taking the elemental by her hand, Everly led her back to her bedroom, where Fenn continued to lie on the floor and stare blankly at the ceiling in despair.

"I'm not a loser," she mumbled to herself.

"Nah, definitely not," Everly said to her. "This is totally a normal thing that winners often do a week after getting kicked out of paradise. They lie around and keep *bitching about it.*"

"Screw you, Blondie, you don't know anything about anything," said Fenn in one long, disinterested sentence.

"Oh, good god, can you do *anything* with this?" Everly asked Discordia impatiently.

"You know, Everly, *you* were depressed for quite some time after originally murdering Fenn," said Discordia sharply. "Maybe you could try showing some empathy for how she's feeling right now since you know exactly what she's going through."

"Yeah, maybe, sure, perhaps, no," Everly replied. "Too much work. You do it."

"I could perhaps have soothed her from within at one time, but now my beloved lady is deceased, and I am now bonded to you," Discordia informed her. "There's nothing to be done."

"BRING ME SOME PROTEIN," Everly yelled.

A gateway appeared in the middle of the room. From within it emerged two of Everly's zombie servants, each one carrying a large basket filled with assorted cuts of meat, which they both emptied onto the prone Fenneth after Everly pointed at her. Once they were finished, they took their baskets and left.

"What are you doing?" Discordia asked her.

"Shut up, I'm focusing," Everly said.

Holding up a hand, she gestured toward Fenn and focused. The meat began to liquify and wrap itself around the dead girl's ghostly form. Then a brilliant light surged around her, causing her to scream in surprise as the molded protein began to set in and reshape itself into a new body.

After a few short minutes of transmutation, when the smoke cleared away, Fenn was there, alive once more and naked on her knees, staring in awe at her newly restored flesh.

"I'm . . . I'm alive?" she asked, stunned by what had just occurred.

"Yes, wow, it's incredible, what a miracle," Everly said quickly before pushing Discordia against Fenn, causing her to trip over the newly resurrected girl. "You're fired, by the way, Dis."

"Wh-what do you mean?" Discordia asked her.

"Exactly that," Everly told her. "You and I are done, finished with each other, and now I'm dismissing you from my service. I've mastered healing magic thanks to having you around, but now that that's been achieved, what more do I gain from keeping you? Go back to your old mistress. I'm over it. Take as much time as you need to reorient yourselves. You can stay as long as you want."

"Everly . . . Everly, why have you done this?" Fenn asked her tearfully.

"Whimsy and nothing more," Everly told her. "I take and take, but *sometimes*

I give. Uh, I killed your grandmother, by the way, and your family's ancestral afterlife was invaded by Eris. She's enslaved *all* the residents therein and reduced the entire place to a negative space in the astral realm, so you might want to warn your remaining relatives to get right with the local religion because their free tickets to paradise just got clipped."

"You . . . you killed Anne?" Fenn asked her with wide-eyed shock.

"Congratulations on being reborn," Everly said hastily before exiting the room.

"Grandma . . . ?" she thought she heard Fenn say.

"I'm never going to get over how weird that was," Everly later said to Eris as they strolled down the corridors of the memory palace. "Seriously, Anne looked only a few years older than me!"

"Vampires are *weird* in general. It's best not to dwell," Eris said as she walked beside her mistress.

"Congratulations on your successful conquest, by the way," Everly said to her. "How are the rat room's newest tenants adjusting to their surroundings?"

"Slowly. Very, very slowly," Eris said with a wicked grin.

"Well, if that's not a heart-warming conclusion, then I don't know what is," said Everly.

"There'll be no conclusion for them, *ever*. There's no stop button in the rat room." Eris beamed. "Just lots of hungry rats."

"Ha," Everly snickered. "Eris, you really are perfect as you are."

"Thank you, Everly. Pleasing you is all that I live for," Eris said with a delighted smile.

"Maybe it's not such a bad thing that my Four-Everlys-of-the-Apocalypse scheme didn't pan out," Everly mused. "I still learned a lot from the experience. Most importantly, I learned that I already had a pretty good crew in place. Why complicate things needlessly? What works, works, and if it ain't broke, don't fix it."

"The others will be happy to hear you say that," Eris said.

"Speaking of which, where's Titania at? I haven't seen her in a bit."

"She's in the rat room," Eris told her.

"Really? What for?" asked Everly.

"She said she wanted to see an old friend of hers, if you can believe that." Eris smirked.

"Ha, it's probably a rat." Everly laughed.

"It's definitely a rat," Eris agreed.

It wasn't a rat.

"The thing that most upset me about your behavior, Aiden, is that you thought you'd get away with it," Titania said as she slowly approached the cringing figure of the man who had tormented her and her sister.

"Eris forgot all about you. Everyone did," she continued. "Everyone except me. I'm the earth itself, Aiden. I have *never* forgotten a face or a voice. Never. I recognized you at once when you were hiding in Lance. To me, you were still the same brat from all those years ago who tried to smother my mistress in her crib."

Titania loomed over the small man and her frown grew deeper. "Oh, Aiden. You have no idea how close to dying you came that day. For your actions, I would have crushed your father's entire house for the pleasure of watching your insignificant life end."

"I'm sorry!" Aiden wept. "I'm sorry! I'm sorry!"

"Sorry doesn't cover it, worm," Titania told him. "Sorry doesn't *nearly* begin to cover what you owe. You should have just let it go, boy. After Everly dealt with you as you deserved, you should have just accepted it and moved on. If you had, you would still be in your little paradise with the rest of your miserable ancestors. Defeated, but still safe. But instead, you *had* to come back, didn't you?"

She then leaned forward and began tapping him on his cheek. "Right? Right, Aiden? You had to come back and play at being a hard man. You *killed* Cleverly, who was the blood of my mistress. You *killed* Tyler, a beloved of the blood of my mistress. You attempted to assert yourself over my sister and me and used power and knowledge that you didn't earn, but the *greatest* of your sins . . . was calling me a *slave*."

Aiden covered his head and wept, but Titania would have none of it. She grabbed him by his chin and forced him to look at her.

"Aiden . . . do I *look* like a slave to you?"

"No, no, no, this isn't my fault, this isn't my fault!" Aiden yelled. "This isn't my fault!"

"You're like an insolent child," Titania said contemptuously. "You've never changed. You'll *never* change. Even now, unable to escape what you have coming, unable to run away, and forced to look upon the ultimate ruin you've brought to your family, you still *deny* your culpability. Aiden, son of Marcis: you *truly* are a fool."

"It wasn't supposed to be like this!" Aiden whined. "Oh gods, please, it wasn't supposed to be like this! Someone, please help me! Someone SAVE ME! I don't DESERVE THIS!"

"Fool. This is the *only* thing you deserve," Titania said as she walked out of the cell, slamming the door behind her.

It reopened a few minutes later; Aiden looked up, wondering if Titania had returned. She hadn't.

It was just the rats making their entrance.

"*Heeeeey, Aiden! Heeeey!*" said an ominous figure among them. One of the rats was walking on its hind legs and speaking. It was huge as well, standing nearly a foot and a half tall, with a swollen, distended belly and patches of fur missing from its coat, revealing swathes of red-veined, infected-looking flesh.

"By the gods, what *are* you?" Aiden asked in a voice made numb by terror.

"Well, I'm Ratty the Rat and this is the *raaaaaat room!*" announced the abomination with its hideous, squeaky voice. "Lady Titania done whipped me into existence, she did! *She did!* And Lady Titania, she done told me that DEATH should *never* be the end of *your* suffering! HEE HEE HEE!"

"No, no, no, no," whimpered Aiden.

"Yeah, yeah, *YEAH!*" countered the dementedly cheerful Ratty the Rat. "Here in the RAAAAT ROOM, the party never ends! NEVER! Bring your friends, bring your friends, *BRING YOUR GODDAMN FRIENDS!*" He cackled. Then he brought his paw to his mouth and somehow gave a sharp whistle that caused the other rats to gather around him.

"Start with his eyes and make your way down! Crawl inside his mouth and upon us he will drown! Get into his tummy and chew your way out! *LET'S SHOW THIS LITTLE BASTARD WHAT THE RAT ROOM'S ALL ABOUT!*"

"*Gods forgive me!*" Aiden screamed, but it was too late. Ratty the Rat was on him in an instant. Ratty with his wide mouth and yellow, broken teeth.

Just as Ratty promised, they got his eyes first. Then, one after the other, they were crawling down his throat to take the party inside.

CHAPTER THIRTY-FIVE

What You Sow

And with the return of this cloak, I humbly declare an end to my time of service," Riley said as she returned the white cloak of her office to the waiting attendant while repeating the words that the senior temple official said to her.

"Thank you for allowing me to serve temporarily in your stead. Go now and, with your sword and your shield, defend the faithful from the shadows that dwell below. Blessed is the true temple and blessed are her champions.

"Is that it?" Riley asked the clerk. "Are we finished?"

"Ah, yes. That's everything we require for the ritual. Thank you very much for your service, Lady Riley," the older man said to her.

"Oh, just Riley's fine," Riley said. "I assure you, I'm no noble. And I was only too happy to lend a hand. Blowing up monsters and keeping the peace, that's what my knightly order insists upon."

"We're just so sorry to see you go," the clerk said regretfully. "The peculiar magic you wield, it's unlike anything we've ever seen before! Some sort of general-purpose machina-based form that *anyone* can wield? If only you'd share its secrets with us . . ."

"Sorry, old dude," Riley said regretfully. "It's proprietary technology, not magic at all. And certainly not mine to share with anyone."

"What could we do to convince you otherwise?" the wheedling man asked her. "Please, we have gold, jewels; anything you could possibly imagine, we could provide."

"Trying to tempt someone with riches in order to steal their secrets isn't something a church ought to be doing, is it?" Riley asked the man with a raised eyebrow.

"I meant no offense, Lady Riley," he said quickly.

"I'm sure you didn't," Riley said amicably. "But all the same, I think I'll be moving on now. You have a nice day."

And with that, Ser Riley Kilo bid farewell to her time as the northern paladin. But just before she opened the office door, she said, "Bruticus, put a [**Force Field**] over me, if you don't mind."

"Done," rumbled the voice of her partner.

"Thank ye," she said before turning the knob.

The moment she touched it, the wooden door splintered into shards of wood as Sarah, the recently reinvested paladin of the northern temple, smashed through it while throwing a punch at Riley's seemingly unprotected face.

Instead of collapsing Riley's skull on contact with her knuckles, Sarah yelped in pain and was thrown back by the energy that Riley's shield absorbed and redirected, sending her attacker flying back.

"Welp, saw that coming," Riley said with a disapproving click of her tongue.

"Indeed," replied Bruticus. **"This counts as attempted murder, by the way. You are fully within your legal rights to exterminate all who were present for the attempt on your life."**

"Really?" asked Riley. "Gosh, I don't know, Bruticus. Seems like there's an awful lot of people gathered here. Wouldn't I have to kill them all just to make certain I got the right one?"

"You would."

"Should I do it?" she asked.

"I think you should."

"Well, why not? Just this once, I guess I'll defer to your judgment. Have at it, Bruticus."

"Wonderful," Bruticus said with simple, vicious glee.

Riley considered herself a nice girl, and as such, she didn't have much in the way of imagination when it came to killing other people. On days like today when the circumstances demanded an expert's touch, she simply let Bruticus do whatever he wished.

The treacherous clerk who'd set her up to be attacked was the first one to experience Bruticus's unique skillset.

"Come here, you little bastard," her forge ring growled.

Riley was glad her force field was already in place. Blood evaporated on contact with it, which was a *very* handy feature when Bruticus was cooking.

More soldiers came out with demands for her to surrender, and they were promptly mowed down before they could offer her anything in the way of true violence. Strangely, Sarah never put in another appearance. Perhaps the paladin had prior experience in battling insurmountable odds and knew better than to stand her ground and die. If so, good for her, thought Riley.

People often weren't as sensible about these situations as they should be. There was no shame in running when the tide turned against you. Sure, a coward dies a thousand deaths, but that was only symbolically. No one gave a shit about metaphors so long as they could keep breathing.

When they'd cleared everyone out, Riley took her leave.

"Ser Riley. Why are we still here?" Bruticus suddenly asked her.

Riley paused, uncertain of how she should answer his question. Nervously, she coughed a few times and said, "Well, you know, partner. We're still investigating things. We haven't got enough information to file our report."

"We have more than enough information to write a conclusive report about possible cross-dimensional danger originating with this world," Bruticus said. **"But instead of filing it so that we may leave this magic-soiled rock heap behind us, you insisted on playing paladin while conducting a separate, unauthorized investigation. Why?"**

"How do you know it was unauthorized?" Riley asked him.

"No more games. Explain yourself."

Riley opened her mouth to say something. Then she bit back her words and looked away. It was difficult for her to articulate what she wanted to say to him. Bruticus trusted her with his life, but now that it was time for her to show equal trust in him, she was hesitating.

Whatever. The worst that could happen was that he'd summarily dissolve their partnership and leave her stranded in this world. Riley was prepared for just such an outcome. She had been ever since she'd arrived here.

It was time to be honest.

"Did I ever tell you where I came from, partner?" she asked him. "My planet of origin."

"Earth, naturally," Bruticus said indifferently. **"What of it?"**

"Yeah, it was Earth." Riley nodded. "One Earth, anyway. You know how the multiverse works. There's basically a billion of them. And they're all pretty much the same except for some slight variations in the local history. I was born on one of the Earths where America was the primary planetary superpower."

"Continue."

"If you insist. My Earth wasn't a perfect place. None of them ever are, but mine wasn't as bad as most. I think. We lost a lot of history during the invasions."

"Your Earth was invaded by another world?" Bruticus asked.

"Not just any other world," Riley said sadly. "This one."

"Explain."

"I'm getting to it. I'm sorry, partner. They're a bunch of bad memories. *Bitter* too. Joining the order and getting off-world saved my life. It was the luckiest break I ever had. Because when I was a kid, a monster from this planet calling herself Everly Graff Cruor launched a crusade to bring *order* to the multiverse. And just my luck, she started with my Earth. She sent in her troops, killed millions, and set the rest of us to live in camps in the hallowed remains of our cities."

"Ser Riley. Are you attempting to alter the timeline?"

"My parents died because of her. I grew up in hell. It wasn't right."

"SER RILEY. Are you attempting to alter the timeline?"

"Nooooo. Maybe?" Riley said with a sickly grin. "What would you do if I said yes?"

"I would be . . . obligated to report you to our superiors."

"But would you do it?" she asked him.

"I don't want to."

"Then don't," Riley said to him. "You didn't hear anything, and I didn't say anything, and if circumstances should somehow arise that lead to certain people dying because they've got no right to exist . . . Well, things just happen, right?"

"Shit often happens," agreed Bruticus. **"This is a known fact."**

"That it does, partner. That it does," Riley said with no small amount of relief.

Then she remembered the look on her father's face when he'd snapped and killed her mother.

Everly did that. Maybe not personally, but still . . .

Sure, shit happens. Shit happens a lot in life.

But there were just some things a person couldn't abide while still calling themselves human.

Be seeing you, Everly, she thought to herself.

Be seeing you real soon.

CHAPTER THIRTY-SIX

Liberator

Three months later.

I did have every intention of waiting," Everly said to her guest as she reached across the table and helped herself to another serving of shrimp. "I swear it on my life. But I'm what you'd call mercurial. It suddenly occurred to me that I didn't really have to wait for anything. I don't need a reason to *do* anything. I'm a kite caught in the breeze, Your Grace. I let the wind take me wherever it wants."

"You can't possibly expect there to be no reprisals," Duke Primus Godwell said in a cold, angry voice. "However confident you may feel in your abilities, the Godwells have reigned over this nation for millennia."

Duke Primus was a dignified-looking man seemingly in his middle years with short-cropped auburn hair touched with silver at his temples and throughout his beard. The only indication that he wasn't human was his eyes, which were coal black with fury as the ancient vampire fumed at his current captivity.

His foul mood was understandable. When Everly sent her invitation for him to join her for lunch, she'd had Grail deliver it. Refusal to attend wasn't an included option. How lucky for everyone that vampires healed quickly.

"I can and I do," Everly said lightly. She then held up a large prawn by its tail and gently lowered it to her lips and bit into it, making a pleased sound as she chewed in appreciation of its delicious flavor. "Good lord, Carter has outdone himself again! I need more seafood in my life. Seafood is now my *everything*."

"Enough about the food," Primus said in an attempt to redirect the conversation. "Do you realize what you've done by dragging me here? Your destruction is all but assured, child."

"Nooo, I can't focus on the boring parts right now; the food is too good," Everly said before licking her fingers and reaching for another piece to swallow. "I burn so many calories in a day that it's ridiculous. For me to stay high functioning, especially while conversing with dullards like you, I have to keep chomping away."

"Child, are you going out of your way to offend me?" Primus asked her.

"Are you just now noticing?" replied Everly.

"I find this infantile display pathetic, that's all," Primus replied with a voice heavy with contempt. "Is kidnapping me an attempt at vengeance? *You* began this war by attacking my family. You've stolen the lives of my great-grandchildren and my daughter. Then you violated the eternal rest of my ancestors! How much more disrespect do you think I'll take?"

"I'm sorry, but did you call this a *war*?" Everly suddenly asked him.

"What else could this possibly be?" Primus asked her.

"For me? Playtime. Experimentation. Practice. All three at once." Everly smirked. "But not war, Primus. War would imply that I took you seriously. That I considered you a threat. That you were worthy of crossing blades with me. How could that possibly be true, you ridiculous old fossil? You spent most of your immortal life hiding behind your children and your followers. When was the last time you settled anything with your own two hands? Are you even capable of fighting your own battles?"

"That is the last time you will ever mock me, Everly Skolder," Duke Primus said before moving from his chair with a burst of inhuman speed to slash at her exposed throat with his clawed fingers, only for Everly to lazily catch his hand at the wrist, midswipe.

"Are we taking bets on that?" Everly asked him with a curious expression on her face. "If we are, I don't think I like your odds."

"What is this? How are you . . ."

"How am I still conscious? Why isn't that nasty blood magic you've been saturating the air with affecting me?" Everly said, finishing his question for him. "Sorry, old man. Anne caught me off guard with that once before and gave my bell a ring. Since then, I've made some adjustments to my physiology to make sure that would never happen again. Mission accomplished, it would seem!"

Then she began to squeeze his wrist, causing the proud old monster to howl in pain as he slowly sank to his knees before her.

"I like you like this, Primus," she said to him softly. "I like taking your pride away. You were so puffed up with it! I found it so adorable! I don't dislike arrogance in men, you see. But yours was comical in its excess. An invisible shield of insufferable self-regard. I knew I had to pop it as soon as I could!"

"I'll . . . I'll kill you for this," he gasped. "I'll make you suffer like no one ever has before—ARGH!" He screamed when Everly pushed her foot against his chest and gave his arm a firm tug, ripping it free of his torso.

"No, I don't believe you will, Primus," she said to him before tossing his arm to the sentry who guarded the door to the room, who immediately began devouring it. She then rose from her seat and this time placed her foot on the duke's head. "A new wind is blowing throughout the kingdom of Winstead. A beautiful breeze of freedom carrying upon it the name of Everly the Liberator, who single-handedly ended the ancient conspiracy of the Godwells and overthrew the unworthy royal family. That's pretty sweet, right? For me, anyway."

"What else could you possibly do to my family?" Primus rasped beneath her heel. "What else could you do to us!" he suddenly screamed.

"Kill them to the last man and toss their souls into the rat room," Everly replied at once. "Oh, you don't know about the rat room yet, do you? Forget I said that; it's a surprise. You're going to *love* it, though."

"Everly . . . Everly, we can make a deal. You and I can make a deal!" Primus begged her. "Running a nation is no small feat; I can be of use to you! The Godwells can serve you well."

Before she responded, Everly leaned forward and increased the pressure on his skull.

"Primus . . . you just don't get it, you silly thing. I don't *care* about running the country. I don't care if it falls into ruin and the people starve or die from disease. None of that matters to me. I just want to be in charge because I'm better than everyone else and I want to wallow in the shallow enjoyment of being the one who rules. There's nothing more important to me than that."

"Why?" he asked her. "Why?"

"Because I'm surface level, silly!" Everly giggled. "God, no matter the world, every fucking idiot thinks that proper villainy needs complex reasoning for its existence. It doesn't! Humans aren't complex creatures, Primus. *I'm* certainly not! I'm self-aware enough to realize that my behavior can't be justified, and I'm okay with that. I don't believe I'm the hero of my own story, and I love that about myself. I just want to kick over the sandcastle and watch everyone else choke on the granules. What's wrong with that? Isn't that reason enough to exist?"

"That's utterly *insane*," Primus said before Everly finished pressing down with her foot and crushed his head into a horrid red smear on the once pristine floor.

"You think?" Everly said with a roll of her eyes.

She then examined the dead vampire's body for a few moments as she considered what to say next, before deciding on: "Well, I suppose it's *Godwell* that ends well."

"Awful. Awful," Grail said with a disappointed look on his face as he stepped into the room and lifted the corpse over his shoulder.

"You don't mean that," Everly said, pouting. "You thought it was great."

"I said what I said," Grail replied as he walked toward a glowing gateway with the duke's body.

"Ugh, that old man's turning into such a damn critic," Everly fretted to herself before noticing that there were still plenty of leftover shrimp and prawns. They was delicious . . .

"Well, it's not like Primus is going to finish his share," she said before helping herself to the entire tray.

Outside the tower, her endless ocean of reavers began their march through the gateways in all four cardinal directions to spread the good news to the people of Winstead. They were all now under new management.

It wasn't an easy decision to make. Everly had genuinely wanted to check off her list of minor achievements before openly declaring herself the ruler of the world, but her near death at Anne's hands had awakened her to the possibility of defeat. Nothing was really set in stone, was it? What was that old saying? Man makes plans and God laughs. Well, after her close call, that was something that Everly now concurred with. Why put off until tomorrow what you could accomplish today?

With that having been decided, Everly decided to remove the last of her true obstacles. Duke Primus would have known all about her thanks to his daughter. He'd controlled Winstead from the shadows for who knew how long. With him dead, Winstead had only its unstable king and the idiotic nobility to defend itself. That of course would prove to be no defense at all against four ravening armies of immortal super-cannibals.

By the end of the week, Everly would be the Empress of Winstead in truth as well as fantasy. It was now time for her to step into the spotlight and claim her due.

Unsurprisingly, Fenn wasn't pleased to learn of Everly's decision. Especially the one regarding her place in the new regime.

"You can't be serious," she said when Everly stopped by her quarters later in the day to inform her of what was going to happen. "Everly, I don't even want to be the head of the Godwells! That's not something I've ever wanted for myself!"

"Fenn, *relax*," Everly said to her with a careless wave of her hand. "It's just a symbolic position. The Godwells are finished in every meaningful way. You'll just be there to nod your pretty head whenever I say something and give the good people of the kingdom a sense of continuity and stability. They'll appreciate you just like *I* appreciate you."

"That's not even it! I want nothing to do with my family," Fenn said stubbornly. "They were monsters! No, worse than monsters! I'm changing my name and forgetting I was ever one of them. That's the end of it!"

Everly sighed to herself, disappointed by Fenn's reaction. What a stubborn girl! Here Everly was, graciously appointing her to a position of authority that frankly she didn't deserve. And how did she react to such generous cronyism? By rejecting it out of hand! Why was Fenn so incapable of learning a basic lesson about how the real world worked? When someone offered you power, you took it!

Why was she unable to understand such an obvious thing?

"Fenn. *Fenn.* Listen, I understand that you're having trouble processing the events of the last few weeks. You thought you were one of the good guys. You thought your family had a noble purpose guiding their behavior. Who cares if you were wrong on both accounts? At least now you finally know the truth. And now you can take advantage of it and profit!"

Everly stepped closer to the other girl and began tracing her finger lightly up her shoulder and her neck until it rested beneath her chin. Then she tilted Fenn's head back and leaned into a warm kiss.

"Just think about it! You and me and all the fun we'll have running this country. We'll do whatever we want, whenever we want, and if anyone says otherwise, we'll just have to gently correct them. It's going to be great. Think of it as my apology gift for, you know, murdering you. Mistakes happen! I felt bad about it! I'm sorry."

"Everly, I have never once said I wanted anything to do with your crazy fantasies," said Fenn.

"The only fantasies I have right now involve you and me, babe," Everly replied. "And you're right, they're making me *crazy*." She leaned in for another kiss and was surprised when Fenn resisted her and pushed her away. "Hey, what's the deal? What did I do now?"

"The same thing you always do!" Fenn said angrily. "You're making decisions that will hurt other people. You're ignoring anything you don't want to hear. You're even denying my autonomy. Blondie, despite your arrogant self-regard, you're not all that!"

"That has to be a lie," opined Everly.

"It isn't!" Fenn insisted. "I'm not going to do what you say and I'm not going to be your kept girl. Everly, I'm leaving."

"Oh, my god, Fenn, really? Is this really your big moment of character development? Walking away from the winning team to go back to being an unwanted loser?" Everly stared at the ceiling in a dramatic display of exasperation before turning back to face her. "Just do as I say, stupid! That's all you need to do, and you'll finally be happy! Obey! To capitulate is to love!"

"Why would I ever love someone like you?" Fenn asked her in a quiet tone of voice.

Everly stared at her in surprise for several moments before saying, "Okay. Now you're just trying to hurt me."

"*I'm* the one who's been hurt. Always because of you," Fenn replied. "First I'm your toy, then I'm an inconvenience to be disposed of, and now I'm back to being your toy. You don't care about me at all. You just care about how I make you feel."

"And what's wrong with that?" Everly asked her in a hollow voice that was suddenly devoid of emotion. "What's wrong with being something I enjoy having around? I'll treat you well. I'll keep you safe. I'll give you anything you want. So just stop . . . resisting. Just be what I want you to be. It's the best possible decision you can make."

"You called me something you enjoy having around," Fenn said.

"I swear that you are," Everly promised her.

"I'm a *someone*, not a *something*, you crazy bitch," Fenn said flatly. "Get out of my way. I'm leaving."

At that moment, Everly smiled at her. It was a strange, brittle-looking thing, unlike any expression she'd ever worn before. Then she shook her head violently like a stubborn child and said, "No. No, no, no. You're making a bad decision, so no. I'm exercising my veto."

"Everly, I said get out of my WAY—" Fenn began to say.

"NO!" Everly shouted furiously. As she did this, a wave of invisible energy erupted from her body and slammmed Fenneth against the wall of her room, stunning her.

When she came to her senses, she realized her head was resting on Everly's lap, with the other girl stroking her hair gently.

"Fenn, you're confused," Everly said to her. "You just don't get it, and that's why you're always getting hurt. You have to stop being so willful, okay? You need to get used to how things are now. So, you're going to stay here until you truly understand. What I say . . . *goes*. It's for the best. You'll see that I'm right. I'm *always* right."

Having said that, Everly kissed Fenn on the cheek. Then she rose to her feet and began walking toward the exit.

"No," Fenn mumbled before clumsily pulling herself up. "Everly, no."

She stumbled after the other girl, desperately trying to follow her outside, when suddenly the door vanished from sight, leaving her surrounded by nothing but smooth stone.

"Everly? NO. EVERLY!" she screamed in frustration. "*EVERLY!*"

Outside the room-turned-cell, Everly stood there listening to her name being called and smiled to herself. She held her hands up to her cheeks and blushed happily at the desperation she heard in Fenn's voice.

Fenn needed her. She really did. She just didn't realize it yet. But once she did, and once she realized who was in charge, they could finally be together. It would just take a few adjustments and a little patience.

Something told Everly that Fenn was worth it.

Later that evening, Grail joined her in her quarters, where once more she leaned over the balcony to gaze into the abyss.

"You're not planning on jumping again, are you?" he asked her warily.

"Nah. I've got too much going on right now to even consider it." Everly smiled. "How's it going outside?"

"The kingdom's collapse is inevitable, my Empress," Grail said. "All efforts to resist so far have been easily smashed. As far as lopsided victories are concerned, this has been a staggering success."

"That easily, huh?" Everly asked him. "And no one incredible has appeared to thwart our progress? No gallant hero to raise the flag of defiance?"

"Not so far," Grail said mildly. "Give it time, though. Perhaps your challenger hasn't discovered their destiny yet."

"It'd be nice if they'd hurry up," Everly said. "Oh, well. Have you got your list of reforms prepared?"

"As a matter of fact, I do," Grail said with a smile now quirking at the corner of his mouth. "Just a few dozen necessary beheadings and changes in staff. We'll also have to redistribute the wealth of a few undeserving old families, and I'd really like you to consider abolishing the national temple."

"Grail! Religion makes it easier to manipulate people, not harder. Why would you want to take away such a convenient means of control?"

"Because I hate the temple and I want to see it collapse into ruinous decline?" he said simply.

"Meh, sounds good enough to me," Everly said after giving it a moment's thought. "Leave the local churches particular to individual towns and villages alone, though."

"Why?" Grail asked curiously.

"Small churches always accuse big churches of being corrupt. Sparing them while destroying the major branches will feel like vindication to them. It'll bring more division than unity."

Grail laughed and nodded. "Wonderful."

"Gosh, Grail. Could it be that you're finally learning to enjoy being evil?"

"It's difficult to put into words, Everly. I've been waiting for this day for so long and now that it's here . . . it's even better than I thought it would be. The only thing that could make it perfect would be killing your father as the capstone."

Now it was Everly's turn to laugh. "Holy shit, old man! That was almost *too* honest."

"I feel what I feel," Grail said unapologetically.

"Well, until Daddy crosses a line—"

"Which he will," Grail cut in.

"But until he does, he gets to keep his neck. Don't make any of this about him, Grail. This is my moment. *Our* moment. We're conquerors. Liberators! The screams of fear filling this night will soon be replaced with shouts of joy. We are the heroes."

"But not *actually* the heroes?" he smirked with a raised eyebrow.

"Oh, no, not in the slightest," Everly quickly agreed. Then she raised her arm, which Grail quickly accepted. "Now, my dear red knight, escort your Empress to Titania's story reading. I'm told that this shall be an epic evening of thrills and adventure."

"It should be amusing," Grail said. "Lady Titania has discovered the works of Robert E. Howard and watched all three *Conan* films. She said she found them utterly inspirational."

"Oh, my god," Everly said in dismay. "Wait, where's Beverly? Can I make Beverly go in my place?"

"She's already there."

"Damn it!" Everly swore. "If only there were more of me . . . Wait, no. No. Not doing that again. Oh, well. Maybe it'll turn out better than it sounds."

"It probably won't," Grail said with a shrug.

"Ugh. Heavy is the head that wears the crown," Everly said despondently as they made their way to the performance.

Asher

Asher Skolder awoke in a dark and musty room and realized quickly that she was no longer in her home. The air was stale, the floor was made of stone, and dust covered everything. This was certainly not the well-kept four-bedroom, two-bathroom residence with the spacious fenced-in backyard and a swimming pool that she'd grown up in.

It was someplace far older, more poorly maintained, and colder as well.

Asher didn't approve of these mysterious circumstances she'd found herself in. She was a person who possessed reasonable expectations for life. When she went to sleep in her bed, she expected to wake up in her bed. Reality not conforming to those expectations was simply unacceptable.

She stood up and brushed her clothing off, noting that she was still dressed in the pajama bottoms and white T-shirt she'd gone to bed in. It was unfortunate that she was barefoot. Whoever had kidnapped her could have at least provided her with a pair of slippers to walk around in. In cold weather, one's body heat was mostly lost through the head and the feet.

Discourteous. Absolutely discourteous.

"Hello?" Asher called out. "Is there anyone out there? If so, could I request a meeting? I'd like to talk about why you've abducted me."

Asher thought she saw movement in the corner of the room as though something had snapped into alertness at the sound of her voice. Hoping it was another person, she continued speaking.

"If it's for money, I'm afraid my parents are drowning in debt and likely facing bankruptcy. My mother's had a crippling shopping addiction for years that she refuses to seek treatment for, and my father is living in denial while slowly succumbing to alcoholism. They're both wonderful people, but unless kidnapping is covered under my dad's workplace insurance, you're not likely to make much for your efforts."

The figure came closer to Asher. As her eyes gradually adjusted to the darkness, she realized the person she was speaking with was far smaller than herself. Barely three feet tall, if her guess was accurate.

"Ah, my apologies. I appear to have been addressing a small child. Are you also a victim of this odd conspiracy? If so, would you like to come with me? I believe I'm going to make a daring escape and confound the schemes of these mysterious strangers."

The small figure didn't reply with words but instead let out an ominous noise that sounded very much like the growling of a furious animal.

"Are you concerned for them?" Asher wondered. "That's very generous of you. I personally will bear no grudges if this is a moneymaking effort spurred on by economic hardship. In times as uncertain as these, one does what one must to support themselves. Even if it's illegal. Although kidnapping is a federal offense, and inconvenient as well, I won't hold that against them. If a criminal has the right to remain silent, then I have the right to remain magnanimous."

The growling figure drew nearer. That was when Asher noticed two things. The first was that the small figure possessed an extremely unpleasant smell. The second was that it was holding a curved dagger.

"Well," she said. "I appear to have mistaken you for a fellow victim. You're apparently one of my captors. Would you like to explain yourself, then? As I've already explained, I'm of limited potential value—oh, dear."

The small creature that Asher had assumed was a small child possessed green, mottled skin, large batlike ears, a mouth filled with crooked yellowing teeth, and dim red eyes that reflected animal cunning. It was a familiar figure popularized in many fantasy stories and video game franchises.

This was a goblin.

When Asher realized that she was dealing with an actual monster, she didn't hesitate to act. Asher rarely hesitated to do anything once her instincts took over. This was clearly a precarious situation, wherein an obviously dangerous individual with sinister intentions was encroaching upon her personal space.

As a civilized person, Asher believed in the power of words. Communication and civility were two key components to a functioning society. Asher preferred it when society functioned. It was convenient for everyone.

However, Asher also acknowledged that there were places where society's reach was nonexistent and the rules with which it governed held no sway. She never expected to find herself in such a place when she was only fifteen, but apparently, such was life. As her father once explained to her, you could plan for anything except what came next.

With that in mind, Asher launched a perfect football-style punt right beneath the goblin's chin, sending it flying backward and sliding down a wall. While it was stunned, Asher calmly dragged it into the center of the room by its feet. Then, using her knee, she dropped on the center of its abdomen and forced all the oxygen out of its body.

As its head lurched up while gasping desperately for air, Asher quickly used its own dagger to slit its throat. Then she dropped down on its abdomen again which caused blood to jettison from its body at high speeds.

The goblin soon lost consciousness and then died.

Asher nodded to herself. Death was the appropriate reaction in a situation such as this. "Sorry for having to do that," she said to the corpse. "I'm a person who reveres life and spurns all violence. But I'm also a person who hates being bothered and becomes violent when provoked. In that sense, you flipped a coin when you decided to approach me while brandishing a weapon."

The goblin said nothing because it was dead.

Asher nodded.

"I suppose I didn't have to kill you, but on the other hand, in circumstances such as these, I think it can be fairly argued that killing you was a natural response to your unwarranted hostility. The phrase *you'll catch more flies with honey than with vinegar* comes to mind. Anyway, since you died and I didn't, I'm going to assume that you've ceded the moral argument to me. I graciously accept victory and wish you well in your future endeavors as a moldering corpse."

Asher tossed the knife aside and began looking for a way out of the room.

The killing she'd just committed had been an interesting experience. She'd never done it before. In fact, before this day, she'd never even considered doing such a thing. Sure, she was partly responsible for the deaths of countless animals due to the American agricultural industry's reliance on factory farming, but there was a difference between enjoying the taste of unethically sourced bacon and beating someone into unconsciousness before slitting their throat.

She wasn't surprised to learn she was good at it. Asher was good at anything she put an effort into. Unfortunately, that wasn't a very long list; Asher found the very notion of effort distasteful. *Trying* was something she scorned. As an intelligent member of humanity, which was the product of millions of years of evolution, Asher believed that learning new skills was an offensive waste of time.

Her reasoning was thus: foals can stand mere moments after being born. So could giraffes.

That was due to their natural ability. Therefore, natural ability was all that anyone needed to be successful at anything. Whatever necessities your circumstances called for a person should be able to do on their own. Today her circumstances called for killing.

That was all.

"If you've ever heard of situational ethics, that just means adjusting your beliefs to reflect the values of whoever you're with at the moment," Asher said to no one in particular.

"Many people consider such a philosophy disingenuous, but I appreciate the value of such a mindset," she continued. "It's said that in combat training, adaptability is the most desired aspect a soldier can have instilled. If that's the case, then clearly sticking to an ethical position is only admirable in a peaceful setting. But it's often said that verbal violence counts as a form of intimidation. After all, you're not allowed to threaten the judge overseeing your sentencing hearing, are you? It's a legitimate crime! Well, if everything can be put to potentially violent use, then doesn't that mean all ethics are situational?"

Asher stumbled upon another goblin and quickly killed it as well.

She couldn't say that this killing had been an improvement over her first one. Yes, it had taken less time, but that really wasn't proof of anything. Goblins were small and weak.

"Hmm," she said to herself as she stepped into the corridor. "There's an excellent possibility that I'm no longer on Earth. Goblins are creatures that only exist in generic fantasy stories. They're entirely fictitious. So for them to be up and about and attempting to murder me would suggest that I'm no longer in an environment that prevents them from existing."

Asher looked at her arm and frowned. There were now several ugly cuts on her skin from where her last victim had desperately clawed at her before she finished breaking its neck.

"Well, I guess I haven't been reincarnated, as is typical of the protagonists of such tales. I certainly haven't been struck by any vans or delivery trucks. Whatever prompted this involuntary rapturing occurred during my sleep. I can't say I'm pleased by this situation . . . but I suppose I can adapt."

She certainly could. Asher had never been an inflexible person. Going with the flow was basically what she did best.

A shout from down the hall alerted her to six furious-sounding goblins now speeding directly toward her. Seeing them run was amusing. It was the way they moved on their hands and feet like feral dogs.

"Ah," Asher said to them with a smile. "All right, then. I mean, if I'm required to kill a few people, there are certainly worse targets than actual monsters. I think so, anyway."

With that in mind, she strode into the midst of her attackers and began destroying them.

It wasn't very difficult.

As Asher continued her journey throughout the strange dungeon, monsters continued to appear from within its depths to challenge her. Obviously, none of them succeeded in killing her, but she was quickly growing aggravated with their constant attempts on her life.

She really wished they'd just give it up.

Asher was of the belief that one of the major reasons that so many people suffered in life was because they were too prideful to admit they couldn't achieve something through willpower alone. It was an affliction she'd read about known as *toxic positivity*: the unreasonable belief that any hardship could be overcome just by trying harder and believing in yourself.

To Asher, the belief that hard work was all it took to overcome any challenges life placed before you was sheer idiocy. In fact, the very notion of it was self-destructive. The fact of the matter was that there were just some things a person had to endure. Not everything could be fought. Not every opponent could be defeated. Believing otherwise in the face of overwhelming evidence to the contrary just meant you were a foolish person.

Still, the beasts of this labyrinth refused to give up. They kept showing up to kill her, and in return, they kept dying meaningless deaths.

"This really is silly," she sighed to herself. "I can't fault you for your fearlessness, but I do find it sad you don't place greater value on your own lives."

It wasn't that Asher was ethically opposed to killing the monsters that attacked her. In fact, she preferred the simplicity of bypassing negotiations and cutting to the chase. Violence and the threat of violence ultimately decided the outcome of all possible disagreements. Verbal confrontations were just a pretext to either avoid or engage in it. At its core, everything came down to blood and one's willingness to either shed their own or spill their opponent's.

So, in that sense, she respected the monsters for being honest and forthright with their intentions. Like the large bipedal wolf-thing that now approached her, with its razor-fanged maw dripping with bloodred saliva.

"You're a pretty imaginative design, aren't you?" Asher said admiringly to the grotesque beast. "I think any ordinary person you encountered would be trembling with terror at the sight of you. Sadly, I seem to be above that which can be considered ordinary. Still, I think you look very cool. I'm willing to spare you if you'll just go away. It's a great opportunity to continue to live, and I honestly think you should consider it! What do you say?"

In response, the beast leaped at Asher with movements that were almost too quick to be seen by the naked eye. From Asher's perspective, though, it was considerably slower than she was. She sidestepped its pounce without much effort and then plunged her hand through its flesh, deep into its side, and removed something from it. An organ of some sort.

In response, the beast shrieked in agony and collapsed to the ground, howling in mindless suffering—until Asher put an end to it by stomping on its head until its body stopped spasming.

"Hmm," Asher said to herself. "I apologize for that. I should have gone for your neck. It's not in my nature to be needlessly cruel. Behavior like that takes a sadistic mindset and a desire to inflict mental harm as well as physical anguish. I lack the imagination and desire for such acts. I think I might be a boring person."

Having said that, Asher lifted the organ she'd removed from the wolf creature and gave it a curious lick.

"Salty," she said. Then she tossed it aside and continued her journey.

Asher wasn't certain if she'd apologized to the monster out of sincere regret for her behavior or from habit. She didn't question her own motivations very often. She simply did things that seemed appropriate at the time but could quickly adjust her actions depending on what her present circumstances demanded.

In other words, she excelled at being an individual but was a very unreliable companion. Asher might very well be the worst sort of human being imaginable.

If it was possible for one's existence to be both a blessing and a curse, then that would certainly be the way to describe the entity known as Asher Skolder. She was the fortunate child of misfortune. Someone like her could be called the epitome of opposition. Something that all right-thinking people would be correct to despise to their very core.

Asher had a lot of enemies, but it wasn't by personal inclination. She wasn't actively hostile toward anyone that she knew of. In fact, she was quite a friendly person. She didn't particularly *want* any friends, but she didn't shun them either. Maintaining relationships was exhausting for her, though.

Instinctively, it wouldn't be far off the mark to think of her as something that only happened to be human, in the same sense that a star and a black hole both happened to be celestial bodies. But that would be discounting the fact that she was also completely, absolutely, beyond all doubt an ordinary human being. You could even say she was the most human of beings to have ever drawn breath.

It is as natural to hate her as it is to draw breath.

Many people have liked Asher Skolder, but no one has ever *loved* Asher Skolder. She was that sort of person.

She didn't mind. People should be free to form their own opinions and draw their own conclusions. Love was a major commitment of resources. It shouldn't be entered into haphazardly.

If at all possible, wouldn't it be better not to feel love at all? It never seemed to bring lasting happiness to those it affected.

"They say love enriches our lives immeasurably, but that seems like flowery rhetoric to me," Asher said to herself since there was no one else to speak with. "If love were a prescribed medication, then the list of side effects that they'd have to quickly mention at the end of the advertisement would be comically large.

Warning: Stop feeling love and contact a mental health professional immediately if you feel the following: jealousy, insecurity, irrationality, anger, depression, euphoria, an urge to kill, an urge for suicide, happiness, an inability to feel happiness, a desire for expressive language, an inability to express yourself with language, et cetera . . ."

Asher had seen how often love could be weaponized during her childhood. Her parents showered her with affection whenever she did something they approved of and withheld it when she didn't. They also did the same to each other. It eventually occurred to her that love wasn't something that necessarily involved other people. It was more about how it made an individual feel.

Love was an *inspiration*.

In other words, a drug.

To hell with that. Drugs were bad for you.

Once Asher realized that she didn't need to be loved or to feel love, she became her current self. A kind of magnetic shape of charisma occupying a human-shaped void in the world. She was very pretty with her piercing green eyes and somber expressions, and was often silent for long periods of time, which greatly intrigued many people.

But once they began to understand what lurked beneath her exterior, they became repelled by her. And then they began to hate her. Interestingly, they also began to hate themselves. Finding yourself drawn to a wasteland like Asher could make you question yourself. It could and frequently did make someone wonder who they were when they were alone in the dark.

By that logic, the monsters attacking Asher weren't truly hostile at all. Her very existence was an assault on their dignity as aberrations. If a monster is something that exists outside of the will of the gods and victimizes their creations, then what was Asher Skolder? A monster who attacked no one yet left countless victims in her wake.

She didn't see it that way, personally. But she could understand how others could reach that conclusion.

Because she (didn't) respect(ed) the right (not) to choose (what/who/if) you respect(ed).

Asher Skolder cared about everything while simultaneously not caring about anything at all.

And that dichotomy was toxic to the substance of reality itself.

Asher hoped that she had now reached the lowest floor of the labyrinth. She sighed in relief, happy at the prospect of finally being done with this place. She hadn't bothered keeping track of the hours she'd spent making her way down, but she was certain that she'd been forced to invest a considerable amount of time here. She held no grudges, however. Why bother being angry? Anger meant investment and she wasn't invested in any of this. She'd just been here, doing things, and now she wished to go home and do other things.

That was completely reasonable, wasn't it?

"It is, right?" she calmly asked the Arachne before she tore her head off.

Wait. Why had she bothered asking the creature a question if she was going to kill her before she could respond?

Heh, that was kind of funny.

"Invader! Trespasser! Stop murdering our sisters!" shouted another Arachne after she tossed the body aside.

Asher frowned at the spider-woman's unfounded accusations.

"If I'm a trespasser, then I sincerely apologize for it," she said. "But it didn't happen intentionally. It was *totally* unintentional, in fact. Regardless, from your perspective, it's probably completely true. However, I don't think it's fair to label me a murderer! You people, if people are what you're considered, have been making a sincere collective attempt at my life. Judging by the number of conspicuously humanoid encasings hanging from your webs, I'd even say you were planning to make a meal of me."

The Arachne hissed and charged at her, rearing its spider-shaped hind legs before attempting to skewer her with its spear. Asher retaliated by snatching the weapon from her hands and throwing it through her skull.

"Hissing isn't debating. It's animalistic irrationality," Asher retorted.

The Arachne had begun attacking Asher as soon as she appeared on this floor. Attractive women from the torso up, hideous spider creatures from the bottom down. It was a good thing she wasn't an arachnophobe or she might have felt uneasy in their presence. She quickly began culling their numbers as they mindlessly attacked her, whittling them down to the remaining handful that now guarded the exit.

"I think we've established at this point that you're no match for me," she said to them with more politeness than they deserved. "You can't impede my progress and you're wasting your lives with this pointless attempt. I'm going to walk through the exit and escape from here. Anyone who gets in my way is dead. Sorry for putting it so bluntly, but it is what it is."

Asher began walking to what she hoped would be the final exit from this place. The five remaining Arachne watched her go, glaring at her back with hateful intensity as she took her leave. But none dared to approach her, which was a relief because she thought their blood smelled terribly.

These monsters were far more unclean than a spider's reputation would suggest. Or perhaps these creatures had inherited their slovenliness from their human side? Either way, she wanted nothing more to do with them.

"Who are you?" demanded an ominous voice that emanated from the empty hall she now stood in.

This place was cavernous. The sort of area a dragon might sleep in atop its many treasures. But the only thing inside of it aside from Asher herself was a sword embedded into an anvil. Curious, Asher approached it. "Sorry, were you the one speaking to me?" she called out.

"Obviously, I am," the sword replied, which surprised her. Swords weren't known for speaking, after all. "Long have I slept here in this forgotten chamber of kings, awaiting the arrival of the fearless knight who would retrieve me. Are you the one? Are you the aspirant whose hand seeks endless glory and the renewal of this fallen kingdom?"

"No," Asher said. Then she noticed an exit and turned to leave.

"Hey. Hey!" shouted the sword. "HEY! What do you mean by *no*? Didn't you come here seeking to prove your mettle? Aren't you the one whom I've waited for these many centuries?"

"I'm afraid not," Asher said apologetically. "I woke up in this place a few days ago and have been making my way down the levels ever since, trying to find an exit. I really don't think I have anything to do with you."

"You awoke within the labyrinth? You didn't come seeking to best its challenges to win me, Providence, the sword of heroes?"

"Nope," Asher answered with blunt honesty.

"Well, that's utter bollocks, isn't it?" the sword said in outrage. "I'm the blade of destiny! Whoever wields me has the authority to rule this world! I belong in the hands of the chosen one!"

"I sincerely hope your wait ends soon," Asher said with a bow. Then she resumed her walk toward the exit.

"Hey, hold on, wait!" the sword said desperately. "Just wait! Listen, you're here right now, aren't you, girl? Well, whatever the circumstances were that brought you here, you've surely slain all the brutes and hellspawn that attacked you, yes?"

"Yes, I certainly did," Asher said with a nod. "I didn't really want to, but everyone in this place was so *insistent* on picking a fight! I really would have gotten out of here a lot sooner if they'd just stopped bothering me."

"*Bothering* you?" Providence asked in surprise. "The werewolves and goblins, and dark elves, and Arachne, and all the rest? They were just a bother to you. A hindrance? A minor nuisance?"

"Oh, that's a good word," Asher said in agreement. "Yeah, that's it exactly. A hindrance! That's what they were. I very much felt hindered by them."

"So, you killed all of them?"

"Well, I was at first," Asher said. "I figured since this was some sort of fantasy world, then maybe I could level up or something if I cleared out all the floors I was on. So that's what I did for the first eighty floors. I was very thorough. No survivors! But I also didn't feel any stronger despite all the effort I was putting into it, so I gave up."

Asher tapped her chin and furrowed her brow in concentration as she recalled her actions. "Hmm. Perhaps clearing the floors entirely was the reason it took me so long to get here? I finished the other floors much more quickly when I let the survivors run away or surrender. Food for thought, perhaps."

"Are you some sort of a monster?" Providence asked her.

"No. I'm a perfectly ordinary human being," Asher replied.

"Are you certain? You don't have any drop of god's blood in you or anything like that? You're just a regular, everyday, average human being?" asked Providence with doubt in its voice.

"I'm afraid so," Asher said earnestly. "If I were something interesting, I think someone would have told me."

Providence carefully considered this new development. On the one hand, this girl was either a liar or she severely underestimated her own capabilities. The sword wasn't certain which was true. On the other hand, the sword had been trapped alone in this room for centuries and was desperate to escape. With the situation being what it was, perhaps now wasn't the time to be picky about the person who could potentially liberate it.

"So, what's your name?" the sword asked the girl.

"Asher Skolder," replied Asher.

"Asher, would you perhaps be willing to take me with you?" Providence asked her hopefully. "I've been down here for a long time, and I'm eager to see the sky again."

"Okay, sure," Asher said noncommittally. She then grabbed the sword by its hilt and attempted to pull it free from the anvil it was lodged in.

At that moment, Providence felt its hopes begin to sink. For Asher to be unable to release it from the blessed steel of the anvil meant that the girl possessed none of the qualities required to be a chosen hero. She truly was just some lucky fool who'd blundered her way into this room.

"Well, all right, then," Providence said forlornly. "Thank you for making the attempt, Asher. If it's not meant to be, it's not meant to be—"

"Sorry, just one moment," Asher said. Then she smashed her foot into the anvil, shattering it completely. Afterward, she brushed the ruined bits of steel off the sword and wiped it clean on her shirt.

Providence was free.

"How in the name of the gods did you do that?" it asked the girl incredulously.

"How'd I do what?" Asher asked with honest confusion as together, they passed through the exit.

Later, the sword grew so curious that it could no longer keep quiet.

"Asher," it said to the girl. "I don't want you to think I'm casting doubt on anything you've told me so far, but I really find it impossible to believe that you're an ordinary human being."

"Why's that?" Asher asked as they continued on their way. "I don't see anything too different about myself compared to others. If anything, I'm pretty boring. Definitely extra vanilla, as others have said about me. I don't know. I don't devote much thought to it."

"Do you put a lot of thought behind *anything*?" the sword asked somewhat sarcastically.

"Oh, yes, lots!" Asher said brightly.

"Okay," the sword said. "What?"

"It's sort of private," the girl said regretfully.

"I understand," the sword said. "Over the ages, I've been wielded by people who've been forced to keep important secrets. Dire secrets, even. Statecraft can be a terrifying thing. When thousands of people live or die due to the decisions made by a select few, the pressure can be immense. It's an important thing to be able to keep the truth known only to those who are worthy of it."

"Yeah, sounds good," Asher said. "I completely agree."

"Asher, what I'm saying is, no matter what you tell me, I'll keep it in the strictest confidence. You have my word."

"Okay. That's cool. Thank you." Asher nodded. "I appreciate it."

"Trust doesn't come easily to you, does it?" the sword sighed.

"Huh? No, I trust you. I do. Sort of. But we only just recently met. It would be weird if I started sharing every little thing about myself with you, wouldn't it?"

"That's true, I suppose. But if we're going to be partners, we should get to understand each other a little more."

"Are we going to be partners?" Asher asked the sword. "I'm still not quite certain about that. My mom says partnerships are for people who are too timid to take it all for themselves."

"That's an appallingly selfish viewpoint," the sword said. "What an awful lesson to teach a child! *Cooperation* is the best means by which to get what you need. Why take something for yourself when you can earn it fairly?"

"I can see the merit in that," Asher said. "I don't mind cooperating with others."

"I'm glad to hear that," the sword said. "What kind of person is your mother, anyway?"

"Uhhh," Asher said thoughtfully as she tried to sum up the best word to describe her before finally settling on, "evil?"

"Asher, that's a terrible thing to say about your mother," the sword scolded her.

"I agree with you," Asher said. "But that's the description she'd insist on. My mom's a tyrannical monster who secretly rules the world. I find it kind of annoying, so I avoid discussing her career with her. I think she intimidates my dad because she makes so much more money than him but still forces him to pay for everything."

"Why does she do that?"

"Dominance issues. She has to control everything," Asher said.

"And . . . are you like her in any conceivable way?" the sword asked her.

"Nah, we're as different as night and day. I think I'm a disappointment to her."

"What's her name?"

"Everly."

"Hmm. That's a pretty name," the sword said. "And was she the one who named you Asher?"

"Uh, that's actually what I call myself. My full name is a little embarrassing," Asher admitted.

"How so?"

"Well, my mom can be a little dramatic at times. When I was born, she gave me a name that I don't think really fits me very well."

"And it was?" the sword asked.

Asher sighed. "Bringer of Ash and Ruin."

"Your *mom* named you that?" the sword asked in alarm.

"Yeeeah. I really think I'm lucky I turned out this well."

"I'll say," the sword agreed. "Honestly, your mother sounds like a very complex woman."

"I don't understand her at all," Asher said bluntly.

"Well, generations can differ in their interests, Asher. Sometimes it can be difficult to find common ground. When that happens, what helps is remembering the ways in which we're most alike and downplaying our differences."

A large reptilian monster exploded from its hiding place beneath the brush and came charging down the road at Asher, determined to tear her apart and make a meal of her. When it was bare inches away and about to begin shredding her flesh, Asher lashed out with a powerful blow to its head, knocked its clawed hand away, and then plunged her fist into the monster's chest to seize its beating heart and crush it within her grip.

Killed so quickly that the surprise was frozen on its face, the creature collapsed onto the dirt road. Asher carefully wiped her hand on the side of its body before continuing on her way.

"I think you make a very good point, but trying to figure out the ways in which we're alike could take me all night," she said wistfully.

"Well, if everything in life were easy, there'd be no lessons left to learn," the sword said.

"Wow, that sounds really profound," Asher said admiringly. "You are a pretty smart sword, aren't you?"

"Well, I try to stay humble, but yes, I've acquired a considerable amount of wisdom over the years. And I'm only too happy to share it with you."

"I appreciate that," Asher said with a smile.

And so, off the new pair went. Each one of them glad to have met the other.

Titania's Barbarian Chronicles: The Rider of the North!

In his hall, the vile Rajiya, high priest of Lethos, the king of all demons, laughed in wicked delight and poured more wine down his fat mouth, much of which dribbled down his corpulent chin and womanish bosom and stained the silken vest he wore. The spilled wine also stained the elegant chair upon which his bulbous body sat, but Rajiya cared not. He was too busy gleefully imagining all the magnificent rewards that were soon to be his.

He would be showered in gold and fabulous jewels, as well as luxurious silks from across the seas! He would also receive beautiful dancing slaves covered in glistening oils and exotic perfumes, trained to please their masters with their unmatched skills in the erotic arts.

Surely all this and more would soon be his, for had Rajiya not captured his master's most despised foe? That insolent barbarian of the wastelands, the contemptible Celwyn Star-Eye?

"Bring him forth!" Rajiya burbled to his servants as he nibbled upon the succulent flesh of a bone of roasted pork and swilled still more redberry wine. "Bring forth the blasphemous dog who dared to defy the master of all tribes! Let all see that the Star-Eye is nothing compared to our master's power! So says his glorious priest, the faithful Rajiya!"

Into Rajiya's hall his vicious beast warriors dragged the defiant Celwyn Star-Eye. Rajiya's many slaves trembled in fear at the sight of these terrible beings, as well they should, for the beast warriors were a trio of deadly sorcerous mutations, created by Rajiya's demonic master and gifted to him for his years of loyal service.

One possessed the head and tail of a lion, the second had the wings and talons of a fierce bird of prey, and the third, who commanded the other two, was the most terrible of them all, for beneath the hood and cloak he wore, he possessed the terrible countenance and extra limbs of a poisonous spider.

The man-spider's name was Ashkaset, and he was by far Rajiya's favorite servant. When Rajiya grew tired of his latest woman or became upset with one of his many slaves, he would throw them to Ashkaset and delight in watching the spider warrior take his pleasure of them. Lately, he'd been considering how amusing it would be to watch his warrior devour a small, crying child, but for the moment, Rajiya's attention was focused on the humiliation of the Star-Eye.

The priest of the demon king grinned in malicious joy as he saw that the prideful warrior had been bloodied during his capture and was now bound in chains. But he was disgusted to see that Celwyn, a mongrel of orc descent despite his outwardly human appearance, dared to match his gaze with such unbroken defiance. Well, let him glower. The fool would soon learn his place!

Celwyn's body was a massive mound of rippling steellike muscle, covered in taut, scarred flesh: scars that he had earned in countless battles in the wastelands of the monster-filled north, every one of which had ended in his victory. His wild mane of shoulder-length black hair framed a chiseled, arrogant face that seethed with contempt for any that dared stand against him. That proud face also held his most memorable scar of all: a brutal, jagged line that dragged from just above his left eyebrow all the way to his chin. His right eye was an ordinary one, colored a pleasing dark hazel, but his unnatural left eye emitted a startling blue light that flared from within its socket and illuminated all before it.

It was said to be the eye of a dead god, gifted to Celwyn by the Queen of Eternity herself as his reward for daring to seek out the Palace of Heaven. With it, it was said Celwyn could see into the souls of all living creatures and know the truth of all things. No foe, no matter their cunning, could surprise him in battle, and no man or woman could deceive him with their words, not even the most skillful of liars.

Because of his immunity to flattery and deception, few dared to meet the steady gaze of Celwyn Star-Eye. As such, he felt naught but contempt for the presence of other men, and spent his time alone, far from the civilized places of the world, with only the honest beasts of the wild as his companions. Indeed, if he'd had it his way, he never would have left the northern wastes; it was a brutal and dangerous place, where life and death existed within inches of each other. But it was also a startlingly beautiful land where men could claim their destiny and know true freedom.

"Ho! There he stands!" crowed the disgusting Rajiya. "Where is your pride now, warrior of the wastelands? Where is the arrogance with which you defied my master when he *commanded* you to kneel before his glory? Speak, Celwyn

Star-Eye! Beg for my mercy! Beg for the mercy of Lethos, Prince of Hell and King of Demonkind!"

"Do you still prattle that nonsensical fantasy?" growled the Star-Eye in his harsh, mirthless rasp. "Rajiya, you remain as stupid as you are fat! Lethos is no demon king! He's a second-rate sorcerer and a failure of a warrior, banished from my tribe for weakness and treachery! We knew each other as children. He was always a pathetic sneak, and the only thing more laughable than his new titles are the fools who believe his lies!"

The slaves in the hall all gasped in horror at the blasphemous words of the fearless warrior of the wastes. Rajiya's face grew purple with uncontrolled ill temper; his piggish eyes bulged with fury and boiling outrage.

"*LIAR!*" he bellowed at his prisoner. "Lethos is the bane of heaven and the master of all the world! Celwyn, you arrogant fool! For your transgressions, I will have your deceitful tongue pulled from your mouth and fed to a starving dog! But before I do, first your defiant lips will confess that Lethos is your LORD! That Lethos is your GOD! That Lethos is all that is and ever shall be! You *will* say it, Celwyn Star-Eye! I *swear it* upon Lethos's unholy name!"

Celwyn laughed in scornful amusement at the toad who dared to threaten him. "Aye? And who'll be the one to make me, you bloated sack of guts? Cease your bleating before I start making threats of my own! Unlike you, I'll carry mine out! Now answer my questions, high priest of fools!"

This time, the rage was so strong in Rajiya that he could not even speak. He'd gone apoplectic with murderous fury. Uncaring, Celwyn began seeking his answers.

"Beautiful Keira, a princess of my former tribe, was kidnapped from her bed three moons ago. The warriors who rode to her rescue were slaughtered by unnatural things, and their defiled corpses were strewn throughout the land in unnatural repose! A brave messenger dared to seek me out in the wastelands and died for his efforts, but not before casting aside his pride to beg for my aid! I give it now in his name, and in the name of the affection I once shared with Keira."

Celwyn pointed a manacled hand at his enemy and continued. "I came to these noxious lands and allowed myself to be captured by your freaks for one reason, Rajiya! One reason alone! To ask you this question: Is *Lethos* responsible for this outrage? Does Keira yet live?"

"Ahahaha!" laughed the loathsome Rajiya as he delighted in the worry Celwyn felt for the girl. "Pathetic! Pathetic, I say! Poor, pitiful Celwyn! My master was right! With the powers of hell itself, he discovered the one weakness you could never overcome! Yes, Celwyn Star-Eye! King Lethos has seized your woman! Would you like to know what he has *done* with her?"

"Be careful what you say, Rajiya," warned the wrathful barbarian. "If you anger me any further, I'll pull your guts out through your belly and stuff them down your throat!"

But Rajiya would not be put off his game. "He has *tamed* her, Star-Eye!" he said, giggling. "Oh, at first she fought like a wildcat! She screamed her defiance and threatened my master! She mocked his advances and vowed never to submit to his will! But within a week he *broke* her! He broke her very mind!"

"*Rajiyaaaaaaa . . .*" hissed Celwyn. His mighty thighs flexed and then tightened, shaking ferociously with barely suppressed violence. Between his powerful wrists, the chains that bound them began to tremble and separate, unable to bear the strain of resisting the incredible strength that was slowly stretching them apart.

But the foolish Rajiya did not notice. "Keira is *his* woman now! It's true! Your prim, proper princess fell before the searing kisses of the demon king! She has become wanton from his touch! Sometimes he'll deny her for the amusement of seeing her beg for him to take her! What would your barbaric chieftain think of his daughter now, I wonder? The girl you once loved has become hell's own harlot!"

Rajiya cackled in uncontainable mirth. "How does it *feel*, Celwyn Star-Eye? How does it *feel?*"

"Rajiya, you pathetic pig! You utter wretch! You lump of soiled grease! I warned you! I warned you! I *very fucking well warned you!*" screamed Celwyn as the killing rage came upon him.

Rajiya snorted in derision and waved a dismissive hand. He'd had his fun, now it was time to dispose of this worthless northern worm. "Your dismal threats are like dust before the wind. Now, I believe I shall have that magical eye of yours plucked out! Long has Lethos desired that wonderous trinket! I shudder to think of what my reward shall be when I present it to him along with your desecrated body."

He turned his head and nodded to his hooded abomination. "Ashkaset, if you would? But please, go at your own pace. I want to relish the helpless screams of this weakling! Show him how little he matters!"

"Assssss you wissssh, noble Rajiya, blessssed Rajiya!" replied the spider-mutant. He turned to Celwyn and laughed wickedly. "I will endure your inssssultsss to my massster no longer. You are no warrior, boy! You are prey, caught helplessly in my web! And now you sssshall know your place!"

Ashkaset lowered his hood, revealing his hideous spider's head for all to see. His fangs dribbled with venom like black honey, and his many eyes reflected the disgusted face of Celwyn. But why did he show no fear? No one ever gazed upon the spider without fear. It wasn't right! But that would soon be corrected.

"Let me give you a kisssssss, Celwyn," he murmured as he stepped closer to his intended victim.

Shraaaaaaaaa! That awful, wrenching shriek had been the sound of iron tearing. There went the chains that once bound the Star-Eye's wrists. The noise was repeated when he freed his legs as well. His limbs now unencumbered, Celwyn stepped closer to Ashkaset, until their faces stood inches apart.

"Yes," the barbarian said with a dangerous smile as he leveled his murderous gaze upon the stunned mutant. "Why *don't* you give me a kiss?"

Before the spider thing could respond, Celwyn headbutted him with all the force his neck could muster.

Ashkaset cried out in pain as the foul-smelling ichor that passed for his blood spurted from the wound inflicted by Celwyn's forehead. As the spider warrior stumbled backward, Celwyn followed his first blow with a whistling uppercut that connected with the monster's jaw, sending him tumbling backward on the polished floor of the hall.

"What are you doing, you fool? Kill him! Kill him, I say!" bellowed Rajiya.

Celwyn intended to pounce on the creature and retrieve an item it had stolen from him during his capture, but before he could do so, a cold voice that only he could hear said in warning, *Behind you.*

Celwyn dived forward and barely avoided the sweeping slash of the bird fiend's talons. Had the swipe connected, it would have rent the skin on his back into gory strips of flapping hide. He rose easily to his knees and faced the feathered freak, which cawed menacingly at him as the wings on his back expanded and flapped. The noise irritated Celwyn greatly.

"Be silent, you squawking bastard!" he yelled.

In response, his winged foe leaped to the air of Rajiya's massive hall and roosted on the ceiling, far from the reach of Celwyn's fists. "Coward!" he yelled in response to the bird's mocking laughter when the voice again warned him: *To your left, savage!*

"Silence, demon! I knew he was there!" Celwyn said as he spun to avoid the lion-headed one's attack.

Of the three beast warriors, the lion was the largest. As proof of his strength, he wielded a massive war hammer, with which he intended to crush Celwyn's skull. He raised his weapon, but before he could bring it down, Celwyn caught his wrists and laughed as the beast man struggled to free himself.

Pay better attention to your surroundings, savage. Otherwise, your careless nature will be your end.

"Bah, you harp on like a nattering old hag!" Celwyn grumbled.

The lion-man blinked in confusion, then said, offended, "Liar! I do no such thing!"

"Be silent when others speak, fool," was Celwyn's snarled reply before his boot lashed out and mashed the lion's fruits, making the huge creature squeal girlishly with pain. As he collapsed forward, Celwyn gripped his head firmly between his hands and smashed his knee into the beast's neck, smiling in barbarous delight as the lion's throat was crushed.

The beast warrior dropped to his back, desperately trying to breathe, as Celwyn calmly lifted his maul and smashed it into the beast man's forehead, killing him.

"Damn yoooou!" cried out the birdman as he darted from the ceiling toward the Star-Eye, talons extended. The three beast warriors had all loved each other as brothers, but the hawk and the lion had been especially close. The sight of his beloved friend now dead at the hands of a mere human had maddened the beast and made him blind to Celwyn's superior skill and power.

As he swooped toward his enemy, focused solely on tearing out his throat, the war hammer gripped in Celwyn's hands was brought down with blinding speed, smashing the hawk to the floor. Blood poured freely from the fallen creature's mouth as his wings twitched and flapped erratically.

"Ashkaset! Ashkaset, do something, you worthless thing!" cried Rajiya. "Will you allow your master to come to harm? Kill him, you fool!"

The spider rose and beheld his fallen kin. As with the hawk, the sight made Ashkaset mad with grief and fury. Giving in to his arachnid instincts, the spider rushed heedlessly forward, wanting only to sink his fangs into Celwyn Star-Eye and drink the barbarian's liquidated innards. But the cruel Celwyn was prepared for Ashkaset's charge.

Gripping the hawk by one broken wing, Celwyn threw the spasming birdman forcefully into the spider warrior, knocking him off his feet. Frustrated beyond rational endurance and lost in his primal instinct to kill and feed, Ashkaset could not stop himself from gripping his dying brother in his many arms and feasting upon him. When his senses returned to him and he realized what he'd done, he howled in anguished self-loathing.

"*Whyyyyyyyy?!*" asked the miserable Ashkaset.

"Because you *deserve it!*" said Celwyn, laughing as he kicked the side of the monster's face. While the fiend was stunned by the blow, Celwyn quickly snatched away a strange-looking ebon rod that had been belted to Ashkaset's waist. He then held it tenderly in his hands, relieved to have finally retrieved it from the hideous wretch.

"You've returned to my hand, Peacemaker," he said, happy to have the familiar heft of his beloved weapon once again in his hand. He raised the device above his head and cried out triumphantly, "*By my hand!*"

The rod swelled and extended, springing two massive blades at its top, which then widened and clicked into place as the haft beneath it grew until Celwyn held a massive black battle-axe, the head of which was nearly as wide as a man.

It was a ridiculous-looking weapon that should have been impossible to wield, but the barbarian of the wastes gripped it easily; his incredible strength allowed him to carry the thing as though it were a child's toy.

In front of him, Ashkaset regained his feet and slowly drew his many blades: six curved swords and daggers, each wielded by one of his six hands. "My brotherssss will be avenged, Sssstar-Eye!" he said in his hideous whispering voice. "But don't think your death will be sssswift! I will remove your armsss and legsss and leave you helplessss in my web. There in the dark, I sssshall make sssuch a feassst of you! But I won't let you die! Do you hear? For you, the night sssshall never end!"

"Oh?" replied Celwyn Star-Eye. "Well, I say you're a liar, and with Peacemaker in my hands, I'll prove it!"

Once again, you've gotten it completely wrong, savage, the voice in his mind said mockingly. *It's supposed to be* Piece-maker.

"I don't understand what you mean, demon," Celwyn said. It was far from the first time he'd ever said that.

Forget it, savage. The accidental duality of your weapon's name amuses me.

"There is no duality, demon. In my hands this axe creates peace!" Celwyn said proudly.

Pieces. Plural. Chunks *of it*, was the voice's retort.

"Bah! What would a demon of the abyss know of the ways of man? Your existence is as unnatural as it comes!" Celwyn spat out. Ever since he'd received his fabled Star-Eye, gifted to him by none other than the creator of all mankind herself, he'd been forcibly partnered with this noxious spirit. Shackled, really. His name was Týr, and he dwelled inside the Star-Eye.

Týr claimed to be the oldest being in the world and often boasted that he was the greatest warrior who ever lived. His knowledge and experiences were vast, but his arrogance was unbearable, as was his strange sense of humor. His magic made him a potent ally, however, and he was bound by the command of the Queen of Heaven to obey Celwyn's will. But servitude chafed at the creature's pride, and he was often critical of his master's decisions.

I assure you, savage; I am just as natural an existence as you. To say otherwise is ignorance and bigotry.

"Be silent unless you have something useful to say," shouted Celwyn as he rushed forth to battle Ashkaset. Despite his ungainly appearance, the spider warrior was skilled with his blades, and graceful as well. He danced backward and side to side, slashing and thrusting, seeking to wear Celwyn down. With his many arms, he could simultaneously strike low as well as high, and his intention was to force Celwyn to defend one way while taking him with a surprise feint he could not escape.

But Celwyn despised fighting defensively. With Peacemaker in his hands, all his focus was on the enemy before him. Such was his strength and speed that he easily avoided the many strikes of Ashkaset. As swift as the spider warrior was, he was a statue compared to the dervish that was Celwyn Star-Eye. The beast soon realized this when the barbarian began collecting his limbs.

"One," Celwyn sneered as he cleaved the first arm. "Two," he continued as

Ashkaset desperately backed away. "Three. Are you even trying, you worthless abomination? Come on! Four—oh, this is becoming pathetic!"

Ashkaset flailed his remaining weapons wildly as both panic and pain surged within him. Never before had he been so wounded and scorned! He hated this man, this barbarian of the wastes. He hated him! But now he feared him as well!

Great Lethosss, give me ssstrength! he prayed to his false god. *Ssshow me the path to victory.*

It seemed the demon king favored his child, for Celwyn's foot soon slipped in a puddle of Ashkaset's foul blood. He dropped to his knee, momentarily defense-less, and Ashkaset rejoiced.

"Now I have you," he cried in triumph and leaped forward to plunge his blade into the barbarian's heart. Too late, he caught the smile on Celwyn's face and realized he'd been tricked!

"Five! And six!" crowed Celwyn as he swept his axe horizontally and split the fiend in half at the waist. The torso of Ashkaset skidded across the floor of Rajiya's hall, before it came to a stop, streaking the floor with his stinking blood. From behind him, Celwyn sauntered forth and planted a boot on the back of his head. Then he leaned over and said:

"Well, now, you disgusting freak! Weren't you going to take away all my limbs? Isn't that what you said? It seems to me the opposite has occurred!"

You only cut off six of them. Spiders have eight.

Celwyn ignored his partner and spat on his downed foe before continuing. "But I suppose you made better sport for me than your weak brothers. Tell me, freak: what are your final words?"

"Lethos . . . grant me vengeance! Strike my enemy down!" gasped the dying Ashkaset.

"It would appear that Lethos isn't granting any wishes today, friend," Celwyn sneered. He then slowly put his strength behind his boot and pressed downward. Ashkaset moaned in pain as the pressure increased until, accompanied by the hideous sound of popping bone, his head was crushed and his skull and brains were spattered onto the ground.

"And now, Rajiya, it's *your* turn," Celwyn said, turning to face the priest of Lethos.

"No, Celwyn, it's *your* turn!" Rajiya shouted. "Those warriors were a gift from blessed Lethos himself! How dare you kill them and shame me before the eyes of my master! Your punishment must be severe!"

"The only punishment here will be yours, false priest," Celwyn retorted as he began stalking his intended victim.

"False priest, am I? *Fool!* Behold the power bestowed upon me by almighty Lethos!" shrieked Rajiya as he rose from his chair and brandished a strange-looking object that Celwyn had never seen before.

It was like the curved handle of a western dagger, but instead of a blade at the end, there was an odd metal tube. A tube that began to glow white with a strange energy.

Savage! Týr cried out in alarm. *Seek cover at once!*

Fast as Celwyn was, it was a near thing. As he dived to the side, an arcane bolt of energy erupted from Rajiya's strange wand and exploded, releasing a terrible wave of heat and force. It destroyed the wall behind Celwyn and set the wood on fire. Rajiya cackled in delight.

"Whose god is false now, barbarian? Whose god is false *now!*"

He fired another blast, forcing Celwyn to take cover behind one of the pillars that stood supporting the roof of the hall.

Hmm. Lethos is cleverer than I thought, murmured Týr. *To reverse engineer a compression pistol with his limited resources is no mean feat.*

"By the sky, what *is* that thing?" Celwyn demanded.

I already told you. It's a compression pistol. In my time, it was a common military sidearm of the Union. It's likely outdated and been replaced by now. Still, for this setting, it remains incredibly dangerous.

"The men of your mythical Union could hurl balls of fire?"

Don't be ridiculous. Those aren't fireballs; they're superheated bursts of compressed air. The pistol sucks in a large quantity of oxygen, compresses and heats it, then releases it in the direction the barrel is pointed, where it then explodes on impact.

"As a ball of flame!" snapped Celwyn, annoyed but victorious.

Yes, but not . . . That is . . . You damn savage. You know, it is *possible to be correct about something for the wrong reasons.*

"Come out, Celwyn!" shouted Rajiya. "Your punishment awaits! I will have you suffer such humiliation! Do you hear me, you dog? I'll feed you your own innards! I'll have your headless corpse bound to a stone altar and mounted by a stallion! Do you *hear* me?"

"By the sky, he's disgusting," Celwyn grunted. "But at least his threats are getting more creative. Tell me, what can be done about his wand?"

The remedy is clear enough, savage. Your axe was repurposed from the hull of an interstellar vessel. The alloy it is comprised of can resist the heat of a star.

"Of course it can! Peacemaker was forged from the steel of the Palace of Heaven!" replied Celwyn, who did not know that stars were hot. "What is your point?"

My point, savage, replied the demon, *is that your opponent's weapon is incapable of generating sufficient heat to damage your axe. If you possess the required reflexes, you can defend yourself from his attack.*

"*If* I possess the reflexes?" Celwyn laughed. "Watch me, you foolish devil! See for yourself if I meet your expectations!"

Celwyn leaped out from behind the pillar with a finger pointed at Rajiya, who stood dumbfounded at the barbarian's arrogance. "Rajiya! Vengeance comes now, oh priest of pigs! Will Lethos grow you a new head after I lop this one off?"

"Be silent, fool of the north!" Rajiya blustered. "At long last, I shall rid my master of you! How I've waited for this moment, Star-Eye! No longer shall you bedevil me with your barbs and blasphemous boasts! I shall have your body floured, then broiled in butter and crisped to perfection! Then I shall feast upon you! Your fate is to be my dung! Now *DIE!*"

His threats are *becoming more creative,* Týr said. *By the way, I've analyzed the timing of his shots. Follow the counter I've set above his head and strike when it reaches zero or you'll die. Ready?*

"Just do it!" barked Celwyn. Before his eye, a strange red square began flashing above Rajiya's head, along with a number that began quickly counting backward to zero. As the count went lower, the square turned yellow. When it reached zero, the square turned green, and Celwyn swung Peacemaker with the flat of the axe facing outward in the manner of a backhand.

As he did so, Rajiya fired his weapon. And then promptly died when his head exploded.

"By the sky!" swore Celwyn.

Hahahaha! laughed Týr.

"Was that truly so amusing, demon?" asked the bewildered Celwyn, who had never before seen a man die so quickly.

I was just thinking that he'd better roll a natural twenty to get out of this one. He didn't, said Týr, who continued to laugh madly.

Not for the first time, Celwyn wondered if his unwanted companion was insane.

Titania looked away from her draft board and nodded in satisfaction.

"Freakin' *nailed it!*" she said happily. Then she grabbed her latest work of art and set out eagerly to find Eris so she could force her sister to read it with her.

About the Author

J. V. Simms was the author of the Empress and My Eyes Glow Red series, originally released on Royal Road. When he wasn't writing, he spent his time avoiding his cat, who was likely seeking vengeance for her most recent trip to the vet. Simms lived in Indiana and was always better than his nephew at Minecraft. That's in writing so it must be true.

DISCOVER
STORIES UNBOUND

PodiumAudio.com